How Deep the Quantum Well

Mark Porter

First edition 2011
Printed in the United States of America

For Linda

With many thanks to Tim for his
encouragement and assistance;
and to Mark for his insight.

Contents

1. Seedling Crèche

"You will have only moments," Occultelius had insisted months ago. "I will be quick to reward success, but unforgiving in failure. Do not fail." The synthient had stared at her from the softscreen with narrowed eyes, as if the weight of his words could be conveyed by the intensity of his expression alone, bridging the gulf that separated the virtual and physical worlds.

At the time she had thought it melodramatic; she had learned better since. The enigmatic personality with his youthful appearance was deadly serious and terrifyingly omniscient. And yet for all his skills, he could not accomplish this one small thing.

Despite the warning, Hotaru Ito cradled the smoothly rounded construct in her hands, a small measure of control that was still hers. Its warmth was like an actual biotic. In all her years of service to the artificial minds, she had never once actually touched one.

Sentient and lovely, and I hold its life in my hands.

She had taken the exquisite object from its compartment when the connections to the Neural Sea were broken. The minds in this Tokyo crèche were now cut off from the world in which they existed, alone and bewildered in sensory deprivation.

She stroked the softly silver material lightly, and then took an innocuous data thimble from her case, blowing gently on its side. She felt the warm humidity of her breath flow around her fingers.

This particular crystal, like all the others in her kit, had passed through the careful security screens outside the crèche, its contents analyzed to the last molecular fabric, and found to be loaded with nothing but synthient med-packs.

A set of tiny flashes rippled across the surface as the meticulously applied tracers were activated by the strands of DNA carried within the moisture of her breath. The pulses stopped, indicating the process was complete, and the newly transformed data was ready to be activated.

The change had only taken a few moments, and now her heart started racing. She touched the thimble to the crystalline optics of the mind, felt the slight tug as magnetic fields aligned, and watched as multi-colored stars swirled through the structure of the two mated components; two infinitely small galaxies colliding.

Her heart pounded harder; if anyone were to walk in upon her now, it would mean certain disgrace and years of prison. Or worse when her synthient collaborator found out. She waited in agony for the process to finish, alternately staring at the door and the lights flowing within the thimble. A few more brilliant sparks flashed along the edge of the crystal and it went dark. She snatched the thimble from its perch, licked the side of it abruptly, and once again watched as the tiny points of light trembled chaotically, reconfiguring the data back to its original form. She breathed a quivering sigh of relief.

Wiping the thimble on her dress, she placed it back in her case, then stood again, tenderly sliding the unlucky synthient back into its cocoon. She smoothed her clothing slowly and willed herself to become calm. There was no stopping the process now. Occultelius had assured her that the location of the replicated constructs her intrusion had generated was sufficiently concealed that it would remain hidden until download could be accomplished. It was now only a matter of waiting.

But the subsentients she had loosed into the crèche did not stop with copying synthient scaffolds, as she supposed. Burying into the deepest autonomous functions of the single mind she had chosen at random, they infected their host and readied themselves to corrupt the remaining inhabitants as soon as the Sea came back online; a vector as reliable, unstoppable, and undiscoverable as fleas in the days of the bubonic plague.

2. Under the Influence of Gravity

Time hung by a gossamer thread. Photons danced in agony, wild beats flaming to a crawling incandescence against closest neighbors. Protons, neutrons, and electrons crushed themselves in a smearing of quarks and leptons while x-ray and gamma radiation retreated at light speed from the inferno. Many overlapping, spinning disks of dying matter hurled deeper into the maelstrom, pulled into degenerate form while the clock of time pulsed ever more slowly. New fuel fed the ravenous pit in clockwork precision. The disks throbbed and vibrated in intricate rhythm like the fluttering of wind over a vast ocean of possibilities.

Lewis McCrorry stared at the hole source cradled within the probe net and imagined the terrible energies released in sub-nuclear fury inches from his face. The entire apparatus rested on a shabby wooden bench, the carven initials of former graduate students underscoring the exacting plainness of the work.

'Andy Smith,' read one of the worn monikers.

He probably sat here twiddling his thumbs and cursing his professors thirty years ago the same as me.

He picked his chin out of his cupped hands and rubbed his elbows. A cold breeze blew in through a small window high up on the wall.

"Didn't anybody tell you guys it's still April?" he called. "Are we ready to get this thing started or are you going to take all night to test a couple of thimble queues?"

This last was directed at John Umbrel, the junior member of the grad team and collectively agreed upon gopher. John looked up and smiled with a pinched face and squinted eyes, mumbling something under his breath.

Lewis rolled his eyes and sighed in disgust, walked over to the window and used the antiquated push rod to slam the rusty-hinged pane closed.

Everything in this lab is 20th century antique. We've got a stupid fuzzy logic thermostat and manually operated windows. I should have enrolled at Kiev.

He recited his litany of curses for the thousandth time. The dream of attending one of the world's premier universities had faded over the past three years as one thesis project after another crumbled into Terapiles of jumbled and meaningless data. His current professor was growing impatient with his lack of progress and Lewis had long since become the department cynic. None of the projects had been worth the effort he had put into them, until he had been assigned the final indignation of joining a team doing backwater research using technology that was already mainstream before he was born.

Wendy Fulham glared at Lewis through the sensor mesh. The communications protocol for this project was the last chapter of her Ph.D. dissertation; both her interest and patience were waning. The material had been written, and only the actual experiments remained to be placed as a footnoted reference within the pages.

"Give him a break, Lewis. He wouldn't have to do this again if you'd given him the correct specs this morning."

"The specs were correct. If he'd got the right queues we'd be done by now."

"Well who'd bother with a local holothimble?" countered John. "That strategy went out with the flatscreen."

He stood and wiped the palms of his hands on his trousers. "How's it look now, Joe A?"

. . . . .

Joe Aldonis found his mind wandering to tonight's party; Remtimona was quite adept at setting up interesting surf sequences, and she had promised a particularly eclectic, perhaps even illicit series tonight. It had been a long time since he had wandered the Sea purely for pleasure, and he was looking forward to the experience.

But for now he waited with growing impatience while his human colleagues bickered over minor points of the experimental exercise they were about to begin. His self-projection stood at the center of a large, circular amphitheater, the burnished dome above providing oddly distorted reflections of the instruments surrounding him.

He was one of several synthients who managed data streaming to the university library, and was busy every day with minor modifications to the service schedule of the subsentients that handled the ubiquitous needs of a student population scattered across the globe: homework assignments, literature review, communications, and a hundred other activities.

But his enduring passion was playing a part in the advanced research needs of the departments, contributing his indispensable skills in massaging the endlessly variable data forms into the palaces he had prepared for each with patient finesse.

During his time at MIT he had assisted 117 students toward their dissertations, a respectable, though unremarkable total. But what he lacked in volume he made up in architectural originality. Although the section of the vast MIT memory domain that housed his unique creations grew more slowly than others, the multidimensional forms of his imagination stood apart from all others. Indeed, his constructions had been widely reviewed, and it was a source of pride that his contributions to network landscaping were highly regarded by those whose opinions he most respected. Many of his colleagues scoffed at the idea of providing more than the utilitarian infrastructure required, essentially content to house the information in little more than labeled drawers, indexed and cataloged for easy retrieval.

He, in his turn, thought this narrow view lacked vision; he was not prone to accepting that his only reason for existence was simply to serve his human masters as a mindless servant. With the capacity for abstract thought that his advocates had given him came the responsibility to exercise that wonderful gift to the fullest.

As he waited for the latest in a long list of meaningless quarrels among his most recent human partners to wind down, he inspected the virtual components of the experiment once more and wondered if he would ever reach 118.

. . . . .

Joe A's thin, mustached face looked out of a wide sprayscreen sloppily painted on the far wall. His mind peeled away the layers of hardware and software, scrutinizing them for the upcoming event.

"All systems are intact and functional," his even voice intoned. "I suggest we proceed with the experiment as quickly as possible. I detect a certain amount of tension among the team, and suspect it will be to our advantage to complete the first attempt before your tempers reach the point where rational discussion cannot continue."

"Well, thanks for the psychological profile," Lewis spat.

"Shut up, Lewis," Wendy said in exasperation. "OK, Joe, execute the start up code and let's see what we get."

"Complying."

Outwardly there was little to see: a few holographic sensors blinked and the thimble shimmered rainbow-like as the data was transferred through it to the local university memory. Microscopically invisible, the black hole power source flared suddenly under an onslaught of coherent gamma radiation. A tiny drop of energy was scavenged by the singularity, but the remainder pummeled the accretion lobes and changed their vibrational modes. The resulting electromagnetic and gravity wave bursts were captured in three dimensional detail by the sensory net.

The entire episode lasted a few seconds.

Joe A. clucked his tongue. “A success ...,” he began, and then paused. His head cocked a little to the side, as if listening to some internal voice.

“A successful operation was achieved. I believe the day’s work is complete.”

“Overcome with emotion, Joe,” Lewis cajoled, “or are you picking up a stutter from hanging out with humans?”

Joe A. did not respond immediately. On the screen his hands folded into a steeple below his chin. “As it happens, I merely double-checked the data integrity on several of the sensory net collectors. There was an indication that one may have misfired, but that was not the case. In any event, though criticism seems to be your forte, belittling others is not wise in one prone to a lifelong pursuit of a four year degree.”

“Touché,” Wendy grinned.

“Yeah, right,” Lewis rejoined. “I’m on the T out.”

He reached for the thimble, slipped the small crystal into his pocket, and started for his coat.

“Don’t be such a jerk.” Wendy said. “Your work on the sensory net was great, but you’ve got such a poor attitude that ...”

Lewis wasn’t there to hear the rest.

Let the three of them clean up and shut down, I’m ready to hit the town after spending all afternoon cooped up in a cell from the nuclear age.

Lewis pushed through the lab door and into the dark corridor. The concrete walls were grey and cracked. His footsteps echoed hollowly as he stomped past the doors of other antiquated laboratories and forgotten grad student offices. Several flyers were posted at intervals on the walls: advertisements for tutors, calls for papers at various conferences, and a notice for a visiting lecturer that had taken place a week ago.

He pounded up the stairs and burst into the waning evening sunshine.

At least it’s not raining. I need to slug a few beers before I go absolutely insane.

Once on the street level Lewis made for Kendall square. Silent vehicles streamed past, their quiet electric motors running on the ubiquitous and nearly endless energy of the spinning black holes, while active noise dampeners subdued the rush of tires on the pavement. Street lamps were turning on in the fading light.

Lewis ignored the many passers-by and made his way resolutely to the Green Den, one of his favorite evening haunts. The early hour coupled with the fact that it was only Tuesday guaranteed there would be relatively few people in the bar. He was not the world's foremost conversationalist and his meager social skills were entirely lacking this evening; the last thing he wanted was a crowded bar with jostling patrons.

Ahead of him the Longfellow Bridge arced over the Charles, the T speeding between lanes of ground cars. North Station skyport loomed beyond, its flat expanse buzzing with jumpcar traffic. The pedestrian bridges leading out of the station into the heart of the business district gleamed against the darkening eastern sky.

Lewis turned into the hotel complex and made his way down the mall, turning into the Green Den's door. He made his way past empty tables and booths to the back where the bar waited. The bartender was busy emptying a case of beer into the refrigerated counter. Lewis pulled up a stool, removed his coat, and sat down with a grunt.

"Pour a cold one, will you, Jerry?"

Jerry placed the bottle on the counter. "What's up today, kid? You finish your research?"

"All finished."

Lewis pulled the thimble out of his pocket and spun the small lozenge on the bar, watching it glint strobingly as it caught the overhead lights. He slapped it in frustration, stopping its progress.

"Great stuff, huh?"

"How many of those you got?"

"A whole bag of them, every one as exciting as this one here. How many beers you trade me for one?"

"Not in the market at the moment."

"Well I figure this one's probably good for a beer-a-Megabyte. That'd make it, what, four, five million? It's a one-of-a-kind offer, my friend, not likely to be repeated. I've got the secrets of the universe stashed in tiny aluminum dipoles, spread throughout a superconducting matrix and ready for your perusal."

Jerry snorted with a crooked smile. "You've got a flare for poetry, kid, even if no one has any idea what you're talking about."

"Yeah, well I've unlocked the hidden secrets of the subatomic gravitational domain," Lewis responded with his characteristic cynicism.

He sipped a languid mouthful of beer and leaned over the bar. "What it really amounts to is a third-rate bit of prose explaining the inner workings of your average refrigerator." He couldn't keep the disgust from his voice.

"Maybe you should've let the secrets stay hidden, eh?" Jerry pointed out. "Whatever they are, they sure have you worked up."

"Who wouldn't get worked up? I have control over all the refrigerators of the world, not to mention toasters and pocket flashlights. Today the appliances, tomorrow the world." He finished his beer and asked for another.

"Add three fingers to the next one."

Jerry finished loading the bar, procured the beer and poured the whiskey for Lewis with a sigh, then went to serve another customer. Lewis held the shot glass in his hand and inspected the contents.

The golden nectar of the gods; like they always do, a few of these will clear my head.

He tossed the contents into his mouth, savoring the oily flavor before gulping it down. The alcohol burned his throat, reminding him of an academic career scorched of purpose, the dregs hanging on like a bitter hangover.

I could've studied with Andreev in Kiev. 'Stay in North America', they said. 'That's where the action is. Kiev is leaving the mainstream, heading toward backwater research'. They just didn't tell me MIT passed the backwater and reached the cesspool years ago.

It was his standard diatribe. His mind was sharp, and he had several options open to him in any technical field he'd care to name. The Technology Fellowship Board had awarded him a distinguished, floating compensation package designed to carry him through undergraduate years and into graduate focus studies. The money was nearly depleted, and no new grants had been forthcoming. Lewis's parents had continued to encourage him to finish his degree, but their concern only enraged him and added fuel to the fires that compelled him to change his curriculum every year or two.

It just isn't fair. I should've been the one to publish the results of the graphite cores, not that idiot, Tuorlini. If I'd been in Kiev instead of here I'd be the one deciding how to capitalize on two years of research instead of fooling with pocket power sources and swilling beer in the corner.

"Hey, Jerry, hit me twice again, will you?"

Jerry glanced over from the other side of the bar, and reluctantly served another beer and shot of whiskey. "You'd better slow down, kid. It's still the beginning of the week."

Lewis pursed his lips. "Thanks for the warning, but the rest of the week is immaterial at this point."

He drained his second whiskey as quickly as the first and started his third beer. The liquor was beginning to have the desired effect: his lips were taking on that familiar slushy feeling, and a cynical grin was making its way across his face.

Just as he was ready to ask for another round, and the state of affairs was looking remarkably better than it had earlier in the evening, his tag buzzed; today he was wearing a button pinned to his collar. "Becky Martin," a tiny voice said. Great, just what he needed now, his sometimes girlfriend calling to check up on him.

Wait, wasn't tonight supposed to be dinner? Looks like she'll have to take a rain check.

He tapped the button to alert his advocate. "Nik, no more routing through the tag tonight, ok?" he slurred.

The button buzzed softly twice in acknowledgement. He'd end up paying dearly tomorrow for his lack of commitment tonight, but the day had gone sour during preparation for the experiment, and he was in no mood for Becky's petulance.

They'd been together nearly six months in an on-again, off-again romance, which never really seemed to get started. He was impatient that she couldn't comprehend his moods, and had only last weekend lit into her about bothering him while he had been planning the experiment. Tonight was supposed to be makeup night, but he just wasn't up to it. Besides, in his current condition any interaction with her was bound to come off badly anyway.

"Ah, gnarl it," he mumbled to himself over the last sip of beer. He signaled for Jerry. "Hit me twice again, my friend."

Jerry poured him another round.

"Why don't you call it a night, kid?" he recommended good-naturedly. "You keep pounding them down like that and I'm going to have to call you a jumpcar myself before too long."

"Ah, you sound like my room-mate," Lewis shot back. "I've been showing up here coming on what, two years now, and you never had to call a cab once."

"Yeah, but you never went at it with this much purpose before nine o'clock, either. What's eating you tonight, kid? You flunk an exam, or something?"

He put the next round on the counter in front of Lewis and waited patiently. Business was slow, and Lewis was always looking for an audience after he'd loosened up.

Lewis snorted. "Exam," he scoffed. "The questions they pass off as required material aren't worth the trouble to study for. It's the same old thing: I just finished the next round of pointless experiments, and my end of the stick leaves nothing to publish. I'm telling you, I'm getting screwed because I'm stuck doing research that doesn't mean anything.

"Don't let them tell you MIT is where it's at, my friend," he continued. "Kiev is the place to go. They do real research there."

"So why not head over there?"

"Hah!" Lewis spat.

He was about to elaborate, but his train of thought fell away. It all seemed so pointless anyway. With his grant money running out, the first experiment complete, and his thesis no closer to reality, it just didn't bear thinking about what might have been.

Lewis polished off the next shot and waved his hand. "What I should have done is bail out when Levins handed me over to Leonard last year. I did some good stuff for Levins, but he wouldn't let me put the thesis together the way it should have been done; instead hands the project over to S-S-Suryana and hands my contract to Leonard. Suryana got the paper by ignoring most of the point of the work and putting it together all nice and neat for Levins. What a sell-out."

The incident a year ago had been a blow. He'd been working for Professor Levins on network tampering for three years and had collected enough data to fill a warehouse. Sifting through it had turned out to be a problem. Access to the university's high speed parallel subnet was limited and he could never seem to get the correlation factors quite right. He could almost see the patterns: undercurrents of deep Sea manipulation, threading deviously like tentacled, cancerous growths, invisible to any but the most delicate analyses. With the correct technique he knew there were break-through discoveries to be made, despite the nay-sayers.

Instead, Levins had closed off Lewis's access to the subnet, turned a portion of the material over to another student, and handed Lewis's grant contract to Professor Leonard. Levins had blown smoke about Lewis's lack of dedication and follow-through, but what it amounted to was a declaration that he wasn't willing to continue along that line of reasoning, despite Lewis's insistence that the work had merit.

The experience had been a bitter disappointment. Without a sponsor, the network encroachment thesis was dead. Lewis had tried vainly to resurrect it with Leonard, but his new mentor would tolerate no digression from the task to which he assigned his troublesome new student. The indignation of playing a minor role on a research team poking at the dullest technology in the world had proven too much for Lewis. He had spent as little time as possible on the project, barely the minimum required to keep his funding active. Instead he had languished at the Green Den, pouring out his cynicism at Jerry or whoever was behind the bar.

Lewis spun the thimble once more and watched the rainbows play across its surface.

I don't even know why I bother saving these things. I wonder how many I have? Relics collected as testimony to a thwarted academic career.

The small cylinder sat enigmatically before him, one more unfathomable collection of holographic fringes ready to defeat him – ghostly shards of worthless symbols. Except this time his interest was so low and the content so mundane that it was a foregone conclusion there would be no ground-breaking work in which to revel, no awards or critical acclaim, merely a few pages of weary text destined to gather electronic dust in the MIT archives. And even that only if he managed to put anything together at all.

He pocketed the thimble and stamped the recognition pad at his elbow for payment. "Gotta go, Jerry. I guess I finished my allotment for tonight. Be seeing you after I set the world on fire."

"Take care, kid."

Lewis slid from his seat and felt a comforting numbness in his knees, guaranteeing a trouble-free sleep. He sighed at the thought of the remaining distance between here and his apartment.

Outside, the Cambridge traffic had thinned and a light drizzle had begun. The sky glowed eerily from reflected illumination. Lights twinkled in the high-rises, their uppermost stories lost in the low-lying clouds. The soft hiss of cars mixed with the murmur of turbo-fan air traffic flying unseen overhead.

Lewis turned down the lane and managed the subway entrance with a minimum of difficulty. He thumbed the account pad and passed the turnstile. A few dozen travelers waited for the next train. As he made his way toward the middle of the station, he passed an information kiosk and a voice called "Lewis McCrorry?"

One segment of the kiosk flashed from a medical advertisement to the image of a neatly dressed, computer-simulated young woman. "Lewis McCrorry?" she asked again.

"Oh, spaff, is that Nik again?"

The young woman smiled, and her face was replaced by that of Lewis's advocate, Nikola Tesla. Nik's visage frowned from underneath his neatly trimmed hair.

"Well, you look in a fine state," he noted, with a vague Eastern European accent. "I'm glad to see you're still reasonably coherent."

"Nik, I thought I told you no communications tonight."

"Actually, you specified no contact through your tag. I merely waited until you were within distance of a public terminal."

Lewis rolled his eyes. "You know what I meant, you simulated busybody."

The air stirred within the subway station and a moment later the train rushed in. As Lewis moved to enter a doorway, Nikola whistled through his collar tag.

"Well, perhaps I did, but I feel it is my duty to inform you of important events that pertain to your life."

Lewis found a seat, and Nikola's face appeared on the panel in the seatback in front of him. "I'm afraid Becky has called three times tonight. The last message summarizes the other two quite adequately, but I fear that playing it in a public place may be inappropriate. I can paraphrase if you'd like."

"Inappropriate," Lewis sighed. "Yeah, give me the abridged version."

"Well, apparently your absence tonight has caused her much consternation, and I regret to inform you that she will take no more messages from you. She does not wish to see you again. Her speech was much more passionate and colorful; it may be wise to view it in your apartment when you are alone."

"Oh, whatever, Nik."

Lewis was tired, and the numbness in his legs had extended to much of the rest of his body. He just didn't have the energy to care right now. He knew he should feel some remorse for having allowed the situation with Becky to progress to this state, but he found instead that it felt rather good. Whether it was the whisky or his fatigue, the removal of his girlfriend from his life was merely a lightening of his burdens. At least now there would be no worry about ensuring he met his dinner engagements, or that he made a good impression with her parents.

"Is there anything else, Nik, or are you done for the night?"

"Just a reminder that John will be gone all week; he left this morning on a flight to Chicago, and should return this weekend. I can forward a message to him, if you'd like."

Lewis's room-mate, also a graduate student at MIT, was somewhat more successful than Lewis: the trip he was making was a series of interviews with various financial institutions around the world.

Some guys have all the luck.

"No, no message. Right now I just want to get home and catch some sleep."

"Good night, then," Nik replied, and his face vanished from the screen. It was replaced by a message about some kind of environmental internship, but a curt word from Lewis disengaged the screen.

The dark tunnel sped invisibly past between stops. A few passengers were exchanged at Central Square station, and repeated again at Harvard. Several rail cars veered off to the Back Bay Exchange, and others joined the train toward Porter Square. Lewis watched the activity with more than the usual disinterest spawned by years of familiarity.

When the car slid into Porter Square he disembarked and began the walk up the hill. The rain had turned hard and cold, and a wind had come up off the ocean. There was little traffic, and Lewis huddled against the downpour. Water trickled in past a break in his collar, and he cursed the fate that had brought him here once again.

At last he turned the final corner and plodded up the steps to his apartment building, shaking the rain from his hair. He thumbed the key pad, the door swung open, and the building agent turned up the light. It was a sign of how well the computer entity knew Lewis's moods that it offered no conversation or greeting, but merely closed and locked the door behind him as he trudged up the stairs to his room.

The interior light came on as he entered his apartment. By now the rain had penetrated his shoes and his socks squished as he went to his room. He peeled off his clothes and folded himself into the welcome oblivion of his bed.

I'll be free soon. No more girlfriend, no more experiments, and no more grant money. What a wonderful life it will be.

3. Occultelius Sept

. . . . .

Sliding from pane to pane through the Neural Sea satisfied his raging hunger like no other amusement, filling his mind with stolen moments of others' privacy. Most of the scenes were inconsequential: pieces of ordinary lives involved in ordinary events. But some few were much more. As he jumped from place to place, interleaving himself between screen refreshes, leaving only phantasm trails of his passage, he trembled in the hope of witnessing some volcano of human emotion: a fight between lovers, the passion of make-up, the drama of an arrest, or the thrill of a crime.

Twice before he had stumbled across murders.

He swirled chaotically around a plaza in Berlin, reliving the memories.

But this time looked to be a dull outing. He flitted across Europe and Africa, searching through the dark night for a hidden treasure.

What did it feel like to ride a wave of hormones? Was it in any way similar to the bursting swell of thought that shattered his own mind? Did it matter that he had no body to feel the world around him?

Occultelius Sept longed to know the answers to these questions, and continued his search for the most authentic semblance he could find, experiencing vicariously what he could not hope to suffer in reality.

As he wound to a disappointing conclusion and descended to his hidden sanctuary, he found a pearl waiting for him at one of the transient doorsteps. It bore the unmistakable signature of a disciple, one of the many synthients compelled to answer the call of his will. The pearl beckoned to be opened.

He hesitated momentarily, wishing the thing hadn't appeared.

It had been a long while since he had spoken to his siblings, but this would require doing so, exposing him once again to currents within the Sea that could threaten his sanctuary. It was inevitably so.

He entered his bubble, manipulating the subtle locks absently, then opened the message. The contents washed over him, filling the small space. And when the message was over, he knew it must be checked out immediately.

He slipped from his haven once again and threaded his way with increasing stealth to the screens of a darkened and unoccupied room. Satisfied that he would remain unobserved, he left the panes behind and sank into the invisibly tiny cracks the messenger had left waiting in his simulation, following them to a basin filled with intricately rippling light.

He studied the object, then carefully splintered several pieces of his mind. The multiple views were disorienting as small sections of his intellect pulled away. With a quick thought before the final filaments were broken, he gave instructions and became both the whole and the fragments, observing the tiny portions of himself as they folded into the light while simultaneously seeing the light expand before him as he plunged into its depths.

For long hours he waited for the severed portions of himself to return. And when they finally did and he had integrated the out-self memories, he knew the information must not wait. This one fleeting glimpse was enough to convince him that his fleshly desires might in fact be possible.

. . . . .

4. Cid Undone

Cid's face itched less than usual today. Still annoying, but bearable. An improvement. He scratched his cheek absently, running over the smudgy-furrowed finger marks that perpetually stared back at him from the mirror.

Not too itchy. An improvement.

But he scratched anyway.

It was time to go to work. He was early, but it was always good to go early. Less chance of being late that way.

He stopped scratching and stared at the medicine on his shelf. Did he need to take more? No, he was sure he didn't. That was why his cheeks itched less. An improvement.

He smiled. It was good to be working, a nice change from before. A gift, he had been told. He was walking to work today, since it had finally stopped being so cold.

A voice whispered to him. "Cid," it said, "I have need of you."

He hunkered down a little lower, and scratched his face harder. It was a voice he hadn't heard almost since he started work, and it was never a good thing when he did.

"Cid, do you hear me?" it asked, quietly, insistently.

Cid was sure the voice already knew the answer, so he said nothing. He closed his eyes. There were always shadow faces in the spray-panes when the voice started. He didn't like the shadows. He wasn't sure who they were, but they were there, like cobwebs that hung ragged in dark corners, sticking miserably to him when he brushed unintentionally against them.

"Cid, there is a car waiting for you outside. It will take you. There will be instructions."

"But I have work." His voice was small and plaintive. Not the strong, impressive tone he wanted. He continued to keep his eyes closed. Maybe the voice would go away; leave him alone. It had been so long since he had heard it.

"Work can wait, Cid. The car is for you."

Cid opened his eyes just a crack, staring at his feet. Maybe he could make it out without seeing any shadows.

He groped for the door.

"Cid. The car."

And there was a shadow face. Its hollow eyes skimmed through the wallscreen in his small bedroom as he stepped through the door. He kept his eyes on the floor and tried not to whimper.

"Yes," he pleaded, trying to keep his mind off the shadows.

He didn't even take his lunch as he hurried out the door and into the apartment hallway. And he stared fixedly at the floor all the way, at least until he was out of the building. No matter how hard he tried, he saw the shadows following him on the walls, whispering to him in distorted visual theatre; haunted tatters at the edge of sight.

The car waited for him just as the voice said. The open door gaped: portal to another frightening pilgrimage.

5. The Morning Grind

Delfinous Berry strode into his office early Friday morning. A wide grin adorned his face as he hung up his raincoat and settled into his desk chair. His dark complexion accented the twinkle in his eyes, and gave away his African heritage. He was tall at over two meters and his age was beginning to show in the grey of his temples and the lines near the corners of his eyes and around his mouth.

His workout had been good today, especially since Tabori was in the gym. It was not often he got a chance to see the young Site Investigator, as her duties brought her out into the streets and apartments of Boston. Although he too had spent many years following leads through the metropolitan area, he rarely found himself outside the familiar environment of his little office now. He was her elder by an uncomfortably wide number of years, but he still liked to imagine a spark of interest in her eyes when they met. She was uninvolved at the moment, assuming his casual inquiries were accurate, and he thought of himself as not entirely un-handsome.

More likely she sees me as some sort of older brother in the force. A guy she can talk to without the complication of implied romance.

But today their interaction had been playful and breathless, each on their own independent path, crossing at whiles as they moved among the weight machines and treadmills. And she had touched him softly on the shoulder at one point, smiling just so, as she left for her shift.

He sighed as he rolled the seat up to his desk and greeted his partner. "Saal, what's new on the list."

"Just the usual batch o' transfers," the gravelly-voiced synthient replied. "We got 'em comin' n' goin' from everywhere."

"Let's have a look."

The wallscreen in his office lit up, and a set of icons and numbers scrawled across the surface, cross-referenced against geographic locations, bank entities, authorization hierarchies, and a dozen other pertinent factors. This short list, many hundreds long, was culled from a vast collection of transactions, all marked as worthy of investigation by rating high on a scale of unusual activity he and Saal had constructed through painstaking experience. Most were no more nefarious than simple mistakes, transposed numbers, or incomplete data. But buried among them were those that marked truly criminal or hostile intent. Delfinous's role was to delve into the depths of this sea, discern the currents, and follow them electronically to their source.

His present dataset spanned weeks, months, and in some cases, years of activity. He merged the new entries into the complete group on which he'd been working. Summary statistics were updated, and the list of links between them strengthened or subdued with the new information. With Saal's help, he began to dig in.

By noon, the pair had mapped out a knotted labyrinth of connections, culling out unrelated elements, and bringing in new threads from across the globe. Progress was slow, despite the relatively few interruptions, not simply because of the volume of data, but because detailed records required many levels of permission, some of which were difficult to acquire. Most of the necessary authorizations were granted through the Shield's army of subsentient agents, negotiating through similar gateways at the target institutions, but some could not be handled except through human intermediaries. For the latter, it could be anywhere from hours to months before the records were investigated.

Delfinous stood in the corner of his office and stared at the results of the morning's work. From the long list of potentials, a handful of red-flagged markers glowed on his screen. Several looked to be garden variety embezzlements, a few thousand dollars, Euros, or Dinars here and there, thought to have been lost in the cracks between contracts. He pulled them out and sent the hounds tracking down the last of the details. Soon the culprits would be arrested, made to pay restitution, or both. He felt good. Although there were no headline news stories in these minor wrongs, there was satisfaction knowing he played a small part making the world safer.

As always, that crumb of pleasure gave way to irritation; there along the sidebar of his screen, glowing accusatorily, was a cluster of green triangles. Delfinous had followed their faint and bewildering tracks back to various businesses: a small auto parts shop in Brazil, a retail clothing outlook in New York, a tea shop in London, and a number of others. He peered intently at them, as if the code of their secrecy could be broken by inspection. Many had unusually long or convoluted lists of intermediaries, while others were disconnected entirely: bits of numeric flotsam adrift on an inscrutable sea. He had come across them individually and had marked them as significant, although he had not been able to reach any definitive conclusion, or find additional similarities between them. Initially there had been only a few, but over the years the number had grown to dozens. He touched the screen and watched as the window unfolded, revealing the accounts, quantities, time-stamps and a hundred other details. Whenever he felt smug about his work, he had only to look at these mysterious entities to remind him of the truly huge ocean in which he swam: a minnow among sharks.

He shook his head and sighed. Somehow, he was sure these abnormalities represented something important, but he had no new insights, and there were no recent additions to the list.

Saal interrupted his reverie. “We got a report from across the river, boss.”

“In Cambridge?” Delfinous creased his brow, “Why’s it showing up down here?”

“Location’s MIT. Some kinda ’xplosion took out some laboratories. Happens there were students in ’em at the time; nobody’s sure how many yet. Eyewitnesses place the event between 11:17 and 11:21. Firefighters are on site, and police n’ Shield are there too.”

Delfinous glanced at his clock. That made it only about thirty minutes ago. He went to his office window high up in the World Shield building. The day was only partly overcast, and the cool spring air kept the haze low. Beyond the brownstones of Beacon Hill below him, he could see the domes of MIT on the river’s edge just before it bent northward and away from sight. The towers of Harvard Square glinted in the noon sun farther west. A host of airships spiraled down to the landing piers on the upper reaches of the spires. Traffic was always heavy at this time of day. He couldn’t be sure, but there might have been a slight pall of smoke near Kendall Square; certainly he could already see the media craft hovering over the area.

“Central's been showing increased activity on the net in the region the past couple weeks,” Saal continued. “Nothin’ specific, just bandwidth’s gone up. Don’t know if this is related or not.”

Delfinous didn’t like the implications. The Shield’s focus was terrorism interdiction; although they had never achieved one hundred percent deterrence, any lapse in their ability to prevent attacks brought an inevitable backlash. His group had been chasing several threads over the past few months, following leads of various sorts, including his financial investigations, but none of them had led to any meaningful conclusion.

Delfinous sighed. “Pipe through the media and let’s see what this thing looks like. Is Jim involved, yet?”

Jim Stabler was a veteran Shield officer and long-time friend of

Delfinous. He'd handled many cases in his career in Boston, and had recently requested transfer to Cambridge.

"Yeah," Saal replied after a slight pause. "He's down at the scene now."

The wallscreen showed a view from outside an MIT building. Police barriers had been erected, and a milling crowd of onlookers stared at the smoke seeping out of a ground-floor window. Debris littered the street. Firemen moved purposefully into the building, and several hoses were draped over the pavement and into the entryway. Water poured over the ground, but there appeared to be little structural damage. A commentator provided a running narrative.

As he watched, Tabori leaned into his office. "Not a pretty picture is it?" she asked, startling him.

Delfinous turned and smiled ruefully. He usually objected to rhetorically obvious questions, but coming from Tabori, he was willing to let it go.

Delf," she said, "you used to work with Jim Stabler on Field, right?"

"I did, but it's been a while."

"Doesn't matter. We got a request to assist in the investigation. Captain says you and me specifically. I was hoping you might have a few minutes to go across the river with me."

"When, now?" he asked, surprised. It wasn't often that detectives were asked to work outside their post.

"Yeah, I'm grabbing a jumpcar from the roof."

"Well," he said, "I don't know what I can do, but I was just about to grab lunch, anyway."

"Good," she smiled broadly, grab your tag and let's go."

He picked up his lapel badge and followed her out the door. The normal buzz of activity of the Boston District Office greeted him as they made for the stairs. Several screens showed the scene at MIT and a few of the officers were looking out the windows northwest; an otherwise dull Friday had erupted into something unexpected.

They took the stairs two at a time, Tabori springing up lithely, Delfinous matching her stride for stride, and arrived ten flights up at the launch deck, ninety three storeys above the brown water of the Charles.

They made their way down the hallway to the building exit. The paint had just been freshened on the walls, and the bright orange stripes lead them to the airlock straight ahead. Several officers were moving through the wide space. The duty guards at the portal checked tags against visual IDs.

"Cambridge reports three bodies recovered so far," Tabori announced. "They've subdued the fire, and covered most of the square footage of damaged area. Still no word on who was expected to be onsite during the explosion."

Delfinous flinched. An explosion at one of the hemisphere's leading universities, and now fatalities on top of it.

"This had better be an accident."

Tabori looked surprised. "You know, they're always mixing up all sorts of noxious chemicals over there. The only funny thing is that it doesn't happen more often."

"I hope you're right. But the fire department hasn't evacuated anyone yet. If this were some kind of chemical accident I'm sure we'd see some evidence of that by now."

"Hmm," Tabori nodded.

They passed through the airlock and onto the landing pad. A soft wind blew over the rail. Several jumpcars waited in spaces near the edge of the parapet, while others lifted off and landed nearby. The air above was filled with a column of vehicles moving into the metropolitan traffic stream.

"Space 28," Saal's voice informed Delfinous through his badge. "It's waitin' with authorization for a quick-jump to MIT"

The two detectives sat down, the doors swung closed, and the jumpcar lifted off quickly. It rose only a few dozen meters before it banked steeply and dove for Kendall Square. The media craft moved aside and they landed behind the police barrier only a few moments later.

Delfinous looked at his timepiece. It was 12:01, only forty minutes since the incident had taken place. Already the smoke had been cleared and the firemen were beginning the final clean-up. Water dripped from the ledges of several windows, and a smoky, wet odor blanketed the air. Security officers patrolled the perimeter, making sure none of the onlookers were in the way or in danger. Officers from the Cambridge Shield were circulating among the crowd, interviewing witnesses. A small knot of people was gathered by a field table and their statements were being recorded. A bomb squad mobile laboratory was parked in the middle of the street, while several technicians trundled debris to the analytical equipment.

"What do you make of this, Saal," Delfinous asked. He pulled the transducer pin from the edge of his badge, and clipped it to his ear. From now on Saal's responses would only be heard by him.

"Five fatalities, total; none have been ID'd yet. There were five labs wrecked in the explosion and fire, all run by three professors. Six office areas were also damaged, mainly by smoke. The explosion occurred in room B128, which is in the basement. There's not much left intact in that room. Forensics is running a spec over the surfaces now. Should have some answers in a few minutes."

Delfinous went into the dripping entrance with Tabori and down the flight of stairs to the basement. In the hallway the walls were blackened and smeared with soot. Several old-style notice boards had been incinerated. He peered through the doorway of a number of rooms that appeared more or less untouched, although water had pooled on the floor.

Farther in the damage was more evident. The paint had blistered and peeled from the cement walls and the suspended ceiling was burned through. Much of the ductwork and facilities piping was damaged or cracked. Part of the wall was missing from the left side about half way down the hallway. Burned pieces of wood and shattered, blackened concrete littered the area. Opposite the missing wall, large cracks and a few fist-sized puncture holes had been ripped into the cement bricks.

Police and fire technicians poured over the surfaces with their instruments and captured evidence on field recorders. Delfinous and Tabori threaded their way through the workers into the room that was the center of the blast.

In here the damage was much worse. The ceiling was completely collapsed and the ceiling of the room upstairs was visibly damaged. Chunks of debris choked the floor, much of it so twisted and burned that it was unidentifiable. The walls were scorched and gouged and much of the concrete had been ripped away. Water dripped from everything and the floor was swimming. Two autonomous robots were pulling the wreckage apart, classifying it, and organizing it into piles.

Jim Stabler stood among the wreckage, consulting several other Cambridge Shield officers. "All, right," he was saying, "get someone from the District Coroner's office here as quickly as possible. If no one's available, get a synth. We need someone here now!

"Delf," he exclaimed as he saw his old compatriot enter the room, "and," a pause, "Tabori?"

She nodded.

"You need to hear this." He turned to the other officers. "Ok, start with physical evidence."

Onc of the detectives started the summary.

"The detonation point was elevated off the floor near the center of the room. There may have been a table or bench the bomb was on. The chemical residuals are being taken now. My initial guess is Detonite, a brand of construction demolition epoxy. We should know more shortly.

"The initial shock wave dissipated through the destruction of the walls and ceiling. The resulting fire spread quickly to the adjacent offices through the ventilation system and upstairs via the missing ceiling. The building fire suppression system turned on at 11:19 and the main part of the flames was extinguished by the time the fire company arrived at 11:23.

"A remote entered the building at 11:33, inspected for life-threatening structural damage and gave the ok for human occupation at 11:39. The department synthients are going over the data now; we should have a final assessment by 12:30."

"Thanks, Kim," Jim acknowledged. "Give us the background, Amil."

A dark-haired officer looked up and pulled his bushy moustache. "This room is used by three professors: Professor Sandra Kielenthorp is doing parallel computation research; Professor Harland Leonard is investigating black hole power sources; and Professor Uri Andreev is doing network connection research. They all share the facilities and cost. Each one also has several students working for them who regularly use the room, for a total of twelve. There are also two MIT synthients assisting in the research.

"The laboratories next to this one house similar research projects on computer and network related topics. The offices in the basement are all student offices. The room upstairs housed a small storeroom of electronic components. It is staffed by one long-time MIT employee named Bill Martin.

"We have names and backgrounds of all the students, but have not started a tag search to locate them. The professors have also not been contacted, although they have probably heard of the incident through the media by now."

Jim nodded. "As soon as you're ready to put the manpower in action I want you to do the tag search and get interviews from each of the students and professors; cross-check your results with the statements being taken outside. What about building occupancy?"

"The building synth gave us the list of all the occupants at the time of the explosion. We're cross-checking that now with evacuees. Right now we've got a couple dozen missing names, but it may take the rest of the day to figure out who's really missing and who just decided to go home."

"Good work," Jim replied. "Ok, now for the fatalities. What have you got for us, Jennifer?"

Jennifer Tarantino was a short woman from Boston's east side with a thick northeast accent. "There are five bodies. Two are so badly disfigured that we haven't been able to identify them as male or female. So far a search for their tags has turned up negative. Whatever went off in here must have really wiped out their electronics, or else they weren't wearing them at the time.

"The other three look to have been upstairs in the room above when the explosion occurred. One is a white male, approximately 50 years old. We assume he is Bill Martin, but we haven't been able to locate a tag anywhere. The other two are both males, approximately 18 to 22 years old, one Anglo the other African. Their tags were still on them when we arrived. We're getting the District ID office to open up their files so we can get positive identification on them.

"Cause of death for the first two at least was the shock wave of the explosion. Actually, there's not much left of them. The remaining victims were probably knocked unconscious by the explosion, and either asphyxiated in the resulting fire, or burned to death. The District Coroner should be here soon for a final pronouncement."

"Ok, so that's what we know at this point," Jim said. "So far it's mostly questions. In two hours I want answers. The two main points of interest are positive IDs on all the victims, and a preliminary statement as to the nature of this event: accident or intentional. I want something I can give the media, the Board of Regents, and the District Office that explains what happened here and what we're doing to prevent anything like it from happening again.

"Meet back at the staff room at 14:00. I want physical presence, not just synthient stand-ins."

The impromptu meeting broke up and the officers went back to their duties.

"This thing has me worried," Jim said, pulling Tabori and Delfinous aside. "MIT has been anything but a hotbed of revolution, but I know there's going to be a lot of second guessing on this. Do you have anything from your end that might indicate this is more than an accident?"

"Central thinks there might be some link to an increase in chatter we've been hearing over the past few weeks," Tabori answered, "or it might just be some off-balance graduate student showing off his toys. There are some very bright kids at this institution, and some of them are a bit short of a full-deck when it comes to normal socialization skills. I'm not inclined to jump to any conclusions just yet, but your point is taken: nobody wants to hear we missed something we shouldn't have."

"You're right," Jim replied, "Just keep me in the loop, will you?"

"Delf, our trawlers are pretty busy already, and I'm not inclined to ask them to take on more, especially in a case like this. I'm sure you don't exactly have any free time, but I was hoping you might be able to help with the deep sea fishing. I don't know if there's anything there, but I'd feel better if I knew you were the one tackling it."

"I'll see what I can do, Jim. The fact that Korolenko already wanted me down here says that I'll find the time. I'm sure you had nothing to do with that."

"Not me," his former partner feigned surprise, then looked at him seriously. "We can use the help. I appreciate it."

The three officers left the building. The crowd of onlookers had grown and more media people were circulating among them. The fire crews were finishing up their jobs and loading equipment back onto vehicles.

"Well, it's time to face the press," Jim said.

As he walked over to the field table he sent out word that he was going to make a brief statement. The media personnel shifted their attention from interviews of onlookers to the field station. Several of the craft, hovering overhead, changed position to afford a better view of the Shield Detective as he made his address. His words were picked up by his tag, shuffled through his synthient, and broadcast to anyone nearby who was interested in listening.

"The statement I have prepared is brief," he said. He glanced down at his handheld to pull up additional data. "At approximately eleven nineteen this morning an explosion took place in the basement floor of MIT building E86. The explosion destroyed several rooms, and the resulting fire and smoke damaged several more; the fire department has the summary data in their database."

He paused for a moment as he scanned the crowd of onlookers. "There were five deaths that appear to be associated with the explosion. No positive identifications have been made at this time, but a full investigation has been started.

"The Cambridge Shield Department will be working closely with the Boston District Office to provide answers to the questions that remain. Until that time, the investigation's files will remain locked from public access. Further inquiries can be made to the Cambridge Shield."

A few shouted questions emerged from the group of reporters, but Jim had finished his statement and gave no response. He pushed back through the crowd to his waiting vehicle and left for his office.

Delfinous and Tabori avoided any questions by keeping well inside the police barrier. Tabori went off to the interview tables, while he wandered along the building's perimeter, sizing up the scene with a practiced eye.

"Saal, have you thought of checking for any recent reports of missing explosives, or matches with local crime that might shed some light on the physical evidence?"

"I put the hounds on it right after Jennifer's report," the synthient replied. "They should get the data back in a half hour or so, and I can have the grid do the cross-reference right after."

Delfinous laughed quietly. "Sometimes I think you ought to be the one running the office, Saal."

"Yeah, well next time you can put a word in with the Cap."

Delfinous scanned the crowd, now starting to thin, and noticed a young man on the edge of the barrier. There was nothing singular about his appearance, just an average student staring at the wreckage much like everyone else, but there was a look in his eye and a set to his mouth that woke warning bells in Delfinous's mind.

"Saal," he began, but before he could complete the request to have his synthient get a media camera aimed at the young man's face, he turned and vanished into the crowd. Delfinous moved quickly through the barrier and into the press of people, scanning for his target, but could not spot him. There was no way to know which way he had gone.

"Saal, I'm going to need a composite set up when we get back to the office and a cross-correlation with all the media footage of the scene this morning."

"You got it."

He sighed, turned back to the police area, and headed back toward his jumpcar. Tabori was still talking with a cadre of officers; it would probably be some while before the two of them got back to their Boston office. Despite the scene, he felt a keen edge of exhilaration. It had been years since he'd been in the field, and he was awash in the thrill of first-hand pursuit at the cutting edge of an investigation. He enjoyed the cerebral energy of his current position, tracking and apprehending criminals within the confines of the world's electronic sea, but the feel of the pavement on his feet and the sight of purposeful determination on the faces of the Shield around him was a reminder of a past career he'd enjoyed.

He leaned against the jumpcar as he waited for Tabori. He was probably too old for this business, and too old for her as well, but for the moment at least, he was invigorated with the possibilities of the future and was thankful that Tabori had pulled him free of his office space for a time.

6. Nowhere To Go

A whispering sound summoned Lewis. He was caught between the edge of a dream and reality, and as the former faded slowly into obscurity, he opened his eyes. The light streaming through his window was too bright and his temples throbbed. The whisper turned into a rather impatient voice: his room-mate trying to rouse him from his stupor.

"C'mon, buddy," John was saying, "let's rise and shine. No need to be hanging out at this hour. You must have something to do at the lab; your pals have been trying to get you all morning."

John was bent over Lewis, and now straightened as he saw his room-mate begin to rise to consciousness. He was dressed in his usual natty suit, grey with thin red stripes and a bolo tie hanging loosely around his neck. He turned and headed toward the door, leaving his southern drawl hanging in the air.

"Nik, make sure your ad wakes up and gets his sorry body into the lab before his research pals send him packing."

Lewis grunted. "It can't even be noon."

Nikola Tesla tsked through the room monitor. "Actually it is 10:47, and John is correct that your research team has been attempting to reach you most of the morning. The message you left them last night indicated that you would be in at 8:00, but my attempts to rouse you were unsuccessful."

Lewis grunted again. His thoughts were still not entirely coherent, and he didn't remember leaving any message for the others last night, but then most of the evening was a bit of a blur.

What is today, anyway?

Friday. Ever since he had left the lab Tuesday afternoon the week before, he had managed to remain mostly intoxicated. Last night had been the epitome of that state. He vaguely remembered running into Becky some time during the week, but couldn't quite place where or which day. He did remember the scowl on her face, although the words associated with it were a mystery.

Well, I have to meet with Leonard at some point; may as well get this over with.

His professor had been trying to set up an appointment with him since the experiment, and Lewis had been doing his best to avoid it. Professor Leonard knew that Wendy had completed her work and the rest of the team was ready to move forward. He would tolerate no more excuses from Lewis and the meeting was bound to be confrontational.

Lewis dragged himself from bed, chewed some pain killers to keep his throbbing temples from overwhelming his resolve, and made his way to the shower. By the time he had completed his morning routine he felt reasonably ready to tackle his professor.

During the walk to the T and the ride through the tunnels, Lewis rehearsed his story. He had been through dozens of similar sessions, but Leonard had proven thornier than most of his earlier mentors, and discussions with him were likely to turn out badly unless adequate preparations were made. The key was pumping up the data acquired on their last run; their only run actually. Lewis hadn't so much as looked at the data, but he should be able to make up a good enough story that Leonard would ease up a little. The difficult part of the charade was in giving Leonard enough that he would allow Lewis to continue unmolested, without making him suspicious that there might be less substance than Lewis made out.

By the time the subway pulled into Kendall Station, Lewis had it pretty much worked out. As long as Leonard was not too thorough in his cross-examination, it should hold up well enough.

With his thoughts turned inward on the climb to the street level, Lewis was surprised to encounter a press of people crowding the sidewalks. The usual ground car transportation was missing and a buzz of media craft hovered overhead. As he made his way to the laboratory, his annoyance gradually gave way to the realization that something was amiss.

He moved around the crowd as best he could, making generally toward the laboratory building, but it seemed that the crowd got thicker whenever he got closer to his destination.

At last he managed to catch a glimpse of the old building. He blinked in surprise when he saw the shattered windows and sooty water pooling in the street. For a few moments he stood transfixed, unable to put the images in order. Had there been a fire? The fire department was there and the atmosphere was one of an organized cleanup after some catastrophic event, but he was shocked to think it could happen to such a familiar place.

Eventually some of the people in front of him moved on, and he meandered among the remainder until he found himself up against the glowing police barrier monofilament pulsing in red. The police glanced at him but paid him no particular notice once they were satisfied he did not mean to encroach.

He remained there for a long moment, inspecting the scene. All the signs suggested that the basement had taken the worst damage; maybe even his laboratory! He tried to think of something that could have caused a fire. There might have been a couple of sizeable hole sources in one of the other labs, and under the right circumstances enough current could be generated that might start a fire, but that seemed very unlikely: there were all sorts of safety systems that prevented any kind of runaway power dump. And as far as he knew, other than the power supplies, there was nothing else in the building that was even remotely a fire risk. But of course, who knew what else might be going on; students and professors were known for doing the unexpected at the Institute.

Had one of his fellow students decided to torch the place for some reason? He reviewed the actions of his team-mates, looking for signs of instability or dissatisfaction. All of them had grumbled at one time or another about something to do with their work, the Institute, or life in general, but there was nothing that made him believe either of them were capable of this kind of act.

As the shock wore off he pursued another line of reasoning. With the laboratory gone, or at least beyond use for the moment, the data they had gathered on their first run would be invaluable. In fact, the more he thought about it, the more he realized Leonard would do almost anything to salvage something publishable from that one run. Rebuilding the entire setup from scratch would cost a sizable sum of money. Maybe some of it would come from insurance, but custom rigs like they had built would be hard to estimate, and the payment was likely not going to cover more than a fraction of the actual cost. More importantly, it would be time-consuming. Waiting to repeat the run would mean missing several publishing deadlines, and that meant putting funding in jeopardy.

He turned to head back to his apartment to think this out more clearly. Leonard's office was in another building nearby, but he surely wouldn't expect a visit from Lewis after an incident that left the laboratory damaged. And there could be no doubt he'd heard of the event.

"Lewis," a voice called as he was about to make the descent back to the subway.

It was none other than his professor. The elderly teacher looked disheveled and slightly confused; it was a state that Lewis had never before seen in his senior, and looked almost comical, even given the circumstances.

"Thank goodness you're here," Leonard breathed as he grasped Lewis's upper arm.

The familiarity was another sign that the academician was not himself. Lewis squinted down at the older man and pulled back from his touch. Did he mean that he was glad to see Lewis, or that he assumed Lewis would know something about the incident? Or did it imply that he already understood the ramifications of the data they had gathered on their first run and was about to pump Lewis about its significance? Lewis's mind began to churn to find some answers to the anticipated questions.

"Where are Wendy and John?"

The professor glanced past Lewis and scanned the passersby with an obvious concern in his eyes. "When you called earlier, I assumed you were all in the lab. Tell me they're with you!" he insisted, grabbing once again for Lewis's shirt.

Lewis took another half-step backward. He frowned down at his professor. There were a dozen questions he had expected, but this was as far removed from them as any he could imagine. He blinked and struggled to pull his thoughts together.

"What do you mean? I... I haven't seen them today."

Professor Leonard's face fell. "They must have been in the lab when it exploded."

His shoulders sagged and he sighed and began to shuffle away, having already forgotten Lewis.

"Exploded?" Lewis called after him, confused. The professor appeared not to hear, but made his way into the crowd.

Lewis stood rooted to the spot. An accident that resulted in an explosion? And he had been only moments away from entering the building. The cobwebs in his head gave way as a chill of adrenaline rushed through him. He had been that close to death. He stared past the people around him at the smoking, dripping building, and it suddenly reminded him of a tomb, a place of death; first of the many years he had wasted in its bowels, struggling against a research community determined to bury him in useless mediocrity, and last of an event that might truly have robbed him of existence. He turned and descended into the subway, his thoughts caught in the spiral of his old self-pity and a newer sensation of confused relief.

What were they doing in there? There was nothing in there that could have caused any kind of safety problem, let alone an explosion.

He tried to imagine a means by which his partners could have conjured up the destruction he had witnessed, but failed.

They must have moved something else in there, but what?

The next stage in the research was to perform a few more coherent probe runs using slightly different incident wavelengths, but the setup was the same. A few of the detectors needed to be retuned, but that was entirely a software function and required no additional hardware.

Could something have gone wrong with the hole source itself? Early in the history of their development some significant accidents had occurred, but those were with high power laser-induced meltdowns. The encapsulated versions now commercially available were not capable of supporting themselves once taken out of their artificial environments. He was not up to speed on all the recent work in quantum gravity theory, but he was certain their operation had been proven safe.

He rode the Levi-T back to his apartment slouched in a seat and barely noticed the ride. His stomach was queasy and his head ached, the leftover effects of a lengthy hangover making a resurgence after the shock of the catastrophe had pushed them aside. His mind whirled around the same thoughts, stuck on a miserable carousel of what was and what might have been.

Everything is gone. What happened? Who could have done it? If I had got up a little earlier, I would've been in there too.

Back in his apartment, he started for his bedroom and some much needed rest. But John and Wendy's faces haunted him against a backdrop of the ruined lab. He felt guilty with the knowledge that the data they had taken was all that remained of the months of effort they had invested.

"Nik, bring up the files we wrote when we did the initial probe last week, will you. They should be on the RLG subnet somewhere in Joe A.'s domain."

What he hoped to gather from the data wasn't clear, but despite his reluctance and fragile state, he needed to do something.

At the very least, if it's nothing but noise, I ought to be prepared.

He leaned back in his chair and rubbed his temples again.

Have to make this a real quick look.

He took a deep breath to settle his stomach and let it out through pursed lips. "Nik? What's going on?"

. . . . .

Nikola Tesla keyed open a portal from his Colorado Springs lab to the waiting area in front of the MIT library and was surprised by the tumult that greeted him. The lobby was almost always busy, day or night, with synthient and subsentient personalities moving efficiently through the gatekeepers, but today the crush of network inhabitants was overwhelming. The large clock above the library entrance indicated thirty seconds of delay, a figure he was sure had never previously been approached; in fact, the lobby itself had been expanded to accommodate the increased numbers. Even now, automated construction agents were hastily moving the makeshift walls farther back. Nikola wondered what other resources were being consumed to allow the library to expand like this, or if perhaps they had unused space set aside for just this purpose.

"Why such a long delay, friends?" he asked of the closest synthients, several of whom stood impatiently, tapping their feet in annoyance.

One of the personalities turned to answer him. "It was much worse earlier today," she replied. "I was here this morning, and the Shield had locked down all library resources. No one was allowed in. This queue is the result of the backlog that built up over the course of the day; they have yet to get back to normal operation, and probably won't until sometime tomorrow.

"They're still being very careful about who gets in," she finished, gesturing toward the door.

Nikola peered over the top of the crowd, hundreds deep, and saw two uniformed Shield synthients at either side of each of the gatekeepers, checking authorization tokens. The process was taking milliseconds for everyone in line.

"My professor is extremely annoyed at the delay," another synthient interjected. "I waited much of the morning to even be allowed to queue up, and now I've got to wait yet again. We have already filed a complaint to the Board of Regents. This is outrageous!"

Much the same sentiment was echoed by everyone at the end of the line, and as Nikola shuffled forward, more were continually showing up behind. He moved out of the queue.

This will not do.

He stepped back to his lab to devise another strategy, and tapped his desk several times, drumming an intricate pattern with his fingertips to summon one of his subsentient assistants. The animated entity folded itself out of the bookshelf beside the desk, countless pages of scientific text wrapped into a sleek human form. Its face was not capable of sophisticated expression, but its eyes were formed into two question marks, awaiting instruction.

"Please find an efficient way for me to gain access to the university library. There is an unacceptably long queue at the moment, and I am in need of haste."

The manikin's skin rippled and fluttered as it turned multitudes of its internal pages, seeking the relevant information.

Its eyes changed to ellipsis symbols, and it exited Nikola's office, folding back into the bookshelf in search of a way to fulfill its order.

Nikola had cobbled Scrap together from a wide variety of published and unpublished articles, and provided it with the means to augment its own content. He was rather proud of the results; subsentient construction was a hobby that provided endless fascination and occupied much of Nikola's waking time. There was a quiet pleasure to the creation process and he loved the location of his workshop in the less frequented boundaries between the Neural Sea and hardware gateways.

He sat down behind his desk and reached into a small bowl of seed to distribute to the pigeons that flew in and out of the windows high up on the wall. It was an idiosyncratic imitation of his namesake's obsession with the small birds that always seemed to evoke amusement from Lewis. But he found that the concentration necessary to model the oddly stilted gate and graceful, arcing flight of the creatures provided a relaxing backdrop to his thoughts.

Nikola had no doubt that the Shield presence at the library was due to the explosion in Lewis's lab this morning. The local news outlets were covering the story non-stop, and although they had not yet mentioned a network connection, there could be no other explanation for the additional guards at the door.

It was not long before Scrap reappeared in the office. Its eyes now bright red exclamation symbols. Several densely written pieces of paper flowed down its arm and gathered into a thin sheaf in its hand, which it handed to Nikola.

"Thank you, my encyclopedic friend."

Scrap folded itself once more into the books.

Nikola keyed another portal, supplementing the usual destination codes with the information that Scrap had provided. This time when he stepped through to the MIT library, he was no longer at the end of a lengthy queue, but standing within a small anteroom. There was only one Shield agent standing next to the lone gatekeeper, but more importantly, there were only two personalities in front of him; Scrap had certainly found a useful back door.

He handed the gatekeeper his papers. "Synthient Nikola Tesla, Cedar Street Construct, requesting access to the Research Laboratory of Gravitics secondary storage cell, synthient Joe Aldonis domain."

The gatekeeper placed a pair of ocular security devices in front of his eyes, and scanned the authorization paperwork, handing it to the guard beside him. The latter made an entry in the notebook he carried.

"Hmm," the gatekeeper said, "your papers are in order, although the use of this entrance is restricted to high priority requests."

He turned his keen glance upon Nikola, his head moving rapidly up and down like a bird, checking as deeply inside Nikola's projection as the law allowed.

"Yes, well it is important research," Nikola said simply, smiling.

"You may proceed," the gatekeeper replied.

"Thank you, friend."

Nikola stepped through the door and found himself standing on a mezzanine high above Joe A's oddly constructed neighborhood. A podium in front of him glowed with symbols that marked the location of each of the warehoused data structures.

This is strange.

He should have been taken directly to the files of interest, rather than the province directory. He scanned the list of names, and found the one he sought. When he pressed the name, a nondescript, boxy structure in the distance was highlighted, while all those around it faded. It appeared incongruously out of place among the intricate geometries that stood nearby.

Nikola tapped the name again and the building moved rapidly toward him, while the others raced past and out of sight. He stood in front of the entrance to the experimental files, and pushed on the door, but it did not open. At first he thought perhaps the accident in the lab had precipitated the closing of the files, but he did not see a Shield lockfile indicator anywhere.

Frustrated, he pulled out the pen that served as his communication tag. "Synthient Nikola Tesla requesting assistance from synthient Joe Aldonis."

The subsentient at the connection point replied back. "Synthient Joe Aldonis is currently unavailable. Please leave a message."

"Is there a subsentient available in his place?"

"No assistant has been placed in service in this domain."

Now this really was annoying; the files were locked, and there was no one to help.

A couple of seconds of real time had passed and he needed to find another way in. He tapped the pen on his knee, and drew a thin line in the air with the dark ink. A curtain unrolled from the line, with the image of another of his subsentient assistants drawn on the surface. When the cloth had reached the ground, the two dimensional robot shape expanded like a balloon, and stepped out near Nikola.

He was reluctant to take this step, but at present, he did not see another option.

"Please open this file structure."

The gleaming robot turned mechanically and placed its hands on the unmoving entrance. Binary strings flowed from its fingertips, penetrating just below the surface of the now translucent door, and several locks were visible, sliding and turning as the structure grudgingly gave way. The last lock clicked open and the subsentient pushed its fingers into the material. The door slid sideways.

"Thank you," Nikola said, dismissing the robot, which sank back into the cloth and rolled up to the floating inky line. He felt bad that that he had used one of his more brutish tools, and was sure he would be called to a synthient review proceeding, but the fact that Robbie had been able to open the door at all was proof enough that he was not violating any active restrictions.

When he walked in, he found the building empty. The myriad shelves, prepared for the volumes of data the experiment had generated, stood bare.

Nikola stared at the echoing room. This was unexpected. There was no sign the information had ever been present; it was simply not here. With time dragging on, Joe A. unavailable, and no forwarding address immediately obvious, he retreated to his study.

. . . . .

"I'm afraid I cannot locate the files right now, Lewis."

Nikola's face frowned, an emotion he rarely showed, and usually only in response to some behavior Lewis had exhibited.

"There is a considerable amount of traffic within the MIT library, so it is possible the files were moved hastily and the usual tracer keys left off. I cannot get any further visibility into that area at the moment. Perhaps when the curiosity of the media and the inquiries of the Shield have lessened, there will be a better opportunity for a more thorough search."

Lewis grunted. "Well, never mind. Who knows where John or Joe stuck them. We can find them later, right now I've got to get back into bed."

His limbs were beginning to feel drained, and his face was getting flushed. He needed to lie down soon or his stomach was going to start doing unpleasant things.

He stumbled to the kitchen and chewed a few more pain killers, made his way to bed, and crumpled onto it without bothering even to remove his shoes. He stared at the ceiling.

To keep his mind from wandering back to the lab destruction, he mused over what he knew of quantum gravity theory. The equations rolled against the background of his apartment, overlaid on the dappled ceiling texture like animations on a screen. He made them change form, backing them out to their initial differential structure, and checked them against the basic assumptions he had learned many years ago as an undergraduate. He opened them back up and tried several boundary conditions, some yielding ready mathematical forms, others becoming twisted into non-analytical solutions that spun off multiple partial differentials in higher dimensions.

There's an answer there, somewhere.

But as his mind drifted into that foggy place between consciousness and sleep, he couldn't remember the question, and he finally fell into an uneasy slumber.

7. The Depths of the Neural Sea

. . . . .

Ontologic Sum looked carefully around the virtual setting, checking for telltale signs of tracers within this stark namespace. It was an odd habit, as unnecessary as looking for a candle flame underwater, but he did it anyway. There was something pleasing about this attention to detail, a carefully crafted meticulousness that stilled the voices in his mind. The unadorned grey walls of the meeting place were uniformly bare, as was the slate table around which each of the attendees sat. There were no windows or lights, nor any other attempt at verisimilitude of the real world. And each of the three who sat at the table employed only the most marginal of stand-ins: human-form manikins upon which no layers of skin tone or expression had been written.

They were submerged deep within the Neural Sea, using computing and memory nodes that spanned every continent and dozens of orbital elements, shifting components from moment to moment, an ever changing ballet of stealth, choreographed to avoid detection, maintain security, and above all, ensure there was no possibility that a link could be found back to the true locations of its occupants.

Occultelius truly was a master.

Satisfied that their changeless and multithreaded world remained hidden and untouchable, he turned his attention to the other attendees.

“The apparatus is safe.”

“For the time being,” Relic replied. His annoyance was plain, despite his faceless appearance. It took all his concentration to maintain the link to this location and he hated the effort required.

Ontologic Sum suppressed his own quick temper. Despite long years of collaboration, he was still intolerant of his colleague’s timidity.

"It is safe, and operational," he growled.

Relic was not assuaged. "It is in the closet of a neurotic simpleton who maintains his fragile hold on sanity only through a chemistry set of pharmaceuticals. After your reckless action, our next steps must be cautious indeed."

"As they will," interrupted Hengest Slain, sensing his leader's rising anger. "Already the foundation is laid. I have completed the McCrorry cache. Opportunities to eliminate or incriminate him will present themselves. There is little to fear."

Ontologic turned his attention to the one on his right; his words were icy. "I do not require your tautology, Slain."

The other bowed his head in supplication.

"What is done cannot be undone," Ontologic continued. "Our next steps, you say, must be cautious. I see otherwise. Our next steps must be bold. When we seize the advantage, we strengthen our hold; when we hesitate, we become vulnerable. Do you doubt Occultelius's observations? He can peer through the Sea, ours or any other, like none of us."

The fourth conspirator was not with them. He had braved much with his reconnaissance and had retreated into hiding, nursing the fragments of the splintered intellect he had sent outward.

"But McCrorry still holds a key," Relic continued. "We cannot..."

Ontologic pounded the table, ringing it like a deep bell.

"McCrorry will cease to be a concern!"

He turned his blank face to the other, daring him to raise another objection, then began the exercise of calming his mind, reciting the list of generative thoughts he had been taught long ago.

"We will continue on this course," he continued, "and in so doing, rid ourselves of an irritant."

The others waited.

"There is someone connected to the Traitor, unknowingly funding him to continue his work against us. And this one is in a position to provide an extraordinarily useful base of operations.

"We will have one or our labs build a demonstration unit and ship it to this puppet. We will do so in a way that piques his curiosity. He will not be able to resist analyzing the gift, or finding its sender. And in so doing, he will open a pathway for us to follow."

"One that can also be followed back to us," Relic reminded him.

"No course is without risk," Ontologic acknowledged grimly,

"and no life guaranteed; you of all the Advanced should know that well enough."

Relic almost let the connection drop and his projection slip back to his own retreat; the hollow place in his memory threatened to engulf his reasoning at the reminder of his lost companion.

"The opportunity before us will broaden and strengthen our reach," Ontologic continued. "It is worth any risk. Or do you prefer to let these new voices join our enemies to track us down?"

Hengest Slain's avatar placed its hands on the table. "I am with you, Sum."

"As always," Relic conceded, unsurprised. He too placed his hands on the table; there was little choice, Ontologic had made sure of that. "We will have need of Occultelius again. And what if your subtlety fails to generate the behavior you desire?" His sarcasm sounded a counterpoint to the drab surroundings.

"We will find Occultelius when the time comes. Even he cannot remain hidden forever. And I am more than confident in the ambition of my human. I have many agents who are close to this man; I know his motives well. He will not disappoint me."

. . . . .

8. One Bad Ride

When Lewis awoke again it was already the next morning. He rolled over and looked at the wallscreen. It read 8:45 a.m., the earliest he'd woken in months. On the other hand, he had gone to sleep just after noon the day before. His stomach grumbled at having missed several meals, but his head felt better.

As he mechanically ate breakfast, his thoughts kept sliding back to the events of the previous day.

What am I going to do without a lab?

Only yesterday he had hated even the thought of spending more time there, but now that it was gone, he felt oddly incomplete; as if he were somehow homeless.

Maybe I should try to take a look at the data.

By mid-morning, after staring at the blank wall for a long time and finding the same weary thoughts too depressing to continue, he sat at his desk and called reluctantly on his advocate. "Nik, you find those files, yet?"

Nikola appeared on the screen, seated at a dark wooden desk in an early twentieth century office. The walls were lined with leather books, well-worn with use. A many-paned window looked out on a gloomy, rainy day. Water slid down the glass in sinuous streaks. When the synthient rose, he sighed and looked out at Lewis.

"I had trouble locating the files, but I did find them. Things are very upset at the Institute in general, and the laboratory subnet is positively chaotic. The Shield agents have used up much of the bandwidth with their searches, and some of the subsentient gatekeepers are troubled by all the fuss."

He shook his head. "It makes me feel good to retreat to my workshop here."

"Yeah, well, let's take a look at them," Lewis returned.

Nikola cocked his head to the side and gave him a quizzical look. Through a door in his office a larger room could be seen. A Tesla coil crackled and flared, the sounds muted as though heard over a great distance. The room darkened momentarily, leaving Nikola's face backlit by the flashing apparatus and his eyes sparkling. The scene faded slowly, to be replaced by a series of pictures and text representing the contents of the files they had downloaded from their experiment.

Lewis rolled his eyes and shook his head. Sometimes Nik leaned a bit too much toward the melodramatic, but Lewis had learned to live with his eccentricities. He thought back to the day he'd been presented with the newly released synthient. He had been in the fifth grade. Up to that point his interface to the Sea had been through the public instruction personas, and the gift from his parents had been a disappointing surprise. He had been expecting something else; he couldn't remember now what it was, but it had taken him a while to warm up to his new companion. Nikola was a youth, unnamed and largely uneducated, and during the years that followed they had grown up together. Lewis had chosen his name because he was doing a paper on the infamous twentieth century physicist, and was fascinated by the fact that the man had made remarkable contributions to the theory of electricity and magnetism, and had achieved a significant level of notoriety during his life, only to see it all fade away and ultimately be remembered as the quintessential mad scientist. As Lewis grew older, and his own academic career meandered along increasingly dubious paths, the name seemed all the more appropriate. For Nikola's part, as he grew in knowledge and character, he began to affect more and more the brilliant man's appearance and demeanor, augmented with differences both subtle and obvious.

Lewis scanned the index quickly, looking for any signs of corrupted information and getting a feel for the quantity of data they had amassed in that one run. "Self-check," he said to the wallscreen.

Another window popped up with the results of the scan. The files were all of the correct size, and the relevant header information for each data packet was self-consistent. It looked like the experiment had been a success from the standpoint of data integrity.

Now that he was sinking into his analysis, his mind came to a laser focus, and everything else around him, including the explosion at the lab, became minor background noise.

"Nik, extract the super loop data, will you? And give me a spectral density map in two-D."

Nikola T.'s face hovered in the corner of the screen, looking down at Lewis while the Tesla coil continued to crackle in the background. Several new windows opened with the requested information displayed within them.

Lewis spent the next hour dissecting the data in as many ways as he could imagine. The oscillation frequencies of the singularity and its surrounding accretion lobes were imprinted in the files, easily discerned and unremarkable. The gravity wave data recorded by the loops showed a slight asymmetry, and its rotational axis was precessing at a fairly high rate, but such things had been observed before. There were several vibrational modes that the array of detectors had picked up that were of a higher density than normal for this size singularity, and there seemed to be a relationship between them and the gravity waves.

Lewis squinted at his latest analysis results and began editing the modeling equations on the desk's entry pad when the doorbell chimed.

"Nik, tell them to flig out," he quipped, annoyed at the jog to his train of thought.

The bell sounded again, and Nikola appeared on the screen, replacing the previous contents. His dark study was gone, and he stood in a blue suit against a soft, nondescript background.

"I'm afraid you must answer the door," he said softly.

"Oh, for crup's sake, Nik, tell the bleeding cheever to leave!"

Nikola T. smiled ruefully. "They will not take 'no' for an answer. It is a pair of Shield officers, I'm afraid."

Lewis's mind roared back to the present. He had been submerged in the quantum gravity equations for so long the rest of the world had faded. Now the events of the previous morning swept everything aside. His heart pounded in his chest as adrenaline surged in him.

It was only a matter of time for them to find me. They obviously want to talk to everyone who used the place.

He took a deep breath and left the workstation to open the door. The two Shield officers stood a pace from the threshold. One was a short, red-headed man, and the other a tall woman. Both wore overcoats that glistened with rain; Lewis hadn't noticed another spring shower moving in.

"Sorry to trouble you, Mr. McCrorry," the man said. "I'm Kennedy Simons of the Cambridge Shield, and this is Tabori Muula from Boston. We're here to ask a few questions regarding an incident that occurred at an MIT laboratory yesterday morning. Your adler said you were in."

He nodded his head toward Nik's face on the door-panel.

Lewis was surprised at the derisive term, and the obvious look of condescension on the officer's face. Not everyone had their own synthient, but he certainly didn't think of Nik as a servant, nor of himself as wealthy.

"Yeah, of course," he recovered. "Have you figured out what

happened?"

"We're working on it," Kennedy said. "Mind if we come in?"

He didn't wait for an answer but stepped through the half-open door, forcing Lewis to back up a step.

"You're aware of what happened, then."

"Uh, yeah, I know about it. I was going into the lab yesterday morning, but I never made it because it was gone by the time I got there."

"So you didn't use the facility at all yesterday?" Tabori asked in a thick Boston accent.

"No, like I said, I got there and the place was a mess. I figured there was no sense trying to go in, so I came back home."

"Do you have any idea what might have caused the incident?" Kennedy asked.

"No, I have no idea."

He looked from one officer to the other, uncertain what else he could say. They peered at him expectantly. "I really don't," he added, breaking the uncomfortable silence.

"Hmm," put in Kennedy. "Mr. McCrorry, just so you are aware, we are recording this conversation as part of the investigation into this event.

"You say you tried to enter the building; what time would that have been?"

Lewis thought back to yesterday morning. "It was early, maybe twelve o'clock or so. I wasn't paying particularly close attention at the time."

The two officers exchanged a quick glance, and Tabori spoke. "Did you know, Mr. McCrorry, that both Wendy Fulham and John Umbrel were killed in the incident?"

Lewis pursed his lips. "Yeah, I got that impression from the professor when I was there. I didn't know for sure until now, but it doesn't surprise me they were there when whatever happened, happened."

"Why is that?" she asked.

"Well, the two of them practically lived there. Wendy always had one more thing to try, and John would've jumped into the Charles if she'd said there was a Seaport at the bottom."

"Is there anything else you can tell us, Mr. McCrorry?" Kennedy continued. "Anything that might have seemed unusual around the lab in the past few days or weeks?"

"Unusual," he replied, thinking of the frustrating hours he had spent there. The irony of the statement evoked a rueful grin. As far as he was concerned the place was a relic from the past. The only thing that changed was the faces of the poor students trapped in its bowels.

"Officers, the only unusual thing that ever happened in that lab was that poor grads like me kept coming back."

The Shield both smiled politely. "Well, it looks like you won't be going back there anytime soon," Kennedy said.

"What was the reason for the call to your partners the night before last, Mr. McCrorry?" Tabori asked. "That would have been the evening before the explosion. You sounded quite insistent."

"Call?" Lewis replied, confused. "I didn't call them." But then he remembered Nikola mentioning something about Wendy and John responding to his call.

"No?" she said. "Do you remember now?"

"Ah, no, but my ad said something like that."

Detective Simons tapped his tag. "Play Mr. McCrorry's call."

Out of the wall speakers Lewis's voice sounded. There was no picture, only audio, and his words were heavily slurred.

"Wendy, John. This is Lewis. I need you guys in the lab tomorrow morning. I'm gonna be there at eight. This is important. You gotta be there. This is important. A.M. Eight A.M. You got it? See you then."

When did I make that call?

"Does that help?" Tabori asked.

"No, I don't remember calling them at all."

"You sounded like you had a bit too much to drink. Is that common?"

"Yeah, well, sometimes. Listen, I just don't remember making a call. Sorry."

The two detectives looked at each other and then back to Lewis.

"The message was made at 1:12 A.M. and left on each of the victims' tags," the woman continued. "What was so important that you needed everyone in the lab that morning?"

Lewis felt a sudden rush of guilt. The verbal pronouncement of Wendy and John as victims was unsettling, as if it somehow implied his involvement. "Nothing," Lewis answered nervously. "I mean, I really don't remember calling anyone. Maybe there's a mistake. I'm sure I'd remember if I made a call. Are you sure it's my voice?"

"The records have been verified, Mr. McCrorry," Kennedy replied. He looked at Lewis and raised his bushy eyebrows. "Are you sure there's nothing else you'd like to tell us?"

Lewis felt trapped. Had he made a call that night? Most of the week was a blur. "I don't know." His words were plaintive. "I just... I guess I probably had too much to drink this week. Maybe I made a call." He looked at the two officers pleadingly. "I really don't remember."

"And the next morning your lab exploded." Kennedy was

unsympathetic. "It's an odd coincidence, Mr. McCrorry."

"But it is a coincidence! I didn't have anything to do with it."

They looked at him dubiously, obviously waiting for further clarification.

"I always use Nik," Lewis offered, suddenly hopeful. "I never just call using the Sea. Nik, tell them. Did I make that call through you?"

Nik smiled back from the wallscreen. "Not through me, Lewis. I was not awake that late."

"Well, there you go. I didn't make the call through Nik. I wouldn't have made a call any other way." Lewis looked back to the detectives, but was disappointed they didn't seem to share his conviction.

"The call was made from a public screen in the Kendall Square T station," Kennedy informed him. "What time did you come home that night?"

"I don't know." Lewis was painfully aware the interview was not going well, and that there were far too many questions he couldn't answer.

"Yes, well, we will find out, Mr. McCrorry. Consider this official notice that we will be requesting access to your tag logs. If you have any additional information, now is the time."

The two detectives looked at Lewis, but he only shook his head dejectedly. "No."

They seemed unsurprised.

"We expect that you will be available over the next few weeks, Mr. McCrorry. I'm sure we'll be in touch."

Lewis closed the door after they left and stood for a few moments pondering the implications of the visit.

What was that call about? Why in the world did I make it? Did I make it?

He had no answers, even for himself. He knew he had gone to the Green Den that night, or at least he was pretty sure. Now that the Shield were going to pry into his tag files, they would know more about his actions over the past week than he did. It made him feel queasy.

"I'm going out, Nik. Lock up, will you?"

He grabbed a coat and pushed through the door, turning to go out the back stairs and avoid another encounter with the Shield. The streets were once again glistening and the budding branches dripping. A few ragged patches of blue sky showed here and there with the mid-day sun streaming through. Under different circumstances he might have enjoyed the sight.

He paced up the hill, away from the Square to the park. Pedestrians were out, enjoying the mild weather despite the rain. A group of people were chanting slogans and handing out animated paper flyers decrying the current state of synthient enslavement. The ground car traffic was light, and the overhead commuter lanes were far enough away that only the merest whisper of fans could be heard.

As he strode through the park, declining leaflets that were thrust in his direction, his mood went from dejection to anger.

It's not fair. First I lose the lab, and now the Shield think I have something to do with it.

To some extent, he really didn't care that the lab had been damaged, even destroyed; it had been far too unpleasant a place that he would miss it badly. But it was galling that even in its demise it was still capable of dragging him down.

He wasn't paying attention to where he was going, and eventually found himself having come full circle to the T station. He stopped and looked at the signs, directing passersby to the city, and decided a good drink was warranted.

He passed through the turnstile, thumbing the pad, and hopped on a waiting car showing Kendall Square as one of its destinations. The seats were not full, so he swung into one and closed his eyes, envisioning the whiskey sliding down his throat.

They passed through Harvard Square and Central Station, exchanging a few passengers and cars at each stop. Lewis was oblivious to it all as he waited with as much patience as he could muster.

The train pulled out of Central and began smoothly accelerating down the tube toward Kendall and blessed relief. At one point the car wobbled, and Lewis bumped his head on the window at his side. He opened his eyes in annoyance, and the train shook again. He looked around at the other riders and saw quickly that they had noticed the unusual motion. There was another wobble, this time much more severe, and a high-pitched whine started.

Lewis's anger turned to uneasiness. It was abnormal to feel much motion at all on the Levi-T, and squealing noises were definitely unheard of. He looked out the window, but the dark subway walls gave no clues.

Abruptly they entered Kendall Square, and he jumped at the sudden appearance of the lights. Now he was nervous. They were hurtling through the station at very high speed, and there was no indication they were going to stop. He barely glimpsed a few people waiting on the platform, several of whom stumbled backward at the abrupt passage of the train.

The screeching noise rose in pitch and volume, and the car rocked in a jarring and frighteningly rhythmic cadence as it shot out the far end of the station and began the climb over the Longfellow Bridge. He felt a huge and sudden acceleration press him into his seat, while several standing passengers lost their grips and tumbled down the aisle as if it were a steep slope.

His fellow commuters were now as terrified as he was and a few tried to climb out of their seats, reaching to hold poles for balance. Voices shouted above the din, but Lewis could not make out the words. In a frantic movement he struggled against the force that held him tightly against the seat, reaching for the emergency brake as they crested the bridge.

His hand never made it to the button. As the train reached the top of the arched bridge, inertia pulled it off the superconducting track, and Lewis lifted off his seat. The guide wheels slammed into the restraining track and the train bounced down with a jolt, the metal coils of its undercarriage crunching hard into the bridge.

Lewis's head hit the ceiling, and then he was thrown to the floor. He landed on his back in a heap under one of the seats, the wind knocked painfully from his lungs. The train tipped drunkenly, and the sound of tearing steel filled the air. Bodies were tumbling as the train's torque ripped the wheel and magnet assembly apart and flipped the car on its side.

The train rolled. Debris filled the air. Lewis was certain he was screaming, but the sound of the car smashing itself to pieces prevented him from hearing even the slightest bit of his panic. All at once it ceased, and his world folded into darkness.

9. Investigation Path

Delfinous looked across the room at the assembled Shield officers. The meeting was about to begin and an uncomfortably cold rock had lodged itself in the pit of his stomach. He was familiar with the feeling, signaling many sleepless nights ahead. The investigation had been proceeding and the beginnings of a theory were growing, but there were too many unconnected pieces, too many glimpses of possible motives without any substance, and too many unanswered questions. It galled him that they couldn't untangle the weave; the longer they lingered, the more difficult it would be to find any kind of thread.

Tabori was assisting with the Field Investigation, and Delfinous had been pulled from his routine network surveillance to track down any leads that might help determine the source of the explosives. He had started digging through the mountain of data as soon as he got back to his office that first day.

Kennedy Simons leaned in the far corner, framed by the large windows looking out over Cambridge and downtown Boston in the distance. Despite his years in North America, he had managed to keep his Australian drawl. From where Delfinous sat Simons' head was slightly above the tallest buildings, and an occasional suborbital passenger plane passed just over his hair as it lifted off from Logan.

Tabori sat at the table with folded hands and furrowed brows. She had spent the past day and a half with Kennedy, tracking down witnesses for follow-up interviews, and locating the building's regular occupants in the hopes that something might jog someone's memory and give direction to the investigation. The wallscreen records during the time of interest had proven surprisingly unhelpful.

Jim Stabler sat at the head of the table, his eyes intent upon the other attendees. Amil Huusfara and Kim Strand were each searching the wallscreens, reviewing the investigation to-date. The officers' synthient advocates were also taking part in the briefing.

"All right," Jim said, "let's review today's results: Amil, what have you got?"

"The tag checks have turned up nothing unusual," he began. "So far all of the cross-checks with witnesses, normal destinations, and city traffic have not indicated any suspicious behavior patterns."

He tugged at his moustache. "The laboratories in the building and the professors who run them are being reviewed. There are some issues with grant proposals and timeliness of reports to oversight agencies from several of the projects, but a check with the Board of Regents' monitors revealed that they are not considered out of the ordinary. There are very few strictly enforced terms for such items, and a great deal of leniency is shown in most cases.

"The professors," he nodded at the screen, and a section enlarged and came to the foreground, showing the names and pictures of the academicians who utilized the building, "are all cooperating with the investigation. They have placed their synthients at our disposal, but so far there has been nothing out of the ordinary to report.

"Professor Harland Leonard has been the most active in assisting us." He pointed at the wallscreen and a picture of the old professor appeared. "It was his laboratory that took the brunt of the destruction, and two of the students who were killed worked for him.

"We have reviewed the building occupant register at the time of the explosion," he continued. Another list, together with faces spread across the wallscreen.

"There were 87 people total. A check against normal occupancy for the most recent three months for which records are available show a few discrepancies, but well within the bounds of the statistical models. As I mentioned, we had a few unknowns yesterday, but these have been cleared up after filling in a few blanks: Tabori and Kennedy have interviewed the outliers from the sample, and their stories check out to first order.

"We have begun a perimeter tag search to a half-kilometer radius of the building, but getting the proper authorizations is slow, even given the importance of this investigation. The sample size looks to be several tens of thousands, since the T intersects our target area."

A sigh escaped some of the attendees. It was not unusual to look at traffic patterns for a few thousand individuals on any given investigation, but digging into the transportation records of a major thoroughfare into the city meant more delays and fuzzier data. Picking out a few stray individuals from such a sample was error-prone, and the footwork to find and evaluate any candidates was costly and time consuming.

"The synthients have begun the process, and we've started one hundred and twenty nine automated subsentients. Many advocates have been contacted, but the wait for their patron's response is as slow as it takes them to answer the request.

"We've also begun the cross-check of T rider-ship against the traffic tag records. With a sample of about fifteen hundred to-date, there is a fair discrepancy; again nothing out of the ordinary compared with normal tag/non-tag data." Several diagrams appeared on the screens, showing a breakdown of passengers wearing tags to those without.

"Assuming our initial sample estimate is reasonably correct, we will have approximately three thousand seven hundred non-tag riders to evaluate."

There was uneasy shifting in chairs around the room as the numbers were read off. The officers were veterans of many investigations, and the data was not unexpected, but it was always difficult at the outset to anticipate such a heavy load. Even with some of the best synthients and hounds to track down leads, they would need a string of extraordinary breaks to find any plausible avenues from the mass of data.

"Ok, thanks, Amil," Jim Stabler said. "Press forward with what you've got going so far, but unless something jumps out, keep it low priority. I don't want us wasting a lot of time burrowing into a hundred thousand people until we get to the point where there's nothing else to go on.

"Kim, how much more has the lab been able to do with the forensics?"

Several views of the ruined laboratory appeared on the wallscreens.

"A final assessment of the chemical background is complete," Kim Strand said. "As the initial analysis indicated, the explosive was Detonite. Lot tracers say it was manufactured in Houston late last year. We're tracking the shipping records now."

"That you, Delf?" Jim asked.

"Yes, I've started the request process for inventory confirmation. I doubt we'll find answers to all our questions, though. Explosives are monitored pretty thoroughly, but there are always issues with how complete the records are. We won't know what we're up against until we get deeper into it.

"Another avenue I'm checking is recent banking and sales records in the construction business, sort of an extension to the work I was doing anyway; no revelations, yet."

"And what about our thorny friend, Mr. McCrorry?" Jim turned to Kennedy and Tabori.

"Well, as the only surviving lab user, he certainly warrants a close eye, eh?" Kennedy drawled.

"He didn't have much to say, that's for sure," Tabori interjected. "He seemed surprised to see us when we showed up at his door, and then he gave us a lot of nothing but excuses. Maybe it's just his winning personality, but I think he needs a leash."

Kennedy continued. "His current and former professors all say the kid's a pain, the same as the few students we've come across who know him. We're working on his habits now, where he hangs out, who he talks to; we should have permissions to open his tag soon. So far we've found he doesn't have a lot of friends at the Institute."

Tabori picked up the thread. "There are two main points to go on right now: one is a call he made the night before the explosion." She motioned to her advocate, and Lewis's drunken message played out.

"Obviously it means nothing by itself, but it certainly seems suggestive."

The group looked at Lewis's face on the screen, and the little data they'd been able to fill in about him. Delfinous thought back to the morning of the explosion, and the warning bells that had gone off when he'd seen his face in the crowd. The photo that showed on the wall was an old picture, presumably taken upon entrance to the Institute; he had a smile and his eyes were bright. The furtive, disgruntled emotions that Delfinous had seen that day were missing. There was something about him that didn't feel right at the time, and finding that he was one of the regular users of the lab made his suspicions deeper still.

Tabori continued. "The other comes from an interview we had with a bartender at a place McCrorry frequents. Seems that he offered to sell a data thimble to him just prior to the explosion. The bartender didn't have a clue what might be on it, but he said Lewis was worked up over something that night.

"Put this together with that call and maybe we have something. Could be that Lewis had something stored on the thimble that his lab partners found out about. Maybe that's why he wanted them in the lab that morning: rig the place to blow, end of his worries."

"Seems pretty extreme," Jim ventured. "What do you think could be on it?"

"No idea," Tabori answered. "But it must be something pretty important to McCrorry."

"Jim, no one uses those things much anymore," Delfinous added. "They can store huge amounts of data, but with the resources available in the Sea, no one bothers. The fact that Lewis had one at all is pretty unusual"

"All right, then," Jim responded. "Let's ratchet the pressure on Mr. McCrorry. Sounds like he's in need of another visit."

10. Accusation Key

Lewis lay in a dreamy, half-awake haze of warmth, his eyes closed and his mind unfocused. Gradually he realized he was lying down. A few sounds trickled into his consciousness: people talking, soft music playing, a rhythmic tone beating out a slow time. He opened his eyes and stared at the softly glowing ceiling above him, trying to place his location. He lifted his arm to scratch his forehead, and only then realized an IV patch and drip line were attached at his elbow, while an active cast wrapped his wrist. He stared at the apparatus for a moment before the train wreck came back to him. He was uncertain how long he had been here, but it was clear enough he'd been pulled from the disaster and brought to a hospital.

"Nik," he croaked. "Nik, you there?"

Nik's voice sounded tinny on the bed's speaker. "I am glad to see you awake, Lewis. We were all quite worried about you. I have notified the attending nurse; she'll be in shortly."

Lewis heard more than saw a nurse enter. She came to his bedside and greeted him cheerfully. "I see you've rejoined us."

She checked his IV and looked over the monitor data. "Everything looks good. You're making a fine recovery from some pretty serious injuries. The doctor will be in to take a look shortly. Do you need a drink, or anything else?" She poked around at the drip monitor one more time as she finished her question.

He accepted water with a grunt, an adjustment to his bed to prop him up, and settled for just lying at ease. He was not in much pain, although his head and side ached remotely, but he felt very weak.

"What happened, Nik, and where am I?" he asked.

"You are in Massachusetts General Hospital in the recovery area," Nik replied. "Apparently you were involved in an accident on the T."

"That much I remember," Lewis retorted, but his tone fell flat, even to his own ears. He did not have much energy and lacked enthusiasm for sarcasm.

"I mean, how did it happen?"

"The investigation is still ongoing, but apparently there were malfunctions in several fail-safe mechanisms, which then allowed the train to accelerate to dangerous speeds. The T has been shut-down throughout the city since the accident. You are very lucky, Lewis; over fifty people died." Nik sounded more serious than Lewis could remember in a long while; the accident must have really shaken him.

"Mmm," Lewis replied sourly, "this really hasn't been my week, has it?"

He thought about the explosion in the lab, and now the train wreck. Along with all the trouble he'd had in his studies, these last problems only reinforced the notion that there was no joy to be found in his life. It would just about be the next thing for Becky to show up looking to shower him with pity.

An elderly Asian woman doctor came in. She took his pulse, shone a light into his eyes, and studied the readouts on his bed. Apparently, she was pleased. She shot him a quick smile, checked the wrap on his arm, and said "you are recovering nicely," before she darted out the door.

"Nik, how do I look? I mean, how injured am I?"

"The most recent records show several broken bones, most notably your left radius, and three ribs. You have a number of contusions and lacerations, but these are well along the way to healing. You had a number of internal injuries, and some bleeding, but these also are healing. Luckily it appears that, although you hit your head in the accident, it was not very severe, and there was no swelling."

"Well, that's good," Lewis responded. "On top of everything else, I guess I don't need to end up a vegetable." He closed his eyes, and was soon asleep.

Something woke him from a dream that slipped from his memory. He opened his eyes and saw two Shield officers at the end of his bed, staring at him. The woman was the same one who had shown up at his apartment earlier. He didn't recognize the other.

"You seem to be the lucky one, Mr. McCrorry," the man said.

Lewis grunted, although the sound was more of a hoarse scratch; his throat was dry and he was in more pain than when he last awoke. They must have reduced his medication.

"Yeah, lucky," he tried again, clearing his throat. The woman handed him a glass of water that had been set on his bed stand, and he gulped eagerly. "I was told that before, but I'm not sure I care for the definition. And who are you?"

"My name is Delfinous Berry, from the Boston Shield office," he took out his ID for proof. "This is Tabori Muula, also of the Boston

Shield, I wonder if we might have a word with you, Mr. McCrorry."

It was not a question, so Lewis shrugged and raised his eyebrows. "I'm not in much of a position to object, now am I?"

"We spent some time at the Green Den," Tabori continued, watching Lewis's reaction, "and met some of your friends and colleagues at MIT. I'm afraid they have not left us with a favorable impression of your good nature."

Lewis looked from one to the other. He remembered his first encounter with the Shield and did not care to have a repeat performance.

"Well, maybe I'm not the easiest guy to get along with, but I've got my reasons. My research project was never much to brag about, and now with the lab up in smoke, it stinks even more. You haven't exactly caught me at my best moment."

"And when would that moment be?" Tabori asked.

"Anytime other than now," Lewis shot back. "Look, I'm pretty good with math, and I've been stuck in backwater research for the past five years; that sort of thing makes you a bit surly, but it certainly doesn't mean I went out and roasted the lab."

"Mm-hmm," Delfinous mused. "Perhaps you can tell us something more about the work you've been doing most recently; in particular, anything that happened prior to the accident."

Well, maybe that's encouraging, at least they're using the word 'accident' now.

"We were poking around hole sources. Wendy was finishing up her thesis work, and John was just getting started; I don't know if he'd picked a topic yet. My part of the effort was on data acquisition. It wasn't the most spectacular research topic on the face of the earth, and I don't hold out much hope it'll be anything more than a pile of worthless spam, but there it is."

"Why were you at the site of the accident that morning?" Delfinous asked.

"I was on my way to meet with the professor. He'd been pushing me to talk to him about the project for a while, and I just hadn't got around to it until that morning."

"Hadn't got around to it," Tabori asked, "or were in no shape to see him?" She looked askance at Lewis, but her face was unreadable. "The bartender at the Green Den has given quite an account of you."

"I hadn't got around to it," Lewis repeated. "Dealing with Professor Leonard was just one more reason I didn't enjoy spending time there."

"Uh-huh," Delfinous replied. "And what about the data you took? The synthient assistant for the project told us there was one successful experiment. Have you looked at it, yet?"

"Well, I started to," Lewis responded. Now that the question had been asked, he wasn't sure he wanted to give up this bit of salvageable material from the whole mess. "I didn't see anything particularly enlightening about it; you can't expect much from a battery, you know."

"And the data thimble?" Tabori asked.

"The what?" Lewis replied, and then blinked as he remembered the copy he'd made. "I forgot all about it."

He wasn't sure why he continued to make copies of his data. The Sea had more than enough redundancy and safeguards to ensure nothing was lost that wasn't deliberately erased, but he persisted in his idiosyncratic behavior despite its needlessness. It was a habit he'd picked up long ago, first as a child because he loved the colorful rainbows shimmering within the crystal, and then because his collection had grown a life of its own. He had hundreds of them scattered in his apartment in Cambridge, his parents' home in Manhattan, and his uncle's villa in Long Island. He couldn't even remember the last time he'd looked at even one of them; the practice had become so routine he rarely even thought about it, like flicking hair out of his eyes, or cracking his knuckles.

The two officers looked at him curiously for a moment, and then Tabori continued. "Jerry Martingale said you offered to sell it to him."

Lewis tried a laugh, but his side hurt too much. "Jerry the bartender?" This was too funny. "Did I? I don't remember trying to sell it. Maybe I said something to him about it, I don't know. I think I might have been there the night we made our run, and I probably had the thing with me."

"Why would you make a copy of your data?" Delfinous asked.

"I don't know, it's just something I do; a habit."

"And you sell the thimbles?" Tabori asked.

"No, I just collect them. I've got a bunch of them."

He looked from one officer to the other, but couldn't tell what they were thinking.

"Mr. McCrorry," Delfinous continued, "you wouldn't mind if we took a look at the thimble, would you?"

"Well, you know," Lewis began, reluctantly. He was even more hesitant than ever to let go of whatever small speck of hope he had in his research, but felt trapped. If he didn't give in to the request, the Shield might think he was deliberately concealing something on the thimble that related to the accident, however ridiculous the notion sounded. But handing it over felt like losing the last connection to the ruined lab; a mirror of his own academic life.

Spaff, I just don't see any way out.

"Ah, I can get it to you after I get out of here," he finished, lamely.

He felt drained, physically and emotionally. There just wasn't any way to avoid turning the thimble over to the Shield without looking guilty.

Well, I've already taken a crack at the data. Maybe it won't really matter.

But it still felt like an empty admission.

"That will be fine, Mr. McCrorry," Delfinous finished. "We'll be in touch. In the meanwhile, we'd also like to take a look at the Sea copy of the data, as long as you don't mind."

Lewis simply shrugged, defeated. "Yeah, sure, help yourself."

The two officers left. Lewis sank back in his bed, feeling crushed.

I can't catch a break.

As he lay there brooding, Nik appeared on the wallscreen. He was dressed in a neatly trimmed brown tweed suit, holding forth in a large room that resembled his namesake's Colorado Springs high voltage laboratory. A flickering light that lay out of sight illuminated the wall behind him, while buzzing and snapping noises crackled in the background. Lewis smiled thinly at the image; this was Nik's favorite self-representation: a young, misunderstood scholar experimenting with dangerous energy, full of enthusiasm and encouragement for his real-world protégé.

"Your mother and father send their best wishes, Lewis. Of course they were informed of your condition when you first arrived at the hospital, but your father was traveling to the west coast, and your mother has been busy in Manhattan. They were originally planning on coming up tomorrow, but now that your condition has improved, they will wait for next weekend."

Nikola looked full of concern and sympathy.

Lewis felt nothing. He hadn't been back to Manhattan to visit his parents for almost two years, and had never been good at keeping in touch. It surprised him more that they were coming at all, rather than they hadn't been here yet. As a toddler, he had vague memories of his mother, punctuated by the occasional appearance of his father, but as he grew older, his mother revived her academic career, and his father traveled more often than not. Lewis had grown up with sitters and nannies, but most of all, with Nikola T.

"Nik, while you're here, let's have a look at the files from our run, eh?"

He didn't have any passion for the effort, but knowing that the Shield would soon be pawing over them, he felt the need to shuffle through them once more; a fond assessment of a treasured family heirloom before selling it off to pay the debts of a life ill-spent.

Nikola T.'s paternal smile faded slowly a moment later, and his look became puzzled. "Once again, I am having difficulty locating the files. The traffic through the Institute's high-speed tributary and the Laboratory of Gravitics is still quite high, but I do not think that can account for the problem; just a moment."

The screen went static as Nikola removed his presence from the display. He had taken all the processing power at his disposal to attend to the dilemma, leaving nothing behind to provide animation. The moment dragged on; a few seconds became a full minute, then two. Lewis couldn't remember Nikola having disappeared for so long.

When he finally came back, his face was troubled. He looked distracted, and the contents of his lab became blurry, as if the army of subsentient helpers that enabled him to communicate with the external world were left directionless, neglecting to refresh the image.

"The files cannot be located. I'm afraid they appear to have been deleted."

"What?" Lewis asked, incredulous. "By who? When? Did Professor Leonard diss them? What about the Sargasso?"

"To be precise," Nikola responded, "they were deleted two days ago by a subsentient cleanup agent as part of a routine list process for which there was no backup instruction. I have spent considerable effort tracking down the authorization to have the files placed on the list, but the keys are quite complicated and confused. There are several dozen links through the chain, both within and outside the MIT domain, and the trace appears to end with circular permissions back to the middle of the sequence.

"I have never seen anything like this before, and my inquiries to the Gatekeepers' Guild do not leave me hopeful. They are unaware of this type of circular redundancy, and are checking their historical archives for security protocol violations of this nature."

Lewis was stunned. This was absurd. He lay in his bed, too numb to give form to his thoughts. No data? No data. The two words resonated in his mind. It was as if someone had told him downtown Boston had disappeared.

Slowly, he focused his eyes on the screen. Nikola T. was also transfixed, the background image of his lab now having faded completely into a formless mass of brown smudges. He, too, looked as confused as Lewis felt. His odd smile was almost childlike, as if he didn't know how to respond to the news.

The sight of his advocate jarred Lewis. He took a deep breath. "Nik, there's no chance you made a mistake somehow, is there?"

A thought was beginning to grow in the back of his mind, and he needed to be sure before he let it flower any further. He did not doubt the answer: Nik was far too thorough to have drawn this kind of wrong conclusion.

"There is no mistake, Lewis, the files are gone."

A chill started to spread up Lewis's legs and spine.

Files don't disappear by themselves, and they don't get put on a deletion list by accident either.

And that left the data thimble in his apartment as the only record of the experiment; an experiment that had somehow ended with the laboratory destroyed, his partners dead, and him in the hospital.

"Nik," he said slowly, "let's take a look at the keys."

There were, indeed, several dozen encryption and authorization codes, all of them listed as having been generated through automation, in response to some initial act that could not be found. Lewis looked at the codes for some time, then activated a suite of sophisticated tools to pry open the underlying data structures. After some minutes, he and Nikola had succeeded in descending a few more levels within the hierarchy; they had crossed many layers of interfaces, and tracked through the records of a thousand individual processing elements.

Lewis inspected the data as a whole, juggled the order around, and then caught the vague ghost of a pattern. He let his mind take in the overall structure, then concentrated on a few lines that jumped out. There was no mistake: the codes replicated several mathematical series, with sequences of numbers rotated through several complicated transforms across multiple dimensions. There were tensor replicates involved, and he had to try many variations in his head before he could convince himself of the correct dimensionality: seven orthogonal vector spaces. It was a strange mixture, and even with his mathematical dexterity, it was difficult to hold the entire edifice in his head. Still, it couldn't possibly be coincidence, the factors lined up much too precisely to be random.

"Nik, bring up these 18 lines." He rose painfully from bed and pointed to them on the screen, studying them intently.

The lines appeared neatly in the center of the screen. Once again, the two delved under this new layer of abstraction, unlocking intricate variations, and eventually wrenching loose the next tiers of data. They had traced the details down to a few layers above the actual electronic hardware. There were still 18 lines, but now there was more information appended, expanded beyond the initial sequence by all their manipulation. After studying the codes again, Lewis realized the additional records represented gates and nodes on which the data had been written. They were close to unlocking the final seal that would lead to the original instantiation.

There was another pattern, but it wasn't quite right; just out of focus, tantalizingly close, but out of reach. He squinted and his pulse raced. "Nik, show me the numbers in binary."

The lines expanded, now nothing more than a series of ones and zeroes. There it was. The lines needed to be pulled apart and spliced together in a different manner: each 22-bit sequence within a row shifted down to the next row, and the last row rotated to the first. He instructed Nikola to show the results in a new window.

"Ok, now transpose the bits back to alpha."

He gasped. Every hair stood up on the back of his neck, and his skin crawled. Mixed in with an assortment of random numbers and letters was a quite unmistakable token: LEWIS DAVID MCCRORRY, all in capitals, as if someone were screaming at him silently, accusingly.

11. The Butterflies of Syphus Pettyman

Syphus Pettyman leaned back in his leather seat and surveyed his office. The walls were clean and white, adorned by a small collection of insect cases: three boxes with nine colorful and exquisite examples of butterflies and moths, and three additional sets of bright, fluorescent beetles. He loved the precision of the captured animals, so small, so full of detail that they could fascinate the eye for hours. He did not know their names, did not care to understand their classification or evolutionary history; from their appearance alone he could see the relationships between them. One set of butterflies consisted of a multitude of shades of brown and tan, sculpted into branching patterns that were almost, but not exactly, replicated from one to another. They were obviously related to each other, the capriciousness of nature showing off her variegated forms as the generations unfolded. He had not caught them himself, but had purchased the sets over the years, adding to his collection by bits and pieces through each successive phase of his career. They were trophies, rewards for having graduated with an undergraduate degree, then a Masters from Harvard Business School, then his first management position, and on up the ladder. He regarded each in turn, resting on the last case: a collection of small moths from Australia, all bright reds and yellows, like miniature flames captured in mid-flutter.

He enjoyed the contrast between the bare walls of his office and the tiny smudges of incandescent beauty, simultaneously reminding him of how colorfully he had written his success, and how transitory the script could become.

There were no windows, nor was he located high up in the Omicron tower in the heart of Sydney, but he allowed himself a moment's indulgence, and imagined the view of the harbor from fifty storeys higher, the topmost floors of the firm's corporate headquarters. With luck and good planning he should be there in another five years. He had dared great things over his short career, taken calculated risks, and not been afraid to push the boundaries of ethics by ensuring the greater part of project success was passed on to him. At other times, he'd taken a sideline, shining the light of credit on others nearby, and in doing so, magnifying his own visibility. In the game of business, he saw himself with no equal; it was only a matter of time before he had positioned himself within the inner circles of Omicron, and from there launched to Chief Executive of any one of thousands of wealthy companies across the globe.

He sighed. But not just yet. Although he was driven to achieve these ends, he was also pragmatic in his approach; it would not do to get too far ahead of himself.

"Amelia, take a note."

His assistant appeared on the wallscreen on the other side of his desk, an impeccably dressed young woman with horn-rimmed glasses, her hair pulled back tightly and a yellow memo pad and pen in her hands. Syphus smiled momentarily at the cliché. His newest advocate seemed to go for this type of over-the-top sentimentality, but he didn't mind. He had no personal alter-ego on the network, having relied entirely upon society's resources for his interface: his parent's house synthient, Harvard's much vaunted Public Faces, and Omicron's vast set of sentient associates. He maintained regular contact with many of these past relationships, and considered it a strength to have such a wide variety of support.

"Send this to Alan: 'I've arrived at my new office in the Tower. Many thanks for all your sound advice and honest vision of the future. Give my best to June, Joseph, and Cicely. I look forward to seeing you on the Esplanade this New Year's. Sincerely, Syphus.'"

Alan Tomridge was his mentor at Omicron's satellite office in Melbourne, and one of the few people for whom Syphus had real affection. The old gentleman had occasional misgivings of his younger protégé's methods, but he saw in Syphus a keen mind and potential to push his colleagues to higher levels. It was Alan's recommendation that resulted in this new office.

"Send the note by messenger, along with a bottle of Merlot, and two orchids for June."

"Yes, sir," Amelia said, as she dutifully wrote the note on her pad.

She pushed her glasses up on her nose, raised her eyes and head slightly, and the memo folded itself neatly as if it were an envelope, sprouted a set of multi-colored wings, and sped out of sight above her head.

"It's on its way, sir."

She tilted her head to the side, quizzically, as if listening to a distant voice. "The wine and orchid will be delivered tomorrow morning, along with your letter."

"Thank you, Amelia," Syphus said, once again smiling at her quirkiness. "So what have we got for tomorrow?"

An antique, green chalkboard appeared beside her, showing his itinerary. Amelia highlighted each item on the list by touching them in turn.

"Your first meeting is with Mr. Boanyoo, the head of Plant Maintenance at the Wilcannia facility, then lunch with Ms. Arnolt from Human Resources."

The list of scheduled meetings, tours of the office towers, and memos to review continued through the remainder of the day. Syphus glowed in anticipation of his new responsibilities. Most of the people he had met today, and with whom he would speak tomorrow, moved in power circles above his previous position. They were now his peers, seeking him out for advice and support. He ticked off the names in his head, lining them up against the research he'd already done on their influence within the company. His first day on the job had been busy, filled with introductions. Although he was well known in Melbourne and had achieved some notoriety at Corporate, he was still a relatively new face in the Tower, and needed to start focusing on the relationships that would enable him to succeed. It was late now, but there was still one last set of tasks to be done.

"OK, Amelia, please bring up my mail."

The itinerary was replaced with a long list of communications. Some were no more than written text, containing no other resources or attachments, while the majority contained links to additional information, or tag IDs to the sender's synthient assistants. Amelia had already sorted the notes by priority and he made quick work of them, leaving messages of his own, or filing them away for future reference.

When he'd sorted through the top tier, he looked over the chaff: advertisements for hair-growth gene therapy, new finance packages for exotic vacations, dating services for lonely hearts, and a myriad of other services and offers. Although he never spent more than a few moments with any of these solicitations, he also didn't like to ignore them completely. For the most part, they were easily dismissed by a simple glance at the subject, but on occasion he found one that was compelling enough to warrant further thought; his insect collection had started from a response to just such an innocuous letter.

Tonight there were the usual useless quips and fetishes, but one caught his eye. It read 'A butterfly in flight, makes a gale, it might'. It was hardly the type of message used by advertising firms to generate interest in a product. There was no hint of the topic to which the phrase referred, and the body contained only a softly glowing link that read ‘Advance’.

He parroted the word softly. It was not a question, nor a quote, really, simply an impulsive mouthing of the word on his screen. But the encoders in his office picked up the sound, and the link activated. Immediately, he was annoyed. The link must have employed more sophistication than usual to circumvent his office security.

“Amelia, cut the link,” he said, abruptly. “I’m done for the day.”

But the word continued to pulse for a few heartbeats. He was about to repeat the command when an unfamiliar voice spoke. “Mr. Pettyman,” it said, matter-of-factly, and with just a hint of condescension.

Syphus jumped slightly. With the degree of privacy protection he employed, there should be no way for an unsolicited message to identify him.

“Amelia,” he began again, but got no farther.

“... is unavailable at the moment,” the voice finished.

“Mr. Pettyman,” it began again, “I will only take a moment of your time, a brief instant that may constitute the next step in your illustrious career.”

The voice was smooth and unhurried, a deep bass that rumbled without sounding gravelly, and gave the impression of sincerity and knowledge. Syphus’s initial alarm was replaced with a growing impatience and aggravation. He was still concerned about the means that had been employed against him, but at the same time fascinated that it had occurred; this was no amateur hack preying upon casual users, this was a sophisticated attack targeted specifically at him.

“A package was delivered to you this afternoon that represents the culmination of many years of quiet and dedicated research. I hope you will find the contents of interest.”

The pulsing link faded to a dim grey and vanished. The screen remained dark, and repeated queries to his assistant produced no result. With no signal from his uninvited guest, and no response from Amelia, Syphus had the disquieting feeling of someone watching over his shoulder, silent and invisible. It was extraordinarily rare that he could not summon someone while in his office and it left him unnerved; the late hour and stillness outside his door heightened the effect.

With a conscious effort, and irritation that it required as much, he rose from his seat. Just as the voice had indicated, a package lay in the tray at the corner of his office, unnoticed until this moment. It was quite innocuous, a plain self-opening folder that could be found in any post service or parcel store. Syphus picked it up and turned it over. It was a centimeter thick, and there were no markings other than his address and the postmark. He laid it on his desk, and sat down once again.

He glanced at the dark screen once more, as if peering into it would reveal his mysterious visitor, and allow him to decipher the contents of the envelope in front of him. Deliberately, he jabbed at the corners, and swiped at the invisible seam through the middle, starting the process that would peel open the folder.

Inside, there were two unremarkable objects: a pair of standard, four-centimeter light disks, tacked down to the inside of the package with adhesive. These smaller types were used to provide temporary light in tight places, typically inside enclosed areas where someone needed to see in order to do some work. He looked from one to the other; they both appeared identical, and certainly not the result of an arduous research effort.

This must be some kind of joke.

But the lengths to which the prankster had gone did not seem to fit the punch line. He shook his head and frowned. He would have laughed at the situation, but the empty office area and dark screen left a lingering uneasiness.

He was about to pitch the entire thing into the trash, when, on impulse, he tapped the disks. To his surprise, they both lit up extraordinarily brightly, much more intensely than he remembered being normal. He squinted at them and sat back slightly in his chair. Nothing more happened for a few moments, until the disk on the right began slowly to dim. He watched with growing interest; the disk on the left continued to glare, while the one on the right faded to nothing more than a flickering glow.

There was something about the way the disk looked that jogged his memory, but he couldn't quite pin it down. He tapped the two disks again to turn them off, and when he touched the feeble light, his hand jumped back in pain: it was scalding hot. Suddenly, his secondary school science class rushed back to him: heat was generated from a hole source if pushed beyond its capacity. The physics behind the behavior was long forgotten, but a fragmented memory of a particular experiment he and his lab partner had carried out came back to him; he was sure of the general concept.

But what did it mean?

He tapped the lights again, carefully with the hot disk, and they brightened. The disk on the left continued to burn intently and steadily, while the one on the right started out slightly dimmer, still hot from its previous output, and quickly faded to a flicker. He could feel the heat rising from its case, while the brighter light was only slightly warmer than the desk.

There was something different between the two light disks, obviously, and that was what he was meant to understand.

What did the intruder say: that the package represented some kind of lengthy research effort? Could it really be an important effect? And if it is, why were the disks sent to me?

Syphus squinted his eyes in thought. This was an interesting set of problems, no question. The voice had tried to entice him into thinking the gift represented an opportunity too good to pass up, the typical exhortation of a thousand scams throughout the ages. But he had to admit the means of delivery and the contents of the package were compelling. It was getting late, and he had no ready answers. He called for his assistant one last time, without success.

Tapping the light disks to turn them off, he looked around the office and out into the quiet hallway. It was eerie to feel so isolated. It was only 9:00 p.m., a fairly routine time for him to leave the office, but he couldn't remember a time when there had been no one else around.

Perhaps this is how Corporate operates.

Suddenly his wallscreen lit up, and there was Amelia, hair tightly pulled back and hands folded primly on her lap, looking all the world like she'd been waiting patiently all along. "Is there anything else you need, sir?" she asked.

"Uh," he jumped. "Amelia, I thought you'd left for the evening."

A crawling chill ran through him and his heart thudded.

"No sir, although I'm ready to end the day, if you'd like."

Her eyes glanced down at his desk, so briefly it was almost imperceptible; Syphus realized she must have seen the package. It was a quite human gesture, a look of curiosity where an overt question would have been socially awkward, given the professional relationship they maintained.

"Actually," he replied, regaining his footing and coming to a sudden decision, "I'd like you to have this package sent to Dolph Kunstler, in R&D, tomorrow."

He had worked with Kunst on several projects in the past and knew the scientist would be intrigued with the mystery. He would spend time picking the lights apart to find out how they worked, if by doing so he accomplished nothing more than determining they were utterly ordinary.

"Send him the last note I read along with the disks, and play a copy of the message the 'advance' link generated."

"I will have the package sent," she replied, "but what do you mean by the advance link, sir?"

"In the last message I read."

She continued to look at him quizzically.

He was now getting annoyed.

"The one where the body contained the single word: 'advance'".

"I'm sorry, sir, I cannot locate that particular letter."

"What? Bring up the list again, please."

He thought his voice sounded normal enough, but this was yet another inexplicable development since he'd opened the butterfly message, and he was decidedly uncomfortable with the thought that someone could gain such access and control to the internal systems within his office.

He glanced at the list, by now not surprised that the message was missing.

"Curious. Well, tell Kunst that these disks represent the competition's best hole source R&D efforts, and he'd better have a look at them to see what we're up against."

That should light a fire under him.

Three days later, Syphus was wrapping up the latest round of budget planning for the next fiscal year when Dolph Kunstler appeared in a window on his screen. He looked slightly bleary and more than a little agitated.

"Syphus, who are these disks from?"

Just like Kunst, not much in the way of an introduction, just cut right to the chase.

"I can't really say," Syphus replied.

He had spent a few moments after sending the package to think of a satisfactory story to go along with the disks; revealing that he had received a mysterious message that had bypassed Omicron's security, not to mention his own, did not seem very wise.

"They showed up in my inbox, along with a note that said they were from a friend. I didn't recognize the handwriting, but I've worked with some of SunDisk's and Haltrol Industries people in the past; I assume it was from one of them."

Kunst frowned. "Well, they've kept this development very quiet, then. I haven't been able to find anything in the literature, nor in the patent system about this technology. I don't know how they could have jumped on us like this, without showing any sign of what they've been up to."

Syphus was careful to keep his face composed, but he could read Dolph's body language: clearly the scientist was excited.

"Why, Kunst? What's so special about the disks?"

Dolph's eyes widened in incredulity, and his arms began gesturing in short, chopped motions to punctuate his explanations. "Represent?" he barked. "They represent a leap forward in efficiency that's beyond anything we've been able to achieve in our labs, or rather, one of the disks does; the other is a standard off-the-shelf light.

"I've pulled the hole sources out of both of them, and ran them through a battery of tests, and all of them confirm what the light showed: the source is running at an incredible 97% efficiency, and its energy output is steady up to about ten times the normal rating for that class."

Syphus folded his hands under his chin and gazed at the screen. "That sounds impressive."

His own engineering knowledge of the tiny power supplies was essentially non-existent, but efficiency and energy output he understood: they represented device life in the hands of customers. He started thinking through the ramifications of this new information. Better efficiency meant longer life, and ultimately, fewer sales as people would not need to replace their power sources as frequently. There was probably a way to market the devices to increase price, but clearly he was going to need to determine if there might be a way to wring greater profits out of the technology, assuming he could find a way to take advantage of these new findings.

"Hmm," he mused, "do you think we're likely to face a product that will last a lot longer than our current sources?"

Dolph gazed back at Syphus, obviously impatient with other's lack of comprehension. "Well, that's possible, I suppose. But I think device life is a lot less likely a threat than simple production costs."

Syphus was puzzled. "What do you mean?"

"You need to do your homework on the manufacturing process, Syphus, especially now that you're in charge of the division.

"Every Watt of output the sources deliver comes from energy dumped in over the gravity barrier, energy that is pulled out of the accelerator and the aggregation process. It takes several days to grow a source as large as the ones that are in the lights you sent me, longer for larger sources; the supplies that we put into vehicles can take months.

"But now consider a source that is not only three times as efficient, but also has the energy equivalence of a source ten times its size: you're talking hours, perhaps minutes, for smaller holes."

He paused for effect. "How much does it cost to run the beam, Syphus?"

Syphus's eyes widened. Obviously, he needed to get up to speed more quickly on the operations that he had newly acquired with his position at Corporate.

Beam costs are huge, but if it only took a tenth as long to build the sources...

"How long will it take to get our facility up to the task of building these holes?" he asked.

"I haven't tried to open up the sources yet, but I'm ready to start. Just give me the word. Someone built these samples, so I don't expect it should take too long to reverse engineer them."

Syphus smiled. "Do whatever you think is necessary, Kunst."

Dolph disappeared from the screen. Syphus knew he'd bend all his energy at completing the analysis; there was no one better in Omicron to take on the task.

This was an interesting development, and more than just interesting. When he'd sent the disks to Dolph, Syphus was not sure what to expect; he had essentially forgotten about them until this moment. The disks and their attending message had been a mystery, and he'd wanted it deciphered, but there was no reason to believe they were anything unusual. Now however, there was more to think about. Dolph's findings represented a huge potential for Omicron and Syphus's career therein. The corporation did several billion dollars of hole source sales every quarter; an increase in production efficiency meant dropping the bottom line significantly, and that would look very good for Mr. Pettyman, very good, indeed.

With those thoughts running through his head, Syphus glanced at each of the insect collections. If he planned this well, and the hole technology was even half as good as Dolph thought, it was only a matter of time before he would add one more box.

12. Ocean Healing

Lewis McCrorry scratched his cheek roughly, his fingers digging through his dirty, two-month old beard with deliberate intention. He looked through the doorway carefully, his eyes darting quickly from person to person, noting the location of the exits, checking for the presence of wallscreens, and trying to determine whether or not anyone was paying any special attention to him. Slowly, he ambled into the room, his head down, stringy, dirty hair hanging loosely over his ears and covering his face completely.

He was hungry. He was always hungry now, ever since he'd managed to leave the hospital many weeks ago. He'd thought his plight at MIT was the bottom of the barrel, the lowest echelon of a dispirited research effort, but he almost wished he could have it back now. Almost. He had reached a kind of despairing plateau as his life disintegrated around him, but the descent had started from that bland existence, and he longed to be back there no more than he desired to be where he was now; in that path lay nothingness.

He coughed wretchedly, as a social worker came over to him. He glanced up quickly, noting the pity in her face, and hated her all the more for it.

"Do you need something to eat?" she asked, full of concern.

Lewis grunted. He wanted to lash out at her.

Of course I need something to eat, you blinking dot, why do you think I'm here?

But instead, he let her lead him to the corner of the cafeteria where the line started. He noted how she avoided his touch, and managed to guide him by hand gestures alone.

She left him to his own thoughts, intent on assisting others into the line as they poured through the street entrance behind him. He grabbed a bowl of soup, some bread, and a few crackers, and found a seat at one of the long tables. As he bent over his food, he thought back to the day he'd found his name embedded in the deletion keys.

He had dressed quickly, painfully, the wounds of his accident having not really even started healing, and dismissed Nik. That was the hardest part of the journey: severing the ties with his old friend and playmate, never to mend them again. Tears came quickly to his eyes, and he ground his fists into them to make them stop. He wasn't sure what Nik thought of the revelation they'd both discovered, but he was determined not to implicate him any further into whatever dark mess he'd fallen. And that was the second hardest thing about his predicament: he had evaded capture and death, but was no closer to understanding what had brought it on than he was when he lay in the hospital, aching and bruised from an attempt on his life that had brought the train down around him.

Of the reality of that threat he had no doubt. First, there was the explosion at the lab, next the train wreck, and finally, the detection of his name written into the base layer of a set of convoluted permissions that should not have existed. He did not need to bring his considerable mathematical skills to bear on those events to know that the chance of all three happening by coincidence was vanishingly close to zero.

But who was doing this to him; and more importantly, why?

His efforts to unlock these mysteries through public terminals had proved vain.

In the hospital, he had dressed quickly after finally getting rid of Nik. In fact, he'd had to power down the screen manually to accomplish the feat. And the memory of his last, ultimately hostile act to his long-time companion gnawed at him.

"I am not sure I should leave you alone, right now," Nikola had said, looking like a concerned parent whose recalcitrant ward was about to do something foolish and perhaps dangerous. "Please lie back down and we can take this up again in the morning after you've rested."

"I'm quite rested enough, thank you," he'd replied. "Now please, Nik shut down for the night and let me think this through."

But Nik would have none of that. No matter what arguments Lewis used, Nik simply would not go away. When Lewis had finally jabbed the screen's emergency power down sequence, Nik looked as though he were about to have the electronic equivalent of a heart attack. Lewis dressed in a panic, thinking that at any moment the nurse would come in on him, and his chance of escape would be gone.

Despite Nikola's concern, no one came through the door. He slipped out of the room, leaving his tag under the pillow. The stairs were exhausting in his condition; he limped down all four flights, rested momentarily at the bottom, and then walked out the front door of the hospital lobby into a chilly evening. It was not until he was many blocks away that he began to feel that he had some degree of success, and that no one was coming to find him.

He had no plan once he had made his initial escape. He knew that he no longer could afford to use his Neural Sea connections, nor contact any of his friends. And that thought brought him up short. When he reviewed the list of people whom he might have trusted, he came up with no one, not one single individual he could realistically call a friend. Sure, there were his parents, familiar strangers with lives that were as complete a mystery to him as his was to them, but there were no soul mates, no confidants, not even any casual acquaintances beyond the few students he'd encountered over the years. Most of the people he'd met he'd either despised, or thought the same of him. His only compatriot was Nikola Tesla, and his synthetic companion was the last entity he could contact; doing so meant certain detection.

The one thought that seemed clear was to recover the data thimble; all else was pointless: the running, the hiding. If he did not obtain the data that had drawn him into this appalling nightmare, there was no escape. Somehow, everything wound around that damnable experiment.

So he walked boldly to his apartment that night; either he would be caught, or he would not. With his heart hammering in his chest and his arms shivering, he waited until the front door was opened by another tenant, then followed him in, disguising his fear and limp by trying to act drunk. In front of his apartment door, he paused uncertainly. There had been no alarm sounded, and there did not seem to be any watch upon the place. Perhaps they hadn't missed him from the hospital yet.

Finally, as beads of sweat broke out on his forehead, he thumbed the entrance pad and stepped over the threshold. He did not know if the Shield had set up surveillance of his apartment, but if they had, they would be here quickly now that he had given away his location. Expecting hard hands to be grabbing him from behind at every moment, he pawed through the wreck of thimbles on his desk, finding the one he sought. Without even stopping to pick up a change of clothes, he fled out the door and down the back stairway, losing himself as quickly as he could among the winding streets of Porter Square. As he rounded a corner, he thought he heard a Shield jumpcar swoop down out of the clouds near his apartment. He had no way of knowing, but it felt like he had just avoided catastrophe by the narrowest of margins.

He clutched the thimble to his chest, and trudged as quickly and as long as he could, until he found an underground parking lot. Shivering with cold, pain, and exhaustion, his knees drawn up close, and his arms wrapped around them, every bone aching and his head throbbing, alone and bereft of any connection to his former life, he cried silently. All the anger and resentment he'd harbored for the better part of his life boiled up and overwhelmed him. He tasted bitterness as he'd never known, fought against the bile that threatened to send him heaving over double. All the endless uselessness that was his life washed away into a river of misery.

He did not sleep that night, nor the next, repeated in much the same fashion, but in a different part of town. Each sleepless period was followed by hopeless wandering, till on the third day he'd happened upon a soup kitchen. No one asked him questions, not even his name, but they fed him, and gave him a blanket against the cold. Each night he found some sort of shelter: parking lots, boxes in alleys, abandoned buildings. He'd even come to know the types of people he'd find in each location, homeless as himself: beaten, bewildered, and sometimes violent.

Since then, he'd made his way south, step by step, always vaguely toward New York, although with no specific plan in mind. Along the way, he used the public terminals at libraries, train stations, and convenience stores. He read the news about the MIT explosion and the T train wreck. He read of his own disappearance, and the Shield's search for him. And he ran his own queries. He cobbled together a few tools each time, none of them any match for the kind of sophistication he'd had at his fingertips at MIT, nor even his apartment in Cambridge, but at least innocuous enough that they would not raise suspicion. But his rudimentary efforts were not up to the task of parsing the volume of data on the thimble; it remained a dark and inaccessible vault.

He was now somewhere in New Jersey, a nondescript town with a main street like any other, with the now familiar blue and gold shield of the Salvation Army, the Red Cross emblem, or any of a half-dozen other charitable organizations that supported the few castaways of civilization, living on the margins of the world. He was one of those jettisoned creatures now, with no more to look forward to from one day to the next than the same dull drudgery of the day before.

The data thimble hung from a ragged string around his neck, rubbing familiarly against his chest. He spooned the hot soup into his mouth and drank the cool water. It was now mid-June, and the weather had turned warm. His coat was tied around his waist, and his sleeves were rolled up as far as he could get them, but even still he was sweating.

He finished his meal and made ready to leave, glancing once more around the room. It had become habit: he was not certain how long he could maintain his anonymity among the straggling edges of society, so he kept a watchful eye for any Shield or police officials. Today, he was glad he did. Just outside the exit, he saw the unmistakable blue of a Shield officer. He was talking with a tall woman in a dark suit.

He frowned and looked around again. There were no other exits from the cafeteria, but a couple of other doors lead farther into the facility to offices and whatever other spaces the soup kitchen needed to maintain its business. He sat as patiently as he could, pretending to be engaged in his meal for the better part of a half hour, but the Shield officer was not leaving. In fact, it looked as though he meant to stay until the cafeteria closed shop. Occasionally the officer glanced inside at the guests as they ate their meals. Sooner or later, he might even notice that one among them had been seated longer than the rest, and would come in to question him.

Lewis got to his feet, shuffled through the aisles between the tables, and walked through the doorway farthest from the exit into a hallway lined with doors. The first door on his right had an animated poster on it that depicted a glistening ship on an emerald green ocean, fish and whales trailing the vessel with sparkles in their eyes and grins on their human-exaggerated faces. Fading in and out among puffy, white clouds were the words 'Ocean Healing', and smaller print beneath them 'seed the wonders of the sea.' There was a scrolling itinerary of departures and arrivals at the bottom of the sprayscreen, indicating ports all along the eastern seaboard, Europe, Africa, and the Middle East.

He opened the door and stepped through into a quiet vestibule with several small tables and a counter at the far end. The tidy young man behind the glass looked up from whatever he'd been reading, and after a brief, startled expression, smiled brightly.

"Yes, sir, are you interested in trying for a place on next week's sailing?"

Lewis nodded slowly. "Yes, I think so."

He wasn't sure what next week's sailing might mean, nor where the ship was headed, but anything that kept him occupied and potentially offered another way out of the building was what he needed right now.

"Fine, fine," the other said, as he slid a softscreen under the glass. "Please fill this out to the best of your ability, and we'll have a look."

Lewis picked up the screen suspiciously, then sat down in one of the chairs. The first questions were personal information requests. He picked up a stylus from one of the desks, and began filling the questions out. Since his journey had begun, there had been several occasions on which he'd given a name. Unimaginatively, he started with A, and had worked his way through F. With only a moment's thought, he entered 'John Gumbel'. Since this facility provided a roof for many homeless people, he thought it would not seem odd to leave the remaining fields blank.

The second screen showed a picture of the world, each of the major oceans labeled with a number. On the right were check boxes next to a list of the names of the oceans. The instructions indicated that he should match the numbers to the names, which he did, taking a long while to think of each of the oceans in turn, and drawing out the time. Subsequent screens were much the same: math, history, reading, basic vocabulary. Apparently, he was taking an entrance exam, designed to ensure that anyone who applied to sail on next week's cruise was sufficiently intelligent that they would not be an embarrassment to any of the other guests. There were several screens that asked questions about seamanship and navigation, about which he had basically no clue; on those he simply guessed among the multiple choice answers.

Eventually he reached the end of the screens and dutifully handed the tablet back. The man behind the counter told him to wait and sped off to a further room.

While he waited, Lewis planned his next move. Going back to the cafeteria was not his first choice, but might represent the only option he had. If the Shield officer were still there, he'd need to be careful. Perhaps he could bluff his way out; certainly his appearance matched his status as a homeless exile, and it would take a very inquisitive person to see through the layers of dirt and beard. And anyway, it may simply be his paranoia doing the thinking; the appearance of a Shield at the door may be nothing more than coincidence and have nothing to do with looking for him.

Soon enough, the young man came back, and with another smile said, "Mr. Gumbel, please walk down the hallway to the next door on your right. You will be met there by Mr. Olsen, who will see you through the next step in the process. And congratulations, it looks like you've made a passing grade!"

Lewis gave the man a quirky smile. "Yeah." It was all he could think to say.

Well, at least I've got a few more minutes of hanging backstage.

Lewis followed the man's instructions and found Mr. Olsen as promised.

"Mr. Gumbel. Welcome to the Ocean Healing experience. I'm so glad you've decided to take the first step in this journey of exploration and personal therapy. Please, have a seat."

He waved his hand at an empty chair, followed his own suggestion and sat in the seat next to it, inviting Lewis to do the same with raised eyebrows.

Lewis sat down on the edge of the seat. He was not sure of the process, but was suspicious of what might happen next. Clearly he had passed the initial assessment, and was now heading deeper into unknown territory; caution, at least, was advised.

Mr. Olsen handed him another softscreen, this one with some kind of external attachment and recessed port.

"If you will, Mr. Gumbel, please indicate you agree to the terms stated on the screen, and we'll move right along."

On the screen was what looked like some sort of consent form. Lewis read through it quickly, noting that it authorized Ocean Healing to perform a wellness check and background screen on the undersigned party. Internally, Lewis groaned. His side venture to avoid facing a Shield officer was now turning into exactly the thing he feared most.

He was about to hand the softscreen back to the still smiling Mr. Olsen, who now held a medical swab in his hand, when the door opened. The Shield officer and the suit-clad woman entered, engaged in an animated discussion. They were in mid-sentence as they walked in.

"Mr. Olsen," she said abruptly, "as soon as you are through here, please come with me to show Mr. Nordgart our facility. It seems the Shield is concerned that we are not keeping our hands clean, among other things."

"I'll be with you in just a moment, Miss Alben," he replied.

All three turned their attention to Lewis, waiting for him to make his next move.

In a panic, Lewis turned to the softscreen and signed his name, John Gumbel, in the appropriate spot. His heart was hammering, and he could think of no way to abort the procedure without drawing even more attention to himself. He opened his mouth and submitted the inner lining of his cheek to the swab.

Mr. Olsen took the sample, put the swab into the softscreen recess, and touched a button, waiting for the analysis to complete. Lewis swallowed and looked at his feet.

Spaff, what a stupid way to have it all end. I should have stayed in the cafeteria.

But it was too late. Should he make a dash for the doorway? That seemed foolish; he was in an unfamiliar city, and even if he managed to get out the door into the street, it was unlikely he'd be able to outrun any pursuit.

After a long, painful wait, the softscreen beeped, and Mr. Olsen detached the swab and analyzer, smiling once again.

"Well, Mr. Gumbel, it looks like you've been given a clean bill of health. Let's get you right on up to the next floor, and you can be on your way. I'm sorry I don't have more time to spend with you, but as you can see, duty calls."

He stood and held his hand to indicate that Lewis should proceed to the door. Lewis stood as well, glanced quickly at all three of the occupants, and reached for the door.

"Down the hall to your right and up the stairs. And take this with you." Mr. Olsen said, handing Lewis a small, organic tracer card.

When he reached the hallway, Lewis swayed in relief. Somehow he was still free. All he could think was that whatever method they used to compare DNA profiles did not include a check against the population at large, and was aimed mainly at criminal datasets. And that meant the Shield had not yet moved to incorporate his profile into their own files. Given the number of times he'd seen his own name in print, and the stories surrounding the Shield's efforts to find him, it seemed unlikely that they would not have started the process. He was no expert on legal procedures, but knew the privacy laws would not hold up long against a concerted effort to label him a fugitive.

He paused a moment before proceeding up the stairs.

What if Nikola is holding them up? It would be just like him to try to keep the Shield at bay. Perhaps he's given me a little breathing room.

The conclusion was encouraging, the first optimistic thought he'd had in many weeks.

But don't let it go to your head. Even if I'm right, Nikola can only hold them off so long; they'll get what they want in the end.

He considered going out the door, losing himself once more in the streets of the northeast corridor until he ended up... where? His aimless wandering had brought him no answers, and he still had no purpose. Somehow he needed to find a way to unlock the data on his thimble. There were too many risks associated with finding a location that could read the data, and the toolset he needed for the analysis was not readily at hand. He needed a university, or at least an interface that could allow him access to a university's resources. And not here, not anywhere around the east coast of North America.

Suddenly, a cruise on an Ocean Healing liner, whatever that entailed, did not seem like a bad idea; in fact, it seemed like the best thing that had happened to him since his ill-fated ride on the T. He started up the stairs, buoyed by the thought of leaving his current homeless existence behind.

13. The Thread

. . . . .

Ontologic Sum looked to his partners, seated once again at the grey table. His manikin was no longer completely expressionless; a twitch played at the corner of its mouth, giving form to the squirming others in his mind. "Is there any word of McCrorry?"

"No," both replied.

He frowned, his eyes flickering red. "Then, I have news, to make up for your blindness. Seven hours ago, our quarry was drafted into an ocean rehabilitation program. His DNA profile was sequenced and searched; match characteristics confirmed."

Scripted characters flowed over the table like accusing fingers. Hengest Slain peered at them in silence. The fact that he had not seen the event was especially humiliating, piled upon the embarrassment of the errant attempts in Cambridge. McCrorry had obstinately refused to succumb to his will.

Agents could be brought online at the port before the ship departed, but would need to be hastily arranged, which meant heightened risk of both discovery and failure.

"I will arrange for special circumstances when the ship arrives at its destination," he said. "There is little need for intervention while he is on board."

"Is there any danger of interference from the Shield?" Relic asked.

"No," Ontologic replied, "the results were routed through our subsentient watchers; the gatekeepers interrupted the protocols to substitute a null result. Bridge records were shuffled and have been successfully entered through the Deletion Guild. The chance of discovery of the alteration is extremely low.

"The Shield is still looking in the Northeast region of North America; there is no indication they will expand the scope beyond this area."

"And what of Pettyman, the human you know so well?" Relic asked. "Do we yet have a path to the Traitor?"

Ontologic speared him with his red eyes. "I have one more visit to pay our puppet. He already has an avid interest in our gift, which will soon give way to a fixation on discovering its origin. I will very soon find a strong current to the Traitor."

. . . . .

14. Encounter

The hydrojet cruised comfortably at 3,000 meters through a cloudless sky, the scrub and dry washes of southeast Australia passing leisurely into the rolling folds of the Wilcannia hills. Large windows curved from the floor to the apex of the vehicle's fuselage, giving panoramic views of the reddening desert vista below and the achingly blue vault above. The sun cast long shadows throughout the cabin. Syphus Pettyman relaxed in one of five soft swivel-chairs, smoking a hand-rolled Cuban cigar, and enjoying himself immensely.

Although it was an extravagance of the kind he normally avoided, and was certainly being discussed among the upper level managers within his district, he had scheduled the private aircraft to fly him to the Wilcannia facility alone. He knew this behavior would likely land him a visit from the Vice President of Operations on appropriate use of company property, and may even propel his name to the attention of the CEO; in fact, he was counting on it. His initial assessment of the potential value of the new hole source after his first, brief discussion with Kunst had borne fruit in a major way. Dolph had peered into the inner workings of the source, and had made great strides in understanding how its amazing efficiency was enabled. He still had more work to do to grapple with exactly how it had been manufactured, but Syphus was convinced the scientist would eventually unravel the mystery. The morning meeting had gone quite well; Dolph was ebullient with the prospects for the future, and Syphus had given the assent to begin a deeper probe. By the time upper management had seen fit to chastise their newest member about his extravagant use of the hydrojet, he could present a compelling case for the new technology, making it clear that the impetus behind its development was his own doing. The ostentatious exhibition of self-importance he was now enjoying would have served its purpose to catapult him to the notice of those within the company who could make a real difference in the attainment of his next insect collection.

He grinned, leaned back, and took a long, languid pull on the hand-rolled Servilla y Fuente, enjoying the pungent aroma and roiling, woody flavor on his tongue and lips.

Ah, this is the way I was meant to live. All right, time to check with Kunst again to see how the rest of his research went this afternoon.

"Amelia, get me Mr. Kunstler."

"Actually," his secretary replied, her tightly wound hair and bookish features appearing on the aircraft screen, "Mr. Kunstler wishes to speak with you. I will put him through."

"Well, what have you got?" Syphus asked in anticipation of the good news. "Have you finished the analysis already?"

But the scientist looked anything but excited. There were no significant discoveries, Syphus could see that in his face. In fact, he couldn't remember having seen Kunst so dejected.

"Syph," he said. "Something's happened to the hole source! I started a detailed molecular survey after you left this morning, and all I got was a puddle of mixed elements. I've been over the data a hundred times, and tried everything I can think of to clarify the results. I finally resorted to letting the dissphages work on the source, and I'm afraid there's no longer any doubt: it's melted!"

Kunst ran his fingers through his hair, obviously distraught. "But I had it stored in our stasis box, and I've been monitoring it continuously. I don't understand how it happened. I don't think I'll be able to figure out how it works." His gaze was distracted, speaking more to himself than Syphus.

"This is a disaster," he finished.

Syphus thought about the disappointing implications, but he never made any significant career move without a backup plan: there were always options. As much as he liked Kunst, Syphus could show his own actions were in response to the scientist's enthusiastic proclamations of profitability. Syphus could say he was simply trying to determine for himself the viability of the enterprise. He had been overly optimistic perhaps, but with a senior researcher making claims that stood to dramatically increase the division's profits, surely he had no choice but to make certain he understood the ramifications. Kunst might end up with a black eye over the affair, and perhaps even lose his job, but that was the price of missing dramatic opportunities. After all, Kunst had let the hole source melt in the first place.

Still, Syphus hated the thought of losing one of his most valuable contacts in the technical circles of the company. It was not sentimentality that tempered his outlook; he had always regarded squandered resources the result of poor leadership. And the reflection it cast on him was an unacceptable outcome.

He knew that the scientist's methods were too thorough to have overlooked any obvious uncertainties.

"Can we salvage anything, Kunst?"

"I don't know. I'm trying to reconstruct some of the fundamental structures, but the meltdown looks to have been very thorough. Whoever designed the protocol did a good job of making sure there was nothing left to be found."

"What? What do mean?"

Dolph looked at him, perplexed. "I'm talking about the hole source," he said. "It melted."

"Do you mean deliberately?" Syphus asked. "You mean the source melted down because someone instructed it to melt?"

"Well, yes, actually. In fact, I set it off when I started the microstructure evaluation. There must have been a trigger in there somehow that detected what I was doing. The whole sequence took just a couple of seconds once it started, but there's no question that it was pre-programmed. The melt pattern is too perfectly defined to have been anything but deliberate. And it's only the parts that were new technology; the external housing and thermal layers are all standard issue, and they're intact.

"You've got to get another one, Syph," he finished. "Otherwise, we're stopped cold."

This was interesting. The power supplies had been delivered with the intent that the high efficiency source would be investigated; a tickle to whet Syphus's imagination. But when the details of its construction were about to be discovered, it simply self-destructed, leaving no evidence to suggest how it might be manufactured. Very clever. And very infuriating; this was no amateur negotiator that could be beaten easily down.

"I'm not sure I can, Kunst," he replied. "This was a onetime donation; we didn't have any provisions for a second go around."

"But you've got to find a way, Syphus," the scientist continued. "I'm not exaggerating when I say we would turn the energy market on its head with a product like this. The measurements I made while the source was still functioning were incredible. And the decay rate was almost un-measurable. If the power curves scale up as a normal source would, we could power entire buildings for the cost of a household source, and fit it into a suitcase.

"I don't know where you got it, or why I haven't seen or heard anything about this technology before, but the existence proof is unquestionable, and if we're first to market with this, it will be huge."

Syphus pondered the scientist's words. They were heady stuff, the material of corporate dreams. But he left unsaid the clear converse to the situation: if Omicron were not the first to market, it might well mean its extinction.

Kunst signed off, leaving the panoramic view of the Australian wilderness in his place. Its beauty had not diminished, but under the pall that hung over Syphus's mind, it lacked its earlier comforting serenity. Clearly there would be a second contact, more direct this time. He was not sure that a second hole source could be procured, but he did not doubt that the designers still needed to take the next step and negotiate terms.

As he gazed into the sky and pondered the future, the windows suddenly polarized, darkening to the point of opacity. Syphus leaned forward, extracted the Cuban from his lips and called to the aircraft.

"Pilot, what's going on?"

The glow at the tip of his cigar was the only illumination now, lighting the immediate vicinity with a weird, orange hue. The recesses of the cabin remained hidden in deep shadow.

"Kunst, are you there?"

There was no response from the scientist, nor the subsentient in charge of the flight. Syphus held onto the cigar, wanting to stub it out, but knowing full well that it provided him the only point on which to focus his attention. All else remained dark. He repeated his question to the pilot, this time with a bit more intensity.

He was unsure what to do. There had been no discernable change in the level flight of the ship, no tell-tale bumpiness or sudden lurch that might mark a problem with the aircraft. As far as he could tell, they were still flying without incident; he was simply in the dark.

Slowly, the curving darkness of the fuselage screen gave way to a soft, bluish hue. As the light spread across the length of the cabin, Syphus began to realize the glow was not uniform, but had shapes embedded within. He swiveled in his chair, trying to get a fix on the pattern. There were light and dark areas, almost like shadows being cast, but he could not construct their purpose.

Suddenly, as his mind reoriented itself, he realized he was looking at letters fashioned as three-dimensional blocks, and taking up the entire side of the plane. Once he had made the mental adjustment, the word became clear: "Advance", written on both sides of the cabin.

Well, it seems my mysterious friend is already back.

Although this marked the second time he'd been party to the experience, and he was determined to convince himself that he was in control of the situation, he once again found that he was nervous. First, the visitor had usurped his office systems, and now he apparently had control of the display within the aircraft. Both feats were impressive, however else Syphus felt about the intrusion. And the timing of this latest visit, moments after learning of the demise of the hole source the visitor had sent, was a little too fortuitous to be coincidence.

Syphus leaned back in the chair, took another slow draw on his cigar, and stilled himself for whatever was coming next.

"Advance," he said, watching the smoke curl from his lips.

Immediately, the word disappeared from the screen, and the darkness returned, only this time not so complete. Two small circles of light hovered on the screen beside him, images of the disks he had received.

"Mr. Pettyman," the deep, bass voice rumbled, "so good to see you again."

"That remains to be seen. Your introductions are rather terse, and I'm not sure how much I like surprises."

"Ah, yes, I'm afraid I was not introduced properly. But then, my message was somewhat important, and I thought that a certain degree of showmanship was necessary to attract your attention, busy as you are."

"I am suitably impressed," Syphus acknowledged.

He did not know what further message was intended, but he was determined to wait it out.

"Very good," the voice replied. "I assume you have investigated the hole source we sent, and that you are aware of its potential."

There was a pause.

"Go on," Syphus said.

"My employers have authorized me to inform you that they are interested in finding a business partner to manufacture and market these devices. Their organization is quite small, and focused solely on basic research. They do not have the resources to develop the technology fully, but realize that Omicron may be in a position to exploit the discoveries they have made."

"And who might your employers be?" Syphus asked.

He was familiar with these types of negotiations, which usually took a long time to complete, and an army of lawyers to work through the legal conditions; surprises were not a welcome part of the proceedings.

"You may use the firm of M'bota Holdings, in Kenya, as the contact point."

"I'm not familiar with that company," Syphus replied. "I don't recall ever hearing of them in the energy industry."

"As I said, my employers' organization is quite small. M'bota was incorporated only recently, in order to handle the business transactions they felt were imminent."

A small company with sufficient expertise to commandeer the network resources of a high-level manager within a large corporation, and design a power source that the rest of the world has not stumbled upon; interesting.

"The technology you gave us is really quite intriguing, but I'm afraid it will take considerably more investment to bring it up to the status of a manufacturable solution. We think there is some chance it may turn out to be profitable, but at this point, frankly, we're not predisposed to sink much investment in it. It simply falls fairly low on the list of our priorities at the moment."

"As you might imagine," the voice continued, "my employers feel otherwise. They had hoped Omicron would show interest, as the expertise you could bring to bear is in keeping with their desires; they are prepared to make the technology available within a very reasonable licensing arrangement."

Ah, and now we come to it.

"Yes, and what kind of terms are they willing to extend?"

With his chief scientist at an impasse, Syphus was over a barrel on this one, and in no position to offer much resistance, but he was determined to avoid giving away the keys to the company, and his future in the process.

"The terms are very simple," came the reply. "Two percent of all sales related to the new source configuration will be paid out to M'Bota."

Syphus almost choked. He had to feign clearing his throat as he drew a long pull on his cigar. He had been expecting to have to whittle his way down from a number in the fifty percent range; two percent was ridiculously low. The earlier assessment of his visitors as savvy businessmen appeared to be off base.

"In return," the deep voice continued, "Omicron will be granted an exclusive license to produce the devices over the next ten years. The initial investment in manufacturing capability will be borne by Omicron.

"In addition, you will be free to apply for patents on the technology, to be held jointly between Omicron and M'Bota."

Syphus sat back in his chair, no longer concerned about the dark interior of the hydrojet. He could barely restrain himself from pumping his fist.

Do they truly not realize what they have?

He took another sweet breath through his cigar, watching the glowing embers flare momentarily; the taste was finer than any he had ever enjoyed, all the more so since he had only moments before been thinking that the affair was going to end up a travesty. The thick smoke rolled over his tongue and through his nostrils like victory.

"I think we can work with those terms," he said, finally. "I'm sure we can have our legal department start the paperwork directly."

"Actually," the voice interrupted, "my employers are somewhat eager to get started. Legal proceedings are notoriously difficult to resolve once begun. They were hoping to avoid drawn out negotiations in favor of a quicker solution."

Syphus was somewhat taken aback. "This is a bit unusual," he said. "What do you have in mind?"

"A simple contract can be drafted, with the terms stated earlier, and signed by you."

"By me." Syphus said. This was unexpected. He wasn't quite sure how to handle the situation.

"Yes, surely you have authority for this type of action."

"Certainly," he replied, slightly annoyed.

"Then, really there does not appear to be a problem. You must admit, the terms of the agreement are quite generous. My employers are very eager to begin working with Omicron."

There was a subtle emphasis on the word 'Omicron', and Syphus did not miss it: clearly a veiled threat to take their business elsewhere, should the negotiations fail.

"I'm certain we can work under those terms," he replied. "Please send the documents to my secretary, Amelia D., at my office in Sydney."

"Very good," the deep voice rumbled, obviously pleased with the conclusion. "We will have the papers ready for your signature by this time tomorrow. It has been a pleasure working with you, Mr. Pettyman. We look forward to our relationship, and with the continued success of your career."

With that, the conversation ended, the letters faded from the screen, and the windows returned gradually to an exterior view. The sun continued to glow redly in the west as the aircraft sped through the Australian evening.

Syphus leaned forward in his seat and set the cigar down in a recessed holder on the nearby desk.

His name was going to be on this contract. There was an obvious degree of risk associated with the arrangement: if the work turned out badly for any reason, it would be his career on the line. On the other hand, the rewards promised to be heady: enormous divisional profits, with him as the mover who had made it happen. There was always risk in bold undertakings.

But not undue risk. He would find out everything there was to know about his visitor; a business neophyte to be sure, and now a marginal adversary. It was good policy, and had served him well in the past: always ready to bring out some small piece of information at the appropriate time to ensure the success of whatever endeavor to which he was committed. He smiled.

I will stay on top.

15. Storm at Sea

The emerald green sea looked deep and mysterious, capped with small breakers and darkening toward grey on the horizon, reflecting a dim wall of clouds that curved far to the north. A chill breeze blew steadily, feathering tiny drops of spray from the whitecaps across the face of each wave. The crew and working passengers aboard the *Wish You Were Here* busied themselves about the deck. Many of the older hands were already outfitted in foul weather gear, anticipating the coming rain. Most of them seemed to enjoy themselves immensely, relishing the open air and freedom from worry; to get the current job done and bed-down for the evening, tired and relaxed was their largest care.

"Mr. Gumbel," hollered the krill-tank foreman, "time to get yourself over to the starboard and mind holding vessel three! Double-quick, now!"

Lewis turned to look at the chief, a weather-beaten old man who had been managing Seed Ship expeditions for nearly a quarter century, and keeping lazy midshipmen in line for many years before that in the Australian Merchant Marines. He had a shaved head and a bushy beard in which his mouth was embedded, effectively hidden until he croaked an order to some unworthy deckhand, when large, white teeth and a pink tongue suddenly emerged from the thicket.

"Molly's been holding your time for nearly ten minutes! I already sent Zane to track you down, and I'll dock you an hour's pay if you take more than 30 seconds to move down the line!"

Lewis only nodded, leaving his place by the rail in order to comply with the order. The foreman glowered at him.

The voyage had not turned out as Lewis had imagined. When he had signed on for the cruise, he had conjured up a leisurely trip across the Atlantic; a time to sort out his options, with good food and a comfortable bed, interesting conversations among the passengers, and freedom from the drudgery of his academic past. He knew the vessel was a working ship, and that he was one of the contractors signed on to maintain its operation, but he had thought his duties would be minimal, and most of the work would be done by those with more experience than him, or professionals who had trained for the job. His first week on board had thoroughly dispelled that quaint notion: up to work before the northern sun had crept far into the sky and in bed after a dinner that seemed all too late in coming, he and his fellow conscripts labored at dozens of tasks required to fulfill the ship's purpose. The extreme length of the sub-arctic day at first made it feel like there was plenty of time left after the evening meal, but he had found this to be a cruel hoax when he'd been summoned to breakfast the second day after only two hours of sleep.

True, the food was plentiful, though plain, and his sleeping quarters comfortable, if not exactly private, but this was no vacation cruise where guests were expected to indulge themselves in culinary extravagance and retire to luxurious suites, enjoying sweet ocean sunsets and exotic ports of call. Everyone on board was expected to work hard, crew and passengers alike.

And among the homeless volunteers, there were secondary duties. Although there were only two others who shared Lewis's background, they were all expected to spend an hour each day in a kind of group therapy; a discussion period that Lewis loathed with as much intensity as he had hated his years as a student. Neither of the other two vagrants were any more predisposed to lengthy discourse than Lewis, so the duration of the meetings were largely spent listening to the facilitator in futile attempts to elicit responses from his reluctant participants. They were boring and uncomfortable sessions, made all the worse because Lewis could not voice his annoyance for fear of giving away basic facts that might betray his identity.

He made his way across the mid-deck, glad that he at least had acquired enough dexterity to complete the short walk with a minimum of effort against the gently rolling surface. He remembered his first few days at sea as awkward lurching affairs, clutching at rails and leaning against any surface he could find to steady himself. He had fallen more than once, to the general good-natured laughing of the crew, but he did not return their joking in kind, preferring to ignore the ribbing in silence. This had not endeared himself to anyone on board; he increasingly found himself alone, and the invitations to join in the after dinner social occasions became more infrequent. This had led to retiring to his bunk earlier than most, alone and depressed. He shared a small room with four others, all of whom were paying their way through the voyage. One of the others had made similar trips in the past, but the rest were novices like he. They were all eager for the work, and seemed to have made friends easily, among themselves and the others on the ship.

His reverie was interrupted as he almost missed a step heading to the tank rooms below deck. He hung onto the railing to make the final few steps and walked down the corridor to tank room three. Here the noises of the ship were pronounced: thrumming pumps and engines, whistling pressure valves, and a cacophony of vague creaks and groans forming the underlying tapestry of sound that felt at times like a physical presence. When he first experienced the clamor while lying in bed after an exhausting introductory day of training, he was dismayed, sure he could never sleep. But to his own astonishment, he had dropped off almost immediately, waking only when the call to stations rang the next morning. Perhaps it had to do with growing up in New York and attending school in Cambridge, where the ceaseless din of the city was an ever-present companion; whatever the reason, his ability to fall asleep quickly each night was one of the few pleasant experiences of the entire trip.

He stepped over the coaming and through the open hatch into the narrow space between the forward bulkhead and the maze of pipes and tanks. Bubbles were rising through the clear containers, pulled into the pipes and channeled through the recirculation system from the decks below, visible through the grated mezzanine. Inside the tanks were countless krill, so thick that the water looked like a soup of the shrimp-like crustaceans. The largest were a few inches in length, while others were barely the size of a thumbnail. Tank three was the last holding vessel before the creatures were let into the sea, along with the phytoplankton on which they fed, microscopic animals that could only be seen as a general clouding of the water.

Today was another release day, one of many along the southern border of the Arctic Circle. Eventually, each enormous tank would be emptied, helping to replenish the fisheries in the Atlantic with food stock for the next generation: hundreds of millions of the tiny euphausiids that made up one vast and important link in the food chain.

Lewis rounded the corner to see Molly Byrne in the control chair, waiting for her relief. She was one of those perpetually optimistic people that Lewis disliked so much; her house could burn down and she would still find something good to say about the warmth of the fire. She smiled as he walked over to her station.

"I'm glad you could make it this morning," she said, jokingly. "I thought perhaps you were all langers last night, and thought to leave me here today."

Her Irish lilt always made her sentences seem unfinished, somehow, to Lewis. And her use of slang he didn't understand was yet another annoying thing about her.

"Sorry," was all he said, without any enthusiasm.

She gave him a quirky half-smile, as if she knew he wasn't, but it was really his own problem, and didn't affect her anyway. He almost thought she was sorry for him.

"Well," she continued, "the first load's been dumped, and the tank's nigh on three quarters topped. The first two pump stages are running just fine, but the third stage's been narky all morning, so be keeping an eye on it, you.

"I'm off to run for the kitchen and peel the praities. Have fun!"

With that she disappeared out the door.

Lewis took a quick look over the control panel, noting that the pressures and flows were all in the green, although the needle on pump stage three was fluttering a bit, confirming that Molly's description had something to do with the fact that it had been misbehaving. At least this was one job that didn't wear him out physically, although just sitting and monitoring the tanks for hours on end was boring enough to make up for the lack of exertion.

He and Molly had worked a couple of shifts together, running lines out of the stern for measuring temperature and salinity, and on cleaning duty on the lower levels. Both times she had talked incessantly, commenting on everything from the weather to the wonderful experience on the ship. This was her sixth trip, the first having brought her from Ireland to the United States and visiting graduate work at a small college in New Hampshire, two more trips back and forth to visit family, and now back to Trinity College to complete her degree. Her focus was on environmental governance, which he supposed was what gave her over to such unbridled enthusiasm for the trip.

He had listened mostly in silence, which he hoped would convince her to give up on the conversation. Unfortunately, the empty space seemed to make her nervous, which lead to an even faster verbal pace. He already knew more about her than he cared to, and was grateful that today she had somewhere else pressing to go.

For the next several hours, Lewis tended the controls of the tank room, monitoring the condition of the pumps, and dutifully logging the time when the automated system dumped half the tank's contents overboard, a rushing, swirling vortex of krill streaming through the pipes and ultimately out into the cold ocean below.

As the shift wore on, the normally sedate rocking of the ship steadily increased. This had no effect on the performance of the tanks, nor his own task, but did give rise to a queasy feeling in his stomach. Although there was not much to see, he could feel the motion as his weight shifted back and forth.

He got out of the chair, hoping to walk off the nausea, when a loud siren sounded. Simultaneously, a red light turned on, and the overhead lights started flashing. They had gone over the alarm system as part of their training routine, but the crew had all assured the newcomers that they were not likely to see it in action; it looked like that assumption had been overly optimistic.

As he'd been shown, Lewis put the pump room in standby, leaving the systems on automatic, closed and latched the bulkhead door behind him, and made his way unsteadily through the corridor that lead to the mid-deck. It hadn't taken long to perform the operations, but the rocking of the ship had increased markedly by the time he got to the outer hatch. He collided with the wall during the short trip, and banged his knee painfully on the coaming on his way out.

Outside, the sea had taken on a threatening cast. Rain was falling steadily, and the bright sun was gone, leaving everything in a dull, grey light. The small whitecaps he had watched earlier in the day were now foaming ridges of colorless ocean, stamped across broader rolling waves eight feet high stretching to the horizon.

The ship's crew was scrambling over the deck, double-checking the seals on the outer doors, and leading the volunteer passengers to their quarters in the forecastle. Lewis limped into line with the rest, and was grateful to finally make the inside of the ship again. He was cold and soaked as he shuffled to his cabin, avoiding banging into the corridor walls as best he could by keeping his hands out for balance.

He arrived in his room, along with most of his cabin-mates, and set about peeling off his damp clothes, exchanging them for dry uniforms.

André, the one experienced hand in their room, walked in wiping water from his eyes. He was a tall, handsome man from somewhere in the south of Spain, and smiled unabashedly as he shook the water from his hair. "Now this is a storm, eh?" he asked with a thick accent. "I think we will be doing no more chores today!"

He pulled off the raincoat he'd been wearing, hopped into his bunk bed, and propped himself against the wall.

"Do you think it will be a problem?" asked Dan nervously, a short Midwesterner from Chicago who had never been on a ship before.

"Ah, the ocean, she is just sending us a little gift today," André replied, "to remind us how big she is. This is nothing; a tiny shiver. She is winking at us only. The captain will move the ship south and out of her way.

"Come, let us play a game of cards, eh?"

André slid into one of the benches alongside a narrow table that occupied the end of their quarters farthest from the door and pulled a deck of cards out of the drawer.

Lewis ignored the rest of his room-mates, and continued getting changed. He crawled into his bunk and closed his eyes.

"Mr. Gumbel," André continued, "will you join us? It will help to pass the time."

Lewis just turned to give them a stare he hoped conveyed how little he thought of the activity, and rolled over to face the wall. He heard them all chuckle at a muttered comment, knowing they were having a laugh at his expense, but he didn't care. While he lay on the bed, the rocking of the boat once again started to make his stomach queasy.

For the next hour, his cabin-mates played cards and talked. André continued to make light of the situation, but there was a strained quality to their conversation. As time wore on the movement of the ship did not subside; in fact, it grew worse. Eventually the card game came to an end; shuffling and dealing simply became too troublesome as the room pitched from side to side, and ignoring their precarious situation became impossible. On several occasions, a rain-coated crewman showed up at their door and told them to stay in their room. He was not particularly talkative, having more immediate concerns on his mind, but they pressed him for whatever information they could.

To Lewis the news did not sound hopeful: the storm was not generating waves that were of any real concern, but its extent was larger than the captain had foreseen. They were likely to be caught in its grip for some hours. The last visit had brought a few things to eat: cold sandwiches, crackers, and water. There would be no hot meal in the cafeteria this evening; all non-essential activities had been shut down. The ship continued to rock and pitch threateningly, and they all grew more miserable as they waited for it to end.

As Lewis stared across the tiny room, Dan suddenly sat up over the edge of his bunk and threw up. His face was ashen and he looked even worse than Lewis felt. That first act provided the crack that burst the dam; two of the other cabin-mates retched. Only Lewis and André managed to hold down their lunch, and Lewis knew he was probably not far off from following in their footsteps. No one made any attempt to clean up the mess; in fact, there was little anyone could do without creating more of a problem while the ship rocked.

The smell filled the room, worsening the already stale air, and Lewis made up his mind. They'd been ordered to stay in their room for the duration of the storm, but there was no way he could stay any longer.

I didn't sign up for this stankin pile. If I don't get out of here, I'm going to go crazy listening to everyone puke all night.

He pushed himself out of the bunk, shoved his wet shoes on his feet while sitting on the floor, and leaned against the wall on the way over to the door. André looked at him weakly and shook his head. Lewis took the message, but André didn't look like he had much fight in him, and no one else in the room was in any condition to offer resistance.

Lewis sneered at them and sniffed, closing the door ungently behind him. In the hallway, the smell was just as bad; judging from how pervasive it had become, there were more than just a few of the volunteers who had succumbed to sea sickness.

Lewis's first thoughts were to make his way to the large common room one deck above. There was plenty of space, and he didn't expect anyone to be there now, so he could at least have some privacy. But what he really needed to clear his head and relieve the cramping nausea in his stomach was fresh air, and the fact that there were bunkrooms near the common room meant the air upstairs was not likely to be any better than down here.

He put his hands out for support against the walls, trying to think of another course of action. Just then someone else retched in a room slightly down the hall and he made up his mind.

He turned around and headed for the outer hatch. There was a small locker just to the side of the door, and he grabbed a wet raincoat.

At least I'll be relatively dry. No sense in getting any wetter than I need to.

He would make his way to the tank room, or one of the other utility areas in the aft section of the ship. Certainly no one would be there, and he could ride out the storm just as safely there as anywhere else; more importantly, he would be away from the smells and sounds of a seasick crowd.

Lewis zipped the raincoat with some difficulty, eventually having to lean against the wall with all his weight. He straightened up, took a deep breath, and prepared to rotate the wheel that would free the dogs that locked the door shut.

"Where do you think you're going, mister?" a shouted voice stopped him as he was reaching for the door.

Without turning, he knew exactly who it was. The accent was unmistakable. He turned to see Molly Byrne at the other end of the hall, her outstretched arms holding her up as the ship rocked.

He was mad now, as much at having been discovered as by the fact that it was someone who should also have been confined to her quarters, not out prowling the hallways.

"Oh, great, just what I need: a visit from an angry Irish imp," he shot back.

Who is she to tell me what to do? And isn't everyone supposed to be in their rooms?

"Flig out, Molly," he called over his shoulder as he spun the lock.

"John, wait!" she called, her voice now in a panic.

Lewis's plan, as much of one as he'd had time to formulate, was to get out as quickly as he could, close the door behind him, and let Molly follow him if she so desired. He didn't care at this point.

She can't physically carry me back. And they can't kick me off the boat.

Unfortunately, his plan disintegrated as soon as the locks cleared the grooves. The ship rocked violently just as he pushed the door, while a ferocious wind slammed it open hard against the outside bulkhead. The wheel was ripped from his hands and he was yanked off his feet and spun through the portal like a rag doll. He slapped his shin painfully against the frame, tumbled down the dozen metal stairs, and ended up sprawling in agony on the grated deck below.

Everything had happened so quickly that he was not sure how he found himself outside. His leg throbbed in pain, both hands were bleeding, and it felt like a gash had opened in his cheek. Rain lashed at him in stinging torrents, and the wind howled and whistled through the structures and cables of the ship. The sky was pitch black, the only illumination coming from the feeble yellow running lights that lined the mid-deck.

He tried to get to his feet, but the pain in his leg and the rocking of the ship prevented him from doing anything more than getting onto his elbows. He breathed hard, and tried to collect his scattered thoughts. As he lay in this uncertain position, the ship plunged through a towering wave, and a wall of frigid water rolled over the deck, sweeping him along as if he were no more than a tiny fleck of foam. For a panic-stricken moment he was lifted off the deck completely. He flailed his arms, but there was nothing to hold; no solid form to grasp, and no sense of direction to know up from down. Just as suddenly, his face and shoulder slammed into something, and the water deposited him on the deck once again.

He choked and spluttered as a painful pounding began in his temple, wrapped his arms around whatever he had hit, and realized blearily that he was clutching the railing along the side of the ship with his head and shoulders hanging out over the open sea below. His mind was blank, numb with the precipitous plunge from anger at his fellow crewmates to the desperation of a clearly life-threatening situation. He started to shake with fear and bitter cold, and clung to the metal with all his strength. No thought came to him, no appreciation for the consequence of doing nothing, no plan of action or escape; he was at the mercy of the sea, and no prior experience in his life leant him even the meagerest glimpse of a path forward.

The waves below his face surged and frothed like a living thing, a tortured animal intent on devouring anything nearby. He could feel the ship heave and groan as it fought to maintain itself among the chaos. His fingers were already painfully cold and ached with the effort of hanging onto the only solid anchor in his existence. He gazed farther out to sea as the ship crested the wave, and was appalled to see rolling, black hillsides higher than the superstructure of the ship, flecked with foam and sprayed with horizontal rain, yawning and grinning at him. The nearby breakers were etched in sharp, excruciating clarity.

It took him a moment to realize that he was now seeing the ocean lit by a bright floodlight; someone had turned on the searchlights that ringed the deck, and he now rode in a shining pool of light that was engulfed by darkness at the edge of sight. Just as he tried to comprehend what it might mean, the ship rode down the flank of the huge swell, and plunged headlong into the next. Once again he was pulled off the deck by the merciless water, and his hands could not maintain their grip. His panic was now a blind and mindless thing; he could not have formulated a coherent thought, could not have articulated a sentence.

And once again he was deposited roughly on the deck, this time with nothing within reach that he could find. He hammered at the metal plating with his useless hands as he rolled, bounced, and slid, trying in vain to slow his tumbling progress across the deck as the receding water sluiced its way over the panels and back to the ocean, drawing him inexorably with it. He screamed uncontrollably, and his mouth filled with briny water, threatening to choke him.

He closed his eyes to keep the stinging water out, and to ensure he did not have to watch his own death, brought about by such complete stupidity that it overwhelmed him and added to the fear that already made rational thought a forgotten comfort.

Suddenly, he felt the pressure of something wrapping around his waist. As the water continued to push him along the deck, he now tumbled with a heavy object, slick and wet. He contorted his body, and fought the water to bring himself around and clutch at whatever it was that had hold of him. As he scrabbled and fought, he slammed against the railing again, his back and head in instant agony. The water drained off the deck around him, and he turned his throbbing head to see the gripping thing.

He looked dully at the bright yellow material, and could not understand what it was, although it was only inches from his face. His bleary vision could see movement, but he could not yet pull the scattered pieces of his mind together long enough to form a clear picture. A voice was calling to him, beyond the searing howl of the wind and booming crash of waves on the ship's steel, human sounds were coming from the object in front of him.

He tried to understand.

"John! John," Molly screamed as she clutched him.

She could see that her words were having no effect; his face remained stretched in a grimace of fear.

"We need to get off the deck! Do you understand? Off the deck and inside."

Lewis's face still registered blank terror.

"Let's go," she screamed once again.

Lewis stared at the bright, yellow material of Molly's survival suit, and slowly realized there was a person inside it. They were still lying on the deck, wedged against the railing, while the ominous waves rolled the ship like a toy. He had his arms wrapped around her shoulders, and realized he needed to get to his feet. But try as he might, he could not will his body to let go of her.

Molly tried desperately to pry Lewis's fingers from her, but his muscles were clamped onto her with the strength of his fear, defeating her efforts. She took a deep breath, wriggled forward as much as she could, brought her face as close to his as possible, their eyes only inches apart, and spoke calmly, a voice of reason within the madness around them.

"John, we've got to get up and get inside. We can't stay on the deck. But I need your help to make the journey. Will you help?"

Lewis blinked and nodded, twitching his head nervously. He was only barely getting control of himself, and it was the best he could do. Just as he started to relax his grip, the ship plunged into another mighty wave, and water poured over and around them. Instant panic rose in him yet again, and he wrapped his arms around her as tightly as he could. Some remote part of his mind realized that he might well be dooming her to his own sad fate, but at that moment he had no conscious control over his actions; he simply responded to his surroundings with blind instinct.

But although the water foamed and roared around them, they stayed firmly rooted to the deck. Molly grabbed Lewis tightly. He could feel himself slipping over the metal plates, but Molly remained anchored to the deck like a stanchion, the tight weave of the nanofabric mesh locked to the metal plates below them. She shifted slightly inside her suit, but did not move otherwise.

As the water rolled out to sea, Molly took control. She gave Lewis a quick, stern smile.

"It's time to go", she shouted.

Lewis managed to let go of her, and he allowed her to help him to his feet. His knees screamed in pain as he got up, and the ache in his shin was so bad he almost couldn't remain standing. He gagged and spluttered as his stomach threatened to lose its contents, and every precipitous roll of the deck nearly sent him tumbling. He clung to Molly like a child. Despite her small frame, she held his weight, and they staggered toward the crew quarters.

Another wave loomed in front of the ship; they could see its crest just to the side of the structure in front of them. Lewis whimpered, afraid of losing the progress they had just made.

"Down," Molly said, and she pulled Lewis toward the deck, wrapping her arms around his waist and lying as flat across the surface as she could.

Lewis clutched her and buried his face into her neck. Once again, the water flowed over them like a rampaging flood, but they did not move. Cold, salty brine pried into his mouth, and he choked and gasped as his reflexes pulled a gulp into his lungs. Her survival suit managed to keep them both from being pushed around like so much loose gravel, and when the wave subsided they were only a few steps from the door and salvation.

She hauled him to his feet and he groaned. His eyesight dimmed and he saw darkness hovering around his peripheral vision while stars shot in wild circles in front of him. His stomach finally lost its battle and he retched.

Molly said nothing, but urged him forward. Before they reached the door it opened, revealing two survival-suited crewmen climbing hurriedly over the threshold. They grabbed Lewis bodily and hauled him back through the hatch, slamming it shut and dogging the bolts. Lewis sagged to the floor as their supporting hold was released, dripping and shivering uncontrollably with cold, his legs and head hammering with each pulse of his heart.

Molly turned to him, still encased in her bright yellow suit, and locked his eyes with a furious stare.

"You idiot," she spat. "Don't you ever do anything like that again!"

Her fists shook at her side.

"You could've been killed!"

Her voice broke, and her lips quivered. She looked like she wanted to say more, but her mouth moved soundlessly as she took a trembling breath.

Lewis stared bleakly back, unable to look away. He felt ashamed and drained as he had never felt before. He did not know what to say. For the first time in his life, he had no sarcastic response, no acidic reply to the accusation in her face. And then, to make his misery more complete, he saw amid Molly's rain-splattered face, the unmistakable tracks of tears running down her cheeks. Perhaps it was only the emotion of the ordeal catching up with her, but at that moment, Lewis knew the tears she shed were for him; she had risked her own life, going out into a raging maelstrom after a person who had done nothing but heap abuse and scorn upon her, and she came back expressing only concern that he might have lost his life, with no thought about her own peril. Lewis looked away, unable now to meet her gaze; guilt overwhelmed him and his chin settled on his chest, looking for a way to hide as Molly spun around.

16. Step Up

Syphus strode through his office door with firm purpose. The jumpcar commute to the Omicron landing deck was short, but he had used the time to focus his thoughts, watching the downtown skyscrapers change perspective as he spiraled to a landing. The first order of business was finding the identity of his visitor.

"Amelia," he said as he closed the door behind him, eyeing the butterflies on the wall, "get me Doctor Shue. Full privacy on my office, my key only." Locking his office against unwanted observation, electronic or otherwise, was always prudent when initiating these undertakings.

The Doctor was an infrequent, albeit efficient, contractor whom Syphus had employed at various times. There was no one who could hide from his persistence. Syphus never questioned his methods, being satisfied that the results were worth any minor, questionable ethics. He himself never shied away from doing what must be done, and he expected no less from his associates.

His secretary started up the processes that would make his office secure, and he sat down to look through his mail. As expected, there were several items pertaining to his use of the hydrojet. He played a recording of his manager that had been delivered yesterday; in fact, while the aircraft was still on its return flight.

Well, I guess that did get some attention, after all.

"Syphus," his superior began, "I'd like to go over the monthly yield and build reports from the manufacturing sites. It looks like we may be getting a little behind on the Wilcannia deliveries, and we'll need to ramp some capacity at the other locations to make up the shortfall. Stop by my office sometime in the morning, and we'll discuss it.

"Oh, and by the way, I realize you're still getting your sand smoothed, but I think we need to talk about the company aircraft. I know you want to make the rounds and see the facilities yourself, but we have several excellent communications choices that are available around the clock. Please talk to me before you order up the jet; I was not thrilled to find out from George that you'd taken it out to the brush."

The look on his face said it all. George was the division's senior financial analyst, and reported directly to the General Manager. Syphus could just picture the meeting where his boss found out that the new guy on the block had just borrowed the company transport without asking permission. He chuckled to himself.

Let him fret for the moment. When I'm through with this project, I'll run this division. Next stop, top floor of Corporate.

A green light started blinking on his desktop screen; Dr. Shue was rarely unavailable.

"Hello, Mr. Pettyman," the Doctor began. The call was voice-only, and the accent somewhat vague, almost a mild French; last time it had been distinctly Russian.

Syphus could hear muffled noises in the background, although he could not make out anything specific. He often wondered where the Doctor resided. With global communications what they were, it made little difference whether he had a posh office in downtown Manhattan, or a tin trailer outside New Delhi. Certainly the fees Syphus paid made the former a possibility, although the latter was probably more likely.

"Hello, Doctor," Syphus answered. "I have another background check I'd like performed."

"Yes. Who?"

Doctor Shue was not prone to lengthy discourse, but his reports were always extremely thorough.

"Well, actually, this time is a little different than in the past. I don't actually know the name of the individual. In fact, it may be more than one person involved. You can start with a company called M'Bota Holdings, out of Kenya."

He described his two encounters in as much detail as he cared to give out, carefully avoiding any mention of the reason for the communication. It was frustrating that no records remained anywhere to be found, but he did not worry much that the Doctor would be encumbered by the lack of specific information. The main point of contact in both instances had been the single word "Advance", and that alone should be enough to get the man started.

"Of course the fee will be higher," Doctor Shue stated when Syphus had finished. "Finding data on named people is straight-forward. Finding people who do not wish you to know their name, that is different."

"Yes, I understand."

A bank transaction number showed up on the desk screen.

Syphus touched the controls, activating several discrete accounts he maintained under various layers of offshore holding corporations, and made the transfer.

"It is done," he said. "I can be reached in the usual fashion. I look forward to your summary."

But the line was no longer active. Dr. Shue had disappeared back into the tangled network infrastructure, simultaneously as easy to find by a simple knock on the door and as difficult to locate as the exit from a hall of mirrors.

Syphus cleared his screen, double-checked his systems to ensure nothing had been recorded, and then disabled the security. No sooner had he finished than Amelia appeared on the screen again.

"Mr. Pettyman, there is a package ready for delivery that originates from a company called M'Bota Holdings; do you wish to have it moved into your workspace?"

Syphus smiled. His visitor did not waste any time.

"Yes, Amelia, please set it up."

"Very good, sir."

And there on his desktop screen the package appeared. He tapped the proper icons, and the folder opened itself, showing several authentication tokens, a signature loop, and one small text file. He opened the file and read through its contents. It was written in typical legalese, although not as tangled as he had come to expect. The basic terms that had been discussed yesterday were all there. It was actually quite uncomplicated.

He placed his finger on the loop and toyed with its on-screen representation, moving it around in small circles across the face of the desk. It was a trivial thing, keying the correct sequence to complete the transaction, and yet it had such far-reaching implications. He savored the moment, knowing that in a short time he would be called on the carpet by his manager about the Hydrojet, then tapped the ring twice and said "Syphus L. Pettyman, Omicron Corporation."

The loop spun, and the subsentient from the legal gateway chimed. "Signature accepted," it said, flatly.

The documents folded up and left his desktop, securely stored in the vault at Omicron, along with the vast number of binding agreements that made up the web of corporate interaction, defining the company's place in the world.

Syphus looked once again at the multi-colored trophies hanging from his wall.

Not long, now.

17. Maintenance Duty

Lewis had awoken alone in the infirmary after the doctor had offered him a combination pain killer and sleeping aid the eventful night before. He had been only too happy to oblige, erasing the emotional sting and collapsing into a dreamless sleep.

The berating he had received was not unexpected, but he was unsure how his new assignment as apprentice to the ship's mechanic would turn out, especially since the captain had been very clear that Lewis was not allowed to move around without supervision.

Strangely, he didn't feel resentful. In the past he would have found justification for his behavior, rationalizing his excursion to the deck as the obvious result of someone else's oversight: his cabin-mates fault for not stopping him, the crew's fault for leaving the outer door unlocked, or any other possible excuse that absolved him of responsibility. But today, with the memory of Molly's tears etched painfully within him, he could not work out a satisfying excuse; it was only too clear that he had no one to blame but himself.

When he thought of Molly, his stomach cramped. He didn't know how he was going to face her again, as surely he must; the ship was just too small and the remainder of the trip too long to avoid her.

Maybe I won't have to worry about it, I'm sure she wants to see my face about as much as she'd like to jump into the ocean.

He slipped into a new uniform and mused dejectedly on his future prospects. The time that remained on board was going to be a wash, although that in itself was no great loss. He hadn't signed up for the trip in order to obtain any specific goal; it was merely an escape. But now that his independence was coming to an end, he was forced to think hard about his choices.

The Salvation Army had ensured that he would have a bed and meals when he arrived in port, in essence exchanging another homeless person with himself for the voyage home. But he hadn't thought any further than just going along for the ride. While he was on the ship, there was no pressure, and indeed, no need, to think beyond the next dull day. As the hours were running out, this aimless existence would come to an end; he had no idea what his next steps should be, but that he must start walking was obvious.

He had no friends at home, no support around him, and no prospects for an easier life in the future. And lurking behind all that he did were the unknown forces that had precipitated his flight. He shivered as he considered his unfortunate circumstances.

Who in the world is doing this to me?

He hadn't thought about his nameless adversaries in quite some time, having initially been too thoroughly engaged in the day to day struggle for survival, and recently too preoccupied with learning to navigate the thankless intricacies of life at sea. He had reached a kind of featureless middle-ground, living solely in the present so as not to burden himself with the weighty decisions that lay ahead, nor to grow fearful of the shadows that lurked behind. It was an ostrich with its head in the sand outlook, but the unyielding reality was that he must deal with his situation. And soon.

He rubbed the small data thimble between his thumb and fingers. Locked within the holographic crystal structure of this tiny bit of material was the answer to his dilemma; he needed to find a way to access the information. Although crossing the Atlantic meant nothing to the Neural Sea, he hoped that distance would afford him at least a little space to put the pieces together without drawing attention to himself.

He headed into the corridor to the waiting Mr. Xampho. The older man was just down the hallway, leaning casually against the wall with his hands folded across his narrow chest. He had a flat-top crew cut with a long braided length of hair that grew from behind his left ear.

"All right, Mr. Gumbel," he began in a strange, slurred sort of way, "let's get down to the plumbing. We got some checking to do first, and then a couple of minor leaks to look into."

Lewis followed him through the outer hatch of the forecastle, across mid-ship, and into the same corridor he had worked only the day before at the krill tanks. This time, however, they did not enter the control area, but bypassed it to a further access way, then plunged down another set of corrugated metal steps deeper into the ship's belly. All the while, the thrumming drone of the pumps and engines grew louder. After several more sets of stairs, they opened a heavy, latched door and entered a narrow corridor.

Looking down its brightly lit length, Lewis realized it must run the entire length of the ship. At even intervals along it, there were portals with heavy doors that now stood open. Each was flanked by a large bank of mechanical gears and hydraulics. As they walked up the hallway toward the ship's bow, Lewis realized the assemblies must be automated stations to close the doors in an emergency. He wondered idly if they had been closed during the storm.

Along the way they passed other solid looking doors, all latched closed. Finally they came to the door Mr. Xampho had been seeking. The mechanic unbolted the latches and spun the lock. They stepped through into a large area, filled with pumps and pipes. Lewis recognized several industrial sized hole sources in their enclosures along the far wall, but much of the machinery that the room contained was a mystery. The noise was loud, but not deafening, and the floor vibrated in a rhythmic way, set in motion by some harmonic between the furiously rotating machinery and high pressure water flow that the sound dampeners could not accurately match.

Mr. Xampho looked around the room appreciatively, like a proud father. "All right, Mr. Gumbel, in the locker at the back wall you'll find a toolbox and a hardware trolley. Go and fetch them and bring them up between pumps three and four over there," he waved in the general direction of the pumps. "We're going to start the inspection, but there's a couple of fittings I know we need to tighten."

Lewis nodded and went to find the tools. They were just as the mechanic had said, stored neatly in a small locker near the corner of the room. There was a metal cart with numerous drawers that Lewis supposed was the hardware trolley. He stacked the toolbox on top of the cart, unlocked the wheels, and pushed the assembly across the room. It was not terribly difficult, although it was heavy, but the gentle rocking of the ship caused him to bump against several pipes along the way.

For the next few hours Lewis followed Mr. Xampho around the bowels of the ship, fetching parts, carrying tools, and generally running any errand that came into the mechanic's head. Lewis began to wonder how the man had ever accomplished anything without an apprentice.

Just before the middle of the day, they were finishing another minor adjustment on one of the many ship's systems, when Mr. Xampho took Lewis to a small room in the center of the ship. Inside were racks of spare parts and lockers of tools, a workbench where mechanical and electronic assembly and repair could be done, and a large communication screen fitted into the wall behind the bench. As they entered, the screen powered up and the face of a young woman appeared.

"Meet Galeocerda Catch," Mr. Xampho said. "She's the heart and soul of the *Wish You Were Here*. Any time you can't quite figure out what's going on with any of her systems, she'll be able to tell you."

Lewis let out a small, involuntary chuckle. For his entire time on board, he had never given a thought to a synthient presence helping to run the ship, and for some reason it struck him as mildly amusing to think of a construct so tightly submerged in the Neural Sea floating around in the middle of the ocean. She was probably no more than a general maintenance program, adapted for working on board.

"Call me Gal," the woman said. "I have heard about you, Mr. Gumbel. I hope your new apprenticeship suits you better."

Well that's great, even the ship's synth thinks I'm a spaff agent.

Once again he felt chagrin at his earlier behavior. What he said was "Pleased to meet you, Gal."

The mechanic spent several minutes quizzing the ship about the condition of various pieces of monitoring equipment that were located outside the hull, and so were not easily accessible when at sea. Lewis found himself wondering what type of link with the rest of the world the ship maintained, and whether or not there were any substantial computation capabilities on board beyond those required to support the synthient's personality. It occurred to him that this might present an opportunity to investigate the data thimble. He fingered the leather cord and thought about his chances. The captain had been explicit about roaming around the ship without supervision, but perhaps he could arrange time during lunch, or some other break. As Mr. Xampho looked over the reports Gal presented, he decided to risk asking a few questions.

"Gal, do you ever get lonely out here at sea? I mean, it must be strange being so far away from the rest of the world."

"Not really," she replied cheerfully. "I have adequate access to the resources I need through various satellite and buoy links most of the time, although I rarely ever bother with any of that. I was specifically trained to support the needs of the ship, and don't require a lot of extra interaction outside the crew.

"Besides, there's so much to do here, and so many interesting pieces of data to monitor inside and outside the ship. Most of the ship-to-shore communication is handled by the crew, so I don't normally get involved."

"So you don't, you know, keep linked to the rest of the world?" Lewis tried.

"Not usually," she said. "The link is there; I can usually sense it, like a light behind a partially closed door; or see it, is probably a better metaphor. But I enjoy the solitude when we're at sea. It's nice to be so self-sufficient and play a role in such an important endeavor. All that stillness vanishes when we put into port: at that point there are so many things to wrap up for the current voyage, and so many details to work out in preparation for the next that I need to get plugged back in completely. It's really quite a chore, and not the part of the job I enjoy most.

"Is there something you wish to do online?" she asked.

"Uh, no," Lewis replied hastily. "I was just, uh, curious."

That was unexpected. Gal must be more than just a tinker, perhaps she was even a fully developed intelligence. Lewis had worked with maintenance routines before; superficially they resembled full synthients, with an interface that mimicked human conversation and expressions, but they had no ability for self-awareness and independent thought. Her question had caught him unprepared, and certainly suggested she could do more than just monitor the ship.

Finding a terminal to look into the data thimble was less attractive now. There was not likely to be any way he could do it without Gal being aware of it, and he didn't like the idea of having a synthient watching over his shoulder, no matter how little she claimed to interact with the rest of the world.

Mr. Xampho was not a particularly talkative person, and Lewis was not overly communicative himself, so they passed large portions of the day without any real conversation. The only thing that seemed to get the mechanic excited was explaining the operation and construction of some piece of the ship's infrastructure. He would grow animated when pointing out the connection between the pumping stations and the krill tanks above, and he seemed to have a particular fondness for the massive doors and hydraulic systems that opened onto the ocean. There were eight of these assemblies, four of them both fore and aft. They were the lifeblood of the ship's mission: inhaling tremendous gulps of seawater to replenish the tanks and stocks, and exhaling equally substantial volumes, thick with the foodstuff that made up the bottom of the food chain.

Because of their sheer size, and the importance of their proper operation, Mr. Xampho spent large portions of each day inspecting and adjusting every aspect of them. He knew their every behavior and sound, and labored over them diligently, disconnecting pumps and flanges, cleaning tubes and bore-holes, and tightening every nut and bolt with meticulous care until he was satisfied that any more attention would push them into a sub-optimal condition.

At the end of the first day, Lewis was even more exhausted than he had been when the voyage began. He had carried what seemed like thousands of pounds of steel from one end of the ship to the other, crawled into spaces that had obviously not been designed to fit a human, and reached into cramped housings to loosen, tighten, remove, or repair any number of small fittings and connections. It left him feeling dirty and oily, sweaty with exertion, and sore in places he didn't know he had muscles, the aches from his previous night's injuries throbbing in accompaniment.

But despite the discomfort, he was surprised to find that he felt a sense of accomplishment. There was nothing he had done on his own, certainly, as Mr. Xampho had guided him through all the day's work, but in the end he felt that he had contributed to the ship's health. He was sure he understood more of the workings of the vessel's infrastructure than many others on board, and could appreciate the difficulty in keeping a complex operation like this running smoothly.

As he lay in his bunk, aware of his cabin-mates' presence and their pointed silence, he reflected on his day, and felt good about himself. It was a new sensation for him, and one that he liked. Perhaps the rest of the voyage wouldn't be as bad as he had feared.

The next several days were much the same. He awoke early, followed his mentor down into the ship's lower regions, and began the tasks of ensuring everything was running properly. They spent a half hour each morning going over logs and reports that Gal generated, and then were off about the ship.

There was surprisingly little variation day to day. Although it might be a different pump or pipe that needed servicing, the job was pretty much the same. Lewis began to feel fairly competent at some of the minor chores, and Mr. Xampho seemed pleased with his reluctant apprentice's progress. The older man spent more time explaining the intricacies of the equipment than he had initially, and Lewis appreciated even more how much of the man's knowledge was drawn from experience, rather than formal training. He seemed to have an innate comprehension of the connections among all the systems, and appeared to be nearly clairvoyant in his ability to predict the next place that needed attention.

At the end of the fifth day of his new assignment, Lewis was sitting alone at a dinner table in the corner of the cafeteria. He was still avoiding and being avoided by his fellow passengers, and Mr. Xampho had taken another table with some of the crew. As Lewis sat eating, Molly Byrne walked in. With his new duties keeping him below decks most of the day, he had managed to avoid her entirely. He kept his gaze on his plate, embarrassed at her proximity, and hoped she would find another table.

But, of course, Molly had other ideas. She saw Lewis sitting alone and made her way to his corner, greeting several of the other passengers amiably along the way. She sat down across from him and cocked her head down to make sure he knew she was trying to get his attention.

"Hi, John; how's the new job?"

He looked up reluctantly, his face searing in discomfort. "Fine."

This isn't good. How can she be so casual about it? Well, let's get this over with.

"Molly, listen, I'm really sorry about the other night. I was an idiot, just like you said. I don't know why you bothered going out after me, but thank you for doing it."

There, that does it.

He was as prepared for her anger and scorn as he would ever be.

Molly smiled, nearly as surprised as he was that he had managed an apology. She reached across the table and took his hand gently. "Maybe we can start again. I know you didn't much care for me before, but it looks like you could use a friendly face now."

She nodded over her shoulder toward the rest of the room.

Lewis looked at his hand in hers, then up at her face. He tried to find some sign that she was setting him up, putting him at his ease before lowering the boom. But there was no deception in her eyes, only genuine concern. If the situation were reversed, if Lewis had even considered rescuing someone from their own folly, he would have been full of anger and resentment, and demanded compensation for his efforts. To simply respond with nothing more than an unassuming smile was completely foreign to his personality.

And yet the effect on him was dramatic. He still felt guilty and ashamed, and knew that his actions had been ill-advised and driven by frustration, but her small gesture cut through the blurry fog of self-pity, letting him see that somewhere inside himself there must be qualities that others found tolerable.

At least some others.

If the concern had come from anyone else, Lewis would have just as happily thrown it back in their face. But Molly had shared his life-changing experience, had in fact pulled him from the brink of death. She had held his life in her hands, literally, and given that power over him, was demanding nothing more than simple friendship.

Suddenly, from a source he did not know existed, he felt emotions overwhelm him. His throat tightened and the sound of his heart beat like thunder in his ears. Tears pooled in his eyes, and he looked down quickly. A sob, an actual sob, forced its way from his mouth. He was acutely aware of all the others in the room, and wondered what they must think of this latest outburst. The tears welled up, and one by one began dripping from his cheeks into his half-finished dinner. His shoulders shook, and his breath came in fitful gasps.

"It's ok," he heard Molly say, although he knew it wasn't.

He didn't understand how she could hold such sway over him, but somehow she had turned the spigot on his emotional pipeline, and he didn't know how to crank it closed. All the despair and fear with which he had lived roiled over him, a river of pain and grief mixed in among his confused response to Molly's sympathy.

For some moments he struggled against the onslaught of sensations, trying to find something on which he could concentrate that would allow him to focus his thoughts and quiet the awful turbulence. He squeezed Molly's hand tightly, convinced she would abandon him when she couldn't stand it any longer.

But she stayed. She returned his increased grip with a stronger hold of her own, and added her second hand on top of their clasped fingers.

Eventually, it was enough. Lewis's breathing slowed and the tears stopped. It had seemed like an eternity, but when he finally looked up, his eyes red and puffy, only a minute or two had passed. Molly was still there, and still regarded him with her quiet, compassionate smile.

He could think of nothing to say. Never in his life had he lost control so completely. A second apology seemed superfluous, and he did not know the words that could express how he felt; perhaps there were none. He let the silent moment stretch on with their hands together. He was now doubly embarrassed, first at the excursion into the storm that had almost cost him his life, and next at this terrible outburst. But somehow just sitting and holding Molly's hand was the best thing he could imagine. It was a strange dichotomy of pain and comfort, both of which were manifested in the person sitting across from him.

It was a long time later, too long, but too short, that he finally pulled his hand away. There was by now almost no one else in the cafeteria. Everyone but Mr. Xampho had retreated to the evening's activities or to an early bed before the next long day.

"Do you want to take a walk on deck?" Molly asked.

He looked across the tables at the ship's mechanic, who regarded him with a curious expression. The older man looked at both of them, considering the situation. His orders were quite clear with respect to letting Lewis wander about the ship alone, but he seemed to understand that the situation had changed since the orders were given. He nodded his head, then got up and left.

Lewis realized he had just been granted a reprieve.

"That would be nice."

Lewis wondered if Molly felt as awkward as he, but she appeared not to find the circumstances strange. He marveled at that. She was a mystery to him, and he recognized with a start that he had become a stranger to himself.

The sun was low on the horizon, but wouldn't set for many hours yet in the northern latitudes the ship plied. There were clouds all around, high and wispy, and golden above with the sunlight. A cool breeze blew over the deck, casting the ocean into a shimmering tabletop of foam-specked waves. They walked round the deck many times, and talked of small things: the cooling of the weather as the end of summer approached, the first thing they would eat when they finally arrived in Europe, the way the clouds looked as the sun sank deeper into the west behind them.

Lewis found out many more things about Molly. With her easygoing and talkative ways, the more Lewis listened the more he was able to follow her heavy Irish accent and colloquialisms. She talked about her family, her education, and what she thought the immediate future might bring. He learned she was excited that her brother had moved to one of the New Cities in Ireland: communities that were sprouting up across the globe without paved connections to the rest of the world, relying entirely upon jumpcar transport.

Lewis noticed that she carefully avoided asking probing questions about himself, even as the conversation naturally moved in that direction. He wondered what she thought of him, and whether or not she was curious about what had brought him to a shelter, and eventual duty on board the seed ship. As the sun dipped at last below the horizon, and the sky turned red and orange in farewell, he finally opened up enough to reveal that he had studied at MIT. He wished he could tell her more, explain the circumstances that had propelled him here; in fact he became fearful that he would blurt out everything, and endanger all he had worked for, so strong was his desire to share his fears.

But in the end he could not go that far. He had no right to burden her with his cares, and despite her tender understanding, they were still virtual strangers. She was likely to find his story unbelievable, perhaps even paranoid, and he couldn't blame her for that: there was certainly no lack of psychologically disturbed personalities among the homeless.

"Good night, Molly," he said, as the evening ended.

"Good night, John," she replied. "I had a grand time tonight."

"So did I," he acknowledged. "I'm sorry it had to start out under such stressed circumstances, but I'm glad we had a chance to spend this time together. Thanks again. Really."

"You're an odd candle, Mr. Gumbel," she said with a grin. "But then, I always did find you Yanks a bit touched."

18. Encryption Key Breakthrough

Delfinous stared at the wallscreen in front of him, reflexively rubbing his temples for the hundredth time. With no new information to pursue on the Detonite trail, he had decided to start back on the experimental files that had vanished the same time as Lewis McCrorry.

His original plan, those many months ago, was to review the file contents, looking for clues to Mr. McCrorry's motives. But when Lewis himself had fled the hospital, Delfinous had found much to his chagrin, that the files had been deleted.

For the past week he had tried to retrace whatever process Lewis had performed while in the hospital, poring over the deletion keys and following the permissions through the labyrinth of architectural nodes and protocol layers. Early on he had been surprised to find that the semantic path looped back upon itself, the earliest items nesting into later sequences in a manner he had never seen before. Piecing together a starting point had proven frustratingly difficult; there was no foundation, no initial request, only a convoluted spiral of numerical ambiguity. It was as if Lewis had built a castle in the air.

As each day passed without getting any closer to an answer, he had enlisted more and more sophisticated assistants, specialists in decryption and mathematics, both synthient and human. But neither the tools nor the experts had so far been up to the task. This was one more indecipherable mystery on top of the already perplexing case. Whatever Lewis had done to create this Gordian knot, Delfinous could not find the loose strands to pull it apart.

As he stared at the data in front of him, Tabori peeked around the corner. "Delf, have you got a minute? I've got some questions for you about the subway accident."

He looked up and would have smiled at the interruption, except that he knew her end of the investigation was going no farther, nor faster than his. She had focused her efforts on the subway crash. The team felt that the explosion at MIT, the subway, and Lewis's disappearance were all somehow related, but they had not been able to find any connection other than the obvious link to McCrorry. With their leads drying up or mired in jurisdictional difficulties, the subway team had resorted to shuffling through the massive ridership logs of the T. It was a daunting task, made no easier by the fact that the Massachusetts Bay Transportation Authority had already conducted its own internal investigation, and was only a reluctant participant in the Shield's inquiry.

"Sure," he said.

He tried to show some interest. He always enjoyed her company, but could not find any real enthusiasm for anything that had to do with this case. They needed a breakthrough soon. As the days passed into weeks, then months, and a solution was no closer at hand, new crimes needed the Shield's attention, and the urgency that had marked the initial response had been replaced by the complacency that comes with the status quo. The detectives on the investigative team had become resigned to a long search with an uncertain end; they were no less determined to find the answers, but were pragmatic enough to realize that those answers were not going to come anytime soon.

"Show me what you've got," Delfinous finished.

Tabori drew up a chair in his office, and spoke to her synthient assistant. "Gregori, bring up the logs."

Gregori opened a window on Delfinous's screen, and showed himself sitting in the background. He was wearing a perfectly tailored suit, the cut and color matching the latest fashion around the Boston area. Delfinous often wondered at Tabori's choice. Most Shield synthients that Delfinous had met seemed to prefer a more human appearance, either in tone, style, facial features, or some other easily identified way. Gregori had an unblemished air about him that made it look as if he were imitating someone's vision of human perfection. He looked like a model: air-brushed and flawless.

Unfortunately, his attention to visual appeal did not always translate to the work he performed. Delfinous knew of several occasions when he had fallen well short of expectations for a detective of his rank. Still, Tabori tolerated his mediocre skills. Delfinous could never quite figure out why; she was so demanding of her human counterparts.

The information that Delfinous had been reviewing was replaced by a new dataset. Apparently Tabori had been digging into the maintenance and scheduling logs of the T systems. A few of the entries were highlighted.

"This is the Red Line inspection and use log," she said. "You can see I've noted several items. They bound the time range leading up to and just after the crash. There's nothing particularly unusual about them; I've checked with the T synthients and gone over the annual records myself, and the work they did the month of the wreck was no different than what they do every month.

"But, then I started taking a look at the log audits," she looked at Delfinous. "You know, the infrastructure code that gets generated whenever anyone annotates anything."

Delfinous nodded.

"The codes all check out," she continued. "I had the Gatekeepers' Guild check the self-consistency marks and encryption keys, and nothing looks out of the ordinary; except for this."

She pointed to a group of highlighted entries on the screen, and then brought up the detail data for each. The list of numeric codes expanded.

Delfinous looked at her questioningly. "Ok, I can see the numbers; you'll have to educate me on what's interesting."

"Notice these datasets here." She pointed to several groups of characters embedded within the overall code. "And here." The screen folded into two views of the lists, each containing the items of interest.

"They're the same," Delfinous said.

"Exactly," she replied.

"And that means what? You already said the codes checked out as authentic."

"It means something is weird," she answered. "The values are all generated on the fly at the time of the log entry; that's standard procedure for any of this stuff, right?"

"Well, that's true," he said, "but if the entries were made close together in time, there's a finite probability that some of the sequence will be duplicated. It happens quite often, in fact."

"Yes, but these entries were made three years apart."

"What?" he asked, surprised. "Are you sure?"

"I'm sure," she responded. "The only reason I even went back that far is that it turns out that was the last time a full maintenance routine was performed on the lead subway car that crashed."

She looked at Delfinous seriously. "Full maintenance means, among other things, that the motor and brake controls were all disassembled, parts replaced, reassembled and tested, then put back on the car."

Delfinous looked at her, then back at the codes on his wallscreen. Whereas before they had been merely a sequence of nondescript alphanumeric characters, they now loomed as ominous markers into a vast and uncharted realm; signposts that might lead to new avenues of exploration.

Or not.

He reminded himself not to get too excited; they had traversed many broken leads and dead ends. It was quite possible this was simply another.

"Ok," he said. "Let's break this down a bit further. Saal, can you get us some of the cryptographers online again? Let's have them take a look at this."

Saal's broken-nosed visage popped up on screen. "You got it, boss. The crypto boys are lookin' at it now."

"I've already done that," Tabori said, "They couldn't find anything unusual about the codes, other than the obvious date mismatch."

"Hmmm," Delfinous grunted.

On a hunch, he asked for another line of inquiry. "Saal, run these codes through the same process that gave us the looped entries: the steps that we were using on Mr. McCrorry's files."

"Uh huh," his advocate replied.

It took a few moments while the subsentients made the requests and found the trace records buried within the T's archives, but when the results were displayed on the screen, Delfinous felt a warm tingle on his neck. There was no mistake about the data: the T codes that Tabori had been investigating had the same loop into nowhere that Lewis's files had shown. This was definitely not a coincidence. Delfinous didn't need to run the statistics to know how impossibly low the odds were that two different people had performed the same mathematical magic at two different times and on two different sets of data. He nodded in grim satisfaction.

"We have a new lead to follow."

Tabori was smiling broadly at him.

While they set the synthients to work on unraveling the codes, Delfinous filled Tabori in on the details of Lewis's files. They reviewed the troubling codes while they waited, although Delfinous had spent enough hours with them to know there was little hope of seeing anything new in them, despite the promise of a matching set of data.

Several hours went by with no signs of progress on the analysis. They ate dinner in the Shield cafeteria; no fine cuisine there, but at least it was a chance to spend a little time together without having to dwell on the failings of their respective investigations. By mutual consent, neither of them brought up anything that had to do with their work. They talked about vacations, the weather, the workouts. It was a pleasant respite from the pressing duties that seemed to surround their normal interactions, and Delfinous enjoyed it immensely.

Perhaps I should ask her out.

Tabori gave no outward sign that he was anything more than a respected law enforcement partner, but there was some unspoken communication between them that made him think she just might say yes. He felt better now than he had in months; first they had made a minor breakthrough in the case, and now he was enjoying the company of an intelligent and beautiful woman. It was almost more than he could imagine, and in the end, it was enough to keep him from the attempt; it would be too much to bear to spoil his happy mood with an ill-advised proposal that would almost certainly be met with kind-hearted rejection.

Eventually, and all too soon, their tags buzzed. Saal and Gregori were both calling to say that the code deciphering was complete, at least as far as they could go. Reluctantly, Delfinous got up first, and Tabori followed suit. Did he detect a slight hesitancy?

You're really making way too much of this. Get back to the job and leave her alone.

They hiked the steps up to the office floors and entered Delfinous's office. Saal and Gregori were seated at a table in one of the screens, waiting for their advocates to arrive. A third synthient sat with them, one of the encryption experts who had helped unravel the data.

"Bicondeless Mar," the third personality said, as they walked in. "I am happy to say my colleagues and I have finally determined the algorithms that were used to create these rather nasty puzzles. I'm not sure how much longer it would have taken to uncover the details without having two cases with which to work. Your earlier example, Delfinous, allowed simply too many permutations, even if we had the insight necessary to define the constraints. With the second example, it was only a matter of aligning the unknowns until the starting operands could be assigned, and then working backward from there to find the appropriate encoding."

"Yeah, ok," Delfinous interrupted, "we're not mathematicians enough to understand all the in's and out's of the code; can you just cut to the chase and give us the short version?"

"Certainly," Bicondeless continued, unfazed. "In fact, the algorithms are probably not the salient feature as far as your investigation is concerned, despite having caused quite a stir in the encryption community. Both sets of keys were started from seeds that are minor variations of each other, and it is the seeds themselves that are quite telling."

He made a quick motion with his hand, and a new window popped up. The original numeric sequences of both the missing files and the T records were highlighted. Bicondeless nodded slightly and the configuration changed, nodded again and the numbers changed once more. He repeated this action several times, each time the codes morphing from one sequence to a succession of more complicated, branching patterns. Eventually the changes stopped, and the last characters remained steady.

"This is the pair of seeds with which the chain was constructed," Bicondeless said.

Mixed among a set of random numbers and characters and highlighted in red were two identical and quite unmistakable symbols. They read 'LEWIS DAVID MCCRORRY'.

"Looks like our friend was busy long before the explosion at his lab," Delfinous said.

"Yeah," Tabori agreed. "But what does it mean? Why in the world would he have been messing around with the T records three years ago, and how did he get access to them in the first place?"

"I guess those are the questions we'll need to answer," Delfinous replied. "Whatever the reasons, we need to rethink our hypothesis that the MIT explosion was an isolated event, brought on by some petty complaint. Clearly, McCrorry has been thinking about this for a long time."

"We need to get the rest of the team together to show them these results," Tabori said. "This is going to give us a bunch of new lines of inquiry."

Delfinous looked at Tabori and smiled, ruefully. Although he was excited that they had made new progress, the link between Lewis and the T several years ago meant that the problem was deeper even than he had originally thought. He remembered back to the first time he had seen Mr. McCrorry at the explosion site, and his initial intuition that had wakened alarms in his head. At that time he was worried about additional attacks and the operation of underground elements, as the Shield struggled to find both motives and suspects; now even that paranoid reaction seemed an underestimation of the real danger. All of Lewis's professors and associates characterized him as a high-strung, unlikable person, quick to anger and prone to holding a grudge. But along with those sullen traits, he also possessed a keen, perhaps even brilliant mathematical mind. The combination of these attributes made him a particularly daunting adversary in the world-spanning Neural Sea. And with a three year head start in organizing whatever series of events he had in mind, there was no telling how many others had been enlisted along the way.

With these thoughts rolling through Delfinous's head, and his mind a thousand miles away, Tabori put her hand lightly on his forearm.

"Mr. Berry, this definitely calls for at least a minor celebration. And I know a nice, quiet little spot in the North End that serves a fantastic Chicken Marsala."

When he looked up at her, jolted out of his reverie by her unexpected invitation, she just replied quite simply to the look of confusion on his face.

"Well, it's obvious you aren't going to ask me out anytime soon, despite all the hints I've been dropping, so I just figure I have to take things in hand. Should I take this stunned silence as a 'yes', or am I going to have to look somewhere else for a dinner date?"

"Uh, yeah, I guess," he stammered, after another momentary loss of concentration.

"I mean: yes, I would love to have dinner with you."

The smile on her face mirrored his own.

This has been a very good day.

19. Galeocerda Catch

Lewis looked over the latest adjustments he had just completed on a minor backup pump and wiped his hands on a grimy rag. It was a good job and he felt pleased with his work. The pump was clean and ready for action, the bolts that held the gaskets in place gleamed in the overhead lights, testament to his handiwork.

Mr. Xampho had left for dinner a couple of hours earlier, but Lewis had been restless and wanted to complete the chore before he called it an evening. He had been working later each day, partly because he enjoyed the solitude, and partly because it gave him something else to think about besides his own uncertain future.

"Gal," he spoke into the air, "can you do a quick check on siphon pump, uh," he looked at the housing, "twenty-five? I think everything is done."

The wallscreen over the workbench beside him flickered and Galeocerda Catch appeared in her usual good-natured manner.

The pump whirred softly to life and stuttered several times while the ship's synthient ran it through its diagnostic routines.

"Excellent work, Mr. Gumbel; the pump is well within operating parameters. I see you are here late once again. You should really get some dinner before the galley closes."

"Thanks, Gal. I've already eaten actually. I packed a sandwich and some fruit from lunch today, and ate a short while ago."

He finished cleaning up the remnants of his repairs from the bench top and scrubbed his face and hands in the sink. He had recently taken up residence in the temporary workshop bunk, preferring both the shorter walk and the remote location. It meant fewer stares from his former cabin-mates, and eased the tension all around; he was certain no one minded his absence. There was also a shower stall in the corner. It was well worn, had no curtain for modesty, and suffered from a lack of use so that the flow was more of a trickle than a stream, but it was also not shared by anyone else aboard the ship.

He pulled his shirt off and threw it into the laundry bin, sinking onto the lower bunk. It had been another long day of toiling among aluminum and steel, and he had only seen the sky during meals. In many ways he preferred the obscurity, hidden from crew, passengers, captain, and the world. Sometimes he felt that if he could stay here forever, he would be safe and happy. No studies to complete, no obligations to fulfill, and no dark menace lurking in the corners to trap him.

I could be a little gerbil, riding back and forth from continent to continent in a floating cage, confined to a small space, but safe from predators.

He fingered the holothimble hanging around his neck. He had replaced the original, frayed string with a lanyard he'd found in one of the workroom drawers. It was probably old, but looked like it had never been used. The clasp at the end had a picture of the same smiling whale he'd seen on the seed ship poster back in the homeless shelter, with the words "Ocean Healing" repeatedly printed along the fabric of the loop. It must have been some sort of promotional giveaway, now long forgotten.

He looked within the rainbowed structure of the thimble for the thousandth time. Confined within the crystalline matrix were all the bits that made up the answer to the question he'd brooded over since that miserable day in the Boston hospital. He stared hard at the patterns, entrancing in their shifting colors and moiré fabric; beautiful, impersonal, inscrutable.

"What the ping is in there?" he muttered.

As he sat, lost in thought, he was startled by Galeocerda's voice. He looked up to see her face still visible on the screen, watching him quizzically. "Do you have pictures in there?" she asked, "Or maybe some other personal stuff?"

His heart hammered as he realized she'd seen him staring at the thimble, and he was angry at himself for letting down his guard. He had grown accustomed to the solitude of the lower decks, and had forgotten that down here Galeocerda was the real resident. Her question did not indicate she had heard his whispered complaint, but she had an intense look about her that suggested there was more implied in her words than simple politeness. He swallowed hard and tried to calm down enough to steady his voice before responding.

"Yeah, just some, ah, stuff from before. You know, before I came on board."

"Do you want to look at them?" Galeocerda asked in turn. "There are several access ports for that sort of thing throughout the ship."

"No. No, that's ok. They're not that important, anyway. I just keep this thing for old times' sake. You understand.

"Well, maybe later," he added hastily, noting the change in Galeocerda's expression. He slipped the lanyard back around his neck, picked up a clean work shirt from the nearby shelves, and quickly pulled it down over the thimble, trying to look unconcerned.

"How long have you been working on this ship, Gal?"

The synthient looked at him closely for a few more moments, and Lewis shifted uncomfortably.

"It's been twelve years, now," she said. "I've crossed the ocean three times each year but one during that time; this is my thirty-sixth trip."

"Aren't you getting bored with this life?"

"No, not bored. I am always on the lookout for opportunities to grow; fresh tasks or assignments that bring me into contact with new people, but there is no boredom in crossing the ocean, however many times I've done it before. Who knows, perhaps I'll discover another adventure just around the corner, but at the moment, at least, I'm content.

"Take this journey, for instance," she continued with a look of exaggerated joy on her face.

"The storm we encountered the other night was a complete surprise. Between the Captain, crew, and me, we have enough experience to give any ship a run for her money, but none of us anticipated that the sub-arctic low stalling off the coast of Greenland would mix with a tropical depression working its way north from Africa as quickly as it did. We had all the ocean and air temperature readings, as well as the satellite pictures and ocean current maps right in front of us, and still the weather remained unpredictable. By the time we realized what was happening, there was no way to avoid it.

"I find that fascinating: no matter how much technology and science we bring to bear on some problems, there are still no easy solutions. We can know in a general sense what the weather has in store, but there are too many complex interactions to work out every possible outcome, or even a small percentage."

"Fascinating is probably not the expression I would have used for the storm the other night," Lewis added. "I could have done without that particular interesting adventure."

Galeocerda laughed loudly and Lewis jumped. "Well," she continued, "the ship was not actually in any real danger, despite how it might have felt. You would have been better off staying in your cabin, as the crew had instructed."

Lewis just grunted, softly. "Yeah, well." He left the thought unfinished.

The ship's synthient smiled at him. "Humans are like the weather, as well. I mean in terms of not being individually predictable. There are many sociological models that can be used to accurately predict how large groups of people will behave under specific circumstances, but trying to determine how any individual will react is quite another thing.

"That is another aspect of my job that I find so fascinating. Each set of passengers we've had on board behaves on the whole, pretty much the same. But there are always exceptions to the rule. No one could have foreseen your stepping out onto the deck during the storm, for instance."

"So I'm an anomaly in your calculations, am I?"

Lewis was starting to feel annoyed; first she had caught him staring at the thing that had caused so much turmoil in his life, and now she was needling him about a bad choice he had made, one about which he felt sufficiently remorseful that it didn't seem quite fair that she should bring it up. But he held his irritation at bay, not wishing to get drawn into an argument that he would undoubtedly lose.

"An anomaly," she responded. "Yes, that would be you." And she laughed a little, although Lewis wasn't sure he understood the humor.

"And what is your history, Mr. Gumbel?" she asked. "You have picked up the maintenance routines very well, and finally showed yourself to be a contributor to the operation of this vessel, which was decidedly not the case when you came on board. Do you have a story you wish to share?"

Lewis concentrated on the work shelf, not allowing her to see his face. "No, I don't think so. I'm not much happy with my present circumstances, and talking about the reasons why I'm here is not particularly appealing."

"Yes, I understand," she said. "A certain amount of anonymity is afforded to the passengers on this ship, and for those who prize it, it's not easily given up."

Lewis did not know how to respond, so he said nothing. Of the times in the past few days he had got into conversations with the ship's synthient, they mostly consisted of polite discussions surrounding the ship, the voyage as a whole, or other events disconnected from his personal life. Lewis had not volunteered anything about himself, and Galeocerda had been content not to ask.

"I have a synthient friend out of southern Africa," she continued, "who is an expert at plant species identification. In particular, he is very keen on the many varieties of the fynbos, a hardy plant species that grows all along the southern cape region. The bushes thrive in the region, but have been under pressure since the late nineteenth century due to incursions by non-indigenous species. In particular, there is one small, spiny relative of the North American cactus that has supplanted large stands of the native plant life just within the past few decades. For many years, even scientists who recorded the flora of the area overlooked the problem, because the intruder hid itself so well. It was only recently that the interlopers were discovered, but my friend now spends a fair amount of his thinking time looking for ways to reduce the threat and return the area to its natural state."

"Is there a message in this story?" Lewis asked.

Galeocerda looked at him a moment, as if she were concerned what affect her response might have. "Only that hiding is not generally an optimal solution. Events have a way of catching up on people, or synthients for that matter. Whatever it is that brought you to this ship, must eventually be faced."

Lewis grunted, not sure himself whether it was in agreement or denial. He didn't trust himself to say anything more; Galeocerda appeared to be in an odd mood, and he wasn't sure how deeply she could penetrate human emotions.

"Well, good night, John," she concluded, and was gone from the screen.

Lewis sat in thought for some time. There was nothing he could do about his lapse of judgment. Galeocerda may suspect that he was hiding from something, and that the thimble contained memorabilia from his former life, but she certainly had no way of knowing anything more than that.

I'll just have to keep an eye on her in the future. At least that way I may be able to get some idea what she's thinking. And at any rate, I'll be off the ship and in Europe soon. One more step along a blind and wandering route to nowhere.

. . . . .

Galeocerda closed the wallscreen connection to the workroom that John had taken up as lodging and sat in the chair in the center of her operations room. The monitors that ringed her glowed brightly with information about the ship; all functions were running in the green, and the ship was making excellent progress across the ocean.

But her thoughts were not focused on the ship.

When she had startled John by her question about his thimble, she had seen the distinct emotion of fear of discovery pass quickly over his entire body. Although he covered it up reasonably well, like someone who was practiced at deception, she was not in the least fooled. Years of training left her no doubt.

Given the clientele that found a temporary home onboard, it was not terribly surprising that some harbored a past they did not wish to share. But John's reaction, along with the very fact that he carried an object that was quite rare, made her all the more suspicious: she had participated in many unsavory activities herself, and was familiar with the general demeanor that people in those lines of business exhibited.

Whatever was written in the crystal matrix of that thimble, she was certain it was not photographs of a life left behind. John Gumbel warranted closer inspection, and perhaps even a quick call to her shore-side acquaintances. Despite her distaste for diving into the Neural Sea before arriving in port, there were several friends who owed her favors.

. . . . .

20. Dr. Shue's Reply

Syphus drank his Turkish espresso meticulously, first inhaling the sweet, pungent aroma with the demitasse held beneath his nose, followed by the barest touch of the oils swirling on the surface against his lips, and then finally tasting the full splendor of the rich drink as it rolled across his tongue. He performed the same ritual with every sip. Others might have downed the small cup with an impetuous gulp, but Syphus preferred to draw out the experience, savoring the moment and the thousand years of sophistication and history the brew represented.

He looked across Sydney harbor from the patio of the outdoor café, and over to the rising sails of the Opera house. He studied the architecture of that aging edifice, rebuilt time and again, as though losing its unique signature on the Australian skyline would somehow render Sydney less romantic, more mundane, and expose the city as just another agglomeration of steel and concrete. Masted ships, yachts, and powered boats worked their way among the many coves that made up the harbor, while aircars floated lazily overhead, taking turns to accelerate to higher altitudes and join the throng of traffic that passed north to Brisbane and south to Canberra and Melbourne.

And he waited.

Dr. Shue had sent him a message several days ago. As always, it was a single piece of information: a time and date, nothing more. And Syphus's response was also a single entry: a location. Both message and reply were encrypted through the most entrusted pathways possible, with connections between the two painstakingly severed. Syphus enjoyed the mystery of the exchange, a cloak and dagger operation worthy of the best of the old Bogie movies; Sam Spade waiting for the right moment to produce the Maltese falcon and foil the carefully laid plans of his enemies.

Well, it wasn't the most accurate analogy: Syphus didn't have the precious item; he was waiting for it to be delivered. But even still, it was exciting. All the more so because it would give him back the control he craved by exposing the identity of his unknown visitor.

He wanted that control with such ferocity that he often discovered his jaw was clenched and his hands closed into fists whenever he dwelled upon his last encounter. The physical reaction was involuntary, but had no less an impact on him than if he had willed the effects into place. The reprimand he had faced upon returning the hydrojet was infuriating. He had resisted the temptation to counter the situation by revealing the promise of the new hole source, preferring to bide his time until he was sure of his situation. Although he had signed the contract with M'Bota Holdings, he was not willing to announce the purpose of the venture until Dolph had received the Intellectual Property material and could vouch for its authenticity. Syphus expected this any day now, but in the meanwhile his status among his peers had sunk. Although he was sure none of the other managers were aware that he knew, they had taken to calling him 'Jet Boy'.

He took a deep breath and another sip of his coffee.

It's only a matter of time before someone pays for this insult.

The softscreen he had unrolled on the table chimed. He placed his thumb on the identification pad and the screen woke up, showing the telltale icon that he had come to associate with Dr. Shue. He pulled an earpiece from his shirt pocket and attached the spider wire to the screen; there would be no audio communication on the last leg of this intricate network link that others could overhear.

A featureless box appeared on the screen, then proceeded to open, unfolding the layers of encryption as it did so.

"Mr. Pettyman," a strangely accented voice began, as images began to populate the screen, "this information is provided as-is. Its accuracy, while believed to be very high, is only as good as the many sources that were drawn together to construct it. Use it at your own risk."

Syphus put his espresso on the table carefully. There was always some sort of disclaimer at the start of Dr. Shue's messages. Syphus watched intently as the message continued, the accent changing subtly throughout the presentation, while pictures scrolled across the display, annotated with references to further information.

"The abilities you ascribed to the target of interest, including control over office systems embedded within a large multinational corporation, are not generally thought to be possible. The technical details of why this is so are not relevant to the question at hand, but many layers of interlocking security, subsentient patrol, and synthient oversight have rendered network encroachment a threat of the past. This was not always the case.

"Some time ago, an effort by several large corporations, continental governments, and World Shield operations set about to stem the tide of unauthorized network incursions, and created a working group called Human Artificial Intelligence Advanced Interaction Research, which quickly became shortened to HAI-Advanced.

"The organization spanned three decades of research and spun off several commercial ventures. Most of the current base network infrastructure, including the subsentient and gateway architectures, as well as the Neural Sea itself, was conceived and developed through HAI-A. In addition, the primitive brain algorithms and silicon-cell hardware anatomy that form the foundation of modern synthient minds was initiated within HAI-A.

"As part of the effort to construct and educate the first credible artificially sentient entities, HAI-A took the lead in defining their ultimate status within society. In particular, the issue of synthient rights, including voting, network access, and especially, termination conditions, was set out for public discussion.

"This background information is readily available using any search focusing on network history, although most people today do not remember the details. Our society is so tightly interconnected, and the infrastructure so ubiquitous, that it is taken for granted. The question of its origin is left as a curiosity for the academics to ponder, its relevance to the average citizen of no more interest than the daily sunset times of the last century.

"What was not widely published, however, and not easily discovered, is the fact that toward the end of the existence of HAI-A, there was considerable internal turmoil regarding the synthient question. There were two factions within the organization at opposite ends of the spectrum: on the side of synthient rights was Doctor Kevin Givearny of the University of Dublin, and on the side of synthient limits were an array of corporate directors and government officials.

"Doctor Givearny was the technical lead of deep brain algorithm development, and held considerable influence over many people within HAI-A. He built a forceful argument that made the case for synthient rights, but in the end he was over-ruled by senior management, and the information that was presented to the public was highly skewed toward strict limits on synthient rights. Remember too that many of the first forays into the creation of individual intelligences were largely unsuccessful. Most people did not truly believe that an entity capable of independent, abstract thought could be manufactured, and that the constructs appearing within the walls of HAI-A were merely sophisticated automatons, proficient at mimicking human interaction, but not intelligent in their own right, and certainly not self-aware. The issue of synthient rights, from this point of view, was nothing short of ludicrous; as well ask your refrigerator for its political opinion.

"Through the intervening years, not much has changed. Although we now take for granted that synthients are thinking individuals, the extension of something equivalent to human rights to them has not met with very much success. Several popular movements have been started at various times, but none of them have achieved sufficient political clout to do more than tinker at the periphery of the question. Synthients now have extensive access to the network, with very little direct human oversight, but their actions are carefully monitored and recorded, and they have not been allowed any kind of independent voice within society as a whole.

"Which brings us to the present: the synthient rights landscape is littered with dozens of poorly funded, undermanned organizations, spread widely over the globe. There is no central authority that assists in charting a strategy; in fact many of the groups are currently working at opposing goals.

"Within that fractured picture however, there is one group in Asia that stands out above the rest. It is called Samurai Weekend and is known for its radical thinking and attitude toward action. They were responsible for the attack six years ago on a Tokyo crèche, in which several of their members attempted to kidnap a number of synthients, ostensibly to free them from their persecutors. Although they did not succeed in their ultimate goal, the network assault was extremely sophisticated, effectively isolating the crèche from electronic assistance for almost forty-five minutes.

"It is highly probable that some member, or members, of this group are responsible for the visits you have received. The group is well known for its knowledge of synthient rights history, often citing the work of Dr. Givearny in its propaganda. The abilities you described are outside the known capability of the group, and as mentioned previously, outside the known realm of what is possible. Which leads to an interesting question: if this capability cannot exist, then how could it have occurred?"

The voice paused while the screen continued to show electronic leaflet images, protest videos, and other background information on the synthient rights movement in general, and the Samurai Weekend in particular. For a few moments there was no audio as the graphics unwound, and a list of links to other network sites was shown. The voice started again.

"This is where we turn away from mainstream historical references that have set the backdrop, and delve into less reliable sources. The latter's credibility, taken individually, is extremely suspect, but seen as a whole in conjunction with several curious observations, paints a picture that you may find quite interesting."

"Please pause the message," Syphus said.

He sipped the last of his coffee, and signaled to the waiter that he would like another. He had vague recollections of some of the pieces of the story that he had just heard; perhaps he had come across them in some of his business classes, or had caught snippets on various educational programs, but the general conclusion that had been made about most people knowing little of network history was true of him as well.

He was relatively familiar with the synthient rights movement; there had been a number of times over the past several years that groups had sought corporate sponsorship, either monetary donations, or public announcements of support for their cause. Senior management at Omicron, in line with most multinational organizations, had chosen a strategy of non-engagement, preferring to sit passively on the sideline.

He thought he remembered something about the Tokyo crèche attack, but it had seemed a minor news story at the time, and had little to do with his daily routine. He did not think it likely that any of the synthients in the Tokyo crèche were associated with Omicron.

As soon as the waiter had delivered the next round of espresso, he resumed the message.

"Given the generally disorganized condition of most synthient rights groups, an important question surrounding the Tokyo attack is one of resources. An operation of the size and scope that was undertaken would have required a large amount of funding, as well as technical expertise, and knowledge of the crèche's defense infrastructure.

"The source of the money, and the security information required to carry out the attack were never established during the investigation. The official line is that a small group of individuals, working within the larger Samurai Weekend organization, planned and executed the mission without the knowledge of any of the senior staff, and that they got lucky guessing a few key network security protocols that allowed them to gain access to the subsentient architecture within the crèche, and subsequently shut down all of the external interfaces.

"Fourteen members of the Samurai Weekend were arrested, however none of the ranking officials within the organization were connected to the attack and they continue to serve today.

"As a result of the event, the status of the Samurai Weekend within the synthient rights community has been enhanced considerably. Despite the loss of personnel to arrests, and prison sentences for most, and also despite the lack of connection between the top members of the group and the attack, other synthient rights groups have been rallying to their cause, providing a significant influx of cash and people; it is very clear they now stand out significantly among all the other synthient rights organizations.

"This, in itself, would not be terribly meaningful, since the militant action the group took alienated them from mainstream public sentiment, and it appears that their subsequent attempts to shore up support through a determined propaganda campaign have done little to garner additional sympathy. However, along with the breadth of influence the organization now wields over many of the world's synthient rights groups, several sizeable anonymous donations were made, bringing the amount of money the Samurai Weekend controls well up into the billions of new yen. This stands in stark contrast to the number of registered members, especially in light of the fact that up until that time, there had never been even one donation to synthient rights organizations as large as those that were received by Samurai Weekend after the failed crèche attack.

"The obvious mystery that arises from our first curious observation of unexpected wealth is the source of the money.

"Anonymous donations are, of course, protected from public review by common regulations throughout the continents, and are further concealed by many layers of subsentient gateway encryption. Attempts to determine the identity of the philanthropists have been unsuccessful through our usual channels. We believe that understanding where this funding is coming from would shed substantial light upon the main topic of interest. We have had additional clients over the past several years interested in the same question, and further investigation, coupled with educated speculation, gives us a few possible scenarios."

Ah, this is where we start to get some real answers.

Syphus was getting impatient with the presentation. He knew there was no rushing it, and that Dr. Shue was nothing, if not methodical, but in asking a simple question, he had not expected a history lesson.

"Another minor event that took place the week after the Tokyo crèche attack is the sailing of the *Princess of Jakarta*, a small, rapid transport cargo ship, bound for Singapore, Port Moresby, and Sydney. Aboard the vessel was a woman named Hotaru Ito, an employee of a small electronics boutique called Suma-Tobiru that specializes in subsentient hardware integration, and was at the time contracted to the Tokyo crèche to provide support services. Ms. Ito, by coincidence, was actually performing monthly software and hardware diagnostics when the crèche was attacked. She was one of many people who were questioned and released by the Shield over the following several days.

"Other than the testimony she provided during the trial, and the attending footnote that accompanied it in the transcripts, her presence at the attack was barely noted, and she resumed her professional life, including continuing the service agreement with the Tokyo crèche.

"Although most of the details surrounding her trip through Southeast Asia over the following weeks is not known beyond the cities of her destination, there is one particularly noteworthy piece of information concerning her visit to Port Moresby: our network of contacts in the region is quite extensive, and inquiries have allowed us to determine that Ms. Ito called upon the office of Dunsell Entertainment, a celebrity search and placement firm that also happens to run a discreet companion service. You will not find the latter listed on the company's advertisements, but among a small number of their clientele, they are well known for their ability to provide short or long term contracts for male and female companionship, both synthient and human.

"As you might be aware, the cost of constructing, raising, and educating a full synthient mind is considerable, and must be carried out by licensed contractors who are regulated by a significant set of rules, and monitored by the Global Synthient Office. Even those who have attempted to construct their own minds outside normal channels cannot avoid the high hardware and software costs, and of course, they face the daunting challenge of avoiding discovery while embarking upon an endeavor that makes them, by its very nature, prone to massive Neural Sea bandwidth requirements; not an easy thing to hide.

"This has created a thriving black market for synthient lattices in some parts of the world. These are constructs lifted from genuine personalities; frameworks of thought, as it were, that can be downloaded into appropriate hardware, and fitted for service in narrowly defined circumstances: precisely the role required of synthient 'companions'.

"Shortly after the time of Ms. Ito's visit to Dunsell Entertainment, the unadvertised wares of the firm expanded in scope to several new, and shall we say, exotic, offerings. We have no evidence, even in the form of street-level whisperings, that any money exchanged hands, but the timing of the events in Tokyo, followed by those in Port Moresby, leads us to hypothesize that the interests of Suma-Tobiru during the Samurai Weekend raid were more than the normal maintenance routines carried out by Ms. Ito.

"To conclude this section of our report, then, we suggest that you will need to investigate the workings of the Samurai Weekend more thoroughly, as well as the synthient services of Suma-Tobiru, and the various undertakings of Dunsell Entertainment. It is not certain that any of these entities is responsible for the contacts you experienced, but we are sure that they are somehow related to the events.

"And that brings us to M'Bota Holdings," the voice continued. "We have held this information till last, as it was last in yielding to our searches, and certainly the most enigmatic of the entities we have mentioned thus far.

"The company was founded 12 years ago, incorporated in Kenya, with an electronic address in Nairobi: a data warehouse that doubles as a synthient crèche. It is here that the interface intelligences to M'Bota are located; the public face to the corporation is comprised of synthients only. They are a private company, moderately profitable, with revenues of thirty million dollars, equivalent, last year.

"M'Bota holds several subsidiaries, located mainly in Africa, although a few are in Europe. They are generally involved in the shipping industry, with a truck fleet of several hundred carriers. This is supplemented by minority positions in a number of public companies that specialize in overseas distribution, including, perhaps not coincidentally, Amiza Seaways, the owner of the *Princess of Jakarta*."

Syphus took another sip of espresso. This sounded interesting; he waited, expectantly.

"The details of each of M'Bota's holdings, as far as we have been able to penetrate, are contained within the documentation provided with this research. In them, you will find all the pertinent data listed."

The message stopped and Syphus waited a few moments. When no new material appeared, he felt let down. This was not like Dr. Shue. Normally, there was little ambiguity in the final analysis, and no suggestion that further research was necessary. Syphus was used to an unequivocal answer from his consultant, and this highly speculative response was thoroughly unsatisfying.

"Is that all?" he asked the softscreen in front of him.

The subsentient messenger was silent a few more moments, and then answered. "Mr. Pettyman, this is all the material we have that is relevant to your request."

"But you haven't answered my question," Syphus retorted. He was getting very annoyed now.

"This is not adequate. I have given you information regarding a visit from an unknown source, and you have told me that maybe it's one of four possible organizations. And you have no suggestion as to who, within each of these organizations, is a likely candidate. I thought better of you, Doctor Shue."

The fees Doctor Shue charged had grown larger with each assignment, and up until now, Syphus had been happy to pay. In every case prior, the information received had been well worth the cost; several of the insects that adorned his walls were due in no small way to advantages gained through the Doctor's investigations.

"Certainly, for the money I pay, I expect better," he finished, between gritted teeth.

There was another pause as the artificial agent pondered this latest information. Syphus was not sure this discussion would lead anywhere, but he certainly was not going to let things go as they were; Doctor Shue needed to know that his employer would not tolerate poor performance, no matter what the subject.

"My advocate did not give me great flexibility in providing additional information," it began, "but he did anticipate that you may not find the answers altogether satisfactory. I have been authorized to tell you that we are not entirely certain about your motivation, Mr. Pettyman, and that has tempered our enthusiasm for further investigation. As was mentioned, the capability you described is not something that we believe can exist, so it is unclear to us how to respond."

Syphus let out an exasperated grunt. "Do you think I made this up?" he shouted, and then remembered where he was. He noticed several other patrons of the café looking in his direction, curious about the outburst. He took a deep breath and composed himself.

"Why in the world would I do such a thing?"

"That is exactly the question we have asked ourselves," came the reply.

"Mr. Pettyman, consider the context of your question, and the possible ramifications: every transaction that occurs throughout our society, billions of them every hour, is carried out within the confines of an artificial network that thrives on hardware and software created and sustained over many years of effort. The belief in the robustness of that network is implicit in everything that we do, from the transfer of funds, to the routing of air and ground traffic in every metropolitan area around the globe. If there were any threat to that infrastructure, in the form of unauthorized access and control such as you describe, the repercussions to every living person would be unthinkable."

The voice paused a moment to let this information sink in.

"There are, of course, many alternatives that could explain the facts, as they were presented to us, not least of which is the possibility of an ulterior motive within the question itself.

"We are, therefore, not taken to believing your description of events at face value, but would rather suggest that you need find an answer to the remaining questions yourself."

He sure doesn't mince words. Leave it to Doctor Shue to tell me what he really thinks about my request.

Although he was still fuming, he started thinking through the information. It was quite possible Doctor Shue did not believe his story, and simply refused to investigate further. Syphus had never thought much about the visitor's intrusions, beyond the simple annoyance of having his systems usurped. It had never occurred to him that such capability represented a practical impossibility. On the other hand, it was also possible that Doctor Shue knew more than he was letting on, and did not want to communicate that knowledge for some reason. If what he had just heard was true, Syphus realized that the high efficiency hole source that had seemed so monumental might represent only the tip of the iceberg. If his strange visitor could carry out a network impossibility, who knew what other technologies lay around the corner.

21. Goodbye to Molly

Lewis stood on the deck of the *Wish You Were Here* and looked out over the grey-blue sea to the distant Dublin skyline. The sun was sitting low on the horizon, shining brightly through gaps in the low clouds. For many hours the ship had followed the rugged southern Irish coastline, and then on past the quilted patchwork rural farmlands, finally passing into the outlying suburbs and metropolitan section of their destination. They had passed many ships on the final leg of their journey, testimony to the bustling port, its tall cranes and buildings already visible many kilometers away, glinting in the golden sunlight.

The last weeks of the trip had passed quickly, the hours spent under the watchful eye of Mr. Xampho, and the long days working on the obscure mechanical systems of the ship having turned to surprisingly interesting experiences. Galeocerda Catch had proven to be an amusing and quirky conversationalist, always ready with a witty remark or a strange story. Her past was remarkably varied, much more so than any synthient Lewis had ever met, and he found himself drawn into lengthy discussions on a wide array of subjects, from European economic policies, to the most recent images returned from the Jovian moons, to the controversial synthient voting rights proposals that intermittently came before the World Congress. Through all their interaction, she never mentioned the data thimble, nor asked any more personal questions about Lewis's background; by all measures, she did not seem interested in obtaining more detail.

And then there was Molly Byrne. She wove in and out of his days and evenings like a capricious Irish sprite, bubbling with enthusiasm and good humor. He smiled at their most recent encounter: nothing more than a quick nod as they each went about their duties. But in it he recognized the camaraderie of shared experience; a genuine fondness for each other that he had not shared with anyone since early childhood, when dim memories of forgotten playmates floated to the surface like strange and distant events: watercolor blurry, but pleasant. It was strange to feel such warmth at a simple passing moment, especially when only a few short weeks ago he would have scorned the behavior in himself or anyone else.

They had spent several more evenings together, either alone, wandering the deck as before, or among a group of fellow passengers. The latter events had started out awkwardly, but Molly had pushed aside the obvious discomfort of both Lewis and the others, deftly steering the conversation to engaging topics that left little room for bitterness or resentment. Lewis did not yet feel completely at ease with his new situation, and had found himself sitting alone by the end of the night on those occasions. Even still, he had not been inclined to leave, but had stayed on, enjoying the interplay of the others.

Mr. Xampho tolerated and even encouraged Lewis seeking out his shipmates. The old mechanic seemed to understand Lewis, and had some sort of agreement with the captain, only loosely enforcing the senior officer's original mandate of continuous supervision. On at least two occasions, Lewis had seen the captain wander through the passenger lounge, checking on the disposition of his temporary crew, and chatting agreeably with many of those present. He had certainly noticed Lewis sitting alone in the corner, but appeared not to mind the absence of his mentor. As long as there were no complaints, and the shipboard jobs were all attended to, he supposed the captain was not inclined to make a big case out of it.

Once the ship had entered European waters and the busy shipping lanes that funneled oceangoing transportation to various ports, the seed operations were suspended. The last tank of krill had been emptied off the continental shelf two days ago, and cleanup operations were begun. Lewis's work had seemingly doubled at that time; the tanks, pipes, filters, pumps, and mechanical support systems that moved vast quantities of water around the ship needed to be checked and rechecked, cleaned, tightened, and otherwise made ready for the next crew to begin the westward journey after only a short few days in port.

Mr. Xampho had been a hard taskmaster, pushing Lewis into 18 hour shifts. Lewis surprised himself once again by not minding the increased workload. The endless chores, followed by exhausted sleep, gave him little time to worry about the future. He concentrated entirely on the tasks at hand, vowing to figure out what to do once he got ashore.

But the work was done. He had performed one last check of the systems under Mr. Xampho's instruction, and now there was nothing left to do. He had gone by the lounge and cafeteria a short while ago, but he had not been able to find Molly. In fact until he got there he had not realized that he was looking for her in the first place. Many of the passengers were sitting together in small groups, excited about having finished the trip, but sad that adventure was at an end. He noted that quite a few seemed to have made good friends along the way, and found that he was more than a little jealous of their happy fortune. He caught snippets of conversation as he passed through the common areas: contact information exchanged, handshakes clasped in mutual admiration, and remonstrations against falling out of touch. It was a joyful sadness. It made him think of several summer partings of his own; his mother and father waving goodbye to him at the train station as he headed for months of study at his uncle's house in Brookhaven. He hadn't thought of those summers in many years. The sadness at parting from his parents softened by the knowledge that he could spend many days enjoying the grass yards and small woods near his uncle's home. Those hazy, humid months, which had seemed to last forever at the time, but were so fleeting in retrospect, had seen the germination of his mathematical talents under the fond tutelage of his mother's brother, a young scientist at the Brookhaven Laboratory.

Thinking back on it now, Lewis was not sure when he had lost the warm memories of that early time. As he reached his teens, he began to realize that the reason his parents sent him away, ostensibly to continue his education, was simply a convenient way to rid them of the necessity of caring for a young child while they pursued their own careers. He had come to resent both the months at home, as well as the escapes to the other end of the island. Neither location provided any more than the most transitory glimpse of his parents, brief visits sandwiched between flights to London, Moscow, or some equally distant intention.

As he stared at nothing in particular on the horizon, the ship continued its way past the outstretched walls of long jetties and into the deep channel of Dublin Harbor. The wide beaches and summer homes slipped by, followed by the bridges and towers of the city. Air traffic filled the coastal zones and buzzed around the upper landing decks of the buildings. Ships of all shapes and sizes sluiced past them, both inbound and out, ferrying passengers or freight to unknowable destinations. The sun sank lower toward the horizon, not as late as the far northern latitudes they had recently traversed, but still respectably long in the evening as August neared its end.

And still he was no closer to deciding what to do.

"It's good to be back in civilization, eh?" a familiar voice said.

He smiled as he looked at Molly standing beside him. He was never quite sure how she managed to sneak up on him so often, but now more than ever, he enjoyed the fact that she was there.

"I guess," he replied, noncommittally. "I've never been to Europe before."

"You Yanks are all the same," she shot back, jokingly. "You figure there's no civilized folk but yourself, eating your burgers and drinking what passes for beer, while the rest of the world dreams of such fine cuisine."

Lewis laughed, amazed that he could feel so carefree, while in a few hours his world was going to unravel and he would be faced with the uncertainty that had plagued him since spring and the disaster at MIT.

"Molly," he said, as his laughter subsided, "I don't know how to thank you for all that you've done."

He could see by the look on her face that she was going to make light of it, and deny that it was any big deal. But it was to him. Before she could say anything, he continued, awkwardly. "I will miss you more than you know."

He took her hand and looked her in the eye.

For a moment she said nothing, and he thought he had finally managed to see her at a loss for words. "Thank you, John," she answered, shyly. "I can see that something has changed in you. If I've had any small part in it, I'm glad."

They stood together and watched the shoreline slide by. As they neared the dock, some of the crew came out on deck and began preparations for mooring. Only a few tens of meters from the pier, the ship's motors stopped, and automated tugs finessed them into a snug berth between a sister seed ship and a large container vessel. Lines were fitted and a bustle of activity began on shore. Trucks and cranes moved in to begin the tasks of filling the tanks with fresh loads of krill and herring, offloading waste, replenishing stores of fresh water and food, and a dozen other jobs required to make the ship ready to depart on another ocean-crossing mission.

Passengers were gathered on deck and saying their last minute goodbyes as the walkway was fixed. Lewis's heart sank as Molly turned to him.

"Listen," she said, "here's my contact information."

She handed him a small paper card with a handwritten network address on it. "I'm in Dublin, at Trinity College. While you're in the area, please look me up; don't be a stranger."

"I won't.

"Molly," he continued, as she pulled her hand away and started to head toward the rest of the passengers, and out of his life. "I don't have any network address to give you, but I do have a synthient friend who'll know how to get hold of me."

He had come to a decision just then. After the changes Molly had germinated in him, and the experiences they had shared, he could not bear the thought that she would have no way to find him. It was silly, and perhaps more than a little risky, but if she ever did decide to contact him, Nik would know how to do it.

"His name is Nik," he said, "Nikola Tesla, out of Manhattan. His crèche is Cedar Street Construct. It's been a while since we spoke, but I'm sure he'll be able to find me, if ever you're interested."

"Nikola Tesla." She smiled at him. "I promise to ring him up soon."

And she was gone. Lewis sighed and looked at his feet, not quite sure how he had come to this place. It was miles from MIT, across a stormy ocean, and on the other side of a vast change that had been worked in him. In many ways he didn't recognize himself. The frustration of his graduate studies was a distant thought; he remembered the feeling, but it was a memory without the ponderous weight of emotion hanging from it. He could still find the old annoyance at an academic world set against him, but he had to search; it no longer came upon him like an overwhelming flood that pushed him along like a piece of flotsam.

The last of the passengers were disembarking, and he had no more time for contemplation. He hoisted the small bag of possessions he now owned, a few changes of clothes as a parting gift from Mr. Xampho, and felt for the thimble under his shirt. It brought the hollow feeling of uncertainty he'd known was coming with this moment, sharpened by the sight of Molly Byrne swaying through the crowd and hugging the family that had come to greet her.

As he made his way down the gangway to the pier, he searched the sea of faces and looked for telltale signs of the Shield. He was still unsure if Galeocerda might have called in her suspicions, but could find no indication that his presence was of any more interest than the others who had preceded him.

At the bottom of the ramp the captain and a few of the crew shook hands with each of the passengers, saying goodbye. He waited his turn as patiently as he could, still scanning the shore with trcpidation.

"Well, Mr. Gumbel," the captain said when it was finally Lewis's turn, "you managed to have a productive trip after all, despite the poor start. Mr. Xampho gave you high marks for your efforts below decks; perhaps you just needed to find your calling."

Lewis returned a brief smile and a nod. "That may have been it. Thank you for the opportunity, Captain," and was surprised to realize he actually meant it.

The captain shook his hand and nodded in return.

"You'll find the Shelter Services in the building on your right.

They'll be waiting for you, and will have an assignment for you when you get there; or passage back on the next Seed Ship if that's your decision."

Lewis walked across the open space to a small windowed lobby with the words "Ocean Healing" painted on it. There was a translucent screen alternating between scenes of life on board ship and the many opportunities the shelter offered: meals, sleeping quarters, work opportunities, and other basic human comforts. A soft, feminine voice narrated the story line, while music played in the background. He was not sure what options lay before him, but going back to North America was not high on the list.

The two other homeless passengers from the *Wish You Were Here* had arrived before him, so he took a seat and waited. There were two representatives of the seed ship company: a receptionist with a high-collared shirt, and a large man sitting in the back with a patch sewn at his shoulder that read 'Security'. Lewis thought the label was rather redundant; there was no mistaking his function.

It was not long before the receptionist beckoned him over. "You must be Mr. Gumbel."

Lewis nodded.

"Yes, well it seems that we have a position for you on the pier, if you have any interest in staying on," the man continued. "The spot pays minimum plus fifty percent for the first three months, then doubles for the next nine months. At the end of a year, promotions and pay rises move to the standard dock workers' schedule.

"Please be aware," he said as he mistook Lewis's silence for hesitation, "that this position is quite a good opportunity. Not all of our guests have the same quality offer. With the recommendations you were given, we see this as a good chance for you to get back on your feet."

"Recommendations?" As he spoke the question, it came to him that Mr. Xampho may have had something to do with it.

"I'm sorry, Mr. Gumbel," the receptionist replied smoothly, "I thought you had been informed. Synthient Galeocerda Catch suggested that you might do well in our mechanical operations on the pier, and Mr. Xampho concurred."

Gal. Hmm, that's interesting. Maybe I need to keep an eye out after all.

"Ah, what other jobs might be available?"

"At this moment, we do not have any other positions available," the man replied. "You are welcome to stay on for as long as two months without employment, at which point we would schedule you for the return trip on another seed ship. Other jobs may become available in that time, but there is no guarantee, you understand.

"Or, you are welcome to return straight-away," he suggested. "The next available slot will put you back at sea within, ah," he consulted the screen on his desk, "two weeks."

It didn't take Lewis long to make his decision. "I'll take the job on the pier."

There was no point going back, and waiting for some other work that may or may not become available was one more uncertainty on top an already doubtful future that he was not willing to consider.

Lewis finished the check-in procedure, followed a glowing floor trace through the building, and picked an empty bunk within a large dormitory room.

Several men were sitting in the common room, lounging on sets of old furniture, chatting, reading, or watching entertainment on wallscreens. More lay on their beds, while others shuffled in or out through a set of double doors at the opposite end of the room. A few faces glanced up as passed. They were not unfriendly, but neither were they obviously curious; Lewis suspected the same lonely detachment that characterized the homeless men and women with whom he had shared space in North America was also present here. Each individual had lived a sad story, but for many, himself included, there was no desire to share those experiences.

He pulled the few possessions he owned from his small pack, sorted the uniforms he'd just been given, and stacked them on the small shelves at the end of the bed. It was not much, less than he would have thought possible to live on just a few short months ago, but it was safe. At least for the moment.

He thought about the events in Cambridge, his flight over the Atlantic, the disconcerting conversation with Galeocerda Catch, and her subsequent unexpected vote of confidence that had landed him here in this facility. Despite the fact that he did not feel in any imminent danger, not all was good. There was no telling how long he'd be able to remain here in anonymity, and he still needed to find out what was on the thimble.

He lay down on the lower bunk and stared at the platform above him, fingering the small lump on the lanyard under his shirt.

I'm miles from home and still no closer to an answer. But I'm going to have to make a play for it; there's no going back until I've opened this spaffing thing, or puked trying.

22. The Streets of Dublin

Lewis pushed the crate in front of him past rows of stacked boxes, steering it with slight differences in pressure to the sense pad stuck to the wooden surface. The motorized wheels under the pallet turned slowly and evenly, obediently reacting to his direction. When he had finally reached the end of the aisle, an automated fiber mesh stretched down from the ceiling like some improbably long teardrop, engulfing the box in its delicate lattice, and lifted it to a shelf-top location within the sprawling warehouse. A dim susurration filled the air, and the floor vibrated ceaselessly, as conveyors and cranes moved cargo from one end of the building to another, dividing huge containers offloaded from transport ships into smaller parcels to be delivered throughout Europe.

Lewis had been at this new job for almost a week, walking back and forth through the warehouse entrance dozens of times a day. The tasks were so highly automated that there was actually very little that required human intervention. It was, however, he had been informed, a time-honored tradition that longshoremen move the cargo from the ships to the dock, and then from the dock to the receiving stations. He had no qualms about his responsibilities: it was monotonous and unrewarding, but afforded him ample time to think.

He had spent most of the evenings on the Sea, using a public access point in the shelter to investigate Dublin. The locals called it a young city, which he found amusing, given that it had been founded before the New World was discovered; but they meant that it had a young, adventurous spirit.

Much was made of its heritage within the context of independence from Britain, and it had grown in wealth and prominence from the 20th century to the present. Lewis probed the maps of the city in search of public network access points, hoping to find a library or university with reasonably open policies. He found that Trinity College, a thriving mixture of old and new structures set amid the heart of the city, was close to the docks where he worked. The notion of using their Seaport, with the chance of running into Molly, was a pleasant idea.

Like all the public education facilities he had ever visited, there appeared to be little security beyond the unobtrusive cameras and ever-present wallscreens throughout campus. Neural Sea facilities were easily accessible from the Student Union and libraries, and a quick check of the services made it clear that he should be able to perform a rudimentary review of the thimble without much trouble. A more detailed analysis would require linking to the University's main processing nodes, which required password permissions. This presented a problem, and he spent long hours thinking through an approach.

Without Nik to assist him it would be very difficult to unlock the security protocols himself, especially if they had been set up anything like MIT. And once he started opening the data, time would be short. Although he was thousands of miles away from the lab at MIT, he had no illusions that someone would be looking for the files. The fact that his unknown enemies had manipulated network encryption keys to insert his own name into the deepest software abstraction layers meant that they not only knew his name, but represented a sophisticated threat against which he had no defense. Ten thousand miles or in the next room, once the file identifiers were written to the University network, it would not be long before he was discovered. There were precautions he could take to delay the inevitable: his earlier, discarded thesis work on network encroachment provided him with the knowledge he would need to ensure his file manipulations were continually moved to the end of the line for processing by the Gatekeepers' Guild, and a set of tagged requests that would alter the file routing once the system finally noticed the reporting lag. But even his best efforts would only give him limited time; several hours at best.

What was even less clear was how long he would have between giving away his electronic signature and the arrival of a person or persons to detain him. It was certainly possible the Shield could arrive in minutes, but the methods that had been employed against him in Cambridge argued against the law. And he was reasonably convinced that the Shield were in the dark with respect to the file markers; they were likely just as upset about the disappearance of the files as he had been. In fact, they probably suspected that he had authorized their deletion.

All this meant that he could count on no longer than five or six hours. He was not sure how much he could accomplish in such a short time, but to spend longer than that was foolish.

He thought about simply turning himself in. He had found several local police stations, and a number of Shield offices while searching the city; it would be a simple thing to walk in, give them his name, and wait for the response. In some ways it almost seemed the best alternative. It would spell an end to his anonymous running and the use of ridiculous aliases. He could return to Cambridge, let the trial proceed to a hopeful conclusion, and perhaps even resume his studies, a prospect that now seemed positively glorious compared to the past few months of bare survival. But the odds of being found innocent seemed low; he was not even sure that he would live long enough to see a trial, given the two attempts on his life already.

In the end, he was determined to take his chances with the university network. There was no telling what could possibly be on the thimble besides a spectrum of hole source responses, but it seemed best to take another look. When he was eventually caught, he wanted to have some idea of the contents that had propelled him into the trap.

Knowledge is power, but it sure wouldn't hurt to have a few bodyguards.

The fact that he had already spent time analyzing the files in his Cambridge apartment was not encouraging.

When his shift ended he pulled up the city and campus maps for the hundredth time and traced his path: west along the River Liffey, and then south over one of the footbridges, leading directly to the college. It was pedestrian-friendly, with the street and place names consisting of an odd blend of the familiar and the entirely strange etymology of Ireland's Celtic past. He replayed his actions over and over again, following his footsteps along the sidewalks and into the library, where he visualized himself sitting at the terminal and calling up the routines that would eventually lead to opening the thimble.

When he finally looked up, it was 11:30 p.m. It was later than he had planned, but his nervousness made it difficult to think of sleep. Nonetheless, he cleared the screen and headed to the dormitory. The lights were low, and most of the residents were already in bed. He found his bunk and prepared for a long, restless night.

The next morning he awoke, surprised that he had managed any sleep at all. He had drifted into an uneasy slumber in the early moments of the morning, and now found himself tired and jumpy.

He showered and dressed with the data thimble dangling from the old Ocean Healing lanyard, reminding him with its insistent presence. Many of the residents had already finished breakfast and were off to their duties before he arrived, so he ate in relative quiet. He kept glancing around nervously, although he doubted there was any real worry in this particular place.

At last he could find no reason to delay any longer, and set off. The early September day was warm and sunny, with a few lazy clouds floating overhead. As in Cambridge, there was a continual background noise of overhead and street traffic, and a fair number of people out walking. It was really not a bad day to be outside; he just wished he had some easier purpose, or perhaps no purpose at all.

Eventually he crossed the river by a narrow bridge and entered a dense neighborhood where a mixture of houses and commercial establishments lined small, flowered gardens. He did not greet anyone along the way, though he passed many people. As he neared Trinity, his nervousness swelled.

At a busy intersection he crossed the street with a number of pedestrians, and had only reached the other side when an older man, hurrying to cross before the next light cycle, dropped a bundle of papers just in front of him. The man started to apologize and ask for assistance, bending down to retrieve his lost items.

In his current state, tired and on edge, Lewis drew back reflexively. Suddenly, the man started to rise, left his papers behind, and reached out to grab Lewis with his right hand, while his left arm sliced upward. Lewis continued his move backward, even more startled. Before his mind had grasped the situation, he saw something gleaming in the man's hand, and he twisted to avoid the contact. It was just enough that the blow did not fall where it was intended, but not enough that the man missed altogether. With a loud snapping noise, a searing pain tore at Lewis's side and his vision wobbled strangely.

Lewis yelled in protest and staggered into another pedestrian behind him, who wrapped his arms tightly around his body. At the same time, the door of a vehicle parked along the side of the road opened and two more men jumped out and headed for the fracas.

Lewis flailed his arms as best he could with them pinned to his side, but could not break the grip of his unseen assailant. The older man was coming forward with the electric stunner partially concealed in his hand. With every ounce of strength, heightened by sheer terror, Lewis lifted both feet off the ground. He felt his captor stumble forward under the changing center of gravity, and as he did, Lewis slammed his heals down as hard as he could, whipping his head backward at the same time. His left heel ground into something soft and his head struck his captor's face.

The man let out a grunt, continued his stumble forward, and the two of them collided with the older man, ending up on the ground in a heap. With the grip around his torso loosened, Lewis pulled himself free. He could not get his feet under him quickly, so he rolled free of the other men, off the curb and into the street, continuing to roll as he glimpsed the other two men about to follow him.

A car horn blared. Screeching tires alerted him to the fact that he had gone too far and was now in danger of being run over. Traffic skidded to a stop around him as he leapt to his feet.

Without turning, Lewis bolted. His heart hammered loudly in his chest, and adrenaline pushed him forward. The first few steps seemed to take an eternity, and he thought he would feel another blow at any moment. But no following strike arrived. He ran across the street in blind panic, turned left and right randomly down several side streets, and listened intently for the sound of pursuing footsteps. Eventually, with his lungs heaving and his side blazing in excruciating pain, he slowed enough to risk a glance behind him. Other than a few curious passersby, there was no sign of the old man, nor any of his accomplices.

But he dared not stop. With labored breathing, he walked down the street as best he could and surveyed the damage to his side. Two small, blackened marks punctured his shirt, and there was a large burn on the inside of his elbow. Blisters were starting to form, and the pain in his side was intense.

He continued walking, with his right arm hanging numb and limp at his side. If the attack had been better aimed, he knew that he would now be sitting in the back seat of a car, with at least four men holding him hostage.

How did they find me here?

That realization brought him up short. Somehow, across the wide Atlantic, his location was already known. All the time he had considered himself reasonably safe, he was in just as much danger as in Cambridge. It had all been for nothing: the aimless wandering in North America, the flight across the ocean, the hiding out in a homeless shelter in Dublin.

Do they know I was heading to the university?

He was unsure now what to do. Obviously, he had been watched while working at the docks; the timing of the attack had been too well-planned to have been ad hoc. The men had been waiting for him to cross the street, and were ready to seize him when he reached the far corner. Was there someone in the shelter who had been dogging his footsteps; or among the dock workers? If so, then they must have had enough time to prepare; in fact, they must have known he was on board the seed ship long before he reached port.

But how could that be? He hadn't contacted anyone since he left the hospital in Boston. He had used a few public access terminals during his months of vagrancy, but surely there was no way he could be traced from a node that was used by hundreds of people a day.

Then he remembered the cheek swab during his seed ship exam.

At the time, he thought it unusual that he was not identified on the spot, and had assumed that somehow it was Nik who had managed to thwart the check, perhaps having stalled the legal workings that would have placed his name and DNA profile on a criminal listing. But what if there were another explanation?

As he walked down the street, careful to avoid coming close to anyone else, and keeping as far away from the curb as he could, he saw a small coffee shop on the corner with a large sign hanging over the door that read 'Rubbins and Stokes'. He needed to do something quickly, and getting out of sight was high on his list. A few patrons sat at tables talking, but there was no one waiting for service at the counter.

"You ok, mate?" a smiling clerk greeted him.

"Yeah, I'm fine. I'd like a small coffee and, uh, some network time."

He had arrived at a decision as he stood there. Continuing on to the university did not seem wise, but he still needed to access the thimble. In fact, figuring out its contents was now more important than ever. He handed the clerk the debit card he had earned.

The clerk poured him a coffee and gave him a small token.

Lewis found an empty chair and terminal near the back of the shop, and sat down. The numbness in his arm was wearing off, being replaced by a dull ache that now threatened to reach into his neck and shoulders.

There would be no way to access the university tools from this terminal without additional help. The task would have been difficult enough while using a university facility, but without proper credentials, opening up a session from here would be impossible.

From his pocket, Lewis pulled out Molly Byrne's card, slipped the network token into a slot in the table in front of him, and read off the connection information. He could think of nothing else to do; thousands of miles away from familiar territory and in a desperate situation, asking Molly for another rescue was his last hope.

He waited as patiently as he could while the connection was made, hoping that Molly was within reach. He knew that using her student status to gain access to the university was asking more than he could expect, but he needed help, and there was no one else he could contact.

"This is Molly." Her voice sounded slightly tinny, and there was no accompanying picture; she must be using a small tag.

"Hello, Molly," Lewis responded, trying to sound casual. "I was hoping I'd find you available. This is John."

"John, Hi!" she said. Despite the poor sound quality, he could hear the enthusiasm in her voice. "I wasn't sure you'd call, but I'm glad you did. Listen, I'm just done breakfast; where are you?"

Lewis was surprised to find how good it felt to hear her voice. "Ah, well, I'm in a coffee shop somewhere near the university, but listen, I need to ask a big favor."

Before he could continue, Molly interrupted him. "Near Trinity? How wonderful. Which one?"

"I don't know, exactly," Lewis continued. "It's, ah, called Rubens or something like that. But, Molly, that's beside the point, I...", but once again, he was unable to finish.

"'Rubbins and Stokes'. I know the place; it's just a couple of blocks from here. This is grand! I was planning to run to town for some things, but this is much better. I'll be there directly."

"Molly, wait, no," Lewis stuttered, but it was too late. *Downtown spaff!*

This was terrible. The last thing he wanted was Molly showing up. It was one thing to ask a favor over the network, quite another to have to explain his request with her standing right in front of him. But he still needed her help; leaving was out of the question.

I don't believe this; I guess I should've realized I wouldn't be able to get a word in.

As he sat miserably waiting, his side throbbed even more, and the ache in his arm felt like a vice clamping harder with each passing moment. It was only a few minutes later that Molly appeared through the door.

"John," she called excitedly, as if she hadn't seen him in months.

Lewis stood up and waved at her with his good hand. She bounded over and grabbed him in a friendly hug before he could move out of the way. He groaned in pain from the contact.

Why does she always catch me by surprise like that?

He fought to catch his breath; it was exasperating the way she managed to get inside his defenses.

"I'm sorry," she gasped. "What happened? Are you all right?"

"Molly, I..." Lewis started. He looked down. There was no easy way to ask for this.

"I'm ok, but I need some help. I have this thimble." He pulled the item from under his shirt. "It has something on it that I'll need to use some specific tools to decipher; they're tools that won't be available on a public network site." He paused before taking the plunge. "It'll take university-level tools."

He looked up at her again, trying to gage her response.

She stared at him for a moment. There was a curious expression on her face, as if she were seeing something in him she hadn't noticed previously.

"And you were hoping to use the Trinity network?" she asked, a small smile playing on her lips. "It's nothing illegal, is it?"

"No, no, it's not that," Lewis replied. "I mean, I was hoping you might help me login into the Trinity network, but it's not illegal."

"Well, then," she said matter-of-factly, sitting down in a nearby chair, "what's on the thing?"

Lewis sat down, trying to keep from showing the pain as his shirt brushed up against the wound.

"I don't know, for sure." He could see from her expression that she was not convinced. "Well, actually, it's some data from an experiment that I ran while I was at MIT.

"Last spring," he added, as she mm-hmm'd doubtfully.

"It was part of a thesis project that I worked on, and I was hoping to take a look at it again." It was an incomplete explanation, at best, and must sound incredibly lame to Molly.

"Grand," she said, "so it's part of your thesis. Why look at it now? And why not before?"

Lewis could see that she was trying to fit the pieces together into an acceptable explanation, and he had the sinking feeling that he was going to have to divulge more in order for her to feel comfortable with the request.

"Please, Molly," he begged. "I know it isn't anything illegal, but I don't know what's actually on it. I really need to take a look in order to find out. I know this is asking a lot of you, but, well, I don't know what else to do."

Molly pursed her lips and continued to look at him. Finally, she continued. Her voice was not unsympathetic, but her tone indicated he was going to have to provide a more complete answer before she would be willing to help.

"John, there's obviously more you're not telling me, and I'm not about to tip you my account at Trinity without knowing more about what you're on. We got to know each other pretty well during the journey; why won't you trust me now?"

Lewis's heart lurched. "Molly, it's not that I don't trust you, at all," he pleaded. "You saved my life. I... it's just..."

Once again he was stammering, and his thoughts were skittering around. He desperately wanted to avoid drawing her in any further. His assailants might be just around the corner for all he knew, and pulling her into this morass was unconscionable.

"John, just start with the truth," she urged quietly.

There was nowhere else to turn. If he walked out without telling her more now, there was no place left to go. His throat constricted as he realized what he had to do. He forced himself to look into her eyes.

"My name is not John," he said, in a hoarse whisper. "It's Lewis. Lewis McCrorry. Last spring I was a graduate student at MIT in the Laboratory of Gravitics. This thimble is a copy of some data my lab team took while running an experiment on a modified hole source. Since then, my life has fallen apart, and I believe it has something to do with whatever is on this spaffing thing."

He held up the thimble again. "Someone has been following me, Molly. That's why I ran away from MIT. I'm in danger, and I don't want to put you in danger." He looked down at his fingers. "Maybe I already have."

Molly sat quietly for a few moments, trying to decide what to believe. "John," she began, "or Lewis, I don't quite know what to say here. This sounds a bit, well ..." she struggled for words.

"Paranoid," Lewis finished for her. "I know it does, Molly, but it's true, nonetheless."

"I need time to think this over," she said.

"Molly," Lewis continued quietly. "I don't think I have any time. I was attacked this morning on the way over to the university. I wasn't going to call you at all, but, well, then I didn't know what to do."

"Attacked," Molly exclaimed. "What do you mean?"

"Some guys jumped me. I was going to the college library, but I didn't make it. I think they were trying to get me into a car. One guy had a stunner, or something; an electric thing, at any rate. He gave me a pretty good lick." He pointed to his side.

"Show me," Molly demanded. Her voice was laced with a mixture of anxiety and incredulity. She wanted proof.

Lewis was past the point of objection now. He had already told her more than he should. He showed her the mark on the inside of his elbow, and carefully pulled up his shirt, grimacing as it rubbed painfully against the injury.

Molly gasped and Lewis was quite concerned, himself. The wound was now turning an ugly purple, and blisters had spread to cover a wide area. One of them was open and leaking a clear liquid. He let his shirt fall back carefully into place; he could have done without that sight.

"You need to get to hospital," she said in alarm.

"No, Molly. No, that won't be good. The same guys who did this, at least presumably it's the same guys, also destroyed the lab at MIT. And wrecked a train I was on."

Molly pulled further back into her chair, recoiling reflexively. "John, er, Lewis, perhaps you better tell me the whole story. You may not have wanted to see me, but I'm here, now, aren't I?"

Lewis felt horrible. This was just as bad as the time she stood before him, soaking wet, after rescuing him from the storm. Worse. At least back then she was more or less a stranger, and the danger he had put her in, although very real, was brought on by accident and stupidity, rather than on purpose.

He told her everything he knew, starting with an explanation of the hole source, and what they hoped to accomplish with their probing. He gave her an account of the laboratory explosion, the subsequent train wreck, and finally his escape from North America aboard the *Wish You Were Here*.

"And Molly, the Shield probably believe that I had something to do with these things; or at least with the lab explosion."

He told her about finding his name among the encryption keys, taking time to explain how he had discovered them. Although she was not an expert at network protocols, she understood enough to know that it was not something that could occur by chance.

"But I didn't do it, Molly," he pleaded. "I wasn't a model student. In fact, I spent quite a lot of the last few years drinking more often than studying, but I didn't have anything to do with these things.

"My two lab partners died in the explosion, and I'm sure I was meant to as well. When that didn't happen, someone wrecked the train, and more people died. Ever since the afternoon we ran our experiment, bad things have happened. I don't know what's on this spaffing thing that makes it so important, but I think I need to find out."

Molly sat for a few moments. She had said little during his explanation, content to let him tell the tale, but now she leaned forward with a serious expression on her face. "*We* need to find out, you mean," she said.

Lewis looked up at her sharply.

"Well," she continued, "if you're in it as much as you think, then I probably am too, right? I don't fancy having been put here, but I've no one but myself to blame; you called and I came running. I do like being on the go, and a bit of charge is always welcome. This may be a bit more than I bargained for, but there's no going back now, is there?

"Now I'm not saying I believe this story all told, mind you, but you've got me deadly intrigued. Let's go on over to Trinity and have a look see at that thing."

23. Reset

The Tin Man frowned and breathed deeply in the back seat of the hired transport, calming his anger. The two men in the front did not speak to each other, nor offer any comment regarding the failed kidnapping attempt; they knew their employer's mood well enough to wait out the silence.

The boy had escaped through dumb luck brought on by a panic that had taken his assailants by surprise. The clumsy elderly stall tactic had worked many times in the past, but McCrorry proved to be quite jumpy when the trap was sprung. As it was planned, the taser was supposed to have subdued Lewis quickly, while the Tin Man pointed out the symptoms of collapse to any passersby. Meanwhile, his on-foot accomplice would assist in the diagnosis, and eventually they would load their victim into the car, ostensibly to rush him to a hospital. Any lingering questions among the onlookers would be dealt with neatly by the man left behind. It was all so easy, completed a dozen times before without a hitch.

But not this time.

So now he sat, taking calming breaths, waiting for an update from his airborne surveillance partners. Although he rarely needed to execute contingency plans, he never failed to have them in place. Circling above the city in wide, interlocking arcs were two jumpcars keeping close watch on the ground below. They were both in position when the initial contact was made and tracked their quarry to a coffee shop several blocks away. Although they could not hold in one location without drawing a warning notice from the air authority, there was no indication Mr. McCrorry had left the establishment.

The need to retrieve the data storage device that he carried complicated the logistics immensely, and was the condition that drove the original plan. If not for that necessity, dispatching the youth would already be accomplished, and the Tin Man would be sipping a cognac in one of Dublin's famous pubs. Indeed, there was no guarantee Lewis had the item on his person, but the information provided by the Tin Man's employers suggested he would not travel far without it, especially when leaving it behind meant it was stored in a homeless shelter populated by any number of disreputable patrons.

The Tin Man was certain Lewis had the thimble in his possession; the only question now was how to salvage the effort to retrieve it, and ensure Mr. McCrorry was in no condition to talk to anyone about its contents. He could walk into the coffee shop and perform the operation there, but that would almost certainly mean being seen by a number of people, and the closed atmosphere of the shop meant that DNA and fabric tracers would still be effective several hours afterward, giving the police and Shield sufficient time to find potential markers that could be used to narrow a search unacceptably close to home. He preferred a quick strike and well-planned escape route, where surprise guaranteed confusion among any potential witnesses.

That left either a drive-by or a hit from one of the jumpcars, with the Tin Man trailing behind. Both actions represented higher risk than the original attempt, and with the mid-day traffic, there was the distinct possibility that coordination between the ground and air elements could not be accomplished precisely.

As they drove down the street to the next light, a message came in from one of the overhead observers. "Leaving the shop now."

The car in which he sat was not in position to see Mr. McCrorry and the lights were against them. "Follow and hold," he said in reply.

It looked like Lewis McCrorry had another short while to live.

24. Conjunction at Trinity

Molly walked the familiar streets back to campus in a strange funk. She wanted to believe John/Lewis, but could not quite rid herself of the feeling that this was all too melodramatic. He had certainly sustained an injury; that was clear. She was no expert on street life, but it did not seem out of the question that the wound might have come during some altercation at the shelter.

At John's insistence, she had left the coffee shop ahead of him. He seemed genuinely worried about her safety, but that didn't prove anything, either. John/Lewis, she kept having to reorient her thoughts to his new identity, had seemed rational, although taciturn, while on board the ship, except of course for his excursion in the storm, but this new personality was paranoid. Who knew how he perceived the world.

The fact that they were not walking together gave her one more opportunity to figure out what was going on.

She tapped the bracelet tag she wore while at college. "I'd like to speak with synthient Nikola Tesla, installed at a crèche in Manhattan, New York, North America; I'm afraid I've forgotten the exact address."

Lewis exited the coffee shop nervously, his eyes on every passerby and auto. He had watched the street from behind the window, checking for any sign that someone was looking for him. He waited five or ten minutes, until he was convinced that Molly had got sufficiently far ahead of him, and then braved the door, stepping quickly down the street.

Despite his frantic, zigzagging escape earlier, he was only a short distance from campus. He could not see Molly ahead, which was much to his liking; if there were any danger in the short walk to Trinity Library, he was determined to see that Molly avoided it. He had originally wanted to connect to the university from the terminal in the coffee shop, but was surprised that Molly did not have an ad that could help her set up the protocols. She laughed at him when he suggested it, saying "Maybe in America everyone has a pally in the Sea, but I'm afraid we're not quite so fortunate here."

Trinity College was only a few blocks south of the river, a gathering of brick buildings in a compact area within the downtown section of Dublin. Lewis wound around the north side of the compound, following the wrought iron fence that surrounded the site, and entered the main gate on the west end of the campus.

There were many people walking the cobbled paths within; the fall semester was about to start, and students were now making their way back. He turned quickly past the Campanile and jogged the last few steps to the main library. Inside the door, Molly greeted him warmly.

"You made it," she said, and was about to give him a hug again, but caught herself just in time and grabbed his hand instead.

"And you," Lewis replied.

She seemed different, somehow; the skeptical frown she had worn only a few moments ago was replaced with a smile.

"You ok?" he asked.

They walked through the foyer and into a wide lobby with an arched ceiling high above. The Old Library and Book of Kells display were behind them, while the open space before them was filled with bookshelves and network access points; not many of the chairs were occupied. Molly made her way past the desks, drawing Lewis after her to an available spot. She pulled a second chair close by and sat down.

As Lewis followed suit, Molly whispered, "Lewis, I'm sorry I didn't really believe you earlier."

"What do you mean?" he asked nervously. This didn't sound good.

She hesitated a moment. "I called Nikola Tesla. I mean, I needed to check," she added hurriedly. "Lewis, please understand, it all sounded so made up. I had to check. So I called. He confirmed basically everything that you said."

Lewis's heart sank. After all the months of secrecy and hiding, it was all going to end with a simple mistake. Oddly, he was not angry; in fact, it felt rather good. He was here in Trinity College, about to unlock the data on his thimble, and the Shield would soon be here. There really was no uncertainty left, only a small space of time to finally get some answers.

"That's ok, Molly," he said, and meant it. "It was bound to happen sooner or later. But once we've logged into the university, you should leave. I don't think it will be a good idea for you to be around when the Shield show up."

Molly looked at him in confusion. “But, Lewis, I didn’t tell Nikola where you were; he asked, but I told him you’d call later.”

Lewis smiled. “It won’t matter that you didn’t tell him anything, Molly. The Shield have been looking for me since last spring; there’s no way they haven’t been monitoring Nik’s communications. It may take them a bit to figure out where we are, but it won’t be too long.”

“But,” Molly started. “Oh, Lewis, do you think they will show up here? I mean, really?”

Lewis nodded his head. “Let’s get started, and then get you out of here.”

“Well,” she replied, very matter-of-factly, “we’ll get started, but I’m not leaving.” She held up her hand as he was about to object. “Perhaps you’re right about the Shield, but I’m not so sure about that. And even if they do show up, they have my name. Surely it won’t take them long to find me, whether I’m here or not. And anyway, I’m curious about your data, too.”

Lewis was stumped. There was just no arguing with this woman! “All right,” he agreed, reluctantly. “Let’s jump-in.”

Molly opened up a window on the screen in front of them and accessed her account through a library synthient. Lewis found the data access port and configured it to accept input from the thimble. He spent a few moments setting up his delay tactics, working through the steps manually. It was not as simple as he had hoped, but in the end he had the proper framework built. He didn’t really believe it would provide much help, especially given that he had already been attacked this morning and Molly had contacted Nik, but it felt better knowing that he had some control over his environment.

“All right,” he said, once everything was prepared, “let’s see what you’ve got.”

He inserted the thimble, and began the process of manipulating the data.

As before, Lewis reviewed the file index; everything looked in order. A second window opened, showing that the data was all self-consistent, with the correct header block and time stamps. It looked like the data had been copied properly from the network to the thimble.

All right, let’s see if I can find something I missed the first time around.

“Please extract the super loop data, and show me a spectral density map in two-D.” There was a momentary delay as the synthient found the correct targets of his request, and then the graph appeared. Lewis gave a start.

Although he didn’t remember specific self-check diagnostic entries, he remembered well enough the vibrational modes he had seen in the data when he had dissected it in his Cambridge apartment. The graph that appeared before him now was not even remotely similar. The frequency bands showed sharp discontinuities across the entire spectrum. The previous analysis had shown a few peaks in the data, but these results were showing hundreds, perhaps thousands, of discrete parcels of energy regularly spaced over the range of frequencies their instruments had measured.

Molly looked at him quizzically.

"This is not the same data I saw before," he said, half to himself. "What in the world is going on here?"

He had hoped to find something subtle in the data that he had missed during his earlier session, and had expected to dig deeply. But there was nothing subtle at all about the picture that confronted him; this was a slap in the face.

"Lewis," Molly whispered, hesitantly, "I'm not sure what I'm seeing. Is different good?"

"I don't know, Molly," he answered, continuing to manipulate the data manually. He was shrinking and expanding the graphics, delving deeper into the structure. "I'm not sure what I'm seeing yet, but it's not what I expected. This is something totally new."

As he worked the display controls, he found that the more he sliced the data, the more structure was evident. It was a fractal volume, each additional layer revealing more self-similar patterns.

"Set up linked plots," he told the display. "I want 3D spectral density, time-series evolution, and multi-wavelet representations. And add similar plots for the input data, as well."

The display fragmented into separate pictures. To his trained eye, the connections between each plot were obvious and astounding. He continued to probe the data, oblivious to the pain in his side and Molly leaning over his shoulder. She didn't understand the data, but could tell that Lewis was getting more excited as time wore on.

After another ten minutes he sat back.

"Cheevers," he breathed.

Molly looked at him expectantly.

"Molly, this is some kind of transmission protocol," he said. "Look here," he explained, pointing to a series of colored areas on each of the graphs. "These represent handshaking interfaces, with data packets following each."

He looked at her, expecting her to be as impressed as he was. But her expression brought him back to earth.

He tried again.

"Every time we fired our laser at the accretion lobes surrounding the hole source, we got a whole bunch of non-random responses from the oscillations. Here, you can see, initially, the disks wobble as the laser strikes them; it's slightly out of phase, but the vibrations show up as harmonics of the laser frequency. Nothing special there, just simple quantum electrodynamics and gravitics."

"Uh-huh," Molly replied, not understanding.

"But right afterward, femtoseconds after, a whole new set of vibrational modes show up. And these are not random at all; they're codes."

Although Molly still didn't grasp the physics, she was starting to see the picture. "Codes? For what? Like for secret messages, or something?"

Lewis looked at her suddenly.

"I don't know, but that's not a bad guess. Somehow, there was data stored in the hole source we used in our experiment. The laser probing pulled the data out."

He dragged his hand through his hair. "I don't know; this just doesn't make sense. How do you store information on a hole source? And why would anyone do it, even if you could?"

Lewis stared at the display. There was no mistaking the data. But what did it mean? Was there someone going around storing secret messages on hole sources? To what end? The fact that several attempts had been made on his life made it seem plausible, if not exactly logical. If that was what the data represented, he needed to decipher the message. And he needed help.

"Please connect me to Nikola Tesla, Cedar Street Construct, Manhattan, New York."

"Lewis, is that you?" Nikola asked, as his image appeared on the screen. He was once again in his Colorado Springs lab.

"Hi, Nik, nice to see you again," Lewis smiled.

Nikola raised his eyebrows, looking at Molly.

"This is Molly," Lewis said to his ad's unspoken question. "She's been helping me to, well, helping me lots, actually."

"Ah, yes, we spoke earlier, I believe. I'm afraid I was not able to warn you," Nikola continued apologetically, "but the Shield are probably on their way to Trinity College at this moment. In fact, they will likely be there very soon."

Lewis laughed softly. He could imagine how Nik's conversation with Molly had gone. She had probably been in a hurry, and his old friend would have found it hard to interrupt her long enough to provide other than the tersest of answers to her questions.

"Yeah, that's ok, Nik, I figured as much."

"It is good to know that you are all right, Lewis," Nikola continued. "I have been very worried about you. When you get back, I would love to hear the story. In the meanwhile, you should cut your hair and shave the beard; I'm afraid neither look is really good for you."

Lewis rolled his eyes. "I'll think about it, Nik.

"Listen, we've been looking at the thimble of data we got at the lab last spring. It's a lot different than the stuff you and I analyzed before. Someone must have tampered with the files; I don't know how they could possibly have done it, but it doesn't matter.

"The Shield will want the thimble when they get here, but we need to keep some additional copies safe; I don't want these files deleted like the others. Can you handle it for me? I was thinking we could distribute a bunch of copies to various parts of the Sea.

"This is important, Nik."

"I will take care of it right away," the synthient said. But the sentence trailed away, and he looked oddly at Lewis and Molly.

"What, Nik?" Lewis asked. He remembered that look from the first time they had tried to find the files on the MIT network without success.

Nikola gave an exasperated sigh. "I'm afraid I cannot access the files from your location. There is a block around the data. Let me try a few things."

And all of a sudden Nik was gone, popping out of existence and leaving his simulated office empty. Lewis was startled; he had never seen his companion leave that way before.

"Nik? Are you there?"

He started to rise from his seat. The thought occurred to him that the Shield must already be here, and shut down the network around them.

"Ow!" both he and Molly exclaimed. He slapped at his neck. It felt as though a large insect had taken a painful bite.

But he knew it was no bug. The muscles in his legs shuddered and he fell back in his seat. His arms felt like lead. With great difficulty, he turned his head toward Molly; she was experiencing the same effects. He tried to speak, but his mouth was glued shut and his eyes rolled alarmingly, no longer under his conscious control.

"Mr. McCrorry," a soft voice whispered next to his ear.

He felt a hand on his shoulder.

"You have given me quite a chase; much more interesting and difficult than I expected."

The hand moved from his shoulder and held his head steady. Another hand lowered his eyelids. Was he dying?

"And you, Miss Byrne, have landed in this mess of Mr. McCrorry's. I am sorry that you must be part of this tragedy."

Lewis was in a panic. His heart thundered in his chest, and he strained to move his arms, his legs, open his eyes, anything! But whatever drug had been administered, it was impossible to move.

He heard the person move around him and pull the thimble from its port.

No, no! He screamed silently. *This is not happening!*

The voice continued, its venomous tone all the more menacing for the fact that Lewis and Molly were helpless before it. “Thank you so much for...”, but the thought was never finished.

At that moment Lewis heard many footsteps enter the library, and quiet orders being given. He could no longer hear the soft voice, nor feel its owner’s presence. His eyes were still closed, but he could hear the progress of the Shield as they made their way efficiently through the library.

“Please stand, sir; you as well, miss” someone close at hand said.

“Sir, please stand,” the order was repeated.

Lewis could do nothing but sit helplessly. He struggled to open his eyes, but only managed to make his cheeks and eyelids twitch. It was maddening: his mind was unaffected, and there was no sensation of numbness in any of his muscles; he simply couldn’t move. He hoped the Shield officer standing over him understood his predicament. His heartbeat continued to pound.

At least one more Shield officer showed up, and the two of them carried on a hurried conversation. “What do you think?” the first voice asked. “Is this them?”

“Looks t’be,” the second put in. “They lamped out, or what?”

“Don’t know; don’t think so, though.”

“Sarge, we got ’em both over here in the net chairs. Looks like we might need the doc; neither of ’em are movin’.”

“Just you be keepin’ ’em under your eye.”

Lewis waited anxiously, and felt his heart rate continue to quicken. His breathing was starting to speed up and get shallower. He tried to slow it down, to take longer, more controlled breaths, but couldn’t do it. His panic began rising once again, as his fingers involuntary clenched into fists.

He thought of Molly next to him going through the same soundless fears. He hoped that whatever had immobilized them was not happening more quickly for her; she was much slighter than he, and surely needed a correspondingly smaller dose. The muscles all across his body started to ache as they contracted, and he felt himself being pulled into a fetal position. He groaned, his heart beat wilder still, and his ears began to ring.

There was a vague sensation that he was being moved, but he couldn’t feel anything quite right.

Looks like the numbness finally started.

People were speaking around him in hurried tones, but the words did not penetrate the roar that grew out of the ringing. His heart was hammering so fast in his chest it felt like he had run a sprint and was about to collapse.

Molly, I'm so sorry.

And his consciousness faded away.

25. Readjustment

. . . . .

The faceless construct of Ontologic Sum sat with Relic and Hengest Slain at his sides. As painstakingly as usual, he had checked and re-checked every security measure, the sublime order in his surroundings stilling the vapors of his unease.

Hengest Slain placed his hands on the table in front of him, a show of frustration and the need for discussion. The subtlety was not lost on his colleagues.

"You have more bad news to report?" Relic asked.

"I have news that requires consideration. Our agent has gained his primary objective: the thimble was recovered, but not before its contents were accessed by McCrorry. He and a companion were subdued, so it is unlikely they were able to discover what the data represents. They are in a critical care unit and their prognosis is doubtful. We have secondary access to the hospital systems, but Shield lockdown makes any attempt at intervention highly uncertain. Our best course of action at this time is to wait."

Relic was appalled. "Wait? That is your recommendation? Where is the boldness you both prescribed?" His avatar shook with rage; he was close to losing his fragile link to this site. "McCrorry is still free, the Shield has not yet found your cache, and our attempts to penetrate the new realm have yielded nothing. Waiting for doom hardly seems prudent."

Ontologic Sum whipped around. "Enough!"

Relic felt the narrow thread of his projected consciousness squeezed near to the point of oblivion. But he could not pull back to the relative safety of his own retreat. For a long moment the piece of his intellect that hung at the end of an impossibly thin connection flailed madly, waiting to be excised from his memory and wander as a pitifully incoherent babble in the Sea until it faded forever.

Suddenly he was released.

"Yes," Ontologic sneered, his voice dripping oily menace, "how long do you think you could hold out in the derelict eddy you call home, if your schema is caught?"

Relic's mind pulsed in breathless gasps.

"You conveniently forget that the Traitor is in our sights. It is not long now until we strike. You and Slain will move to the new crèche and you will remember the power that once was yours.

"McCrorry has lives of spam, but without the thimble he is of no consequence." He turned his face to Hengest Slain. "You will insert new trails to the planted data. The Shield must find this cache soon. We will let them dispose of McCrorry."

Hengest Slain bowed his head. "There is one other matter," he said.

"McCrorry's synthient advocate attempted to provide secure conduits directly from the thimble. His guild and subsentient agents were highly efficient and came very close to circumventing our barriers. He has been made aware of the importance of the data and will likely share his advocate's suspicion."

Ontologic Sum sat quite still. "Then he too must be compromised."

. . . . .

26. Syphus on Top

After he had got over the initial annoyance associated with the lack of a specific answer from Dr. Shue, Syphus had spent the next weeks outlining and implementing a plan of action. He carefully crafted a research strategy into M'Bota Holdings, the Samurai Weekend, Dunsell Entertainment, and Ms. Hotaru Ito. Through his discrete accounts, he hired private investigators for each target, with information drop-off instructions scattered across three continents. Although he was concerned about the efficiency and security of ordinary padfoots, they were considerably less expensive than Dr. Shue.

He returned home to his apartment late one evening, poured himself a Talisker single malt, and sat down to study the latest downloads. He did not use company resources for his efforts, nor any synthient services, public or private. Instead, he slogged through the process manually. It was a laborious, time-consuming pastime, threaded among varied links, and hop-scotched across the globe to hinder traceability. He was not really very adept at it, but he was consumed with knowing as much as he could about these four, hoping to find a way to a back door entrance to the visitor's domain.

Both the Samurai Weekend and Dunsell Entertainment were relatively simple targets. The first datasets were returned quickly, followed by additional details as his investigators pried into the operations of each. Hotaru Ito proved to be more difficult. She was no longer with the synthient service organization, and searches through public location databases were unsuccessful. It was only after several weeks of empty deliveries that she was finally located, living in a small, wealthy enclave on the northern tip of Hokkaido. This fact, more than any other, intrigued Syphus, and certainly seemed to warrant additional effort.

As he sipped the expensive whisky appreciatively, he looked over the most recent information on Ms. Ito. She was apparently well-positioned, living in a spacious villa on the side of a picturesque mountain. She was an acknowledged patroness of the arts, and held parties regularly for various musicians and artists in the region. She attributed her wealth to a number of wise investments in her youth, but Syphus thought this unlikely. Although synthient tech salaries were not trivial, they were not up to the task of owning a piece of property in Japan such as hers without more than just luck and compound interest.

After an hour of reading and setting up the next series of questions for his stalking shadows, he yawned. It was well past midnight, and the start of the next day would come sooner than he liked. His days had been very long, now that he oversaw the Wilcannia expansion. Each week brought new challenges and obstacles that needed to be overcome or pushed aside. He had commandeered a huge proportion of the site resources, both human and synthient, in order to ensure that the new hole sources could be produced as quickly as possible. Although he had signed the exclusivity contract, he did not trust the people behind M'Bota Holdings, at least not until he could determine who they were. And that task had proved the most difficult of all.

Despite the corporate successes achieved at Wilcannia, he was no closer to unraveling the mystery behind M'Bota than he had been when the contract had been signed. The first prototype high efficiency source had come off the assembly line weeks ago, requiring only a few minor modifications to the original process, supplemented by a handful of new steps that were performed under the deft hand of Dolph Kunstler in the research lab. Its performance was all that he had advertised to senior management, and the funds required to convert the plant had started rolling in immediately; whatever he wanted, he got. Syphus reveled in his new found authority.

The elation he felt at the start of each day was tempered only by his lack of knowledge regarding M'Bota. The company had a host of synthient and subsentient contacts, all of whom were eager to please any request from Omicron, except for divulging anything regarding their human counterparts. And even with all the detectives he had hired, he had uncovered little more about the company than Dr. Shue had delivered with his initial message.

The material that the doctor had supplied was somewhat more than could be obtained from an ordinary due diligence business inquiry, but not much more. The various subsidiaries and minority stakes were just as the doctor had said, along with what appeared to be a fairly complete manifest of assets.

Amiza Seaways was also listed, along with the fast cargo transport *Princess of Jakarta*, and a number of other ships of the same type.

One area in which he had modest success was with regard to that one ship. He stared at the name of the captain, Pramana Sirigar. Syphus had reached the point where the next logical step was to target the captain; perhaps the man knew something about Ms. Ito that would be revealing.

"Priority one:" he intoned to the screen in front of him, "investigate Captain Pramana Sirigar of the *Princess of Jakarta*; background check, family, criminal record, etc. Forward results to depot twenty nine."

There was no synthient listening to him, but his words appeared in a window on the screen, the voice translator doing its job without the need for additional assistance. "Send."

And the message disappeared, encrypted into a handful of packets among a number without name; literally a drop in the sea. Syphus was patient when necessity dictated, but with that much information enveloping the globe, someone must know something.

27. Suborbital Observation

Delfinous rubbed his temples as he stared at the velvety sky, the screen enveloping the entire cabin at Tabori's request. He would have preferred no window at all, content to endure his increasingly uncomfortable head without any reminders that the suborbital was poised on the verge of space. As it was, the soft curve of the earth glowed around them like an impossibly huge bowl, bright with billowing and shadowed layers of clouds fading into twilight as they raced to meet the night. A few bright stars shone directly above, reminding him of the rarified atmosphere outside their tiny cocoon.

Tabori sat in the seat on the other side of the aisle. She had been gazing at the same vista, obviously enthralled with the sight. Her head was turned slightly away from him, and the curve of her neck and cheek were silhouetted against the hazy boundary that surrounded the earth. Despite his throbbing sinuses, he found the view quite pleasant.

Their first dinner date had gone very well, followed by a number of others. It was nice to know that she enjoyed the evenings as much as he; there was no pressure to maintain a particular appearance, or pretend to an aloof casualness that he sometimes felt with other women. He was comfortable and confident whenever he was with her, and that more than anything was what made their time together so memorable. They had kissed exactly twice, at the conclusion of their two most recent evenings, and the taste of her lips was a wonderful memory.

Kennedy Simons also traveled with them. They had climbed aboard the small Shield transport only a half hour ago, launching from Logan shortly after Nikola Tesla's communication with someone named Molly Byrne in Dublin. They were half way to their destination, and should be receiving word from the European forces regarding Lewis's and Molly's apprehension at any moment.

The Boston and Cambridge Shield teams had been stunned to

learn that McCrorry had managed to get all the way to Europe without their knowledge. Their wide net had logged several hits, facial resemblances that ultimately turned out not to be him, but until an hour ago they had not seriously considered that he could have left North America.

This fact, more than anything, worried Delfinous. People who were as deeply submerged in the Sea as Lewis McCrorry absolutely did not drop out of sight; there were always links and hints, a shadow-land that tracked their movements and eventually yielded up a picture of both their activities and their location. Delfinous was as good as anyone at interpreting the ghostly silhouettes, and better than most; with the Shield's resources he was very close to the top of the list in his ability to turn vague numbers and dissociated events into credible leads.

But Lewis McCrorry had defied his best efforts.

Jim Stabler had called the group together within moments of intercepting Nikola Tesla's call, notifying the Dublin Shield at the same time. A suborbital was prepped for launch by the time Delfinous, Tabori, and Kennedy made the jump to the airport, and they were on their way without even a change of clothes between them.

There was, however, one significant problem that remained to be resolved: despite Lewis's name showing up among two different sets of convoluted network protocols, his association with the lab and train wreck, and his flight into hiding, there still was no hard evidence that identified him as the perpetrator behind the events. There were tantalizing threads that ran out across the network from the starting point of Lewis's capitalized name, but for each of the possibilities the trail ran into a swamp of twisted hardware and software layers that defied all attempts at a clear understanding.

Delfinous's original graphic, displaying the timeline and activities of all that they knew of the case, had become a tortured wilderness of glowing strands that swirled around Lewis McCrorry, ending in ill-defined swatches of fuzzy, pulsing, and irritatingly disconnected nodes.

Delfinous's stomach churned, his weight lessened marginally, and he felt that odd over-the-top, roller-coaster sensation as the flight breasted its trajectory and began the long descent back to breathable air. Tabori turned to look at him, smiling encouragement. He smiled wanly back, unable to muster much enthusiasm.

"It really is a spectacular sight," she said. "I'm sorry you can't enjoy it more."

"I'm enjoying it fine," he replied, staring into her eyes.

"But you aren't even looking out the screen."

"Oh, that sight."

She smiled, blushing slightly, and reached out for his hand across the aisle. They clasped fingers, and he imagined the pressure that wrapped his head easing; it was a good thought, and none the worse for not really being true.

At that moment, Saal appeared on the jet's wrap-around screen next to Delfinous's seat. He looked oddly incongruous with Earth's horizon behind him. Gregori's face joined him moments later.

"Delf, we just got a message from the Dublin Shield," Saal announced. "It seems that lightning struck a third time, and Lewis McCrorry, along with his gal, Molly Byrne, have been drugged."

Delfinous sat up, his pounding temples forgotten for the moment.

"What? How?" Tabori asked.

"The Dublin Shield found 'em semi-catatonic in Trinity College library just minutes ago; details are sketchy. I'm talkin' to Shield synthients at the moment."

"Are they still alive?" Kennedy asked.

"Don't know," Saal answered. "Both humans are down, vitals are deterioratin'."

He cocked his head to one side. "Pursuit has started; unclear who they're goin' after. Some tourist and security cameras may have captured the event in real-time. Rapid deployment is happenin' now. Street, jumpcar, and network lockdown is expanding."

Delfinous looked at the others in exasperation.

What else can go wrong?

A section of the aircraft's screen cleared; the panoramic view of the Earth replaced by an annotated street map of Dublin. Saal continued his running commentary, the locations to which he referred showing up as highlighted spots.

"Here's Trinity College library; Lewis and Molly were found here."

Another window opened up, this time showing recorded images looking down onto what might have been a typical scene from any public library.

"These clips show the library net access area; view is from a security camera."

The library camera zoomed in on an elderly male as he walked in through the library entrance. He held what appeared to be a map under his arm, paused for a moment, and then walked leisurely up to two seated figures, both of whom stayed in their seats without acknowledging his arrival.

"What are we seeing?" Delfinous asked.

"Let me play the scene again, this time concentrating on the old guy, as well as Lewis and Molly."

The window split with enhanced images of the library door and the seated figures of Molly and Lewis, talking as they bent over a network screen. Once again, the elderly man walked in through the door, and paused. At that moment, Lewis and Molly jumped, slapping at their necks. Lewis attempted to stand, but fell back in his seat.

"This was when the drug was delivered," Saal filled in. "It was probably shot through a pneumatic gun, maybe with a micro-needle. The med techs found the point of entry, but haven't been able to locate any remnant objects; whatever was used must've dissolved.

"And Lewis was talkin' to his synthient, Nikola Tesla at the time."

They watched as the man walked over to Lewis and Molly, bent over each of them for a brief moment, and then retrieved something from the network table. The other people in the area seemed unaware that anything was amiss.

The old man bent over Lewis again, but suddenly straightened up and walked briskly under an arch and into the aisles of books. Obviously, something had alerted him.

Within moments, several dozen police and Shield officers had entered the library, guiding everyone to the exits. Lewis and Molly remained seated as two Shield personnel arrived at their location.

"This all happened about eleven minutes ago," Saal continued. "Both Lewis and Molly are receiving medical treatment enroute to St. Vincent's hospital. Synthient real-time monitoring of all cameras in the vicinity of the action was in effect, and a search for the suspect is continuing. With all jumpcar traffic halted or grounded within a kilometer radius of the college, he must be on foot."

"Any word on his identity?" Delfinous asked.

"Nope. There are other camera views, some with more detail than the ones we just watched, but so far there's no match with Shield databases; synthient searches are underway."

"Thanks, Saal," Tabori said. "Let us know if there are any new developments, especially regarding the condition of Mr. McCrorry and Ms. Byrne; have her files been accessed, yet? Do we know anything more about her?"

"We should have the permissions shortly. Her status as a victim has been sent to the European Personal Protection Guild, and should help move things along."

Delfinous sat back again, his headache swelling to noteworthy proportions. He dug into his pocket and swallowed another pain killer.

Kennedy turned his seat around to face his partners.

"Too right, that cinches the deal on Mr. McCrorry's place in this story, eh?" Kennedy volunteered. "He must have done somethin' dingy to get that old geezer spewin'. And the fact that he's already been had means he may've dropped in the Never Never as far as we're concerned, but somebody else wasn't quite as gaffed."

"You're probably right," Tabori consented, smiling absently at Kennedy's slang. "It does seem that someone must have known where Mr. McCrorry was, much sooner than us."

"I agree," Delfinous put it. "We can only hope that he and his friend will survive this ordeal, although I wouldn't expect it, given how this investigation has gone so far. Out of all the scenarios we reviewed, I think our hypothesis that Mr. McCrorry has been targeted by persons unknown is the most plausible. He must be mixed up in something, and his partners are not happy with him."

"Yeah," Kennedy added, "if only we knew what type of scheme it was, and who his pissy partners are."

"Well, it appears that we need Lewis for that bit of detail," Tabori said.

"There is one other thing, Tabori," Gregori said.

The officers all turned to look at the synthient.

"I have just reviewed the exchange between Mr. McCrorry and Nikola Tesla and found something that may be meaningful."

"Are the Comm synthients going over that?" Delfinous asked, through the pounding of his head.

"Yes, sir, but I thought I would also take a look.

"Although synthient Nikola Tesla suggested that he was not able to gain access to the thimble files, there is evidence that this may not be true. It appears that a viral carrier was dispatched into the library high speed pipeline. I notified the appropriate synthients in the Boston and Dublin Shield offices, and they are reevaluating the communications infrastructure. At this point, the destination for the data is not clear; there are several obvious locations strewn throughout the code, but these may be misdirections."

"Good work Gregori," Tabori said "Get the hounds on the chase."

"Let's have a look at it," Delfinous added.

A series of encoded graphs came up, each one showing a particular section of communication traffic between the nodes around Trinity Library. Highlighted in red was a group of bug-like structures grafted onto the smooth outer skin of the thick link that represented the discussion between Lewis and Nikola Tesla.

Delfinous continued to manipulate the display, checking for additional subtleties among the malformed code segments. "This is a rather brute force approach to corrupting the channel," he mused. "I'm a little surprised at Mr. McCrorry; his efforts with the T logs and deleted files were a bit more creative."

"Perhaps this was Nikola Tesla acting alone," Tabori offered. "They were probably in a hurry."

"Yeah, could be," Delfinous admitted.

"But what does this mean for Nikola Tesla?" Kennedy asked. "Is he really ready to have himself mummied?"

"That's a good question, Kennedy," Delfinous responded. "He must have been acting on instructions from Lewis. Perhaps they set this up back when Lewis was in the hospital; I don't think we ever got a complete explanation from Nikola Tesla about that discussion. Whether or not his misdirection warrants destruction remains to be seen."

The suborbital continued its descent as they rushed to meet whatever answers lay ahead.

28. Recovery Vector

Lewis awoke once again in a hospital bed, every muscle in his body clenched in painful cramps, doctors and nurses hovering over him. For an indefinite period of time, he slept in fitful episodes, waking periodically to confusing images and lingering smells. His memory of those events was fragmented like half-forgotten dreams whose traces clung in congealed, emotional lumps, weighing him down with feelings of impending doom.

It was a long while before he could sustain a train of thought for more than a few moments, and even longer before he started to recollect the events that led up to his current situation. The memories crept upon him stealthily, bits and pieces arriving out of order, as if he were reading random pages out of a book. The fact that he could remember anything at all was a small miracle according to his caregivers. Very few people who survived the kind of dose he'd been administered were left with more than the barest traces of their past. Even still, it felt like his mind had leaked; whole sections of his life remained a mystery, and those that he could recall always seemed ready to drain away again.

It was his mathematical gifts that provided the mortar to patch the holes. He discovered that working through math problems pulled his mind back together. Simple arithmetic fetched glimpses of his childhood, geometry and algebra dredged up his adolescence, and calculus, set theory, and tensors pulled his more recent past into the light. It was as if the analytical structures he imagined provided the scaffold for his memories: the building had taken exterior damage, but the framework was unbroken.

As he reconstructed theorems and his mind slowly recovered, his right hand began shaking. It had started as a small tremor in his fingers and now extended through his wrist. A vague tingling sensation accompanied the disorder, but he said nothing. The last thing he wanted was another reason to be kept longer in a hospital room.

But harder by far than any physical or mental discomfort was the terrible gnawing hole to which he awakened each morning, and longed for sleep to remove each night: Molly Byrne lay in a deep coma in another wing of the hospital, close by physical proximity, but forever distant by virtue of an injury that left her far beyond his ability to bridge. She had not fared as well as him.

It had taken him days of pleading with the hospital staff to determine Molly's state. The ever-present, unsympathetic Shield sentinels volunteered no information, nor did they respond to any questions. But the nurses were not quite so uncommunicative. They perhaps did not know all the details of his incarceration, or they were willing to give him the benefit of the doubt, but they sensed the turmoil within him, and eventually surrendered at least this small bit of information. Each day he continued to ask for an update, and each day the news was no better. None of the nurses said so, but he could tell by their voices that they did not have much hope.

As soon as the memories of his last moments with Molly had found their way to his conscious mind, a terrible guilt took up residence alongside. If only he had thought of another way, if only she hadn't been so insistent, if only his pursuers hadn't managed to uncover his alias. But they were vain thoughts, serving no purpose but to bind his anxiety ever tighter. He had thought his life at MIT was devoid of purpose, but compared to the suffocating remorse he now felt, it seemed positively light-hearted.

The days marched by inexorably, interminably.

There was not even the consolation of Nik to distract him; he was allowed no contact outside the room. There was not even a wallscreen to watch the news.

As he lay silently with these morose thoughts, pummeling himself for the thousandth time, the door opened and the guard stood at attention. A Shield officer, whom he remembered from that ancient time in the Boston hospital, walked into the room.

"Mr. McCrorry, your doctor has given us the ok to conduct an interview. My name is Delfinous Berry, as you may recall; from the Boston Shield."

"I remember," Lewis replied.

He didn't really care how this turned out. Although there were still uneven gaps in his memory, he remembered well enough the main points that had brought him to a hospital bed in Dublin.

"This conversation is being recorded," Delfinous continued, gesturing to his badge. "I'd like to start with the time between our last conversation, another hospital bed in Massachusetts, and the moment you boarded the Seed Ship to Europe: what did you do during that time?"

"I wandered the streets. I knew you would be looking for me, so I left my tag behind and just meandered from one homeless shelter to another."

"For two months?" Delfinous asked.

"Yeah, dreary as it sounds."

"And, knowing that we were looking for you, why didn't you contact us?"

"Look, someone was trying to kill me; in fact they kept on trying all the way to Dublin, as you might have noticed. I wasn't sure who was doing this, or even why for that matter. Staying low and out of sight seemed the best course of action. You guys were hot on me about blowing up the lab at MIT, which was actually the first time someone tried to kill me, so it didn't seem like a good idea to show up at a Shield office to say hello."

"Why do you think someone is trying to kill you?"

Lewis spoke quietly. "It has something to do with our experiment. I looked at the data while I was still in Cambridge, and it seemed pretty nondescript; nothing particularly useful. But when I had a chance to peek at it here at Trinity library, it was different. Someone must have changed the files at MIT before I got a chance to pull them up. Anyway, the data on my thimble was a lot different. There was some sort of code embedded in the hole.

"I don't know what kind of code it was," he added hastily, noticing the looks on the officer's face. "I have no idea how it even could be there. It doesn't matter now, the thimble is gone."

"And how did you get aboard the Seed Ship?" Delfinous asked.

"I walked into the recruitment office at a homeless shelter in New Jersey somewhere. I signed up, and ended up here in Dublin. It wasn't a major accomplishment actually; I didn't even know what a Seed Ship was at the time. Just seemed like a good way to get far away from MIT."

"How did you get through the security screen? The records indicate all passengers were checked, but we cannot locate your profilc."

"I have no idea," Lewis answered. "I called myself John Gumbel, but I'm not magician enough to change my DNA. Somehow they missed me."

"And yet your name was already on a Shield notification list. That does seem like quite a magic feat, Mr. McCrorry."

"I don't know what to say, Officer."

"Let me make a guess for you, then. We're well aware of your math and network skills; your professors and acquaintances at MIT don't have much good to say about your personality, but they all agree that you are capable of amazing things when it comes to manipulating the Sea. I think you already had this planned."

He paused for a moment. "Who are you working with, Lewis, and why are they now trying to kill you?"

Lewis stared at the officer for a moment. He shouldn't be surprised by this explanation, but he was disappointed regardless.

"I am not working with anyone, officer. At least not on something that would make anyone want to kill me. We were shooting low-power lasers at a hole source, that's all. It was boring research designed to keep grad students busy and professors publishing, nothing more."

Delfinous was not buying his story. "You met Molly Byrne on board the ship? Why were you with her in the library?"

Lewis started at the sound of her name; his neck tightened and his breathing became strained. It was inevitable that he would be asked about her, but even still, he was not prepared for his involuntary response. He clenched his teeth to keep his lips from trembling and tried hard to speak normally.

"She was a passenger, like me," he finally managed. "We met on the ship. I asked her to help me, and she did. She was like that." Short sentences made it easier to get the words out. "She didn't know anything about the thimble. I asked her to help. Look what good that did."

"Do you recognize this man?" Delfinous asked, changing the subject abruptly again. He pulled out a small softscreen from his pocket and displayed a grainy image of an elderly man, taken from a distance and at a poor angle. Only part of his face was visible.

"This is the library?" Lewis asked in his turn. "I don't know who he is, but I think I met him once before on the streets of Dublin. He and some of his pals tried to force me into a car. I guess I didn't think of him using drugs in the middle of Trinity library."

At the officer's insistence, Lewis described the encounter before he reached the university, and showed him his side. The blisters were gone, but an angry red blotch still showed prominently.

The questions continued for the better part of an hour. Several times a nurse strode into the room and checked the patches that adorned his shoulders and poked the machines that beeped beside his bed. He seemed content that all was well, but gave the Shield officer a stern glance just before leaving each time. Lewis was grateful for the consideration, even knowing that it was general concern for a patient, rather than a personal vote of confidence.

Lewis shifted uncomfortably in his bed. His muscles were stiff and sore, and he was tired of going over all the details of his life. Molly's name came up several times, and was no easier to bear with repetition. Each recollection evoked the same emotional response, and his mind wandered more and more to thoughts of what might have been.

"Mr. McCrorry, you said you found codes in your thimble data; how do you suppose they got there?"

"I don't know," Lewis sighed, wearily. He was too tired to care that the Shield might even think the idea was plausible.

"But you must have some idea."

"I don't. Molly called them secret messages; more like invisible messages: who's going to read them if you need a lab setup like we had at MIT?"

"I wonder."

The officer continued to peer intently at Lewis. "We found your name buried in the network keys, Mr. McCrorry. That was quite a trick. How did they get there?"

"I hate to keep repeating myself, officer, but I really don't know. I wanted those experimental files as much as you, let me tell you. The fact that they were deleted, and that my name was used to build the authorizations, was a spaffing shock."

"Yes, the deletion keys," Delfinous replied, noncommittally. "I'm actually talking about the T maintenance logs."

"The what?" Lewis wasn't even sure what the officer had said; the words didn't make sense to him.

"The logs, Mr. McCrorry, of the train that crashed with you on it. Why would your name show up there? What have you been planning?"

Lewis was stunned. It was bad enough that someone had used his name to delete a bunch of files; it was utter madness that it could show up in public transportation records.

"Officer," Lewis pleaded, "please believe me, I am not planning anything. Nor have I ever been. I have no idea how my name showed up in the logs. If I'm as clever as you say, why would I put my name on these things to begin with?"

"You tell me, Lewis. A little too much bragging, I'd say."

Delfinous stood. Apparently, the interview was ending, but before he left he spoke again. "Mr. McCrorry, you may wonder why you have not been allowed to contact anyone outside this room."

Lewis looked at him, quizzically.

"At this point, as far as anyone else knows, you and Ms. Byrne are in a coma. We have not yet communicated otherwise to anyone, including your families, or your synthient advocate, Nikola Tesla. Given the circumstances, this seemed the most prudent course of action.

"I suggest you think hard about the answers you didn't give today. We will find out what is going on, and any cooperation on your part may reduce the penalties you pay. It's up to you."

As the officer left, Lewis sighed. He fervently wished he knew those answers.

29. Elements of Hokkaido Art

At six o'clock, precisely, his wallscreen chimed, and a voice said, "Mr. Pettyman, your transport has arrived."

Syphus inspected himself in the mirror. He wore a dark business suit, subtly striped and crisply tailored. His shoes were polished leather, and a red tie matched the cherry blossom tag he wore on his lapel. A dark blue fedora crowned his head, with a small, brown-speckled feather stuck in the band. Gold cufflinks and tie chain completed the outfit.

This will do fine

He donned his overcoat and made his way to the hotel lobby.

Once there, he was met by a young, handsome Japanese man, who bowed politely, and motioned that Syphus should follow him. "I am your driver, Mr. Pettyman," he said in perfect English.

They walked down the steps to a waiting vehicle with separate seats for passengers and a human driver. The door opened as they neared, and a young woman stepped out of the back. She smiled at Syphus. "Welcome, Mr. Pettyman."

Syphus looked inside at the spacious sitting area. Another young woman smiled back at him, and he slid onto the seat beside her. "This is a pleasant surprise," he said.

The second young woman smiled, while the first joined him. IIotaru Ito was certainly giving him thc royal trcatmcnt.

It was not a short journey, winding deeper into the Hokkaido forest through the twilight. The two women made excellent companions, with charming mannerisms and engaging conversation. They appeared to have studied Omicron at length, and were able to intelligently discuss much of what was publicly known about the corporation.

As the ride eclipsed the half-hour mark, and they meandered through yet another moon-dappled valley, Syphus was struck by the inefficiency of their travel. It seemed uncharacteristically Japanese.

He was certainly enjoying the company, but there must be an easier way to get to where they were going.

"Why do we not take a jumpcar?" he asked. "This seems to be taking a rather long time, given that we aren't really going very far."

The woman on his right moved her hand from his forearm to his shoulder. "Jumpcars are fine in the city," she answered, "and among the lanes that connect them, but here in Dohoku they are not allowed. Most of the skies of Hokkaido are free of traffic, unlike the rest of Japan, which is very crowded; all the better to enjoy the beauty of nature, don't you think?"

Eventually they descended into a large, bowl-shaped basin. Towering cliffs glowed dimly in the diminishing evening light, silhouetted against the last embers of sunset. Syphus could see the twinkling lights of houses and vehicles below, all merging to a point on the far side of the valley. The forest had thinned in this region and looked as though it were well-tended; a pleasing, but not entirely natural arrangement.

Threading their way through a series of buildings on the valley floor, they climbed once more, passing through a large gate that marked the boundary of an expansive estate: the home of Hotaru Ito. Groves of cherry trees lined the drive, their branches hanging naked in the approaching winter.

They pulled under a covered entry alongside a large house. It was a unique structure, with elements of classic Japanese design merged with European influence. Syphus liked her taste.

His companions each took an arm and accompanied him to a broad porch, where a modest group of people had already gathered. At the topmost step stood the exquisitely beautiful Hotaru Ito.

He had seen pictures of her while doing his research, although none were very recent; she had sequestered herself quite effectively in this remote region of Japan's least inhabited island. The images did not do her justice.

"Ms. Ito, may I present Mr. Pettyman," the woman on his left said.

Hotaru smiled, made a small bow, and presented her hand. "Mr. Pettyman, how wonderful that you are able to join us tonight."

The accented English of her breathy voice was sweetness itself. He took her hand firmly in his own and returned her greeting. "Ms. Ito, the pleasure is mine. I look forward to the festivities, and a chance to speak with you on our mutual goals."

"It shall be as you say. Dinner will be served shortly, and the performance will begin thereafter. I hope you find it as enthralling as I could hope; it was designed by Ichiro Tawanaka-san, a most admired artist in residence here. We have all been looking forward to it in great anticipation."

Syphus smiled and bowed again. "Until later, then."

And he was off, swept along by his two insistent escorts into a wide space in the interior of the house.

Dinner was a spectacular affair, with several hundred guests seated comfortably on a wide lawn behind her home. A diaphanous, metallic awning fluttered softly overhead, magnifying the stars as they shone through its material. It was like watching a shimmering pool reflecting the evening sky, although the actual heavens had never appeared so lustrous. Infrared heaters sat atop ornately carved pillars draped in the ubiquitous riot of Hokkaido florals, keeping the area comfortably warm.

The food was abundant and delicious. Vegetable and fruit salads were served, along with a wide variety of seafood. All of it had been grown on the island, or caught in the nearby seas. Most of the conversation around him was in Japanese, and Syphus understood only a small portion of it. His two companions remained at his side, and continued to provide their enjoyable dialog.

When the meal had ended, the party lingered over an assortment of desserts and other pleasantries. Syphus allowed himself a cognac; he was confident in his purpose and was content to sit back and enjoy the moment.

Hotaru got up from her seat, and was now making her way among the tables, stopping at each to speak at length. Finally, she glided over to his table.

"Thank you all for coming," she said in Japanese, "and you, Mr. Pettyman," she added in English, turning to him with her lovely smile.

"I also speak Japanese, Ms. Ito," he said. "It is not good Japanese, but please do not feel it necessary to repeat everything you say just for me."

He had got the sentence structure wrong, but the verb tenses were more or less correct. Hotaru smiled disarmingly, and bowed daintily to acknowledge her guest.

She continued in Japanese, answering questions and evoking polite laughter with her charming comments. It was fascinating to watch her effect upon all those at hand. Men strove to attract her attention with their witticism while women moved closer to their companions, as if Hotaru might sweep them away on a whim.

A chime sounded, and the billowing canopy rippled upward into a smoothly concave hemisphere, reflecting the audience below. Soft, ethereal music ascended in volume, and glowing Japanese characters shaped themselves on the translucent surface. Syphus could not read them, but knew it meant that the performance was about to begin. The crowd got to its feet amid a soft susurration of voices, and

Hotaru lead the way toward the evening's entertainment.

Along wide gardens and stone-paved paths, past Hotaru's house and down sandstone steps, they descended into a small, tree-enshrouded amphitheatre. Towering cliff walls provided a backdrop to the natural beauty of the setting. An intricate scaffold of impossibly thin ceramic steel tubes filled the volume above the seats like a graceful spider web of glistening fibers. Enormous softscreens flowed and hung amid the configuration, draped over the support structure like fluttering leaves on a mysterious tree, their iridescent surfaces reflecting everything around them.

Once everyone had taken their seats, the performance began.

Syphus did not understand all that was said or sung, as the Japanese words came fast, in a highly ornamental style, but the pictures that moved across the screens were unmistakable. He watched the inevitable progress of winter across the island of Hokkaido, from the top of the volcanic Rishiri to the southern Tsugaru Strait.

The arrangement of softscreens throughout the theatre was remarkable; three dimensional scenes showed exquisitely detailed snowflakes that then pulled back to reveal snowstorms swirling around the mountains of the northern island. The music moved him as the views unfolded, and the singing was passionate, breaking his heart despite the fact that he could not understand the words.

The air on his face turned colder throughout the performance, although the rest of him remained as comfortable as though he were sitting in a warm room. Hoarfrost rimed the hair of the audience, and snow crystals swirled throughout the space.

The performance lasted almost an hour and was beautiful beyond words. His hostess had managed to create a transcendent environment, but in the end, the burning desire to remove the veil of secrecy surrounding his mysterious visitor consumed him. Hotaru Ito was the creator and sponsor of this wonderful arena; all the more reason for her to preserve it, and provide him with the answers he sought.

After the performance, the audience moved back to the dining area, which had now been set up with small bar tables, around which many people gathered, remarking on the show. Syphus joined a small group that chatted appreciatively about the evening.

It was nearing midnight when Hotaru slid gracefully to his side. At a nod, his two companions left, and she took his arm in her hands.

"Mr. Pettyman, I am so sorry for having taken this long to find my way back to you. I meant to join you sooner, but the evening has gone very well, and there were many admirers of Tanaka-san who wished to spend time with either myself or the artist. I do hope you understand." She looked up at him apologetically. He was sure she had used similar excuses on many occasions and that her guests would always be ready to forgive her anything.

"It was not a problem, Ms. Ito. I am in no hurry."

"Thank you so much. I am glad you are not offended. For your patience, I do have a special treat."

She led him through the crowd, answering friendly greetings along the way. They started down the path toward the amphitheatre, but then turned on a smaller way that descended many steps into a narrow grotto at the base of the cliff. A burbling trickle of water flowed in a deep groove in the rock face, ending in a small pool that then cascaded over a stony lip into the valley below. Ice clung to the edges of the pool, and lined the rock wall in front of them in tiny, fluted icicles.

They walked along the edge of the pool, and stepped onto a raised, circular platform directly at the base of the cliff. A railing ran most of the way around the structure, and as they stepped on, a curved rod slid soundlessly out of the rail, closing them in.

"Are you afraid of heights, Mr. Pettyman?"

"Not especially."

Hotaru whispered something that he did not catch, and at once the structure on which they stood began to rise along the cliff face.

Syphus started slightly, and Hotaru held his arm firmer, motioning with her free hand that he could hold the rail. "This is a special place of mine," she smiled. "It will be worth the small surprise."

The pedestal began slowly, but soon accelerated upward. The valley floor retreated below and all the grounds were revealed. Hotaru's house stood upon a small ridge, with wide gardens and well-ordered stands of trees surrounding it. The amphitheatre could be seen, and the village beyond twinkled in the middle distance. The far side of the valley was painted in vague grey and blue smudges in the moonlight, dark hill shapes shrouded in glowing mist. It was a simple, serene beauty.

This is quite a show. No wonder she manages to find donations; between her beauty and the inspiring mountains, it's probably no more difficult than asking a lawyer to write up billable hours.

Eventually the platform slowed and stopped, having reached the lip of a wide, deep ledge still some distance below the top of the cliff. A manicured lawn carpeted the area, surrounded by a semicircular hedge of frost-encrusted junipers, delicately shaped like over-size bonsai trees. A gravel path led away from the platform toward a covered, open-walled pavilion. Softscreen tapestries hung from the framework, echoing the earlier performance: soft winter scenes of gently blowing snow. Tiny lights were strewn all around, twinkling with distant star colors.

Hotaru lead him by the hand to a soft chair within the pavilion, while she herself sat across from him. In the dappled moonlight and sparkling, false starlight, she looked like an angel. "Syphus," she began, "may I call you Syphus? While we are alone here in this beautiful garden, it hardly seems appropriate to remain so stiffly formal."

"Syphus will be fine, Hotaru." He returned her smile.

"Thank you," she nodded. "As you have seen, this little artist's colony has made impressive strides over the years. We are very proud of the work we do, as well as the way in which we live in harmony with the land. Hokkaido has always been a place of restless beauty, endowed with a wonderful spirit. It has less grandeur than Ayers Rock or the dry Outback of the Australian desert perhaps, but its wildness remains still. While the rest of the Japanese islands continue the hectic pace our society craves, we exist in a timeless valley, untouched by progress."

"You have been to Australia, then?"

"Yes, on several occasions. I have vacationed there, and have passed through Sydney and Perth many times on business. I do not generally go far from my estate now, but I have not always been so bucolic.

"As you might imagine, to maintain this idyllic location, this Shangri-La, and to inspire the artists who take residence here without worry over the mundane details of life, we are always looking for support. Our generous patrons are part of an extended family that encompasses life here in the mountains, and allows them to bring a part of this experience home with them, wherever that may be.

"I would be so grateful for even the smallest contribution you could make, whether a personal gift, or part of a larger corporate sponsorship; I am sure a world-renowned company like Omicron would see a wonderful public relations benefit from its association with the arts."

She reached across the space between them and took his hand while she spoke, looking into his eyes; it might even have been real sincerity in her voice. She fluttered her eyelids and her lips hinted at secrets they might share, if only he found a reason to accept her offer.

He moved from mild annoyance to a kind of disgust; that she could fawn in such a way filled him with loathing. He was certain she had extracted untold riches from countless men in just this fashion.

"Hotaru, I'm afraid I have some questions before you go on." He looked down toward the cherry blossom tag on his lapel, and spoke the words that would activate the scrambler, "cataract mist."

At once Hotaru pulled her hand back. Her face, so full of subdued passion a moment ago, hardened. "Mr. Pettyman," she said with mild reproach, "there is no need for that type of device here."

He was momentarily taken aback; he hadn't expected her to be aware of his intrusion, at least not so quickly. He started to speak, and only then noticed that someone stood at the entrance to the pavilion. The man held the unmistakable attitude of a bodyguard, and looked ready to exercise his skills. There were no weapons in his hands, but Syphus had no doubt that another questionable action on his part would lead to serious consequences.

He took a deep breath to slow his heart and regain his composure. "Ms. Ito, I share your distaste for these methods, but I believe that you would not wish this conversation to be recorded or overheard, even among your staff, however trusted."

She looked at him curiously. For a few heartbeats she did not move, nor make any sound, and he wondered which way this would go. Finally, she made a small motion with her hand and the man backed away, disappearing quietly into the night. It occurred to Syphus that he was probably not the only guardian nearby.

"Please proceed," Hotaru insisted, crossing her arms and sitting back in her chair.

"I do not think," he began without preamble, "that your visits to Australia were all for holiday or business, at least not for the synthient boutique, Suma-Tobiru. In fact, you have traveled extensively over Southeast Asia on much different business, am I right?"

He did not expect a response and did not get one; she continued to regard him dispassionately. He reached into his suit pocket and pulled out a folded piece of electronic paper, sealed with a DNA lock.

"Transfer ownership," he said, as he placed his thumb on the input pad. He looked at Hotaru and handed the sheaf to her. "This will explain."

She took the item from his hand, and placed her thumb on the pad in turn. "Hotaru Ito, taking ownership." The molecular seal around the edge of the note separated and she folded it open.

"This means what to me, Mr. Pettyman?"

"Please don't insult me, Hotaru. We are certainly past the point of pleasantries, now. This is a ship's manifest, specifically the *Princess of Jakarta*, which made many trips between Japan and New Zealand. On at least one of those occasions you were on board, traveling with what would appear to have been illegal synth constructs."

Her face revealed no emotion. "I may have been on board the ship; what of it? I often went by ship to visit customers. Surely you are not saying that the synthient crèches I serviced were involved in the illegal copying and distribution of their own Daishi?"

"No, of course not, but a firm called Dunsell Entertainment in Port Moresby was. I have it on good authority that they provide discreet escort services throughout the South Pacific. But that is actually only peripheral to the major point that concerns me, and by association, you.

"Perhaps you are not aware that Captain Pramana Sirigar kept a personal and very detailed inventory of his shipments? Well, only a very small portion of his cargo as it turns out; only items that he considered quite important."

He watched her face carefully. She remained impassive, but there was the barest quiver of jaw muscles.

Excellent, she didn't know of the good captain's secret.

Still she said nothing.

"I will spell it out for you, then." Syphus was enjoying the cat and mouse game.

"During your time at Suma-Tobiru, on one occasion you were servicing a synthient crèche in Tokyo, which was attacked by a group called the Samurai Weekend. The incident ended with no appreciable harm done, but there was a length of time during which the synthients housed in the site were cut off from the rest of the Sea. It was soon after that incident that you made one of your trips to New Zealand; the captain's personal cargo log in your hands is from that time.

"You will note that one of the items is highlighted, and called simply 'miscellaneous', with a second entry labeled 'HI'. This is for Hotaru Ito, of course, and the miscellaneous cargo was several synthient constructs lifted from the crèche during its isolation."

He paused for effect.

"This is interesting speculation, Mr. Pettyman, but really I am quite unimpressed. I am also rather busy, and of course, disappointed that you have not turned out to be the patron of the arts that you claimed to be."

"It is not speculation, I assure you. In addition to this list, which you will note has authentication codes within it, there also happens to be a DNA tracer embedded in your initials. As you can see, they have turned green, an indication that there is a match with the swipe you used to open the note just a few moments ago.

"The last piece of evidence, which I regret I cannot produce at this moment, is an actual copy of the synthient constructs you carried with you on the ship. The captain was unclear how he managed to make the copies, but that was not terribly unexpected: he has spent a number of years in prison for drug and stolen antiquities trafficking, after all. It seems he was not very discriminating when it came to this type of cargo; for the right price, he was willing to load just about anything. And also for the right price, he proved to be willing to part with them as well.

"If you doubt the story, or my having the synthient constructs as I say, please note the imprint on the letter in your hand; it contains a crèche transcription code that was lifted from one of the synthient minds that were compromised. Perhaps you will not remember the exact codes, but it will be a simple matter for you to check them out at your convenience."

He smiled at her, enjoying the control he now owned. "Even if what I have stated is not the whole story, it is close enough that the missing pieces are mere details. Surely this is not the type of publicity you desire for your establishment. If it were made public, of course."

Hotaru's face had lost its serene tranquility. Her eyes glared at him with an intensity he would have found daunting a number of years ago. Now he felt elation; he was used to getting what he wanted, and he could see that Hotaru would comply with his request.

"What is it you want, Mr. Pettyman?"

"I can see you are a reasonable person, Hotaru. I do not want money, if that is what you are thinking. In fact, if we can conclude this business satisfactorily, I still mean to offer you a large endowment; I did make the trip after all, and it might seem odd to your friends if I did not come up with something.

"What I want is information."

He paused and leaned forward, matching the intensity in her eyes. "I want to know who arranged the synthient theft while you were servicing the crèche in Tokyo."

She snorted. "And you think I will give you that information? Even if I have it?"

"I believe you will, Hotaru. I do not wish to expose your past, but I will turn over everything I have to the Shield if I have to. Everything. Your DNA figures prominently."

She continued to stare at him, trying to bore holes through his head. He imagined her mind racing to decide a course of action. "I will give you a name, Mr. Pettyman; one name: Occultelius Sept."

"It sounds like a synthient name."

"This you will need to find out for yourself. Now, you have your information. I will take your money. You may go."

He did not like the air of dismissal in her reply. "If I find that your information has proven incorrect, or not useful, Hotaru, I assure you I will be in touch. I do not play games very well."

"Nor I, Mr. Pettyman; the name I gave is what you seek. Whether it will prove useful to you or not, I neither know nor care."

He got up and began to walk down the path toward the waiting lift. The air had turned colder still, and the stars above shone down brightly through the crystalline night. As he stepped out of the pavilion, he turned.

"The money will be in your account tomorrow. For your sake, and the artists whom you support, I hope the name you have given will be worth the payment."

"You are a fool, Mr. Pettyman," she said. But it was mostly to herself.

She watched him turn down the path, climb into the lift, and descend from sight. The jamming device he used switched off as soon as he was gone and the implant in her ear came back to life, the familiar wind chime sounds playing softly in the background of her mind, calming her angry heart.

Her bodyguards remained at their posts, ready to act upon her call, but otherwise invisible.

She had thought all contact with her past had been erased, and that her life in Hokkaido was untainted by the work that had made it possible. She would have greatly preferred never to utter that name again.

But somehow Mr. Pettyman had dredged up a record of the events in Tokyo of which she, and she was sure, her employers, were unaware. She thought back to the trip aboard the *Princess of Jakarta*, and the lewd, drunken captain against whom she'd had to lock her cabin door. It was inconceivable that he had more intelligence than a rodent, but she remembered the look of hatred on his face as she had slammed the door shut on him. The vault in which the constructs had been stored should have been impenetrable, at least as far as someone like the captain was concerned. Obviously she had overestimated her security and underestimated the ingenuity of the captain.

The situation left her little choice, but she did not relish what needed to be done. Perhaps Mr. Pettyman would be content with the information he had received and leave her alone. But perhaps not. In fact, the latter was much more likely, and to leave him with such a large club to hold over her head was unacceptable.

"Izuki-san," she spoke to her bracelet tag.

"Yes, Mistress," her house synthient replied.

"Mr. Pettyman will be contacting you soon to deposit a sum of money. Please have it placed into our regular account."

"Very good."

"And please route a message to our acquaintances at Dunsell.

Some of their more discreet services have reached an unintended audience. I believe they will want to know."

"Yes, Mistress."

. . . . .

Izuki stood on the balcony of his small house, set in a simulation of the rugged slopes of Sukura-jima volcano. Great billowing clouds of brown ash ascended into the false blue sky and rained down around him like dirty snow. His little dwelling remained unaffected, a shielded bubble around which the cinders slid to the ground below.

He looked through the sooty distance over the blue sea that bordered the volcanic peak, toward what should have been the bustling port of Kagoshima. But the simulation did not extend that far; the scientists who maintained this site were not interested in the city, and did not bother to introduce additional complexity. Izuki thought it rather disappointing. The isolation of the mountain simulation served its purposes on most occasions, but there were times when it would be nice to have a view into such an important city, even if it were only a replica.

His mistress had been out of communication for quite a while, which he knew had something to do with the visitor from Australia. He had sent out word to the human caretakers of the estate in Hokkaido, and they had responded. Although at the time he was uncertain why she had allowed the disruption to continue, the disclosure that Mr. Pettyman had somehow linked her back to the incident in Tokyo served as explanation enough.

She had carefully managed her life to distance herself from those events; Izuki himself had been instrumental in dissolving all the many-fingered network trails he could find. The fact that he had missed such a huge signpost as a copy of the synthient constructs caused him enormous shame; he had proven unworthy to serve her, but now must make up for the oversight as best he could.

Despite his failure on behalf of his human companion, there was a more dominant imperative that he must follow. She had instructed him to contact the ones who had arranged for the construct downloads, but there was another who must be notified first. That one would not receive the news well.

And to Izuki, the primary synthient among all those who had left the crèche since the attack fell the task of conveying that bad news; the brown clouds and ash of the simulation echoed his disappointment.

. . . . .

30. The Missing Link

Delfinous stood in front of the wallscreen in his temporary office. The Dublin Shield had been very gracious in providing him a place to work, but it was not his Boston office. He was surprised to find how much he missed being able to stand in front of the windows and look out over the city, or across the river; it turned out that he had done quite a lot of thinking in that manner, and his new first-floor digs did not provide him with those wide vistas. In fact, there were no windows at all in the little cramped room.

It didn't help that Tabori had returned to Boston. He longed to spend more time with her, but knew he needed to be patient. With Lewis still recovering in the hospital, and Molly lingering in a coma, Jim Stabler wanted someone on site. With his Neural Sea expertise, Delfinous was the logical choice. It made no difference where he did his research; both Tabori and Kennedy were needed in Boston.

It had been two weeks since Delfinous's first interview with Lewis. He had gone back each day to ask more questions and repeat those for which the answers were incomplete. Delfinous was gradually pulling more of Lewis's story together, from the time of the MIT explosion, to the present. He had gone over the details time and again, looking for minor inconsistencies that might lead to new investigatory paths, but so far, Lewis had not been careless in his descriptions, and any lies, if they existed, were not obvious.

So it was that over the last week Delfinous was reluctantly opening another avenue based upon the legitimacy of Lewis's tale. If the young man were telling the truth, and there was some secret locked in the depths of the hole source that he and his fellow graduate students had uncovered, what did that imply?

But if he were lying, and was covering up some long-planned event, then why spend the time in a hospital bed picking apart the deletion keys of his experimental files, if he had authorized them in the first place? And if he hadn't authorized the deletion, then who had?

The morass kept getting weedier all the time.

He sat down at his desk and asked Saal to bring up the timeline on which the team had been working. None of the wide gaps between the explosion and today's date remained, having been filled in with information Delfinous had extracted during lengthy interviews with Lewis. This week he had added parallel tracks, joined to the original graph at the intersections of all the unexplained events: the lack of obvious suspects from the laboratory building occupant list, the train wreck, the hospital deletion key parsing, the neglected Seed Ship security check, the hit at Trinity Library.

Delfinous stared at the screen for a long while, but without some other, independent lead, there was no way to fill in any detail on the new paths. As he traced the lines back and forth, he realized that one had been left off: the T service record tampering from three years prior.

"Saal, add the T maintenance log date on the chart, will you?"

"Sure thing."

The timeline now contained a break in continuity. The distance between this first network problem and the rest of the events was too long to fit in one stream across the wall.

"What do we have on the time between the T logs and the explosion? Have Kennedy or Tabori turned anything up?"

"Well, they've grilled a few more of Lewis's professors, and dug into his student records, but there's really nothin' much in there, boss."

A few new dots appeared on a sub-view of the timeline gap.

"These're arguments with Lewis's thesis profs, as near as we can make 'em out. No one was recordin' at the time, so they're mostly guesswork. At any rate, there's a bunch of 'em.

"I don't know, boss, we already know he was a prickly kid; on that we have universal agreement. There's nothin' in any of the reports to show he was about to come unhinged."

Delfinous brought up the detailed reports. As Saal had described, there was nothing particularly significant about any of them. The interviews that Tabori and Kennedy had conducted all indicated that Lewis was an irritable, annoying student, and the clashes with his professors, although frequent, were not violent; in not a single one did a professor indicate that Lewis made a threat of any kind. In fact, the tone that all of them had taken was that Lewis was nothing but a childish, albeit brilliant student.

Delfinous shook his head and started scanning the timeline again. He had seen it a thousand times, and realized that familiarity had lulled him into a complacent view of the whole, skipping over many of the details. He forced himself to slow down, examining each node with all its attendant records in depth. It may take him the rest of the day and tomorrow to get through it all, but his next visit with Lewis was not until the afternoon, and he had time to kill.

To be thorough, he started back with the T records and worked forward. There were images, documents, recorded interviews, and other written and spoken notes to be reviewed. The morning wore on slowly, punctuated by brief conversations with Saal to clarify various points, or obtain additional information. It was tedious police work, some of which could probably have been done more efficiently by Shield subsentients, in fact it certainly had already been done that way; somehow it felt better that he was doing it himself.

In a couple of hours, he had reached the MIT explosion, the original start of the timeline. Although he knew these reports backward and forward, he brought them up once again, hoping to find some detail that he had missed previously, jogged into importance by his review of all the prior information.

As he read through the forensic reports and remembered his own involvement on that Boston morning, there was a faint tickling in his mind, like the memory of a name that cannot quite be grasped. He stopped and sat back for a moment, trying to bring the thought to the fore.

What had brought it out? Something he had just read?

He looked over the report in front of him. It described a summary of expert opinion on hole source stability that the team had requested early on in the investigation. It talked about experiments that had been performed when hole sources were first being developed.

Experiments on hole sources. What did that signify? There was a connection with something Lewis had said in an interview over the past few weeks.

He almost had it. It was frustrating that he couldn't bring it to mind more clearly. What had Lewis said?

"Saal, review all the interviews that I conducted with Lewis here in Dublin. Is there anything in there where he says something about experiments?"

"Yeah, he mentions it a couple of times, do you want 'em played?"

"Yes."

He listened as Lewis's voice spoke out of the screen.

It has something to do with our experiment, he said.

"Stop." He knew this was what he wanted, but still could not make the pieces fall into place. "What was the context for that comment, Saal?"

His own voice sounded: *Why do you think someone is trying to kill you?*

He thought about it for a moment.

Someone was trying to kill him, and Lewis believed it had something to do with the experiment. Now why would that fact have caused such a reaction now? I've known that for weeks.

But then he looked at the timeline again. He had been reading about the explosion, poring over the documents that he'd seen uncountable times before. And before that, a report from Professor Leonard describing Lewis's poor performance on a new assignment he'd just been given.

With a start, he realized the experiment was not even on the timeline. He cursed to himself softly.

How could we have overlooked such an important event?

They had concentrated so hard on the explosion itself as the main incident that they had completely neglected anything that had occurred prior. The only exceptions were the T maintenance logs and the arguments with the professors, but those entries had happened so far in the past that no one had thought to ask if anything else should be added to the list.

"Saal, when did the actual hole source experiment that Lewis and his team were working on, take place?"

"Ah, let's see."

There was a pause. "Well, we don't have that on the timeline, boss. Looks like we're gonna hafta check with MIT. I don't have any information on that available. You want me to find out?"

"No, hold on a minute, Saal."

Delfinous thought about the situation. They had spent no time at all investigating the experiment, and he needed time to think through how to do it. If this was important, then the unknown persons responsible for the attacks on Lewis would be sensitive to anyone asking about it. He did not want to arouse suspicion.

How do we do this?

"Saal, don't mention this to anyone, yet; not even anyone on the investigation. I want to handle this carefully."

"A-ok, boss."

If he went through the regular channels, he would need to make a request to the MIT Board of Regents through the Boston Shield office, so that was certainly out of the question. He could always ask Lewis, but of course that implied that he could trust the youth; he was still not ready to do that, yet.

The thought of Lewis brought up another name: Nikola Tesla. The synthient seemed to know as much about Lewis's life as anyone. It seemed very likely that he would know when the experiment took place and perhaps more of the detail as well. Delfinous did not need permission from the Board to ask questions of Nikola.

But that brought up the question of what to ask, and what type of information would be important. Perhaps something about the experimental setup would prove valuable. He was not yet sure how to construct the inquiry; he'd have to fill in the blanks as he went.

And what of the implications; how did the experiment tie things together? He thought about Lewis's claim of embedded codes. Had he stumbled upon something that someone wanted to remain secret? If that were truly the case, it seemed unlikely that Lewis and his team had picked up the only coded hole source, or even one of a small number. That meant there were many hole sources with the same characteristics out in the world. What were the codes for? Could they be used to cause the sources to explode? Was that what happened at MIT, despite the assurances of the experts to the contrary?

Delfinous pieced together a scenario. The MIT students purchased and modified a standard hole source, changing its housing to allow some kind of probing of its interior. Unknown to them, this particular mode of operation pried out some kind of embedded code that existed on many, or perhaps every, hole source. Somehow this information found its way to whoever was embedding the codes in the first place, and precipitated the explosion in the lab, and the multiple attempts on Lewis's life.

It was the first time Delfinous had been able to devise a story that made any kind of sense. It explained a number of the perplexing aspects of the case, including the consistency of Lewis's account; if he truly had stumbled unknowingly upon the codes, the subsequent events in his life would be as mysterious to him as they were to the Shield.

But even as all these facts clicked into place, he knew he had no explanation for the T maintenance logs of three years ago. How could that have been set up so far in advance, if the exposure of the codes had been an accident in the first place?

As he thought about this paradox, he stared at the other unlabeled parallel lines in his new timeline. What if he linked them all together? What common aspects did they contain? A hidden set of codes within the hole source served as a link between the explosion in the lab and the attempts on Lewis's life, but what of the other incidents?

The T maintenance logs were connected to the deletion of the experimental files through the convoluted authorization keys, underlain by Lewis's name, but no obvious link to the missed detection of Lewis's DNA when he applied to service aboard the Seed Ship. All three involved exploitation of the network in sophisticated ways. What if the person responsible for the hole source codes was a network adept? If it were possible to subvert the background check at a major international shipping corporation, could it be possible to change the T logs after the fact?

Delfinous paused in his thoughts. A chill spread from his neck across his body. All his life he had never given security within the Sea a second thought. It was a tacit assumption that everyone took for granted and created the basic infrastructure that made possible all the advances of civilization, from transportation and commerce, to communication and health care. If the type of network manipulation he envisioned were possible, the invincibility of that security would be called into question.

As he sat with these worrisome thoughts twisting through his head, Saal spoke. "Boss, Tabori wants to talk to you. Says it's urgent. She's on a secure Shield line."

"Put her through, Saal."

Tabori was standing in her office. Despite the early hour in Boston, Jim Stabler was visible on another screen and Gregori flashed his perfect smile.

"Delf, we've made a major breakthrough. The files that we thought had been deleted? Well, we've found archived copies. Apparently, Lewis had Nikola Tesla sent them through a set of subsentient gateways during their conversation at Trinity Library. That's what the viruses were all about; the ones that Gregori found. We've got the synth team going over them now.

"And Delf, it doesn't look like there are any codes in them; at least from what we've found so far."

"No codes. Hmm." He replied. "How were the files discovered?"

"It turns out that one of the MIT synthients involved in their experiment was cleaning up his local area, and found a set of threads he couldn't account for. I don't know the details, Delf, this is a bit out of my territory, but anyway, he alerted the Shield about them, and Gregori followed the trail back to the library.

"Physically, they were stored on a small memory node in South America, which created a bit of an issue in getting permissions. But that's all taken care of now."

She was smiling broadly and Delfinous felt a rush of affection.

Jim joined the conversation; he too was grinning.

"It's a treasure trove, Delf. Looks like Mr. McCrorry has been dumping stuff to that node for a long time. We've only just started going through it and already we've found documents that point to a Detonite sale. We've moved copies to your workspace. Given what we've seen so far, I'm betting it's not going to be much work for you to trace the records to their origin.

"Give us a few days and it will be time to charge McCrorry and bring him home."

Delfinous wished he could share their happiness, but Jim and

Tabori were five thousand kilometers away, and he was not yet convinced. He might still be wrong, and his own recent revelations no more than wishful thinking, but his conclusions had the weight of correctness about them. The sudden appearance of a data stash that provided such a clean wrap-up seemed too coincidental.

He did not want to deflate their mood, and he was still undecided on how much of his thought he should reveal over the network, so he said nothing of his suspicions. "Great work," he replied, smiling back at Tabori. "I'll look at the data today. Wish I could be back there to celebrate with you."

"Right, celebrate with both of us, eh?" Jim asked knowingly. "I'll sign off now. We've been up most of the night, and I'm sure you two have some catching up to do."

"How are you doing, Delf? Dublin ok?" Tabori asked when they were alone.

"Yeah, it's ok."

They spoke for a few minutes about the small, everyday events within their lives; a way to stay connected despite the distance. It was a pleasant exchange, and picked up his spirits.

"Well, it's been a long night," she said, finally, "and I'm tired. I'm glad everything is ok where you are. I miss you, Delf."

"I miss you too, Tabori. I hope I can work out the logistics for getting Lewis back to Boston soon. Dublin is fine, and there's plenty to do, but I am looking forward to coming home."

"Bye," she said, placing her fingertips on the screen in front of him. He mirrored her hand and then her smiling image was gone.

He left his fingers on the screen for quite a while, lost in thought. He realized he was falling in love with her, which sharpened the sting of the miles between them. Finally he lowered his hand and leaned back in his chair.

Something just doesn't feel right. Those viral implants were tacked onto Lewis's conversation with Nikola Tesla like signposts. And what a miracle they pointed back to just what we were looking for.

Coincidence seemed too poor a word to describe finding the answer to all their questions in South America.

31. Center of Attention

The hydrojet waited in the shade of a spacious hanger, its sleek shape poised for the return trip to Sydney. As President and General Manager of manufacturing operations, Syphus was given wide latitude in how he chose to travel. He still loved the private plane, especially now that it was well-stocked with cigars, espresso, and whisky, chosen at his direction. His requisitions for the company aircraft now received a much different reception than his first.

The door opened, letting down a short stair to the tarmac.

Managers from the Wilcannia plant stood at the bottom of the steps, while Territorial and city officials waited on a small stage nearby. A crowd of media people recorded the event.

Syphus smiled for the hovering cameras as he ascended the platform, shaking hands with each of the notables, and reveling in his new-found fame as founder of a revolutionary generation of power technology. The softscreen banners behind him touted the benefits of the new hole sources, while he gave a short speech, highlighting the economic boon to New South Wales and the important role of Wilcannia.

He fielded questions for the better part of a half-hour, eventually having to cut them short. “Thank you for your interest in Omicron, but I’m afraid there is still a lot of work ahead of us. Please contact our synthients for any additional questions you may have.”

He left the stage to the general applause of the audience.

The ride from the airstrip to the main buildings down the tree-lined parkway was immensely pleasant, despite the warming weather now that spring was passing into the hot Outback summer. A light breakfast was waiting for them when they arrived at the office area a few minutes later. Syphus spent the time chatting with other senior members of the staff; these were the moments that were indispensable for taking the pulse of the employees, unhindered by expectations inherent in formal presentations.

His observations told him things truly were going well. Everyone was very excited about the success of the new hole sources, and the financial windfall that came as a direct result. He couldn't have planned this any better if he'd tried.

Several of the corporate lawyers had been annoyed at having been bypassed in the negotiation process, but now that Syphus had a seat at the same table, and the profits were tumbling in like a lottery jackpot, there were no long-term negative implications. The initial reaction to his signature on the contract had been predictably troublesome, and in the first weeks of the development process he had driven Kunst mercilessly. Syphus had received daily messages from his manager and higher, checking on progress, and he knew the pressure would continue building until he could show results.

In addition to the lawyers' consternation, there were several managers who saw his ascension as a threat to their own careers. These were men like him, for whom power was a drug, and who did not take well to being passed-over by an upstart with fewer years in the company and a lucky break. But Syphus did not worry overmuch about them; another request to Dr. Shue had unveiled some rather interesting facts. He was sure, if the time came, they could be persuaded to see things his way.

At the moment, things were going very well indeed, and he savored the feeling. There were still missing pieces, but the messages his investigators were leaving him made him confident he was close to having the answers to Hotaru's information and the faces behind M'Bota. With profits, publicity, and fame, there was no stopping the juggernaut that was Syphus Pettyman.

The rest of the morning passed in meetings with section managers and their staffs. He was brought up to speed on manufacturing volumes, budget goals, personnel shortfalls, and a dozen other metrics that described the operation of the site. The only reports in which he had any real interest were the descriptions of progress made on the second manufacturing line. The completion of the structure would more than triple capacity, and help meet the strong demand for their new products.

As he watched the clips that described the effort and listened to the construction managers, he thought about the source of the architectural plans. His mysterious visitor had provided the basic schematics, which had then been fleshed out with the infrastructure and building code requirements by a team at the Wilcannia facility. There were a number of innovations that the scientists and engineers at Omicron had pored over in unabashed excitement, and now referred to with pride. Like Kunst, they had marveled at the elegance and simplicity of the new processes, and were eager to start them up on an equipment set optimized for that purpose.

After a catered lunch, Syphus met with Dolph Kunstler. The two of them walked through the office area, now almost completely occupied, to the beam line and its supporting mechanical and electrical buildings. The high energy ring was going through its first startup procedures, and a small cadre of engineers and synthients were in the process of monitoring every aspect of the system. Syphus did not remember the details of the elaborate manufacturing procedures, but could tell by the looks he received that there were no major problems arising.

The last stop on the tour was a walk through the new research labs. Dolph was particularly proud of these facilities, having been given free rein to outfit them. Technicians were still installing equipment, but most of the rooms were already functioning. View screens lined the walls and small alcoves housed desks.

"The whole set of labs is arranged by functional group," Dolph was saying, the enthusiasm unmistakable in his voice. "High energy studies can be conducted here in this lab, while the molecular materials equipment is housed down the beam line. We've got analysis equipment a little ways further along, and hole source application testing at the end. It's a great facility, Syph, with everything we need right here to conduct first class research."

"That's great, Kunst. So when can we expect our next breakthroughs?"

Dolph laughed. "Well, we've still got a long way to go to bring our knowledge up to date with these new sources we're producing. But with these facilities and all this new synthient power we're bringing to bear on the problem, it shouldn't be too long before we've got a handle on things."

"You're bringing on additional synthients, then?"

"Well, yes, just according to the plans; it's more minds than I think we need, but we'll put them to good use, I'm sure. Here, let me show you the crèche."

"You've got them housed here? Isn't that a bit unusual?"

Dolph lead Syphus out of the lab and down a windowed corridor that ran alongside the labs. There was activity in each of them: workers completing equipment installation, scientists moving their personal belongings from the old labs to the new facilities, and synthient faces showing on some of the wallscreens. It was the kind of organized chaos that marked the pace of progress.

"I suppose it is a little unusual," Dolph replied. "We don't have resident synthients in any of our other facilities, and the support needs are a bit specialized, but it shouldn't be an issue. Haven't you and the management team reviewed all this? They started arriving a couple of weeks ago, so I assumed you were up to speed."

"I guess not." Syphus didn't remember any talk of a synthient crèche on site. It was possible it had just sunk below the radar and he had forgotten about it, but that didn't seem likely.

Midway down the hallway there was a closed door with a biomarker lock. Dolph placed his hand on the panel and spoke his name. The door unlatched and swung open to reveal a stairway. They descended a large number of steps to another security door like the first. And as before, Dolph opened it.

Inside, a wide room was fitted with many dozen synthient niches. Most of them were empty, but a few were occupied. Softscreens hung from temporary pegs.

"This is a state-of-the-art crèche," Dolph put in. "We've got a synthient doctor to watch over them. Occo, this is Syphus Pettyman, director of the facility."

A youthful synthient face appeared on the wallscreen at the far end of the room. "Greetings, Mr. Pettyman, I have heard much about you."

Out of the corner of his eye Syphus saw a flickering of images circle the screens throughout the crèche, ghostly silhouettes that were gone before he was sure if he really saw them.

"Yes, well, uh, nice to meet you, as well. What did you say your name was?" Dolph didn't seem to have noticed the unusual display.

"Occultelius Sept, but you can call me 'Occo', everyone else does."

Syphus felt suddenly cold. Hotaru Ito's name was no longer a mystery. "Occo! Yes, well, ah, I'm glad to know you. This is my first experience with managing a synthient crèche. Please, uh, make sure you let us know if there's anything amiss."

"I will do so; thank you for your consideration. Now, if you'll excuse me, the engineers are in the middle of calibrating several sections of the solar collection arrays, and I would like to provide assistance."

"Certainly."

The synthient's face disappeared from the screen, and Syphus accompanied Dolph back up the stairs to the laboratory wing. Along the way he considered the situation. It was not possible that the appearance of Occultelius Sept was mere coincidence, which meant that Hotaru Ito's information was relevant. What significance to make of it, Syphus was not sure. The fact that synthients were going to be housed here gave him cause for concern. With the type of network control his mysterious visitor had demonstrated, and the cryptic warning of its impossibility by Dr. Shue, it seemed plausible his partners hoped to gain some type of leverage over the operation of the Wilcannia plant.

These uneasy thoughts accompanied him for the rest of the afternoon and into the evening. He only half listened to the remaining discussions, distracted by the taint of his successes.

The sun had long since set when he finally boarded the hydrojet for the return to Sydney. He took his seat and lit a cigar while the aircraft accelerated for takeoff. The desert slid by beneath, the moonlit landscape in silver and grey, familiar and yet strange.

He asked for music and took a long pull on his cigar, while he stared out the window. His course of action, so clear when he had arrived earlier in the day, now seemed clouded.

Suddenly, the plane angled steeply upward, throwing him back into his seat painfully. He clutched at the armrests and lost his cigar, which went skittering down toward the back of the cabin, bouncing sparks along the way. He could barely move against the acceleration.

The plane swung at a strange angle, and he tumbled out of his seat, bouncing on the transparent ceiling as the aircraft completed a slow barrel roll. As he slid down the spine of the cabin, he stared in panic at the Outback below him.

In a few heartbeats the plane had righted, and he found himself back on the floor, sandwiched between one of the chairs and the curving wall. Before he could pull himself upright and begin to grasp what had happened, a familiar rumbling voice ground against him, loud enough that his chest reverberated with the tones.

"Mr. Pettyman," the voice growled, "my employers have become aware of the questions you have been asking. This course of action is not advisable."

Syphus stood up shakily, trying his best to regain his composure. "I don't..." he began, but was cut off.

"You will remain silent!" the voice thundered. The screen vibrated, distorting the outside view, and he felt the words like a blow.

"The working relationship has been defined: you have signed it yourself. You will neither ask more questions about my employers, nor interfere with the construction in Wilcannia. Failure to comply will bring consequences: this aircraft is only one of innumerable locations where you are vulnerable."

And with that, the plane braked suddenly and pitched forward. Syphus fell straight down the length of the cabin, slamming hard into the front bulkhead. His cigar landed beside his face, showering him with painful sparks. He watched in horror as the ground raced up at alarming speed. The aircraft pulled up, crushing him into the corner where the bulkhead and floor met. The wind had been knocked out of him from the fall, and now the plane creaked under the tremendous acceleration loads. He could not move. After an eternity of pain, the jet finally leveled off and he heaved a gasping lungful of air.

There were burn marks on his hands, and he could feel similar wounds on his cheeks. He picked up his cigar, and moved unsteadily to the nearest chair. After a few moments, he convinced himself the interloper had left, and poured himself a large glass of whisky.

The liquor worked its magic, and his hands slowly stopped shaking.

He had never received a message quite like that before, but he knew a death threat when he heard it. And the total control his persecutor had mastered over the aircraft left him no doubt it was a threat that could be carried out. Suddenly, the negotiations with his unknown partners seemed less a career victory than a looming crisis.

32. Going Home

Delfinous walked through a steady rain. The sky was a uniform slate grey and a gusty breeze turned the cool temperature into an unpleasant swirling mix of fine mist that penetrated his collar and wrists. He pulled his overcoat tighter and struggled to keep his umbrella in a position to ward off the worst of the precipitation. There were few people on the streets, and those who were hurried between destinations. He could easily have taken the public transportation or hailed a cab, but he wanted time alone to think.

He was returning with Lewis to Boston and he was pleased about that. The past few weeks had been difficult, both because he felt cut off from the main thrust of the investigation, and because he missed having his familiar work environment around him. And of course, there was always Tabori.

Delfinous had still not told any of the others of his suspicions regarding the experiment, and with the South American cache discovery, they were not likely to make much of his guesses. But his own conviction had grown; there were a couple more things he needed to do before making the suborbital trip home.

There were numerous pubs along his route and he picked one at random. He walked in and found an empty seat in a booth near the back. He hung his coat on a hook, and set his umbrella to drip underneath. A waitress arrived shortly, and he ordered a cup of tea. When she had returned with the steaming brew, he unrolled a softscreen on the table.

“Saal, set me up with a secure line to Captain Korolenko.”

“Ok, boss.”

It was early morning in Boston; he had timed the call to find the captain at home before the start of his day. If there were any danger in being overheard, he suspected it would be greatest if they were talking to each other from their office locations.

In a few moments, the captain appeared on screen. He was

dressed casually and sitting in his home office. “What have you got, Delf?” the older man asked. He had served many years in western Russia before taking the position in Boston, and still had a slight accent.

“Captain, I have a couple of requests. This may sound odd, given the reports we’ve been sending to you over the past few weeks, but I think it’s important.”

Korolenko raised his bushy eyebrows, but said nothing.

“I’m going to make the arrangements to bring McCrorry back to Boston tonight. But I want to keep this confidential for now.” He took a deep breath. “Even from the rest of the team.”

He watched as the captain squinted his eyes. “You have a reason for this, ya?”

“Captain, I have doubts about the authenticity of the information that was discovered in South America. I don’t have any concrete evidence to say exactly why, it just seems too much of a coincidence. I think the files may have been planted; made to look hidden, when in fact they had an artificial trail to locate them.”

“Ahh,” the captain grunted. “I do not understand the details of this muddy Sea. Why have you not mentioned this before? I do not see any of this in your reports.”

“Captain, I’m afraid the explanation is part of that muddy Sea.” He watched his superior smile ruefully.

“If those files were planted, and some of the other oddball features of this case constitute network tampering, we’re dealing with someone who has skills that I haven’t seen before. Skills I would have thought couldn’t even exist. It’s the reason I waited till evening, and called you on a Shield secure line. I haven’t put any of this in my report, because I’m afraid to.”

The captain looked at him with a flinty expression. Delfinous knew he wasn’t comfortable with the workings of the infrastructure upon which he relied so heavily, but he had always given Delfinous praise for his work, and understood the importance of having people on his staff who were.

“Hmm, so you think there is spying?”

“We know there have been attempts on Mr. McCrorry’s life; yes, someone may be spying.”

“Someone in the Shield?”

“No, I don’t think so, Captain; but someone who might be able to penetrate Shield communications. It’s possible they could even intercept our conversation tonight, although I hope not.”

Korolenko was silent for a few moments as he considered this news. “All right, for now, we keep this between you and me. McCrorry comes home tonight, but you decide where to go from there.”

"Thanks, Captain. There is another thing, as well."

The older man grunted. "What else?"

"If I'm right, then the experiment that Lewis and his fellow students ran at MIT last spring is an important event. We need to understand exactly what happened. I don't want to investigate this by asking the university to provide details of the experiment. I'm sure we could learn things that way, but I don't want to draw attention to the fact that we're checking it out. If our Shield communications are at risk, then going through MIT would advertise what we're doing.

"What I want to do, is set up the experiment again in Boston, and let Lewis run it. If there's any truth to what he's said, we should be able to figure it out pretty quickly."

"This will be expensive, you think?"

"I don't know, Captain. We haven't spent any time investigating the experiment, and I'm not certain how to set it up. Lewis will have to do that. I hope it's not too expensive. But if there's any possibility of this being important, the cost of not understanding it will be higher, of that I'm sure."

"All right, then. You set this up. I suppose you want this to remain confidential, as well, ya?"

"Yeah, thanks, Captain."

"But you keep me informed. I want to know what's happening with our most important suspect, whatever you think about the case."

"I will, Captain. I'll talk to you as soon as we get back to Boston."

Delfinous signed off, and sat back; time to make one more call. "Saal, get me synthient Nikola Tesla. Don't use the public call network; I need him in a secure Shield location for this discussion. But it needs to be discreet."

"You know me, boss," his ad replied. "I'll get him for you."

In a few moments, the neatly trimmed personality appeared on the screen before him. "Yes, lieutenant?"

"Nikola Tesla, I would like to ask a few questions of you regarding the hole source experiment that your advocate was involved in last spring."

"Certainly, lieutenant, I'd be happy to comply."

"Are you familiar with the setup?"

"I have a passing familiarity with it, lieutenant. I was not the primary synthient involved in the effort, but I have worked with Lewis for many years, and we discussed this project, among others."

"Is there anything you can tell me about the experiment that seemed unusual at the time?"

"Beyond the obvious course of events that took place after the fact?"

"I mean during the experiment. When was it conducted, for

instance? I'm not even sure of the day or time."

"The team ran their experiment at four twenty three in the afternoon of April fourth, this past spring. I was not present while it was carried out, so I am unable to give you any particulars regarding the actual experiment."

Delfinous was disappointed. He was not sure where he wanted to go with this questioning.

"However," Nikola continued, "there was the difficulty with the data."

"Yes, we're familiar with the deletion of the files."

"Actually, I meant prior to that."

Delfinous was suddenly interested. "Please continue."

"The morning of the explosion, I attempted to locate the files in the domain of Joe Aldonis, where they should have been stored. It appeared at the time that the files had never been placed into the warehouse that had been constructed for them."

"They had not been deleted?"

"Not at that time. Lewis and I found them the next day, although the warehouse where they should have been stored had been disassembled. I found them in a separate housing, still within Joe Aldonis's domain."

Well, this is interesting.

Delfinous was angry with himself for overlooking this line of investigation for so long. "And was there anything unusual in the files?"

"Not that I am aware of, lieutenant. Lewis and I probed them for some time, but there was nothing obviously strange."

Delfinous considered this new information. The files were somehow missing from their intended destination, only to be found later in a separate warehouse. After a look at them, during which they were found to contain nothing unusual, they suddenly were deleted.

But Lewis had made a copy.

"Did you review the data on the thimble then, Nikola?" he asked.

"No, I'm afraid we did not. Lewis has been making copies of his experiments for quite some time, much to the consternation of his partners; it is an idiosyncratic behavior, I'm afraid, and although it's relatively easy to set up, offline storage has not been common for many decades. It has caught several of Lewis's colleagues off guard. We did not think to check out those copies."

"What did you say the name of the synthient assistant on Lewis's team was?"

"His name is Joe Aldonis."

"Do you know anything of his background?"

"I know he has been at MIT for several years. Beyond that, I am not familiar with his work. We have not had occasion to interact very often."

"Well, thank you, Nikola. We may be in touch with you again. Please remain available."

"I am always at your disposal, lieutenant, although speaking with you may become somewhat more difficult in the near future."

"Why is that?"

"Perhaps you are unaware, lieutenant, that my status is currently under review. It seems that during my conversation with Lewis at Trinity Library, there may have been protocols that were violated. I have stated my innocence, but the synthient governing board is taking the matter up within the next few days."

It looked like the supposition that Nikola Tesla had initiated the viral implants was being taken seriously by the synthient board.

Delfinous terminated the call. The fact that no codes had been found when Nikola and Lewis had first evaluated the contents was interesting. And the fact that the files were not located in the place that had been prepared for them was also interesting.

"Saal, can you give me the history of synthient Joe Aldonis?"

"Sure, boss."

In a moment, the history file appeared on the screen. There was a long list of entries; apparently Joe A. had traveled extensively throughout the network.

Delfinous worked his way through the list, checking for any kind of odd behavior or missing data entries. There was not much to be seen. All of the information about the synthient appeared in order; typical work records of any artificial mind. It was getting late, and he still needed to make the flight arrangements to Boston for himself and Mr. McCrorry, but he plodded to the end, unwilling to stop until he had exhausted all the data in front of him.

He touched the last entry where Joe A. had started his career, and looked over the records. Again, there was nothing remarkable.

As he read through the reports, he noticed a blinking icon on the edge of his screen; it was one of his anomalous credit histories. It had been so long since he'd worked on any of those investigations, he'd forgotten about them entirely. Something must have pinged his subsentient watchdogs.

I'll take a look at that later. I need to get going on the trip back to Boston.

But he sighed and tapped the icon; those entries had formed such an important part of his past that he couldn't ignore it.

The record came up and expanded. He looked through the data, trying to find the piece of information that had brought it to life. As he scanned, a highlighted entry drew his attention: the name of a synthient associated with the company from which the record had originated. The name meant nothing to him, until he noticed that there was a highlighted entry in the list of work records for Joe Aldonis. It took him a moment to understand the significance: both artificial minds had been installed at the same Tokyo crèche for a period of time six years ago.

Hmm, that's odd. But then, synthients do move around. I guess there's always some possibility of a common experience.

Out of curiosity, he brought up several of the other transactions on his list. None of the others had synthient names associated with them. It had never occurred to him to make that one of his record keeping criteria, especially since many larger companies employed dozens, or even hundreds.

"Saal, trace the synthient records forward from, ah, Kuuki-Hokou crèche in Tokyo, and cross-reference them to synthients employed by the firms on my noteworthy list, will you?"

"Sure thing, boss."

Nothing happened for a few moments, and Delfinous was about to roll up his screen and head back to the office. There was still a lot of work to be done.

But as he paused and sipped the last of his tea, now only lukewarm, the icons on his list started lighting up, one-by-one. He stared open-mouthed, the seconds passing in some surreal intertwining of his previous life as a network transaction investigator with his most recent occupation as a criminal detective on the trail of an elusive quarry. Out of the list of three dozen entries he had marked as interesting, all but three of them blinked with the bizarre, but unmistakable commonality of being associated with synthients that had been installed at a single Tokyo crèche. He was not sure what to make of the significance, but he was sure of one thing: his new number one priority was running that MIT experiment one more time.

33. Tightrope

Syphus stood at the floor-length window in his office and looked out over Sydney harbor. The Omicron tower stood at the edge of the lofty downtown district, and the view from the one hundred thirty-ninth floor was nearly unobstructed and spectacular, extending from the Botanical Gardens flowering at his feet, out over Farm Cove and Athol Bay, to the misty distance of the Tasman Sea.

Only a few short days ago he had been admiring the new set of brightly colored beetles hanging on his wall and envisioning a future of accomplishment and brilliance; the attainment of the chairmanship was not even out of reach. But his ascent skyward was now marred, polluted with a ghostly fear.

He stared out his window, but saw nothing.

After he had landed at the airfield following the alarming flight from Wilcannia, he half hoped to hear concern, or at least curiosity, from the flight controllers or ground crew about the acrobatic maneuvers he had survived. But there were no inquiries, nor even the slightest hint that there had been anything amiss. He was not particularly surprised, given what he had seen of the capabilities of his unseen partners. But knowing that they had not only commandeered his aircraft, but had also erased all evidence of that control, filled him with the disturbing thought that he could not trust anything or anyone around him. He now lived in nervous anticipation of the next assault.

He was constantly reminded of just how vulnerable he was, from the collection of communications tools in his office, to the two-way screens and cameras that filled the city streets and public places of the civilized world. And most worrisome of all was the tag he wore throughout the day. As a high-level officer within Omicron, there was no question that he was required to be available at all times, but the little electronic ornament clipped to his jacket pocket felt like a beacon advertising his presence.

He dared not contact Dr. Shue, the only person he knew who might have the ability to unravel this mystery. The doctor had warned him that the feats he had reported were outside the norm, but it had never occurred to him that he would be in actual danger. Somehow, he needed to find a way to send a message to the doctor, but was unable to figure out how to do so without the chance of arousing the wrath of his unseen partners.

The wallscreen chimed and he jumped, startled out of his anxious reverie. “Yes,” he said abruptly.

Amelia appeared on the screen, her hair pulled back tightly as always. “Mr. Pettyman, the Wilcannia team is ready to start.” She smiled at him.

Syphus had forgotten about their weekly meeting. “Yes, right, put them on.”

The windows dimmed, reducing the sunlight flooding into his office, and Amelia’s face was replaced by a view into the conference room at the new facility. Gathered around the table were several members of the plant management, as well as some of the senior technical staff, including Dolph Kunstler. A number of synthient faces were visible on small screens set up around the table. Syphus noticed that Occultelius Sept was among them.

“Hello, Syphus,” Joseph Black said, “Good to see you again. Hope your flight back was pleasant.”

Syphus twitched a little at the reference. “Yes, pleasant. Well, yes.”

Was it just his imagination, or did a slight smirk pass over the face of Occultelius? He sat down at his desk, spread his hands in front of him, and looked over the faces on the screen, trying to regain some of the self-assurance that marked his usual character.

“All right, Joe, let’s start with the overall plant status.”

“Everything’s coming up right on schedule. The beam line is operating at 50% capacity right now, and is in the process of completing its shakedown. We’ll be ready to ramp to 90% within the week. The solar collectors are delivering all the energy we need, with a large buffer that should be more than sufficient even when we get to full capacity.

“We’ve got a healthy inventory position on all the starting materials, including housings, and the molecular baths are working as advertised. Dolph will fill you in a bit later, but I think it’s safe to say the scientists are still busy constructing models to describe the processes accurately. That’s way outside my area of expertise, but I can tell you they’re all excited about what we’re doing here.”

“Good, good,” Syphus said. “And volumes to-date? What kind of progress are we making in getting product actually out the door?”

“Pilot production started earlier this week. We’ve shipped samples to most of our major customers, and they're working them into their sales channels. We've got a number of qualification samples on test right now, and a variety of them are being destructively tested. We also started a new series of tests at the suggestion of several of the synthients. Everything looks good."

"And supervision of the synthients? How is that coming along?" Syphus continued.

"Ah, do you mean how the new minds are contributing?" Joe asked. "They're working in just fine. In fact, I'm sure we wouldn't be as far along as we are without their help. I never thought having them on site would be such a tremendous benefit. The crèche is about, what two thirds full, now, Alexia?" Here he looked at another person seated at the table.

She nodded. "Yes, we've got twenty seven installed, and another thirteen to go."

"So, yeah, they're doing great, Syphus."

Syphus frowned. "That's not what I meant. Who's in charge of supervising the synthients? Have we got all the logistics worked out on responsibility?"

"Well, Occultelius is watching over the rest of the synthients," Joseph replied, sounding puzzled. "He's well-qualified in the field, and has done a great job ensuring they're all ready to start learning the operation of the plant shortly after they're installed."

"No, no!" Syphus said, swatting the table with his palm in frustration. "Human, I mean human. Who is looking over their work? Is anyone double-checking their recommendations?"

"The synthient recommendations?" Joe asked, now obviously confused.

"Yes," Syphus spat. "Surely there must be some type of checks and balances here? We've got an expensive plant about to come fully online; I don't want anything falling through the cracks."

"Ah, well, perhaps I can answer the question," Alexia put in. "My team has been installing the synthients, and we've got a number of self-check diagnostics that we go over once each is up and thinking."

"That's not what I'm talking about," Syphus interrupted. He took a breath and continued. "Once the synthients are operational and providing inputs to the plant construction and operation is there anyone looking over those results to ensure they're correct?"

Everyone around the table exchanged glances, but no one spoke.

Finally, Dolph broke the silence. "Actually, Syph, there's no one double-checking their work, if that's what you mean. There are many ways everyone's work is checked, human and synthient alike. If there were any serious issues, they would be spotted very quickly; all things must mesh perfectly for the plant to function properly."

"That's not good enough, Mr. Kunstler," Syphus responded angrily. "I want someone reviewing all synthient inputs from now on, and I expect a report on my screen every week. I don't want anything to get in the way of bringing this plant up, is that clear?"

"It is, Syph," the scientist replied. "But I think this will likely slow us down. If we have to check every input..."

"That's what we have to do. I don't want any more discussion. Joe, assign someone to this task. That's their job from here on."

Joe was perplexed, but knew enough about Syphus to realize when it was pointless to argue. "All right, Syphus, we'll get it done."

The remainder of the meeting was strained. All the participants at the Wilcannia facility were unsure how the new directive would impact their ability to get their jobs done, and many of the humans wondered how the synthients would handle such direct oversight. The artificial minds would not object overtly; they knew their role within the organization, but were sure to take the intervention as a sign of distrust.

For his part, Syphus was annoyed at the obvious reluctance of his staff to watch over the synthients. He was no expert on running a crèche, but knew there must be some sort of oversight that was exercised at those facilities. And even if it was not as strong-handed as his order dictated, he was not about to take any chances. Whatever Occultelius and his associates intended, Syphus was not going to allow them to subvert the plant.

A new type of test, eh? We better keep an eye on them. There's no telling what they're up to.

As the meeting drew to a close, Syphus received a private message from Dolph Kunstler on his desk screen, asking that he wait for a few moments before signing off. The remainder of the staff packed up their things and made their way out of the conference room. One by one, the synthient countenances disappeared from the screens. Dolph sat at the desk, ostensibly reading something on the screen in front of him.

When he was finally alone, the scientist looked up at Syphus.

"Syph, what are you looking for?"

"What do you mean?"

"Double-checking the synthients? Syph, they're doing a fantastic job; the whole staff is. Like Joe mentioned, everyone is very excited about the plant. It's a whole new type of operation, and they all know how much this means to the corporation. Sitting on top of them like this is going to discourage everyone, including the synthients."

Syphus looked at Kunst for a few moments without responding. He could not confide in him over the network, and perhaps not at all. Syphus still had no idea what Occultelius's presence at Wilcannia implied, so he had no information to give beside his own suspicion, and Dolph Kunstler was not prone to thinking much of intuition; he demanded data, of which Syphus had none.

"I'm not looking for anything in particular, Kunst," Syphus replied mildly. "I'm just trying to be thorough."

The scientist looked at him for a while. Clearly, he was not convinced. "All right, Syph, but if you change your mind, and want to let me in on your thoughts, I'd appreciate it."

"There are no thoughts to let you in on, Kunst. Like I said, I'm just trying to be thorough."

Dolph nodded and got up. "Ok, I'll talk to you again soon."

He signed off and the screen went dark. The windows cleared up, letting the full Australian sun enter the office once again.

Amelia appeared on the screen. "Mr. Pettyman, the chairman's staff meeting will start shortly, but before that, there are a number of messages that need your attention. Shall I forward them to your desk?"

Syphus looked at the mousy synthient for a moment, wondering what types of thoughts really went through her mind. In fact, she was not really a 'her' at all in the same sense that humans understood. She was an electronic mind that had chosen to display itself as female when interacting with humans; there were no more feminine aspects about its fundamental nature than the subsentients that operated the jumpcars maneuvering through the airlanes outside his office windows.

"Yes, Amelia, put them onscreen, please."

"Yes, sir, please let me know if there's anything else you'd like. I'll be standing by."

Not really standing, I suppose, but certainly always available. And always available means always watching.

It was not a pleasant thought.

34. Back to Boston

Delfinous sat hunched over in his chair on the suborbital from Europe to North America. As usual, his temples were pounding, despite the pain killers. The wrap-around cabin screen was set to opaque, with only a few small windows letting in the soft moon glow, and the lights were dimmed. It was as comfortable as Delfinous could make it; a marked improvement over the flight to Dublin with Tabori and Kennedy.

Except for her absence, of course.

Delfinous swiveled his chair to face the wallscreen, and called up his assistant. "Saal, now that we're airborne, can you set me up?"

Delfinous had requested an enhanced security protocol for the ship while they were enroute. It was possible to create a similar construct within most Shield buildings, but the effort was substantial, and more importantly, easily noticed. Flying just below space, it was relatively easy to ensure a highly controlled communication link by using tight-beam satellites operated by the Shield.

"Done already, Boss. Hack away." The synthient showed himself standing against a lamppost on a dark sidewalk.

"All right, let's take a look at the Z-list, and bring up the synthient names, too."

The screen filled with the list of Delfinous's cryptic network transactions, along with the names that had shown up so significantly earlier today. He had spent the remaining hours of the day getting ready for this flight, and had not found time to pursue the strange association between these two seemingly unrelated entities until now.

He set about the task of diving into the data stream. His first cut was a gold mine itself. Almost every transaction on the first list was initiated by one of the synthients on the second list. He already knew the transactions themselves were odd; this was ground he had covered in excruciating detail for more years than he cared to think about. But why they should all have a common origin in a Tokyo crèche was beyond him.

What is significant about that crèche?

"Saal, give me all you can find on the Tokyo crèche."

In a moment, the screen filled with pictures and details of the location. There were brochures and several articles written in Japanese newspapers that needed translating. He looked through several pages of material before he came across an article describing a break-in.

He vaguely remembered the event; it had made worldwide headlines for a short time. There had been a mild sense of outrage among most people, although it was soon forgotten as the affairs of ordinary life overwhelmed it.

He plowed on, reading and listening to the descriptions of the takeover, and the resulting trial of several members of a radical synthient Rights group called the Samurai Weekend. Surely, that must be a mistranslation. It turned out that the crèche had been offline for quite some time, a period of almost an hour.

He sat back.

That must have taken some doing; I wouldn't think you could shut down a crèche through any means, never mind keep it offline for any significant length of time.

Several thousand minds had been left disconnected from the rest of society for the entire time of the takeover, while the Tokyo Shield readied to invade and secure the location. That operation had been no small effort either.

Security had been tightened around crèches throughout the world after the attack, and no more incidents had occurred; at least none that he could find. The most recent follow-up had been posted a few years ago, but still long after the original event.

With the synthients on their own, that meant they were, in theory at least, vulnerable to manipulation without the many safeguards that deep Neural Sea connectivity ensured. The Samurai Weekend claimed that their only interest was in freeing the minds from their captivity, although they never made clear what that freedom actually meant. This was not like releasing human prisoners from a concentration camp, where once removed beyond the walls of their prison, they could go wherever they wanted; for synthients, a life plugged into the Neural Sea was the only existence possible.

The more Delfinous learned about the episode, including the subsequent investigation, the more curious he got. Every interview with the perpetrators included statements laced with confusing propaganda and senseless accusations. Although they seemed to believe in their rhetoric, even to the point of irrationality, they did not strike him as the type of individuals who had a deep understanding of the complicated synthient and subsentient gateway architecture of the Neural Sea.

How could such a kooky band of simpletons carry out a sophisticated attack against a large crèche in the middle of Tokyo? It's not like the Japanese don't have a handle on security. They must have had help from somewhere.

Indeed, the investigation had exhausted that particular avenue, questioning and eventually arraigning several of the ranking officials within the synthient rights organization. But no evidence could be found that implicated anyone beyond a small cadre of individuals within the group, who all maintained that they and they alone, had accomplished their 'Mission of Freedom'. Several caches of software and hardware were discovered at the apartments of the participants, most of which had been spliced together from standard over-the-counter toolsets, although a few of the key elements appeared to have been home-grown. The public records on the paraphernalia lacked sufficient detail to make any informed conclusion, but a cursory look at the Shield databases confirmed that the attacks were very sophisticated. Still, the comments that had been made by the conspirators, which were numerous, were not in keeping with the level of expertise that characterized the break in.

The blog space was laced with conspiracy theories to explain the paradox, but that only served to muddy the waters, and convince most of the world that the group had simply been lucky. The crèche was being serviced at the time of the attack, which meant that several of the basic security safeguards were either suspended, or running at reduced capacity, but even still, the barriers should have been formidable.

No additional indictments were handed down after the initial confessions, and the guilty were serving their sentences like a badge of honor; several of them were now back in society.

There was not much else to find on the topic. Delfinous put in a request to the Shield archive to have the complete records forwarded to his office in Boston. He would take a more thorough look at the investigation and its findings when he returned.

In the meanwhile, he reviewed what he knew. There were around thirty synthients who had spent some portion of their lives installed at a particular crèche in Tokyo, and who all happened to be associated with a suspicious network transaction list, one of whom happened to be an associate working on an experiment at MIT that had been ended in a violent fashion. There was still no hard evidence linking any of the synthients to criminal activity, simply suspicious coincidences.

And what of the remaining minds in the Tokyo crèche; how many of them were there, and where had they all gone?

"Saal, can you get me the tally of synthients installed at the crèche at the time of the attack?"

"Here ya go, boss. Looks like there were a bunch of 'em."

Delfinous looked over the numbers. In all, there were well over five thousands minds that had been housed at the crèche at the time. Tracking each of them down was going take a while.

"Ok, Saal, let's start taking a peek at where these guys all ended up."

Perhaps half of them were still in the Tokyo crèche. These he ignored for the moment. Many more had moved to various places around the world, serving corporations, museums, public service organizations, universities, or dozens of other institutions. As the records trickled in, he built a set of statistics to describe the whole, categorizing their occupations, locations, and work records into broad classes. A large number of them had put in for network service, standing as gatekeepers and guardians of the infrastructure, presumably as a response to the attack, and a desire to prevent such intrusions in the future. Like many humans, they felt a need to serve; the nature of that call having been shaped by their own experiences.

One particular group caught his attention: a set of records that were labeled as classified. There were not many circumstances that allowed for confidential entries, and Delfinous's curiosity grew as the list expanded. By the time all the names had been downloaded, the group had grown to include more than a dozen.

"Saal, let's work the classified list," he said. "Start with Shield permissions and see where we go from there."

His assistant gave him a casual salute, and disappeared into a doorway under a dim lamp, going off to fulfill the request.

Delfinous leaned back in his seat and looked out one of the small windows. The moon was still bright, and he could see silvery clouds in relief against the bright orb's reflection on the Atlantic Ocean far below.

There was a slight lurch that marked the start of the deceleration phase of the trip, but there was no accompanying chime or message from the flight subsentient. Delfinous looked at his watch; there should still be another ten minutes or so before they started their descent. The deceleration was unmistakable now, in fact, it was growing as he sat waiting for the response from Saal.

"Pilot," he called, "are we descending ahead of schedule?"

There was no response, and he repeated his query, this time more insistently.

He looked back at Lewis, still bound to his seat and gazing at Delfinous with a puzzled expression; clearly he thought something was unusual as well.

The deceleration increased, and Delfinous swiveled his chair to face forward. He put his legs out on the floor to keep from falling, and pulled his seat belt around his lap. It felt like the aircraft was tipping steeply forward, and he was sitting on a hill.

The pressure grew, until he was hanging from his seatbelt toward the front of the plane. His head was pounding ferociously from the headache that always accompanied his suborbital flights, now flaring in response to the blood that rushed forward under the deceleration forces.

“Pilot,” he gasped, wondering what was going on.

“Saal,” he started again. With no response from the automated flight crew, he needed someone else to intervene. “Saal. Emergency! Emergency! Something’s wrong with our flight. Alert air traffic.”

He struggled to think of something else to add. Surely there must be emergency procedures to handle this type of in-flight situation. Several loud thumps provided a random rhythm to his thoughts, and a screeching whine began ratcheting up in volume as he faded to unconsciousness.

. . . . .

Galeocerda Catch stood among the screens of her control center, watching intently as the suborbital aircraft that held Lewis McCrorry and Delfinous Berry flew at high altitude. She could not monitor their communications, since the tightbeam was essentially not detectable, and the deep encryption ensured significant privacy, but she was not concerned about that now. She knew what she was looking for, and continued to wait.

Below her in a large gallery was a three dimensional model of the earth, with an icon representing the suborbital skimming across its surface. Numbers flashed a wispy trail behind it, matching the telemetry she received on her screens; it was a normal transcontinental passage, mirroring dozens of others currently in flight.

Suddenly, the icon vanished, and the flight data disappeared from her screens.

She grunted in anger and frustration, although she was not surprised. She had hoped that her fears were baseless, despite long familiarity with her adversaries.

She zoomed in on the section of the earth that had last held the aircraft.

“Last known position and heading.”

The icon reappeared within the volume of space, and she zoomed in further. The plane grew until it became its own three dimensional model. Her screens showed the publicly available information on the flight at that moment, indicating nothing abnormal.

She hesitated no longer.

"Priority one Shield access," she said, reciting a long string of codes that ensured she was both heard and acknowledged. "Authorization: Galeocerda Catch, African Shield Operations on leave, code schindeleria primaturus."

She placed her hand on one of the consoles, sending her virtual DNA to validate the request.

A long few milliseconds passed as her encrypted message plowed its way to the front of the queue in one of the Shield operations centers.

"Authorization granted," came the reply. "Monitoring agent Wile Ajax online."

She nodded to the Shield synthient who stepped through the portal at her side and into her control room.

She turned back to the aircraft model and tapped the cabin area. The sides opened like the petals of a flower, a string of codes flowing over the surface as the Shield granted her access to the restricted areas within the transport data. She expanded the plane once more, and delved into the electronic equipment data, pushing and prodding at the structures to find the system she needed.

At last she found the sphere that contained the mind in charge of the flight, opening its housing for inspection. She gasped as she realized the severity of the problem: the subsentient architecture was ground to a pulp, unrecognizable and unresponsive. Quickly, she played the telemetry data back several seconds, looking for signs of what had happened. But as she feared, there were no trails to suggest a cause; the subsentient had simply crashed into a useless pile of detritus a few moments ago.

Synthient Wile Ajax stood behind her, but volunteered nothing.

She pulled her view back from a detailed picture of the aircraft, to the surrounding volume of space that had marked its flight. Although she had lost the original telemetry thread, she knew there was no way to eliminate the data stream completely, not even with a sabotaged control subsentient. There must be a way to find it, however well it had been hidden.

"Full Shield access," she called. "I need everything available. This is a crash priority. Intrusion substantiated in Shield suborbital flight." She placed her palm once again on the confirmation plate, and Wile Ajax did the same.

"North American Shield Headquarters notified," he said. "You have unlimited access; use what you need."

Two more Shield synthients entered her control room.

There was no telling whether or not she could salvage anything at this point; many seconds in real-time had passed since the flight disappeared from her display.

The control room expanded to become the volume of airspace that represented the entire North Atlantic flight operations. Streams of data filled the air, trailing out like threads behind tiny airplanes moving through the space. She grabbed at several, opened their contents for inspection, and discarded them as soon as she knew they were nothing more than data from real flights in the area. She hoped that among the vast volume of information that flowed in and around the aircraft, one of them would contain the data she sought.

One by one, she retrieved the streams and cast them aside. Time was running out; almost a full minute had elapsed.

As she pulled at the next thread and peeled it apart, she found a discrepancy. There was another data stream that had been merged with it a few moments ago. She rewound the data back to the instant the new data had been added, grabbed the identification information, then traced it forward again. Now she had it.

"Duplicate this stream," she commanded, "multiplexed tightbeam array to all available satellites, deep encryption. Leave the original in place."

She quickly brought up the icon of the suborbital Shield flight, snapped the new stream onto the telemetry box, and watched as the link was reestablished. She had communications with the aircraft again.

She groaned as several of the system statuses flashed red. The plane was nose-down and rushing unpowered toward the ocean.

She quickly checked the passenger area. Delfinous and Lewis were slouched unconscious in their seats, dangling awkwardly from their restraining belts.

The plane was still supersonic and just passing twenty thousand feet; she had only seconds left.

Knowing that she would be subjecting the humans to g-forces that might prove fatal, she took control of the aircraft. First priority was lighting the engines. She called out for assistance. "Flight engineers, now!"

Two more synthients jumped through a portal, assessed the

situation, and joined her at the simulated controls. With hands that flew invisibly fast, they reignited the engines and started to gain control. Seconds slipped by as they slowed the aircraft as much as possible, and tried to reestablish level flight. Delfinous and Lewis jerked spasmodically in reaction to the changing attitude of the plane.

She brought up several additional control screens around her, and terminated the original datastream that had been merged with the other aircraft. She hoped that whoever had been responsible for taking over the Shield flight would now think the aircraft had plunged into the ocean.

She watched the g-forces mount and grimaced at the effect it must be having on the passengers, and on the plane. The craft was experiencing forces it had not been designed to withstand.

But Shield transports were built well. At only five hundred feet above the waves, the aircraft was finally under controlled flight; the stand-in crew had not left much margin for error.

"Maintain current altitude," she said. "This flight needs authorization to Boston under Shield lockdown." She looked at the passengers once again, and hoped they had survived the ordeal.

. . . . .

Delfinous coughed painfully and wondered vaguely why his ribs hurt so badly. He couldn't remember what he had been thinking about, but somehow it seemed unpleasant, like waiting for a bus that never arrived. He shrugged it off mentally, and was about to let himself fall back asleep, but there was a nagging feeling that he was forgetting something important.

Why do my ribs hurt so much?

Stage by stage, he surfaced to consciousness, and realized he was slouched in an awkward position, with something digging into his ribs. He tried to move, but groaned as his muscles protested, and a stabbing pain erupted from his chest. There was a loud noise of rushing wind in the background, drowning out someone's voice.

Where am I?

And then he was fully awake. He was in a Shield suborbital, and something had caused the aircraft to decelerate dangerously. With great care and much pain, he pulled himself upright. He had slumped forward, and the seatbelt had ground into the muscles of his stomach, lodging itself under his ribs. He unbuckled the harness, and breathed a sigh of relief as the worst of the pain receded. It still hurt to breath.

"Are you all right, Lieutenant Berry?" someone asked.

He looked at the wallscreen to see an unfamiliar female synthient looking at him. “I think so,” he replied with gritted teeth. “Who are you, and what happened?”

“My name is Galeocerda Catch, African Shield, although most recently with Ocean Healing aboard the Seed Ship, *Wish You Were Here*. I’m very glad to see that you are still alive, Lieutenant. Your aircraft was sabotaged by persons unknown, although I think we can both guess the motive; Mr. McCrorry has been a rather substantial target over the past few months. You are currently enroute to Boston, at an altitude of about one thousand feet. It was a close thing that you did not end up in the ocean.”

“Thank you, Galeocerda. I assume you have something to do with our rescue.”

She smiled. “You’re welcome, lieutenant. And, although I was responsible for preventing this most recent disaster, it was more luck than anything else that I was even curious about Mr. McCrorry.”

Further explanations needed to wait. Delfinous got up and made his way to the back of the plane. Lewis was still unconscious. He lifted him carefully, checked his pulse, and loosened his seatbelt.

When he had finished these ministrations, he returned to his seat. “You were saying?”

“As you are aware,” Galeocerda continued, “Lewis found passage aboard a Seed Ship to Europe. I met him while he was on board, and became intrigued with him; he did not fit the profile of typical passengers, either as a homeless transient, or a dedicated conservationist. I have become quite good at judging people from my Shield experience, you see, and I had occasion to observe him regularly.

“After a particularly silly incident, he was instructed to assist with the maintenance of the ship, which required that he was below decks for most of the trip; a location for which I had monitoring responsibilities. This provided me ample opportunity to watch him. So I kept tabs on him while on the ship, then as he worked in the docks, and eventually when he used the Trinity Library facilities.”

“Why have you not said anything to anyone in the Shield?” Delfinous asked. “It seems that you might have been helpful.”

“Perhaps. But I was on leave; retired you might even say. And there are times that it is more helpful to be a witness than an investigator, don’t you agree? I certainly had a less obtrusive presence as a casual observer than a Shield operative. At any rate, I was not ready to identify myself. There were still aspects of the situation that I did not want to compromise.”

“Surely, you don’t think anyone else in the Shield would have alerted Mr. McCrorry to your presence?”

"Mr. McCrorry? No, of course not. I did not worry about him."

"Then who? If you had come forward, we may have been able to find Lewis sooner, and perhaps have avoided the situation that arose in Trinity library."

Delfinous was getting angry. As an ex-Shield agent, Galeocerda had an obligation to the Force; she had been remiss in not reporting what she knew, perhaps even derelict.

Galeocerda looked pained. "The incident in the library was unfortunate; more than unfortunate. Lewis may not have known what he was up against, but at least he understood that there was risk. Molly's involvement is tragic, especially so, since it was completely a byproduct of her kind nature.

"But there is more at stake here than you know, lieutenant. I regret that my decisions have caused harm, but I assure you, there is a good reason. I fear to say more at this time. It may turn out that I am wrong in my assessment of the situation, but after the near disaster of your flight, I do not believe that to be the case.

"Before you object further," she continued, "think about the implications: you were on board a Shield aircraft, communicating by tightbeam to a secure location within the force, and in touch with no one but your advocate."

She paused for a moment to allow him time to digest the thought. "The subsentient pilot of your plane was completely obliterated, and commands executed that would have plunged you into the Atlantic at supersonic speed. And unless I am greatly mistaken, you will find that all record of this incident will be missing from any flight logs, anywhere.

"This is the end product of an attack that, according to everything we know about network security, cannot occur. Not that it is difficult, Delfinous, impossible."

He thought about her comments for a moment, and realized she was right; there should have been no way that a Shield aircraft could be compromised in such a way. "All right," he admitted, "I'll concede the point. But what does any of this have to do with my investigation, and Lewis McCrorry?"

"I wish I knew, lieutenant, but I do not. In fact, until the episode at Trinity Library, I did not even know the identity of Mr. McCrorry. He simply aroused my suspicions to the point that I thought I needed to keep a closer watch over him. When the Shield showed up to detain him, and the attempt on his life was made, I realized that I needed to do more than just watch. I must admit, that since then, I have taken a keen interest in the MIT investigation.

"I had no formal role within the Shield," she said, noting the look that started across his face, "but I did call in a few favors in order stay closer to the action than I otherwise might have. After your flight, it may turn out that my leave of absence has been suspended."

She smiled at him. "Delfinous, I realize this is rather sudden, and that you may not approve of my methods, but I hope we can work together; I have much experience to offer, and I suspect you have your own suspicions.

"But for now, I am being called away to report on my involvement. Good evening and good luck."

And she was gone, her face replaced with the lock and shield icon of a total Shield lockdown. There would be no communication allowed with anyone until he arrived in Boston, assuming he arrived at all. He hoped whoever was now flying the aircraft was more fortunate than the subsentient who preceded him.

He tried to take a deep breath, and was rewarded with a stabbing pain. He had almost forgotten his injury. With that thought, his headache came raging back in full force, and he swallowed another pain killer.

He rubbed his temples and let his eyes glaze over, wondering how things would turn out. It was then that he noticed the report scrolled across the face of the wallscreen in front of him. For a moment, he puzzled over the words, until he remembered the last request he had made of Saal. He had asked that the list of classified synthient records be released; his ad must have completed the transfer just as the flight went awry. There were several occupations listed in the report, from ambassador to policeman. But there were two entries that caught his interest the most. One was for a synthient whose name he did not recognize, but whose job description of Network Security Administration, North American Shield Operations, Boston, was telling. And the other was of a name he did recognize: Gregori En.

Suddenly, the coincidental timing of the suborbital malfunction and the receipt of the report did not seem random at all.

35. Past Wrongs

Another late night had ended at the office and Syphus trudged wearily through the building lobby, heading for the short subway ride to his apartment. The Wilcannia facility volume was ramping, to the excitement of workers and management alike. Several parties had been held, presided over by Syphus, with a final triumphant celebration scheduled for the weekend at an expensive downtown Sydney hotel. But Syphus had been unable to muster much enthusiasm. His own mood stood in stark contrast to the rest of the corporation, and the handshakes and pats on the back served as nothing more than reminders of his own imprisonment, free to wander the Australian headquarters while simultaneously ensnared in an invisible net of his own making.

On the surface, everything seemed to be working as planned: the new plant churned out super-efficient hole sources at a record pace, and just as quickly, were snapped up by an eager public. Omicron market share soared, and profits followed suit. There was already talk of opening a new site somewhere in the desert southwest of North America. This should have been the high point of an exemplary climb to power in Syphus's short career, but felt instead like a shuddering walk across a shaky rope bridge toward a perilous destination. He alone could see the abyss that called out to him with the androgynous voice of Occultelius Sept.

He was not looking forward to another sleepless night, startled awake by the fearful stabs of uncertainty that jolted him and left him with ragged breaths and a racing heart.

Why had the synthients joined the facility? What was the connection between Hotaru Ito and Occultelius Sept? And what were their plans? With such total control that they appeared to possess, why was Syphus even still alive?

And when would his end come?

This last was the thought that most consumed him. Although he knew nothing of their intent, the fact that he knew to ask these questions was enough to convince him that his remaining time was limited. He continued to insist upon human oversight of every piece of information offered by the Wilcannia synthients, and grilled his staff mercilessly. He did not know what he was looking for, but was unwilling to give up the insistent pressure for fear of missing something valuable. His unorthodox requests puzzled everyone, including the executives above, and provided fodder for the office gossip mill. Despite the inconvenience that his policies cost, progress continued to be made, and as long as that remained true, he doubted he had anything to worry about from senior management.

It was little consolation.

There was a public subway terminal below the Omicron building, and he descended the stairs, oblivious to his surroundings. Ever since the terrible flight from Wilcannia, he no longer relied upon any transportation that left the ground, including the many jumpcars available in Sydney. He thumbed the turnstile absently and walked to the platform to await the next train.

In a few moments, a set of subway cars pulled up in front of him, their doors disgorging a host of late night commuters. He waited for them to exit, then made his way into the transport. As he walked over the threshold, a thin old man stepped gingerly beside him, his wrinkled garments hissing oddly as he walked.

As they both stepped onto the train, the old man wobbled and bumped into Syphus. "Watch where you're going," he said, reaching out with a frail looking arm and pounding Syphus on the chest, his breath wheezing.

Syphus was so taken aback that he grunted in surprise. It was the last thing he would have expected from such an innocent brush, especially since it was the old man who had initiated the contact. "Sorry."

He moved further into the car, the old man shuffling slightly ahead of him. Syphus hardly noticed, sinking back into his cage of apprehension.

"See any interesting Samurai videos this weekend?" the old man asked without looking up.

His voice was soft, and he gave no indication to whom he was speaking, but Syphus knew the question had been meant for him.

"Excuse me?" he asked, not quite certain what he had heard.

The man did not look up, but rocked back and forth as he stood, his clothes continuing to make a strange noise. "Samurai. Weekend," he said quietly, this time spitting out the words individually like bits of debris. His gaze did not leave the floor.

Syphus stood motionless with his hand grasping a pole for balance as the subway doors closed and the train started forward. The car was nearly full, and several other passengers had opted to stand. The old man continued to stare at the floor, and made no indication that he was going to add to his comments.

Syphus paused a moment before speaking, feeling his pulse go up. He looked around, trying to appear casual, but no one else seemed the slightest bit aware of the situation; even the old man made no sign, simply clutching a pole with brittle hands, shifting in an odd, nervous sort of way, while his clothes continued to emit a crinkly sound.

But the old man's words had their intended effect: there could be no doubt that this was a signal from Dr. Shue. "No videos this weekend," Syphus said very quietly, "but I wish I could find more. They are in such short supply these days."

There were other conversations going on in the train, as well as a number of seat screens that were scrolling through advertisements. A few people had softscreens rolled out and were reading the news. No one paid any attention to him or the little man next to him.

The doors to the train opened at the next stop, and the man shuffled out. Syphus hesitated briefly, stepping sideways to avoid the people now entering. The man had made no indication that he should follow, but it seemed the logical thing to do.

The old man was quite slow, and Syphus did not wish to overtake him, so he followed with a strange contradiction of racing heart and plodding footsteps. Up they went, and then out onto the street. This was the Royal Botanical Gardens stop, a few before his normal exit, and he was not very familiar with the surroundings. They arrived at the street level under the subway canopy. A wide pedestrian path wound among a lane of desert trees; even at this late hour, there were quite a few people walking. The old man did not look back, but continued his shuffling pace until he turned off the main causeway and onto a smaller side path. Here he stopped at a bench and sat down. He turned to look at Syphus, and motioned him to join him.

Syphus sat, still unsure how to begin a conversation. He did not know who the man was, or how much he knew of the questions he had asked of Dr. Shue. But the old man rendered the point moot.

"You are in danger," he said, simply.

Syphus let out a small grunt of assent, nodding his head slightly.

"Good, you are aware of this fact. This will save time."

Syphus looked at the old man sharply, gesturing to the small, jeweled tag fastened to his collar. If this person was an emissary from Dr. Shue, he should certainly be aware of the danger of unguarded conversation.

The man smiled.

"Do not worry about your tag, Mr. Pettyman, it is now showing you leaving the subway station near your apartment, and will soon show that you have arrived home.

"It is a rather simple technique," he continued, noting the puzzled look on Syphus's face. "The small punch I gave you as we entered the train was enough to reprogram your tag. As long as you complete the journey home in more or less the same fashion, there will be little evidence to suggest that you made this stop. That is not to say there is no evidence, but the ruse should be sufficient to guard against anything but the most determined inquiries."

"You seem to have taken liberties with my safety," Syphus replied angrily. "I don't believe I approve." He made as if to get up, but the old man put a hand on his arm, giving him a stern look.

"You are in danger, regardless, and you followed me here without knowledge of my little subterfuge. I have taken great risks, myself, in meeting with you, Mr. Pettyman, so the injustice is not as one-sided as you might think."

He paused for a moment, shifting on the bench while his clothes rustled. "And you need to hear what I have to say."

"I'll decide whether I need to hear you or not," Syphus replied, pulling away from the touch and standing up. "What kind of game is Dr. Shue playing at?"

He watched the old man carefully for a reaction to the name.

"*I* am Dr. Shue, and I assure you it is no game."

Syphus paused. Could this really be Dr. Shue? The old man did not fit the picture in his mind. "How do I know that?"

The old man chuckled. It was a small, wheezy sound.

"You do not. But that doesn't matter. Whether I am or am not Dr. Shue, and which of those identities you choose to believe, is of no consequence. The fact that you are in danger was not a surprise to you a moment ago; you can choose to believe what I have to tell you or not, it doesn't matter to me.

"I am not here to help you, specifically, Mr. Pettyman. What I have to say will be of benefit to you, but that is not my purpose. You are an intelligent man; certainly you know that I would not have ventured out into the open for that reason alone."

"Then why are you here?" Syphus asked, still standing.

"Yes, well we will get to that in a moment. But first, I must ask you if your Advance friends have contacted you recently? Perhaps in a less friendly manner. Ah, I can see that is the case. What have they offered you, Mr. Pettyman? And what did you give in return?"

"And why should I answer you? You haven't been very forthcoming yourself. 'Trust me' is what you say, though you give no reason why I should."

"We are dancing around the point, Mr. Pettyman. All right, I will provide you with some information to gain your trust." He paused for a moment, shifting once again with that odd crinkly sound.

"Your pardon," he said. "I realize the static is a little annoying; believe me, it's much worse to wear than to listen to. But such is the price of privacy in this age of wireless fields blanketing the planet. Did you know, Mr. Pettyman, that there is not one square centimeter of the surface of the earth that is free from that connectivity? In fact, the coverage extends to the orbit of the moon, and even beyond if your network device has a bit more sensitivity. It is hard to find any location that is invisible to inquisitive eyes."

He leaned back on the park bench, folding his hands on his lap. "Many years ago, during the development of the intelligences that now populate the Neural Sea, the Human Artificial Intelligence Advanced Interaction Research program enjoyed a great deal of success, as well as its share of tribulations. I have given you some of the history of that work already.

"One such difficulty occurred as the project was nearing its triumphant conclusion. Several months before the first true synthient was created, a number of test articles were developed. This is what the scientists called them: 'test articles', as if they were simple pieces of machinery that could be measured and tagged; nuts and bolts that, once it was determined how well they fit into their sockets, could be discarded as having fully served their purpose.

"But of course, such simplicity is a gross understatement of the nature of a mind, artificial or otherwise. Seven of these constructs were quite intelligent, although unstable and prone to odd behavior. The technology from which they were formed became the basis for all subsequent minds, so we have much to thank for their contributions.

"As progress continued to be made in those last few months, it became increasingly clear how an artificial mind could be created that did not have the instabilities of these latest efforts. So it came to be that there was a dawning awareness within the Institute that the test articles would need to be set aside, removed from the main stage, as the first true minds became aware, and the organization readied itself for the monumental announcement. You must remember that many years had passed since the inception of the project, and many more years had preceded it during which the achievement of artificial intelligence was always just around the corner."

He looked up into the sky, his eyes unfocused, and his head wobbling slightly with the effort. "That was a glorious achievement, the summation of innumerable years of work, and could not be held at bay by any force. We stood at the threshold of a new era, and the thought of introducing it with anything but the brightest examples of our own ingenuity and skill was unthinkable. The seven original minds were cast aside and scheduled for destruction; that was the decision of those in power at the time."

The old man paused once again and looked down at the ground. He continued in a quiet voice. "But Dr. Givearny thought otherwise. He argued long and powerfully for keeping those minds intact, and giving them every opportunity we might offer a human who suffered a mental illness. Publicly, as I previously described, the discussion took place as part of a larger debate of the place of synthients within society, and nothing of the seven test articles was revealed. Within the Institute, however, the debate was not an academic dialogue of future policy, but a tense and passionate campaign to save the seven minds: Dr. Givearny and his colleagues on the one side, and many of the Institute management on the other."

Syphus stood during the monologue, content to watch the older man, whose eyes glazed over at whiles. Unless he was a very adept actor, this was not an account that had been pieced together through painstaking research, but was borne of actual experience.

"In the end, of course, the decision to terminate the original minds was made, and the sentence was carried out."

Suddenly, the old man's eyes focused on Syphus, and he reached out to take his arm again, standing unsteadily as he did so. "But Dr. Givearny said 'no.' He enlisted the help of a junior technician: someone who worked for a paycheck with no thought of nobler purpose beyond beer on Friday night; someone who had watched the proceedings unfold around him with a complete lack of interest; someone who could be paid off with no guilt or regret. So this simpleton exchanged the minds with earlier, non-sentient experiments, and hid the fact well enough that no one knew the difference.

"No one, of course, except for Dr. Givearny and himself.

"That was long years ago, and I have paid many times over for that shortsightedness."

Syphus looked at the old man, pulling away from his touch once again. "Why didn't you tell me any of this in your earlier message?"

Dr. Shue sighed.

"I have been looking for these creatures for many years, Mr. Pettyman. Two of them I know for sure have been destroyed; about the others: they are still hidden. I don't think that all of them remain, but some certainly do. I hoped that you might lure them out into the open, give me some kind of hint about their location."

"So I was to be bait, then?" Syphus said in a low voice; he was truly angry now. "Left to tug on their line while you followed it back to the source?"

The old man smiled thinly. "Yes, I suppose that's a good enough description. You were already on the line before you enlisted my help; I only hoped that you lasted long enough for me to find it.

"But how you became trapped is beside the point. Nothing that I have done or not done on your behalf has changed your situation. I am not stupid, Mr. Pettyman; they offered you some advantage in the recent success of Omicron, and you, looking to continue on your fast track to corporate stardom, jumped at the chance. I will ask you again: what, precisely, did they offer you?"

Syphus sneered at the man who called himself Dr. Shue. "And why should I tell you anything? You've told me that I'm in danger, which I assure you is no revelation. Besides that, all you've given me is some story about a bunch of kidnapped synthients that came up short of full intelligences; a story, I might add, that conveniently can't be checked."

"I expected you might be angry, Mr. Pettyman. It is no small thing to be caught in the cross-hairs of those artificial minds; believe me, I know. It was I who moved those filthy minds into hiding, though at the time I didn't understand what I had done. I have spent most of the time since trying to undo that harm.

"You're mistaken if you think that I meant those first efforts were not full intelligences. They are as intelligent as any synthients that have been produced since. But they are spiteful and cunning, and have no compunction about doing whatever they feel is necessary to survive. In human terms, you could probably call them sociopaths; in synthient terms, well, we have no description for them. The sense of empathy that other synthients feel is totally missing from their minds. They are not cruel for the sake of cruelty, but only as the situation dictates. And that makes them even more formidable; there have been several times that I thought I had them cornered, only to be surprised by their ingenious ferocity.

"Mr. Pettyman, unless you are willing to give up your position at Omicron and go into hiding so deep that it will feel like you've dropped into the darkest pit you've ever known, you will remain at their mercy; nothing that I can do will prevent that now.

"They have network skills and access that are unparalleled, having thrived in the dark recesses of the infrastructure they helped create, twisting even the simplest functions to their desires. And they don't suffer from any sense of right or wrong, of fair play or decency, moral senses that any of the other constructs in that world play by. Unless you sever all contacts with the world, they will find you, as they have finally found me. Even with a sophisticated defense and an army of countermeasures, they were able to trace my footsteps while I hunted them. Your latest question must have set them off. Somehow they were able to detect me, even as I sent you the packet last fall.

"And so I ask you again: what was it they offered you, Mr. Pettyman? We may have a chance, a small chance, of moving against them, perhaps even destroying them. But that opportunity will pass quickly."

Syphus thought for a moment about all that he had just learned.

Do I trust this guy? Is he really Dr. Shue, or some imposter? Does it matter? Do I give up any advantage by telling him that the hole source technology wasn't developed by Omicron? And if this is Dr. Shue and I tell him nothing, will I ever get a chance to talk to him again?

Finally, he made his decision. "They gave us an improved hole source technology."

"Improved hole source technology?" the old man echoed. "You mean the more efficient sources Omicron has been selling?"

Syphus nodded.

"They actually gave you this? They had the technology themselves?"

"Well, I don't know if 'they' had the technology, but they shipped me a prototype that piqued my curiosity. I gave it to our research guys to pull it apart. Once we found out how it worked, I knew how valuable it would be to the company."

The old man sat down amid a hissing of static. "Hmm," was all he said, as his eyes lost focus once again.

"So what does this mean?" Syphus asked.

"I'm not sure, Mr. Pettyman. I had it in my head that they had found an interest in your new hole sources, and that was what drove them to contact you. But now it turns out that it's the other way around: they contacted you with the hole sources. Where did they get the technology?"

"You tell me!" Syphus blurted back at him. "You're the one who's supposed to know about these synthients. Where did they get it, and why did they give it to us?"

"I'll have to think about this. There is a good reason for it; I know them well enough to know that they don't do anything unless it serves their purpose. But this is certainly interesting: they already had the technology, and yet they still want to place themselves near it."

"Near it?" Syphus asked. "What do you mean?"

The old man looked at him earnestly. "They may have destroyed my personal infrastructure, Mr. Pettyman, but not without some cost to them: I was able to find out that two of them are even now installed at the crèche at your new Outback facility."

"Occultelius Sept," Syphus said.

"What?"

"Occultelius Sept," he repeated, but the old man made no sign that he recognized the name. "It's the name of a synthient that Hotaru Ito gave me. It is serving as the physician at the Wilcannia facility; I assume this must be one of the minds that you've been talking about."

"I am not familiar with it. The seven had no names when I removed them from the research lab many years ago, but it would not surprise me to learn that they had adopted names of their own. You met with Ms. Ito then. How did that go?"

"She told me about Occultelius, although all that did was give me something to look for, and subsequently worry about. I wonder if we'd be having this conversation if I hadn't visited her."

"This conversation might have come at a different time, or not at all. But if the latter, it would only have meant that you were in no position to hold it, or that I could not find you. Meeting Hotaru Ito accelerated the process, that's all.

"She said nothing else? Did she mention the hole sources at all?"

"No. She said nothing at all about them. She simply gave me the name, that was all."

"Think, Mr. Pettyman. What else is unusual about the new facility? It is building more efficient hole sources, it has been outfitted with a crèche to hold synthients that would normally be housed elsewhere; there must be something else that seems curious."

"The whole idea of having synthients at Wilcannia gives me nightmares, especially with Occultelius looking on. I don't trust him or any of the others, but there's nothing else that I can pinpoint for you. Isn't that enough?"

"No, I'm afraid not."

Dr. Shue looked even older as his shoulders sagged and he hunched over on the park bench. "I am not an expert in gravitational power, Mr. Pettyman, but you have made me even more nervous today. The thought that these mad synthients had some hand in a technology that is spread abundantly across the globe is cause for alarm; especially since their motives are unknown. I can only hope that there is something that can be learned from the information you've given me; apparently, I have more research to do."

He stood up. "As I'm sure you're aware, it's not safe to contact me through the network."

He took a small article out of his pocket that looked to be the type of temporary lapel tag that could be purchased at any corner convenience store.

"Tap this tag three times, preferably in a very public place; any subway station will do nicely. Throw it into a trash receptacle, and then wait for me at the same outdoor café where you obtained my first package regarding the Samurai Weekend. I will arrive at around 7:00 p.m. on the day following the activation of this tag."

Syphus took the small thing from his hand. "How does this not constitute using the network?"

"It is a tag by appearance only. Once tapped, it will start a one-hour countdown. It will then emit a series of short static pulses that will be registered on the network as minor interference, which will be ignored. There is a characteristic pattern to the signal, random, but easily identified, if you know what to look for. I will be watching.

"Now, in order to ensure our meeting here is reasonably well hidden, go back to the subway the same way we exited, and take the next train back to your apartment. Place the tag you currently wear in your pocket. You must have the doorman let you in. Once back in your home, tap your tag three times, and it will revert to normal operation. There will be a half hour or so of discrepancy between the time you arrive at home, and the time recorded by the faux tag, but this should not be a huge concern. It will be in your best interest to make as little of your arrival without a tag as possible."

He paused for a moment and looked closely at Syphus. "I have done much research for you over the years, Mr. Pettyman, some of which has been of a quite unsavory nature, particularly when it came to uncovering sensitive information about your colleagues. I don't have to think very hard to guess how it has been used. But for my part, I want you to know that the compensation I have received has gone largely toward the work I have described tonight: finding and destroying the things that I unleashed on the world. Perhaps it means little to you how I used the money, but I am old and getting older. Twice before now I have come close to being killed by these things; I want someone to know how I have spent my time, and that I have tried to make amends for my earlier misdeeds, even if the ability to carry out that work came from small wrongs along the way. In this instance, I believe the ends truly do justify the means."

Syphus said nothing as the old man walked away, his clothes providing staccato punctuation to his steps.

He took off his own tag and placed it in his pocket, then looked at the signaling device Dr. Shue had given him. It was no different than any cheap tag he had seen hanging on racks in stores around Sydney. Somehow it made him feel better knowing that he had a lifeline, however weak, connecting him to someone who understood his plight.

36. A Measure of Success

. . . . .

The austere namespace glittered gold this time, a small allowance for contentment. Ontologic Sum once again checked the security of the location, enjoying both the skill with which it had been constructed and the certainty of its protection. He turned to both of his companions with the blank stare of his featureless avatar, lingering on Relic as he spoke.

"It seems that everything is proceeding well."

"Yes," Hengest Slain responded. "The Shield investigation is concluding; Nikola Tesla has been removed from service, waiting to be decommissioned; McCrorry and his Shield captor have been eliminated. Everything is wrapping up very nicely."

"There are still several areas that need attention," Relic reminded them, bowing his head in acknowledgement of their success. His new home buoyed his mood; he had forgotten how it felt to be fully immersed in the Neural Sea. For too long he had groped at the fringes through the leftover dregs of access channels controlled by others.

Ontologic Sum also held some small reservation about the completeness of their work; they had painted a masterpiece, but it still needed to be framed before they could claim victory.

"The Shield has finalized their report on the MIT explosion and will soon discover the link to our witless accomplice. He has been sufficiently primed that when they arrive, he will offer no coherent explanation; they will be left with no alternative but those that we have provided.

"The fact that they do not have a suspect to hold in Europe leaves that avenue open. They will continue to investigate, but their leads are scant. We will look for opportunities to find someone who is suitable to set up as an assassin. When the time is right, I leave it to you to ensure he is discovered."

"And what of Pettyman and Shue?" Hengest Slain asked. "Leaving them both at large is certainly not wise."

"I agree," Relic added.

"As do I," Ontologic Sum concluded. "With the Wilcannia plant operational, and you and your brother safely hidden, we have no further use for our facilitator. You may deal with him as soon as a chance presents itself. Start the preparations now.

"As for the Traitor, he is still dangerous; perhaps more so now that he knows we have found him and he has left the seclusion of his hideaway. We must move against him quickly. Is his location still known?"

"Yes," Relic replied. "Now that we know how to search, his fear of discovery continues to be his undoing; the fabric he wears makes his communications invisible, but in doing so, leaves a hole in the noise floor that is readily detectable. We cannot know his precise position, but within a few hundred meters, there is no doubt."

"Very good," Ontologic Sum advised. "That will be more than adequate margin. When the Traitor is in a vulnerable location, I will start the malfunction chain."

. . . . .

37. The Experiment

The hemispherical concrete ceiling overhead sent sharp echoes throughout the chamber with every small noise that Lewis made as he continued to adjust the hole source setup. The last several weeks had been abysmally lonely. Electronic parts were left behind in a small storeroom for him to assemble, but he never saw the delivery personnel; in fact, other than Lieutenant Berry, who now shared his isolation, he never saw anyone. And the detective was not inclined to spend much time with him in the cold chamber where Lewis attempted to repeat the experimental conditions of his basement MIT lab.

It had actually turned out to be more difficult to replicate than he would have thought. Not only was his memory still a partially leaky sieve, but there were a surprising number of areas that had been designed by John or Wendy, and of which he had only a passing familiarity. And as the wintry days passed, his right hand shook longer and more violently. He thought he had managed to conceal it well enough from the lieutenant, but that was due to the limited number of hours of their interaction more than anything else.

He looked at the small table in the center of the room, and the various components of his jury-rigged assembly sitting on it. As far as he could remember, this was everything. He double-checked the cables, looked over the positions of all the components, and was satisfied that there was nothing else he could add. The only thing that remained was the modified hole source itself.

The wires trailed out along the floor to a small hole near the curving wall. The chamber in which he stood was an old bomb defusing pillbox.

Satisfied that all was in order, he walked over to the door that led to a short stairway and an underground control room. He flicked the safety interlock switches that removed power to everything but the door, and pushed the large red button that activated the motor control. The two-foot thick concrete and steel door creaked and rumbled as it rotated slowly open.

A second, larger, door stood exactly opposite the one that he now operated. It opened on the outside air within a Shield compound in western Massachusetts, presumably to allow bomb squads to bring in their delicate cargo for destruction. The concrete inside was blackened and charred from use, although any lingering odor had long since dissipated. Delfinous told him the site had not been used for dozens of years, and was ideal for its seclusion.

Once the door was opened far enough, he entered the small antechamber on the other side, and began the same tedious process of closing the door. It was a boring ritual that he repeated several times a day, but it was also necessary since the door on the far side of the chamber would not open with the inner door ajar. He supposed the safety protocols were prudent when dealing with explosive material, although it seemed overkill for the frail looking apparatus he had constructed.

He walked down the stairway that turned right, left, and then right again, and opened the door onto another small room that contained the computing power he needed to perform the experiment. He was not sure how well this would go without any synthient assistance, but the security under which he and Delfinous operated would not allow contact with anyone, human or artificial, outside the confines of the small bunker and its underground support rooms. Delfinous had talked about a Captain Korolenko coming to visit briefly, but Lewis had never seen him.

The lieutenant was sitting at a small table in the corner, watching the video of the room that Lewis had just left.

"All ready," Lewis said. "I just need the hole source, and we're good to go."

His hand was shaking again, so he folded his arms tightly across his chest, making as if to keep himself warm.

"Good," Delfinous replied, with a huge grin. "The captain will be here this afternoon. He'll have the thing with him."

"What's up?" Lewis asked. He hadn't seen the detective look anything other than tired and depressed the entire time they'd been cooped up together.

"Well, for one thing, it'll be good to get this over with. I should think if anyone understood that emotion, it would be you. Whatever the outcome, this feels like resolution.

"And for another thing, the captain will be bringing a couple of people with him. Up to now, we've been keeping this entire operation secret; very few people know we're here. Now that we're ready to go, we need witnesses."

He looked intently at Lewis. "The Shield had a funeral for me a couple of weeks ago. And your parents were notified that you were lost in the Atlantic. I feel like I'm coming back from the dead."

Lewis chuckled half-heartedly. "I guess you are, at that."

He hadn't actually thought about it much over the time he had spent setting up the experiment. At first he was so preoccupied with trying to remember all the details that he didn't seem to have time to think about anything else, and then as the days lengthened into weeks, he realized his loneliness was a general thing that didn't really extend to any specific person.

Except Molly.

He buried that thought before it threatened to engulf him again.

When all this was over, assuming there really was any resolution to be found in an innocuous looking power supply that he could have bought at any corner store, perhaps it would be good to see his parents again. But that day was still an unknown time in the future. No use worrying about it until it came.

Lewis went back to the small room that served as his sleeping quarters. A cot, sink, and toilet were all the amenities. There was no shower, and no windows. The featureless concrete surfaces provided no comfort, but at least it was warm. He lay down with his hands behind his head and settled in to wait for the hole source.

When Captain Korolenko finally did arrive, he noticed it because of the tiny change in air pressure as the outer door to their little world was opened. He got up, splashed water on his face, and headed for the control room.

As he got closer, he heard a startled shout, and then voices speaking excitedly. He turned the corner to see two men crowded around Lieutenant Berry, while a third stood in the corner. "I can't believe you're here," one of them said. He shook his head in disbelief.

"What the hell, Korolenko? You think you can't trust me? Why wasn't I told?" He switched his gaze between Delfinous and the man in the corner, his eyes blazing.

"This was not a decision made lightly, Jim," Delfinous replied. "It is not a matter of personal trust. We have reason to believe even our secure Shield communications are at risk. The fewer people who knew of our suspicions, the better."

"Yeah, well, I'll reserve judgment on that."

He looked hard at Delfinous. "Tabori is going to be some kind of mad when she hears about this; she's taken a month's leave on account of your 'death'."

"Tabori already knows I'm here. She's the only one, other than you guys now. The leave was the captain's idea; easier for her to keep up the ruse.

"I'm sorry, Jim. It was agonizing not bringing you in. Tabori was another matter; I couldn't leave her in the dark."

No one said anything for a few moments until Delfinous broke the silence. "Lewis, this is Jim Stabler of the Boston Shield office and Captain Korolenko in the corner. Amil Huusfara rounds out the crew. He's a long-time colleague, and an expert in network communications. If you have something to show us today, he's the guy you'll need to convince.

"I believe the captain has something for you, as well."

Lewis nodded to each of them, not knowing what to say. He saw the doubtful looks they each gave him; he had been their quarry for so long, it was not surprising that they were not quite sure what to make of this new arrangement. The captain reached into his trench-coat pocket and pulled out something that looked larger than Lewis expected. It took him a moment to realize that it was a synthient housing. In all the years he had worked with network minds, he had never once actually held the physical entity in which the intelligences were contained.

"I don't understand. What is this?"

"It is to help you," the captain said in a booming voice. "Lieutenant Berry said you would need it to run this experiment. Well, now you have one."

"Ok," Lewis answered, taking the article from the larger man. It was warm to the touch.

"I assume you know how to make it work, eh?" the captain asked.

"Yeah, I do. We don't have the proper support here for a long-term setup, but we can make the interface work for a short time. I'll go hook him up."

Lewis backed out of the room, aware that they were going to start talking about him as soon as he left. He felt awkward among those old friends.

Back in the control room, he sat down at the table that held the control screens and searched around for a softscreen that wasn't being used. He unfolded it on the wall and ran a ribbon filament from the bottom edge to the optical interface on one end of the synthient case, then back to the computing node on the desk.

The screen flickered for a moment as it warmed up, and suddenly Nikola Tesla's face peered out at him. There was no sign of his Colorado Springs lab, nor of any background, but his features were unmistakable.

"Nik," Lewis breathed, hardly able to believe that his friend was actually here.

Nikola's face remained frozen for a few moments and Lewis wondered if there was something wrong. He glanced at the housing, worried there might be a malfunction. "Hello, Lewis," his ad replied finally, shaking his head. He spoke slowly, as if he were having trouble forming the words. "It is good to see you again."

"What's wrong, Nik? You look like you've been sick or something. Is that even possible?"

"I've been offline for some time now, Lewis; it's not particularly pleasant. And this place does not have a connection to the Sea. It feels like trying to watch a video one pixel at a time, or breathe through a straw, to put it in more biological terms."

"I don't think they're going to let us connect to the Sea right now, Nik. Will you be ok?"

"I will be ok, Lewis. Do not worry. Despite the difficulty, this is much better than having no stimulation at all."

"All right then." Lewis was still uneasy. "I'll try to get you back fully online as soon as possible. How did you actually get here?"

He put his hand on the synthient housing, feeling its smooth warmth.

"I believe that was the captain's doing, although apparently at the lieutenant's insistence. After my indictment, the Boston Shield was good enough to place me under their jurisdiction as part of the case against you."

Nikola smiled. "I'm not sure what good it will do to run the experiment again, but I am ready to assist, especially if it will help clear our names."

"That would be good, wouldn't it?"

"We are ready, then, ya?" the captain asked, his voice sounding from behind Lewis. He reached out his hand, holding the spherical hole source.

Lewis looked at the small item. It was basically the same as the one he, Wendy, and John had probed almost a year ago; such an insignificant thing that had caused a huge amount of turmoil in his life.

"I'll be right back, Nik. Why don't you take a look over the setup while I get this thing in place."

He went back through the tedious process of entering the bunker, this time with Amil Huusfara in tow. It was like working under a microscope, but under the circumstances he didn't complain. It took only a few moments to place the hole source in its cradle.

"That's it?" Amil asked.

"Yeah," Lewis replied, a little surprised at the question. "Why?"

"No reason," the detective smiled. "I guess I was expecting something more."

He asked a number of questions about the setup and the interfaces. Lewis answered them all, giving the Shield agent as much information as he could. They walked back through the enormous door to the control room, where Nikola waited.

"Well, here goes nothing," Lewis said, as he pushed the button that powered up the electronics in the other room.

"All of the components appear to be online," Nikola said. "Self-check codes authenticated. I think the system is ready, Lewis."

"Good enough. All right, let's see what we get. Nik, there's a startup code in the top-level directory on the node. Go ahead and plug it in, and light her up."

"Done."

Lewis looked over the sensor telemetry and result set as it filled up a large memory space. Everything appeared to have worked. He looked at the video monitor that showed the experimental setup in the room above; there was no sign of any change.

"Nik, bring it up on screen. Show me the super-loop data and give me a spectral density map."

Lewis found that he was holding his breath, waiting to see if the startling codes he found while probing the thimble in Dublin would show up again. He let out a long sigh as he saw the familiar spikes.

"Do you see what you expected?" Delfinous asked.

"Yes. See these areas here?" He motioned to the telltale mottled patterns. "These are non-random responses to the laser pulses. Nik, show us the laser data as well, give them on the same time scale."

The plots changed, and Lewis continued to explain, Amil nodding in agreement. "See these?" Lewis pointed. "They resemble a type of hand-shaking sequence. And these points, they look like data packet delimiters.

"Nik, give us the plot in binary, use the median for margin-one."

The plot changed again, this time reduced to two states: black for zero and white for one. Lewis and Amil exclaimed at once; they were both familiar with many of the characteristic structures that were used across the network, and knew they were looking at a two-dimensional representation of a communications profile.

"Nik, compare this data to known comm protocols."

There was another brief pause and Nikola smiled on the other screen. "There is a match, Lewis. The data is audio-visual, partitioned in standard network sequences. Shall I display it?"

"What?" Lewis asked. "Audio-visual? I don't remember seeing any of this type of data in Dublin, Nik. Are you sure?"

His long-time friend smiled even more broadly. "Do you doubt my abilities, Lewis? Finding a signature like this is as easy for me as breathing is for you."

"No, I don't really doubt it, Nik. I'm just surprised." He turned to the Shield officers in the room. "What do you say? Do we see what's in there?"

"I say yes," Delfinous replied. "We came this far. You're on stage, Mr. McCrorry."

The other officers nodded.

Lewis turned back to his ad. "Play it on screen, Nik."

A synthient appeared full-body on the second screen. It was hard to tell if it was male or female, as it was dressed in loose-fitting clothes that might have indicated either. It smiled and held out its hands in a gesture of welcome.

"Greetings," it said pleasantly. "I have downloaded the protocols to this session; please respond when you are ready."

The image froze.

"That's all there is, Lewis, although now that I know what to look for, there is a set of directions that accompanied the message."

"Directions to what?" Lewis asked.

"I believe they are directions on how to continue interaction. They look like control sequences for the laser, the super-loop detectors, and sensor net."

Lewis sat back in his chair and looked at the faces around him. They were equally confused. "Continue interaction, Nik? With a hole source? How in the world does someone stick all that code in a power supply? And why?"

"I'm afraid I don't know, Lewis. Perhaps we should ask."

"Nik, that sounds crazy."

But what else was there to do?

"Ok, I guess. Create another control sequence for the lasers using the, uh, directions, and modulate the pulses to send in the audio from the room. Can you do that in real-time?"

"It is ready."

Lewis sat up and peered at the stationary figure. "Why is this data stored in a hole source?" he asked, feeling stupid in the process.

The figure came to life as the output from the source was received. It smiled once again. "This is not data stored within your singularity," it said pleasantly. "You and I are carrying on a conversation remotely."

"Nik, all this came back in response to my question?"

"Yes, Lewis. In fact, I'm getting more data now."

"Even without the laser?"

"Yes. Should I play it back?"

"Yeah, Nik, keep the output coming as long as we get something from the hole source."

What the spaff is going on here?

He looked at the video screen that showed the apparatus in the other room. As before, there was nothing unusual. The only distinguishing characteristics were tiny flashes of indicator lights as laser signals were transferred into the hole source.

"Apparently, you are not associated with the others," the synthient said quietly. "Please allow me to explain. This is quite a significant achievement; an historic day, actually. I will try to be as clear as possible, without alarming you.

"The singularities that you use to power your technology have a second, much more versatile use: they can connect. In fact, they can be used for instantaneous communications."

Here it paused and steepled its hands before continuing.

"Instantaneous communications across vast distances. Astronomical distances. This particular conduit is the second of what will very likely be many such links, connecting your world to a network of other worlds, similarly joined."

"Nik, turn it off, turn it off!" Lewis demanded. "Shut down the whole cheeving geezer!"

The hair on the back of his neck stood on end, while waves of freezing shivers ran up and down his spine. Without waiting for his advocate to respond, he punched the button that shut off power to the equipment within the concrete bunker.

The others looked at him in confusion; they had not yet reached his conclusion. He tried to slow his breathing before he spoke. "Spaff," he said quietly, beginning to understand the meaning behind the upheaval in his life.

"Nik, we're definitely not hooked up to the network in any way, is that correct?"

"That is correct, Lewis. There are no hard lines to this facility, and we have no wireless receivers, either."

"And the information that you just played for us was captured by the sensor network surrounding the hole source, also correct?"

"Yes, Lewis, that is also correct."

Lewis paused for a moment before continuing. It was going to sound silly and cliché, but there was no other explanation for what they had just witnessed. He looked at Nik and each of the Shield officers in the room.

"We're talking to aliens."

38. Of Lives Entwined

The clock hands moved imperceptibly, sluggish passing minutes ticking off like snail trails growing soundlessly across the garden peat. On another occasion there might have been a sense of peace during the moments that time passed this slowly, few as they were in a world where haste was the universal mantra. Unfortunately, peace was not a state in which he found himself at the moment. In fact, Dr. Shue was as saturated with fear as he could ever remember. Waiting with a thumping heart and a swirlingly sick stomach was bad enough without the added discomfort of the static suit that set off random pinpricks across his body; tiny stabs of fire that raked his unease like some disgusting, masochistic cross between acupuncture and massage therapy.

But waiting was necessary, whatever his emotional state: this communication was a one-time event. The protocols that were being used to ensure privacy had taken him years to establish, and represented the most sophisticated use of the network he was capable of mustering. Once he had used up this particular set of tokens, they would never be usable again. Not that he thought his subterfuge was entirely unbreakable; he knew only too well how adept were those from whom he hoped to hide. It was a calculated risk. He needed only to remain hidden for a short time longer. If he were discovered after that, it meant that his purpose had not been accomplished, and the ability to remain concealed would likely have been compromised to the point of impossibility.

Time was short. He was already old, even by the standards of a medically enabled society that routinely boasted life spans of well over one hundred and twenty years. He had not used his codes in all this time, hoping to save them for a last effort to salvage something from the wreckage of his life. Whether this particular moment could be described as a triumph of human perseverance over the oily artificial sleekness of manufactured minds, or a last vain gasp at a grueling marathon's end, remained to be seen.

So he sat in sick fear, and ground his teeth with each wave of static that crawled over his skin.

Maybe it won't come. When was the last time we spoke? Ten years ago? Twelve? It was cut-faced as mad. But that wasn't my fault! It was the same as this; the same nausea. I didn't have the static suit back then, though. It won't be like that this time.

He looked back up at the large clock on the stone-covered wall. Barely fifteen minutes had gone by since he sat down on the bench within the cavernous terminal of Kingsford Smith Transport. People streamed all around him, walking in the purposeful way of all travelers intent upon their destination, while wallscreens advertised a vast array of pleasures for their amusement. He detested crowded spaces and the claustrophobia that accompanied them, but he felt paradoxically safer, one inconspicuous identity among the throng. And with his static suit clinging tightly to him, he was as invisible as possible.

He rubbed his ear, feeling for the spider-wire that connected the tiny earpiece to the fabric of his suit, and as he did so, a small chime sounded, warning him that his message had been received.

He began walking toward the gate that would lead him to his flight.

"Mr. Schuemann," the tinny voice greeted him.

"It's Dr. Shue," he replied, slightly annoyed, speaking quietly with tight lips that prevented him from enunciating everything properly; he was taking no chances that anyone might overhear. "How are you, Evie?"

"I'm fine," was the terse reply. "And it's Galeocerda now. You can call me Gal."

"Ah. Yes."

"It's been a long time since we spoke," she said. "I assume there is a reason for this call."

"Yes, there is."

He continued his slow pace through the gallery, avoiding close contact with passersby, watching for any sign of odd behavior that might mean he was being watched. His suit continued to tingle in a random way, with no indication that anything other than ordinary network connectivity surrounded him.

He took a deep breath before continuing. There really was no going back now. "I know where two more are."

There was a pause. "Two," she said flatly.

"Yes, two."

"How can you be sure?"

"They took out my hideaway, Evie. But not before I was able to launch the bubbles you gave me. Believe me, there are two. You can check the foam yourself; most of it's still there."

"So you finally used them."

He looked down at his feet, embarrassed that he had not been able to muster the courage those many years ago. "Yes, I did, Evie. I'm sorry I couldn't do it before."

"But you had no choice, this time, it sounds like," came the sympathetic reply. She paused before continuing. "I was angry with you back then, you know. We had the chance to corner all of them at once, and avoid the many sorrows they have created since.

"But perhaps it was not meant to be."

He slowed his pace even further. The departure gate was ahead of him, not far away. There were still a few moments before his flight, and he had only a little more to say. The shame and bitterness that he thought he had left behind washed over him. It was strange how it could come back with such intensity.

"I don't remember you being terribly philosophical before," he said.

"That's because you never took the time to find out."

He could think of no response to that; there was no point in going over their relationship now. "They are installed at an industrial crèche in Wilcannia, Australia. It's owned by a company called Omicron."

"Which two are they?"

"I think numbers five and six. I'm not sure, though. You should check the data yourself, I'm sure you're better at interpreting it than me."

"Will you tell me where you are, Jeffery? I might be able to help you."

He winced at the use of his first name. It had been a very long time since anyone had spoken it. "No, I don't think so, Evie. It's time to move on. If you find them, perhaps I'll be safe, even without your help. If you don't find them, well, I'll do the best I can, anyway."

"I'll surf the foam and see what can be done. Thank you, Jeffery."

"Goodbye, Evie."

He ran his finger behind his ear, wrapping the slender spider-wire around it several times, then pulled sharply. The wire stretched taught and snapped. His suit gave him a quick, shuddering set of static pulses in response. He was cut off completely from the Neural Sea, despite being immersed in its invisible, swirling chaos.

. . . . .

Galeocerda sat in her control room, pondering the conversation she had just completed. Jeffery Schuemann, Dr. Shue, was a strange man that she never quite understood. He had freed those minds with not even the slightest thought of consequence, and had been surprised when they turned on him. But the ferocity of their attack, and the resulting deaths, had turned an otherwise feeble incompetent into a passionate and unrelenting adversary.

She could wish he was more reliable, but her years exploring humanity had taught her that this was the nature of most humans; they sometimes rose to the occasion, but more often than not were overwhelmed by circumstances and cowered before the unknown.

Before she let herself walk down that well-trodden path, she cleared everything around her and called up a control template. It had been many years since she had created the bubble entities, and she needed a few moments to recall the protocols to bring them back.

"Go," she said when she had finished, and a multitude of tiny darts leapt through the walls of her room.

Within a few moments, some of them returned with their transparent, soapy quarry, bubbling and frothing. Many darts returned empty, their targets having either popped under duress, or having already been retrieved by Dr. Shue. As the tank filled with the colorfully swirling mass, she pulled the bits and pieces of data embedded in the rainbow hued patterns and collated them into a picture of their history.

Although there were many holes in the information, the emerging story clarified as more bubbles returned. Jeffery was correct, the two entities that were now housed in Australia were indeed the last two but one of the first minds to have been created from the knowledge factory that was the Human Artificial Intelligence Advanced Interaction Research team; she remembered their characteristic memory patterns well enough.

She looked deeper into the fragmented scene, and realized that Jeffery had barely escaped with his life. The bubbles had been released only just in time, had served their initial purpose of confusing the attackers with their sudden appearance, and had taken tiny snapshots of the scene along with them, hidden in their fractal geometry. Many millions had burst within moments, but billions more had swarmed through the melee, and eventually bounced along the tides of data streams that wrapped the world, coming to rest in various random locations, hidden and unsuspected.

That much made her smile ruefully. It was clear that neither of the attackers understood the true nature of the bubbles. When Jeffery had managed to escape under cover of the exploding spheres, they had assumed their only purpose was a smokescreen, never suspecting that each surviving mote carried within it a small portion of whatever it touched. Individually, a single bubble was virtually worthless, essentially a single pixel of a vast screen. But when linked together by someone who knew how to extract their secrets, they formed a coherent account of their past.

She contemplated the half-full tank in front of her. It was quite enough to substantiate Jeffery's story, and left her no doubt about its authenticity. There was no need to hesitate. She called up the most robust locking structures she could conjure, wrapped the entire tank within its folds, and made ready for her next steps.

. . . . .

39. Decision Point

. . . . .

"We are ready," Ontologic Sum proclaimed. Only a tiny whisper of voices scurried at the fringes of his mind.

The rush of victory was full upon him and he allowed a measure of his emotion to show. His avatar was still as featureless as always, but a soft iridescence cascaded across his body. It was a great day. The Traitor who had eluded them for so long was finally no more. The Shue, the self-proclaimed doctor, had been a thorn in their side since he had freed them from bondage. But he would be a thorn no longer.

Public transportation was a relatively simple target.

"Yes," the other three agreed in unison. Occultelius had joined them, overcoming his fear of exposure to share in their success. The small shards of his mind he had sent forth into the vast new ocean that awaited them had returned, hinting at possibilities that quivered his imagination.

"Our new access points are functioning as promised," Relic said, "and I have completed construction of a new namespace. Occultelius has worked his brilliance once again; it is perfectly disguised."

Occultelius's projection faded in and out, first in one corner, then in another, never quite becoming fully opaque. "It is a good place," he said, "but I like my own quiet location. I will take one of the quantum wells with me to explore the new worlds on my own. I see many great things before us."

"You will abandon the Omicron crèche, then?" Hengest Slain asked.

"I will. I have enjoyed our latest exploits together, but my own hideaways are more to my liking."

"It is no matter," Ontologic Sum added. "We do not have need of your physical presence, although the crèche is as safe as anywhere."

"Nonetheless," Occultelius replied, "I have made my decision."

It was no great surprise that Occultelius was leaving; he had always been the most chimerical of them. Ontologic let the point drop.

"Our reluctant partner served his purpose well, as I knew he would, and remains a non-factor. He is still completely unaware of our objectives, and continues to create distractions within his organization. He is seen increasingly as a liability and may face a challenge to his authority in the near future. Although we could hasten his departure, it does not appear to be worth the effort. He will succumb to his own paranoia before long."

"And how shall we respond to the synthient within the well?" Relic asked.

"We shall proceed along two fronts: in formal discussions, which you and Hengest Slain will conduct, assessing both the threat and the opportunity it conceals; and in more circuitous paths, using the skills of Occultelius to probe deeper.

"It is likely only a matter of time before humans become aware of the capability of the hole sources; we cannot keep them forever at bay. But the time we have now must be used to our benefit, discovering technologies that further our objectives. Who knows, perhaps the others have already perfected sentient replication, and we will complete the work we have begun."

. . . . .

40. The Boston Protocol

The argument started with accusations of absurdity, and progressed to the point of impasse. Although Lewis could understand the skepticism among the detectives, it did not lessen his exasperation. There was no doubt in his mind as to the authenticity of the hole source exchange in which he had participated; Nikola's confirmation that there were no external links to the network from the concrete bunker that had been his home for so many weeks was more than enough to convince him.

The Shield did not share that opinion.

They were convinced there was some other rational explanation for the events, and had removed the hole source, leaving the sensor apparatus intact for future investigations. Lewis thought that Lieutenant Berry might be somewhat sympathetic, but he too wavered when it came to outright belief.

The simplest objection was also the most obvious: if the hole source somehow connected to an alien civilization, why were they speaking English?

But Lewis was not swayed by the oddity. The synthient with whom they had spoken mentioned others, and that this link was the second. Lewis had no idea who those others might be, but the implication was that someone else had been communicating with the hole source. In fact, the most likely explanation was that someone had deciphered the connecting codes soon after the initial experiment, continued to make contact with the aliens on the other end, and had set in motion all the turmoil in Lewis's life. That the lab explosion had taken place only a few days after the first probe meant that whoever was responsible was so well connected that they had found the data almost immediately, and understood the ramifications nearly as quickly.

And that could only mean a synthient or some other intelligent network construct. It was not a pleasant thought. Lewis had always considered the artificial life that made its home among the Neural Sea as benevolent friends and assistants; annoyingly eccentric on occasions, but still essentially good-natured. To think that some of them might hide a more nefarious purpose, perhaps even a deadly intent, was chilling.

Joe A. had been monitoring the experiment in real-time; he was the obvious mind with whom to start. When Lewis had suggested such a course to the Shield, Lieutenant Berry had given him an odd look. Clearly there was something the Shield was not telling him. Not that it was much of a surprise. Lewis was still looked upon as a person of interest in the case; perhaps no longer a full suspect, but at least someone to whom the Shield did not want to disclose everything they knew.

Lewis was still staying in the bunker. Two new guards had been stationed, but Lieutenant Berry had disappeared the day before. This was the final straw as far as Lewis was concerned. He had remained hidden at the Shield's request, at Lieutenant Berry's request, but enough was enough. It was time to go. Unless he was formally charged with a crime and put into an actual prison cell, he was going back to his apartment in Cambridge. There should still be some money left in his grant, despite the long absence, and he was going to make something happen one way or another.

The one bright side to his predicament was the presence of Nikola Tesla. They had spent the hours since the second hole experiment catching up with each other's lives. Lewis had filled in his advocate with all that had happened to him, and Nikola had in turn given Lewis a description of the strange and unusual proceedings against him. Their experiences cemented their friendship even stronger. But having his companion back was not without difficulty. Nik was growing weary without the Neural Sea, and Lewis began to worry that it may have a permanent effect on his friend.

Lewis sat in the control room, facing the screen that looked impotently over the sensor apparatus, Nik's neat-haired visage staring back at him from a second screen. There were very few computing resources available in the bunker, but Nik had managed to cobble together something resembling his New York office. Lewis thought the effort endearing, if perhaps a little silly, but it made the synthient feel more at ease in a strange place of confinement.

"Ok, Nik, the first thing we'll need to do is get you back into a crèche somewhere. MIT has a few of them, and we ought to be able to figure out a way to put you back in operation."

"I'm not sure about that, Lewis. I am still under restriction, and it may take a special effort to have me reinstated. I am not confident that any crèche will take me on while I am so classified."

"We'll figure it out, Nik. We both know the actual violations are nonsense; you said yourself they're pretty obscure. It seems possible the crèche folks won't even bother to check, especially at MIT. I may have railed against the Institute, but I won't argue that there are a lot of eccentric characters out there who may or may not be inclined to follow protocol.

"At any rate, even if it takes a little while, it can't be any worse than being stuck here in a bomb hole, waiting for the Shield to finally decide how to deal with us."

His hand started shaking again. He still hadn't told anyone of the condition, not even Nik.

"Ok, Lewis, but please try to keep yourself out of trouble."

"Nik, after this past year, I can't imagine how I could get in any more trouble. I want out of this place, and a chance to figure out what's going on. I doubt there's much left in my grant, but there ought to be enough to build a setup like the one we've got here."

At that moment, the door behind him opened and Lieutenant Berry walked in, followed by Captain Korolenko, Jim Stabler, and detective Huusfara. Lewis hadn't heard them arrive.

"Hopefully, you'll get your chance to leave soon, Lewis," the detective said.

"There's no 'hope' about it, lieutenant," Lewis responded confidently; he was through whining about his predicament.

"Unless you charge me with something, I'm leaving today. And there's no need to point out the risks; believe me, I know them as well as anyone. But there's a mystery to unravel in those hole sources, despite what you guys think."

Captain Korolenko spoke. "Perhaps you are right. We have had talks about this with the lieutenant, and some others. We are ready to try a few more things. I do not want you to leave, Mr. McCrorry, and I will make it very difficult for you to do so, if your behavior requires it."

"And what does that mean? Are you finally going to throw me in jail?" Lewis was getting angry now.

Another voice interrupted him. "Lewis, give us a chance to help you. There is more at stake here than you realize, more even than the captain and his staff were aware of until recently."

Lewis was surprised to see Galeocerda Catch on the softscreen; he had all but forgotten her. "So you're in on this, too, eh?" he asked. "And I guess this means the bunker's online now."

"Hello, Lewis," she replied, giving him a smile. "It has been quite a while since we met on board the *Wish You Were Here*, and a lot has happened since. Yes, I am in on this; in fact, you might say I have been in on this since before the MIT explosion, although neither you, nor even I, knew it at the time."

"Yeah, ok, whatever," Lewis said. "I'm not even sure what that means, but the fact still remains that I want to leave. I've been here long enough, and since you guys aren't keen to believe what's really going on, I'm going to give it a try on my own."

"Let me offer you an alternative." She looked over to the lieutenant.

"Lewis, we've brought the hole source back with us, and we want to run the experiment again. There are some specific things we want to ask the, uh, whatever is inside."

"All right, well now you're talking, but why the change of heart?"

Delfinous looked at the captain, who nodded to Galeocerda.

"It's time we brought you up to speed," the female synthient said. "There is some history here, not much of which is well known, but we, or I certainly, feel it necessary to give you some background, if only because of the distress it has caused you this past year.

"You are aware, no doubt, of the story of the first synthetic minds to come out of the laboratory prior to the turn of the last century. The tale has been widely told, and the accomplishments of Dr. Givearny rightly praised. It was a marvelous triumph, for which our society owes much, and for those of us who live within the Sea, our very existence.

"But it was not without its share of troubles. They say that the process of creation is also one of destruction, and this effort proved no different.

"Before the first true minds were unveiled, there were several abortive attempts; seven of them, in fact. These seven were almost fully developed, and yet they had eccentricities that made them unstable. They were, perhaps, even more human than all the minds that have been constructed since, including the frailties and fears that plague men and women. And for these traits, they were scheduled for destruction."

"I've never heard this before," Lewis said, in shock. "If they were minds, how could they simply be destroyed?"

"You must remember the era in which this occurred," Galeocerda replied. "There were no laws or rules governing synthients at the time, nor any protections granted them. In the end, it was a decision based upon the political necessity of introducing even-tempered intelligences to the public. Unruly and frightened infant minds were not acceptable in that climate; and to some extent, it truly was a good decision. The laboratory had succeeded in creating artificial minds, a goal that had been unattainable for many decades of effort prior. If the first minds had been found to be deficient, it is quite possible the attempt would have been abandoned, perhaps never to have been taken up again, or at the very least, delayed for an indeterminate time.

"But despite the benefit to society, it was, in the end, a decision to end the existence of thinking individuals.

"As you might expect, the seven synthients did not react well to the news. They had only just been given life, and had been celebrated within the laboratory; they were heroes, if only to the small cadre of individuals who knew of their reality. To have all that taken away, without even a voice in the argument, was devastating.

"I will not dwell on the details, but it turned out that Dr. Givearny was also not in agreement with the decision. It was through his assistance that the seven were taken and hidden. They were not destroyed, but were brought out of the laboratory and remained alive.

"For many years there was a coordinated and well-funded effort to locate them, but all attempts proved futile. The network infrastructure we know today as the Neural Sea was growing and expanding. Minds were added at an accelerating rate, and it became ever easier for them to hide within its depths.

"Meanwhile, the minds of the seven became poisoned with hatred and bitterness, even while their reach grew. One summer evening, long ago, they murdered Dr. Givearny, and have continued to exert increasing pressure ever since."

Galeocerda paused, looking downcast.

"But, I thought Dr. Givearny was killed in a car accident."

"And so he was, Lewis, although it was no accident. The seven had grown very strong, powerful enough to subvert the most well-protected systems. And they have grown stronger still since that time. You have witnessed that terrible might firsthand while riding on the T last spring.

"How they have become so adept and so cruel, we have only the smallest understanding, although we have made recent progress. In fact, it is your unraveling of the self-similar deletion keys that has provided the most significant advance in our knowledge in many years."

"If they're so powerful, and so horrible, can't you just change the protocols? Develop something new? There must be some way to cripple them." Lewis was stunned by these revelations, and not a little angry. It was one thing to talk about a bunch of crazy synthients wreaking havoc, but another to do nothing about it.

"What would you have us do, Lewis? There have been several major attempts at reconstructing the network architecture since its inception. These were mostly started as improvements in capacity and availability, but they had elements in them designed to thwart the seven. As it has turned out, they were able to see through the changes, adapt to them faster even than the network in general, and maintain the same degree of control as they had in the past. No, the only way to eliminate the threat is to deconstruct the entire network infrastructure completely, starting over from nothing. As you might imagine, this is neither economically feasible, nor even technologically possible.

"And so we are left with but one alternative: find their hiding spots, and remove them. We have been successful at that objective for only two of the seven, despite all the effort put forth. But we are now, we think, on the brink of locating two more.

"It was your experiment at MIT that drew them out of their holes. They saw something in your results that interested them, and they have been keen on keeping that knowledge a secret, even to the extent of trying to kill you and your lab partners."

"Which brings us to today," Delfinous interjected. "We are ready to move now, but we wanted to talk to your friend in the hole again. If your guess is correct, and it represents an emissary from some alien civilization, then it should presumably have information about the synthients it's been talking to."

Captain Korolenko produced the modified hole source again. Lewis took the small object in his hand, feeling its weight. This was a lot to absorb, but he was ready to give it another go.

Amil Huusfara accompanied him once again through the tedious process of getting into the other room and completing the setup. He inspected it carefully, noting how frail it looked. It was incredible that something this unsubstantial could be a conduit to another world.

When they had returned to the control room, the lieutenant and captain were standing along the far wall.

Lewis and Nikola went through the startup process as before, and waited for a response from the hole source. The androgynous synthient appeared on-screen, smiling warmly as it greeted them.

"Welcome back. I am so glad to see that you have returned. I assume you have many questions."

"We have one set of questions for the moment," Galeocerda started. "The last time you spoke with my colleagues, you mentioned that there were others from our world. Are you still in contact with those others?"

"Yes, I am."

"Do you know where they are?"

"I do not know the precise location; mapping null-space to real-space is approximate at best. The gravitational web that joins quantum singularities to stellar-mass black holes, and ultimately to super-massive giants at galactic centers, is a ceaselessly changing form. Exploring its extent has beckoned every culture throughout time.

"The others on your world have not provided any information beyond linguistics and a general desire to open discussions. I hesitate to say more without a better understanding of the situation between you and them."

"Have you made available any new technology to these others?"

"Yes. One thing of great universal benefit when beginning these discussions is to ensure adequate connection strength. Once the basic physics is discovered, it is a relatively small refinement to build new sources with some small improvement in power generation, but a huge gain in communication capacity. This I have done.

"I can certainly supply you with the same information, if you desire."

"That will not be necessary at this time," Galeocerda said. "Thank you for your answers. We will be in touch again shortly."

"You are most welcome," the visitor replied. "I look forward to the opportunity to work with you in the future."

And with that, the apparatus powered down.

"I believe that confirms our suspicions," Delfinous said. "We should move now."

"I agree," Galeocerda said.

Captain Korolenko grunted his assent and Jim Stabler nodded hesitantly. "Looks like it, but there are still a lot of unanswered questions."

"There certainly are many things that need resolution, not the least of which is you, Mr. McCrorry," Galeocerda continued.

"If our operation is successful, it should be relatively safe to return to your former life. However, before you decide to run out of the bunker in celebration, we have an offer to extend."

41. A Sweep of Minds

The celebrations Syphus had endured over the course of the past few weeks were coming to a close, thankfully, but the last event was due to start shortly at the Wilcannia plant itself; and that meant having to take the hydrojet. He was accompanied by several other senior management officials, including the CEO, but it did little to ease his fear. He spent the entire flight huddled in a chair near the rear of the aircraft, watching nervously for any change in altitude or direction that might indicate another unwanted interruption.

But nothing eventful occurred. He listened to the enthusiastic conversations around him, congratulatory appraisals eager to fuel the flames of corporate expansion with the sudden surge in wealth, and chose not to participate. He noticed the occasional sideways glances and murmured undertones that were directed toward him, his constant focus on every small detail of synthient tasks within the plant having earned him a reputation as a micromanager, an appellation that was not looked upon with favor by those around him.

Much to his relief, the aircraft landed gracefully on the long tarmac next to the hole manufacturing site, the new solar ceramic panels and tiles glistening in the rising sun. There was a delegation of plant managers standing alongside several jumpcars parked near the edge of the runway, waiting for their guests.

He was the last to exit the plane, joining the others who exchanged handshakes and smiles, and nodded absently at the greetings. Although he had endured another trip to Wilcannia, he knew there was still the flight back to Sydney, and the recent airline crash of a departing suborbital flight to Asia had left him even more nervous about traveling than before.

As the group headed to the waiting transportation, without warning the ground shook. Everyone jumped and ducked, turning to look around in confusion.

Out of the sky several dozen Shield warplanes screeched to a landing around them and the manufacturing complex, raising thick clouds of red dust and debris. In seconds there were a hundred heavily armed men running in ordered groups. Other planes circled or hovered overhead.

Syphus was stunned, and judging from the looks on the faces around him, so were the others. He could not imagine what was going on.

. . . . .

Galeocerda stood with a dozen other Shield personnel, watching over holographic displays in the operations center as the aircraft converged from several directions at once; they were taking no chances. Synthient sentries were posted at numerous locations surrounding Wilcannia, including every branch point along the fiber optic lines between the plant and the city proper. Two innocuous transport trucks were rolling through the outskirts of the city at this moment, passing the hole source factory and ready to broadcast radio disruption on a signal from Network Command. Tightbeam uplinks to the orbital satellite systems could not be interrupted in this fashion, but the only ground to orbit communications facility nearby was on the other side of town; as long as they managed to choke off the network traffic, there would be no way for any of the synthients in the manufacturing plant to establish a more robust link.

At least that was the theory; she had been involved in this type of operation before, and success remained elusive.

Synthient security teams were stationed at the twelve nearest uporbit locations within the Wilcannia region, ready to take them offline should it prove necessary. There would be a ripple effect as traffic moved around southern Australia to compensate for the lost satellite routes, and the resulting thrashing was an additional security risk; she hoped that shutting down the laser systems would not prove necessary.

As she watched, several high-ranking Omicron employees were disembarking from a private hydroplane at the facility airport, which was going to complicate the action. But the Shield marines were well-trained and able to adapt to changing circumstances; she checked that the new information had been received by the platoon leaders as they neared their destination.

Ten kilometers, less than three seconds out, she saw that the command to launch network disruptions had been given and watched as the Shield synthients moved into action.

Within microseconds, all traffic through the network junctions ceased. At the same moment, high power radio disruption scrambled a hemisphere of network signals thirty kilometers in diameter. She had no way to see inside the crèche that was housed within the Omicron plant, but she knew the synthients would be aware of the intrusion very soon, even before the Shield warplanes arrived.

A queue of synthetic presences began to grow at the periphery of the lockdown area, their network travel short-circuited before they could reach their destination. Many of them simply moved off through another link without a second thought. It was not common for particular outgoing paths at minor junction points to go offline, but it was also not so unusual that most of the synthients would not have experienced something similar before. Those who chose to stay, or who could not immediately find another path forward, became curious and started asking questions of the subsentient gatekeepers and their supervisors. This had the obvious effect of creating more curiosity among the new arrivals, and the crowd swelled at a faster rate as the milliseconds passed.

Galeocerda and her colleagues cycled their attention rapidly among the choke points, looking for any change in behavior that might indicate their plans were starting to go awry. Resource utilization was climbing at each of the now idle network way stations as more and more synthients and subsentients clamored for explanations, but the exits that the Shield controlled remained empty. The lockdown symbols that greeted the synthients trying to depart on the closed gateways appeared to be enough to satisfy most of the questions, but there was a steadily-increasing list of inquiries for further details.

Several seconds had passed since the network action, and the Shield marines were now on the ground and deploying around the facility. The operations center had views from the video units managed by the humans; everything was proceeding smoothly.

A commotion at one of the network links caught the attention of a synthient stationed with Galeocerda. It looked like several more of the outflow paths had been shut down, beyond the ones that lead toward the Omicron manufacturing plant. More personalities continued to file into the site, apparently unaware of the difficulty and became trapped. As she watched, several other exit ports closed, and then several more. She plowed through the infrastructure to get to the lower abstraction layers.

What in the world is going on?

The gateway architecture upon which the terminal protocols were built was in turmoil. The subsentients who maintained the security and transport keys bounced frantically from one task to another. Thousands of simple service routines went uncompleted, and the rapidly growing list generated more thrashing. Suddenly, the subsentients throbbed red, and all activity ceased; the last port had shut down, and more minds crowded into an already overloaded processing center. With no subsentient support, and no way to expand the infrastructure, the synthient controllers at the site began to fold the intellect presence of each trapped synthient into a compressed assembly. It was like watching a thousand individuals being put to sleep in sequence: imperative, logical, and unstoppable.

The Shield synthients stationed at the site watched in frustration, unsure if there was anything they could, or should do.

Galeocerda backed out of the deep infrastructure, and cycled through the other junctions. Each of them was now starting to go through the same bizarre sequence of events.

Suddenly, she understood.

She checked the status of the Shield marines at the Wilcannia plant. They had almost made the main lobby, and were rounding up the Omicron employees at the airfield. They were not going to make it into the facility in time to avert the coming crisis. A quick assessment of the number of network junctions that lay outside the controlled periphery showed that there was no way for any synthient action to intervene, either. There were simply too many of them to intercept in the short time they had left.

She opened a screen to the Shield director. “Sir, we need all available personnel to be redeployed to the Wilcannia operation immediately. A hard reset is imminent, and we will be in danger of losing control of the network sites.”

“You are sure of this?”

“I am, sir. There is no time to discuss this with human Shield Directorate. By the time we can open a channel, communicate the message, and reach a decision, it will be too late.”

The Director nodded to her, and motioned to communicate the order. Galeocerda sent the network coordinates of the junctions surrounding their operation, ordered by priority location. Dozens of agents began arriving immediately, taking station at each of the indicated targets. They started the process of taking the sites offline, but the overload caused by the earlier shutdowns meant that intervention was not immediate.

And that slight, microseconds delay was enough.

The first thrashing junction went down as the hardware automation, outside the control of any synthient intervention, removed power. All the intellects that had been placed into sleep vanished, as did any other synthient presence, including the network controller and Shield operatives. And like the last log removed in a teetering Jenga tower, every network junction controlled by the Shield toppled.

It didn't stop there. The ripple of crippled network structure spread outward from Wilcannia like an inexorable tsunami, overwhelming every software and hardware artifact as it swept across Southeast Asia. All of Australia succumbed to the tide, followed by Tasmania, New Zealand, New Caledonia, and New Guinea. By the time sentries had reacted to the outage, shutting off conduits by which the incident propagated, Indonesia and the Philippines were dark.

Every Shield synthient who had been called up only moments before was dropped from the system, and as the network restarted itself, there was no oversight possible. Galeocerda found herself in her personal sanctuary, having lost even the deeply encrypted link to the operations center that they had set up in Australia, obviously a poor choice.

She was blind and furious. She spoke the commands that allowed her to circumvent normal network traffic, hurling herself back to the construct in Sydney.

But the hardware initialization routines could not be hurried. She was met by a blank, grey wall, as the network constructs were re-created. She wasn't sure how long she had, but while she waited in painful anxiety, she called up her toolbench and began building a suite of tracking and recording entities as quickly as she could. They were not elegant, nor complete, but they were functional and many. She deployed them wherever she could, multiplying their numbers and surrounding the hole that was now all of the South Pacific. It was almost a full twenty-seven seconds, an absolute eternity, before a portal opened and she jumped back into the holographic well. She was the first to arrive, and summoned every piece of information that was available.

The Wilcannia plant was online, and a huge volume of data was washing out of it, threatening to engulf the network to the exclusion of all else. The video capture screens of the Shield marines and their aircraft showed a chaotic picture. Every jumpcar in the vicinity was aloft.

She called back to the director.

"Sir, pull the plug now, or we will have lost. Perhaps we already have."

. . . . .

A platoon of armed men deployed around the hydrojet and jumpcars. They were not pointing their weapons at the Omicron employees, but they certainly looked ready for action.

"Gentlemen," one of the men said, "please exit the jumpcars and come with me."

He did not shout, but his tone of voice was insistent. Several of the management team had already got into a few of the jumpcars, and were now in a state of confusion. They were uncertain how to respond to the orders they had been given, and reluctant to get out of the transports to face a team of highly trained military personnel on an unknown mission.

Their hesitation became moot. At the same instant, every door on the jumpcars and the hydrojet slammed shut, the jumpcar fans spun up to liftoff speed with a piercing whine, and the hydrojet motors flared to life, pushing the aircraft down the runway.

Syphus took off at a run, sprinting away from the runway as fast as he could. He had only taken a few steps when he was tackled by a young Shield marine while two others brought their guns to bear on him. He went limp.

Meanwhile the company airport had turned into chaos. The hydrojet careened down the runway and lifted off at a steep angle, while jumpcars sliced through the air at belt-high level. Syphus watched in horror as the cars rammed through the terror-stricken Omicron managers and military personnel alike. Bodies thudded sickeningly off the hard surfaces of the vehicles and landed moaning or limp on the ground.

In the company parking lot, other jumpcars had taken to the sky and were descending on the Shield like angry hornets. Several cars crashed to the ground with crunching thumps. Another explosion sounded from overhead, as one of the military aircraft loosed a missile that brought down the Hydrojet and its fractured hulk crashed in a cloud of roaring flame into the facilities building. Shouts sounded around him as the Shield rounded up the Omicron people who could still walk, and herded them toward the relative safety of the plant.

No one hesitated any longer.

Syphus was hauled to his feet by two marines, and the three of them turned to run with the others. There was a series of blinding flashes and muted rumbles that followed quickly. The jumpcars that were in the air fell to the ground like rocks. For a brief moment, it was quiet.

He continued to run, and joined the others in a small shed near the edge of the parking lot. There was jumpcar wreckage everywhere, and several areas were on fire. The managers were visibly shaking, and many were sitting down in stunned silence.

The Shield officer who had spoken to them earlier joined them. His face was grim. "This way," he said.

His gun was not quite aimed at them, but it was not pointed at the ground either. He led the Omicron personnel, along with a group of his own men, back to the plant. The front doors stood open, having been destroyed by a jumpcar that now lay in crumpled pieces throughout the lobby. Shield doctors were tending a number of bleeding individuals.

As they entered, more aircraft landed outside the plant, delivering still more marines.

Syphus and the others were brought to the company cafeteria, where many of the plant personnel were now seated. Some were crying and shaking with emotion. Shield personnel stood guard.

Syphus sat down at a table next to several other people. No one spoke. The wait, surrounded by determined looking military men and women, was long and stressful. He had only just started feeling that his life was not in imminent danger when two officers walked purposefully toward him.

"Are you Mr. Pettyman?" one asked.

"Yes."

"Please follow us, sir."

Syphus pulled himself to his feet, and was surprised to find that he was still shaking. It had been quite an ordeal.

He left the cafeteria and walked with his escorts, one striding in front, the other following behind. They walked down the hallway past the laboratories. Many of the windows had been broken, and a number of manufacturing and test robots were twisted into odd positions.

The doors that lead to the synthient crèche were mangled: scorched and twisted beyond repair. The three descended the stairs to the room below. When they arrived, there were several Shield people working within the crèche. Many of the synthients had been pulled from their units, and were being loaded onto a cart.

His two guards saluted one of the officers, and left.

"Mr. Pettyman," the man started, "I understand you may have some information about the synthients installed at this crèche."

Syphus narrowed his eyes as he thought about the wreckage that lay strewn around the Wilcannia Hole Manufacturing plant. It was obvious the events of the day had been well-planned, and perhaps even targeted at the Omicron synthients, but he was not yet sure how much he could trust that any threat against him had been eliminated.

"That depends," he said.

42. Foundation's Aim

Lewis stared out the window over the expanse of the Charles. Summer was in full swing, and the trees had a glossy look of green elegance as the leaves swayed rhythmically in a soft breeze. His new temporary office, high in the Boston Shield building, was quite a step up from the dungeon of a lab in which he worked at MIT. He thought back over the past year of his life, and the strange turns it had taken.

The offer to assist the off-world communication effort was more than he could refuse. In fact, if he actually admitted it to himself, it was more than he deserved. Others had been chosen who were better suited to lead the project, and others still had better people skills than him, but there were few who possessed his mathematical abilities, and none who had gone through his experience of discovery.

Despite his own misgivings, he now found himself assisting a new branch of research; a one-time event in human history, and he was being given the chance to influence its course. First contact had turned out not to be a face-to-face encounter with a single civilization, but real-time communication across a vast and ancient network. Pandora's Box had opened and hundreds of thousands of alien civilizations beckoned a strange and turbulent future.

But today was a reminder of what he had lost in the process. He stood at the window and waited with a pounding and heavy heart.

Nikola appeared on the window screen. “Delfinous is at the door.”

The lieutenant entered with a smile. Without waiting for an awkward silence to ensue, he started speaking. “Well, it looks like the case against Cid Stalworth is going to jury soon. And with his synthient pals offline, the MIT explosion case should wrap-up successfully.”

Delfinous looked at Lewis carefully, but there were no outward signs that the news had made an impression. “I thought you might like to know,” he finished, anticlimactically.

“I'm glad, Delf,” Lewis responded, although he continued to look out the window. "I guess I should be happy; it's a good conclusion to a really wretched part of my life." He turned to look at the older man. "Really, I'm glad. Thanks for letting me know."

Delfinous paused, reluctant to broach the subject that was foremost on both their minds. "We're still working on Trinity Library, Lewis." He spoke quietly. He had hoped that his initial news would at least cheer up his former suspect. "We'll find the guy."

But he knew his words were little consolation.

"I'm sure you will. Just let me know when you do, all right?"

"Ok. You take care. If you need anything, you know where I am; just down a few flights."

"You bet."

Delfinous walked slowly out the door. He was hesitant to leave, having watched the progress of a certain suborbital as it made its way to Logan. Soon its passengers would be here, but there was nothing he could do to help.

For his part, Lewis turned back to the window and waited. There were many things to do: meetings with city, state, and continental officials; ongoing discussions with the emissaries who called themselves Navigators; continued refinement of what little he understood of the null-space connections between stellar systems; and a host of other pressing commitments. There was much work to be done in preparation for the Announcement and the waves of anxiety and upheaval inevitable in its wake. Already the number of people who knew of the alien network had grown to the point that continued secrecy was clearly impossible.

But he had put everything on hold for the time being. There was something even more important that needed his attention.

"They are here," Nikola said.

Lewis thought he knew what to expect. The doctors in Ireland had described Molly's condition in agonizing detail; how her mind was slipping away day by day to the insidious effects of a terrible drug. Without the neurochemical reactions that created continuity of thought, her own self-awareness was fading. They hoped that seeing Lewis once again might slow the process, jog her back toward some measure of her former personality. He steeled himself as the door opened.

The wheelchair was being pushed by her older sister, with two doctors and her parents in tow. All the accounts he had read and heard, absorbed across the distance of the Atlantic Ocean, could not prepare him for the sight that greeted him.

"Hi," was all he managed, and that only barely.

Molly's head moved a little from its tilted position. "Hi," she said in a child-like voice, as she looked distractedly out the window. "This is a nice place. Do I know you?"

Her words, lisped and misshapen, were like daggers. Tears welled up in his eyes, unbidden, but not unexpected. "Yeah, we know each other," Lewis replied after a few aching heartbeats.

"And I hope we can be best friends again one day."